QUEEN'S SACRIFICE

FINAL BOOK OF

THE GODDESS'S SCYTHE

COLIN LINDSAY

Books by Colin Lindsay

QUEEN'S SACRIFICE

for Katherine

PREFACE

The gnome-like man closed his eyes and dropped the torch onto the powder. A trail of flame sped down the corridor behind him.

"Run!" Kala yelled and raced to the heavy door, wrenching it open and darting through. She slowed to let Grey and Seline catch her, and together they hurried down the ramp, every step an eternity.

They had barely made it to the bottom when the building erupted in a massive fireball. Kala shoved her companions out of the way as the blast funneled down the ramp and lifted her off her feet, depositing her in a broken heap.

She lay on her back, contemplating the starry sky. She couldn't feel any part of her body, but at least she didn't feel cold when the life left her.

PART I
BAYRE

1

Kala

Kala stood atop the ramparts of the formidable wall that surrounded Bayre. She hopped up on the parapet, earning her disapproving looks from the nearby guards, which she ignored. She sat down, dangling her legs over the wall, and gazed out at Soren's army. He was down there somewhere, and of the ten thousand sets of eyes that might glance up and see her contemplating them, his might be one.

It had been a long siege, and the soldiers sat around fires talking, or they moved about the camp on errands intended primarily to stave off boredom. While the army as a whole was enormous and threatening, Kala couldn't help but think of it as a collection of individuals, each with families, hopes, and dreams. Somehow, these people had decided that Bayre was its enemy, which made *her* friends their enemy, despite their having done nothing more to them than live their lives. That made those soldiers *her* enemy, and it would be her duty to cut them down, snuff out their hopes and dreams, and deprive their families of loved ones. It made her angry – she didn't ask for this – the mantle of 'Angel of Death' had been laid on her by persons and prophecy, and she had been given no choice but to wear it.

Kala drummed her fingers on the stone. An arrow sailed up at her that she batted away absentmindedly. The guards around her drew their bows to return fire, but she waved them to stand down – she was in no danger, and they certainly weren't under attack. They reluctantly returned to their posts. Kala gave the army a last look and swung her legs back over the wall and walked across the rampart to take in the view of the city inside. It was quiet and motionless, its citizens hunkered down in their homes. Resignation had eclipsed fear. Their immediate concern was now simply surviving another day. Food was scarce, and people were hungry. As always, the vulnerable suffered most. The young, the old, the weak, and the alone – their stomachs were empty as they huddled in the cold and dark. Kala clenched her fists. For them, she would fight until there was no fight left in her. Someone had to be their champion, and if it had to be the Angel of Death, so be it.

Her world felt desolate with her friends scattered in search of allies. She felt Skye's absence most profoundly. He was the rock that she clung to when she felt like the storm might sweep her away. He and Hawke were somewhere along the coast when she desperately needed him at her side to give her the strength to get through this. She craved the feeling of him holding her and making her feel like the person she felt slip away more and more every day – a girl with her own hopes and dreams. When he looked at her, he didn't see a monster or a savior, he only saw her.

Amber and Eden also made her feel human, but they were so far away. Amber was clear across the continent, safe in the tiny village where Edith had nursed Kala and Skye back to health. Eden was closer but in mortal danger, thanks to Kala's dragging her into a scheme to copy a forbidden book, right under the nose of the Priestess. Kala was awash with feelings of guilt.

She missed Forest too, who had become like a little sister to her. She was somewhere to the northwest, with Jarom, Nara, and the rest of her adopted family, and Kala was happy for her to have found them. Forest's sister, Lily, was here in Bayre, but now that she had been reunited with Cera, her world resumed revolving around her. While it warmed Kala's heart, it also reminded her just how alone she felt.

Her only family was her grandfather, and she didn't know if he was alive or dead, having fled Soren's army into the wild with a party lead by Emrys and Fayre. Worse, she couldn't even go search for him, as she yearned to do, so long as the responsibility for opposing Soren remained thrust on her.

The last of her friends, Calix, was somewhere to the south with Dhara and her sister Kaia. Dhara was courage personified, and at the moment, she was everything that Kala wished she could be, rather than being consumed by worry and self-doubt.

Kala closed her eyes and leaned over the city. The flags atop the walls flapped in the wind, sounding like beating wings. Kala imagined herself flying away on the wind, sailing high above lands that were not embroiled in conflict. The dream faded, and she opened her eyes to the cold reality of a city under siege.

She turned from the wall and walked toward the stairwell that wound down to the city streets. It deposited her into an empty laneway, and she started off toward the temple, where Celeste had relocated the orphanage. Roaming the city alone wasn't safe for most people, given the desperation of its residents, but Kala welcomed the thought of being beset by thugs – so much anger was pent up inside her that begged for release. Whether it was the invitation for trouble that she radiated or the weaponry she carried, no one dared bother her.

The streets were deserted, except for patrols of guards and the occasional furtive movement of someone avoiding them. Windows were boarded up, as though that provided any protection from the coming storm. Signs were plastered at regular intervals informing the public that the city's store of food had been closed to the public. What meager supplies remained were reserved for the city's defenders – by order of a Council that struggled to maintain control over a city in which order was increasingly breaking down.

A handwritten sign caught her eye. It read, 'Take my children, please – just feed them.' Kala hadn't thought her heart could break further, but she was wrong. She knew that Celeste did her best to help the city's poor and downtrodden, but there were too many, and Celeste had run out of help to give. They could not survive the siege much longer.

Kala walked past the tavern that Celeste used to sing at. It had long since closed its doors, having run out of food to serve, then alcohol, then finally cheer. It had been taken over as a place of worship to the God of Chance, one of many shrines to Him that had sprung up around the city. The God of Chance was a trickster, they said, and if they prayed to Him fervently enough, perhaps he would trick the God of War and get them out of the predicament they were in. Kala placed little stock in Gods and Goddess's interfering in the lives of people, at least to their benefit.

She mused as she walked back to the temple that she and her friends had taken over when the Church had vacated the city that the God of Chance from her village was more like a God of Luck. In the north, He was more of a capricious god. Other places, he was a God of Bounty. It made her wonder if gods shaped people, or if people shaped their gods.

Kala walked up to the temple gates and knocked the coded knock that Celeste had devised and regularly changed. A moment later, the massive gates creaked open just wide enough for a person to shimmy through. A girl's head poked out, one of Celeste's charges, and Kala smiled at her as she squeezed through the gate.

"Good to see you back," Twill called out as he rolled forward and gestured to a pair of children to pull the gate closed and re-secure it. They struggled to slide into place the heavy wooden beam that braced the gates, so Kala gave them a hand.

"Your security is top-notch," she congratulated the children, but it was more of a compliment to Twill, who smiled at her words of encouragement.

He looked around mournfully at the dusty courtyard. "It's a far cry from my studio," he lamented.

"You should bring an easel out here," Kala suggested.

"I would, but the surroundings don't exactly inspire me. My paintings would be pretty dark, and there's enough darkness in the world already."

"Good point," Kala agreed and placed a hand warmly on his shoulder. "Is Celeste inside?"

"No. She's around back with Lily, tearing up the remains of the gardens."

"Thanks. Keep up the good work defending us from invaders," Kala said, with a wink.

Twill grinned and called the children back over to him. They sat around him as he resumed telling them stories.

Thank the gods for Twill and what few other lights still shine in the darkness, she thought and headed toward the gardens. She arrived to find Celeste and Lily on their knees in the dirt. They had started at one end of the former garden and were meticulously digging up the roots of whatever had been planted there before.

"Waste not, want not," Celeste explained, spying Kala's approach.

"It's a damn shame," Lily added. "Nothing is going to grow back after we're done."

Kala smiled that after everything they'd been through, Lily reserved her strongest condemnation for the murder of plants.

"Come sit with me," Cera called over, patting the seat of the chair beside her.

Kala hadn't noticed her sitting in the shade, a basin in front of her. She was washing the dirt off whatever Lily and Celeste pulled out of the ground, and laying it to dry on an adjacent table.

"I should help Lily and Celeste," Kala replied.

"Sit," Celeste authorized her, wiping sweat and dirt from her forehead. "Regale us with stories from the wall."

Kala sat down and pulled her chair closer to Cera. "Not much to tell. It is still sad as hell in the city, and scary as hell outside."

"I miss the view from the wall," Lily sighed.

"It would be prettier without an army at our doorstep," Kala suggested.

"I, for one, am happy that you got yourself banned from the wall," Cera told Lily. "I'll never forget the look of you waving from the battlements like a crazy person. You were the talk of the camp. I think a thousand soldiers wanted to date you," Cera teased.

"I'm spoken for," Lily responded, smiling. "By the way," she began, turning back to Kala, "we're having a concert tonight. Celeste is going to put on a show for the children."

"It'll get their minds off how hungry they are," Celeste explained.

"Sounds like great fun," Kala responded.

A shrill whistle sounded from the temple gates.

"Twill!" Kala exclaimed, burst from her chair, and broke into a run.

Kala had just left the courtyard, when there was a second knock at the gate, identical to the one that she'd just used. *Curious*, thought Twill, *Who else is out there?* He motioned for the children to unbar the gate, which they did with great effort. The two boys pushed it open a crack, while a little girl readied herself to peek out and see who had come calling. She'd no more than poked her head through the opening when it was shoved roughly back inside, and two sets of gloved hands reached in to grab the gate and open it wider.

"Close it!" Twill called urgently to the boys, but he knew with a sinking feeling that there was precious little they could do against determined adults.

Five rough-looking characters pushed their way through the gate and into the courtyard. They surveyed the place hungrily.

Twill rolled toward them. "I'm sorry, but we're not taking visitors," he told them, trying to sound firm, but not flip or rude.

"Shut up, boy," the group's leader responded and walked past him. "What do you have to eat in here?" he asked, looking around.

"Nothing – same as out there," Twill replied, gesturing to the gate.

"Weren't you told to shut up?" A second man said, advancing toward Twill menacingly, and using his foot to upend his wheelchair, sending him sprawling to the ground. The rest of the party laughed and fanned out to look around. Two of them advanced toward the frightened children.

"You kids will show us to the food, won't you?" one of them asked the cowering children.

"Leave them alone," Twill demanded from the ground.

The man who had upended his wheelchair pulled out a club. "Looks like I'm going to have to *make* you shut up," he said, tapping the club against his hand.

Twill scrambled to pull out the whistle that Celeste had insisted he keep tied around his neck. He brought it to his lips and blew a shrill note.

"For the gods' sake," the leader declared, covering his ears. "Shut him up for good, will you?"

The man with the club advanced, placed a foot on Twill to hold him steady, and raised his club.

Twill closed his eyes and readied himself for the impact. When it didn't come, he opened an eye hesitantly to see the man clasping his hand, his club dropped and lying nearby, his eyes spitting fire. Twill followed his gaze to where Kala stood, gravel still spraying from where she'd screeched to a halt. A moment later, she was joined by Cera, then Lily and Celeste, brandishing trowels, but only looking feebler for it. Kala motioned for them to stay back, and advanced a step toward the men.

"We have no quarrel with you," she told them. "You're welcome to leave the way you came," she added, gesturing toward the open gate, "and we won't hold it against you."

The men stood belligerently, but uncertainly. They looked to each other and came to the collective decision to stand their ground.

7

Kala sighed. "Children, help Twill up, then go inside, please." She unsheathed her swords and stuck them in the ground. She pulled the daggers from the sheaths at her thighs and another pair from her belt. She handed them to Cera, who was standing closest and unencumbered by a trowel. Kala rolled her shoulders, and seeing that the children had run inside, she turned her attention back to the five men.

"I can't promise I'm not going to hurt you badly, but be thankful I'm not in the mood to kill you. Last chance, if you have any brains between you." She stared from man to man, giving each the chance to reconsider. None of them did. *Damn masculine pride*, she thought.

The men pulled out whatever weapons they had, ranging from clubs to knives – nothing that marked them as particularly threatening, just desperate men.

Kala breathed in to center herself and opened her inner eye to the path of combat. Even as the first man swung at her, she raced into it. Her fist broke his nose. Her elbow caught the next man in the temple. A leg sweep took out the third man of his feet, a kick the fourth, and her forehead shattered the nose of the fifth man. They lay about her or stood hunched over, cradling their wounds. Kala held out her hand to the man lying on the ground in front of her.

"I'm sorry," she told him, "but I did warn you."

The man looked up at her angrily, but deflated his puffed-up chest, and accepted her hand up.

"We're not your enemy, and I'm sorry we have nothing to help you," she told him as she shepherded his group to the gate, escorted them through it, pulled it closed, and hefted the brace to secure it. She turned to see Celeste, Lily, and Cera staring at her, and Twill too, off to the side. "What?" she asked.

Lily shook her head. "I can't reconcile what I just witnessed with the Kala I grew up with," she said.

Kala looked down, embarrassed.

8

"I didn't mean it that way," Lily corrected herself. "You're a force of nature, that's all."

"Kala's always been a force of nature," Cera added.

"I for one," Celeste interjected, "love having an assassin under our roof." She strode over and put her arm around Kala. Cera walked over and handed her back her daggers.

Twill dusted himself off, prompting Celeste to rush over and help him back into his chair.

"I'm sorry there are so many assholes in the world," she apologized.

"It's okay," he replied. "I'm sorry I let them in. They used the right knock."

"They must have seen me use it," Kala added. "I should have noticed that I was being watched instead of being lost in thought. I'll be more careful from now on."

"No harm done," said Celeste. "I already have a new scheme of secret knocks worked out."

"You really should have been a spy," Kala told her.

"With these good looks?" she replied. "I'd hardly pass unnoticed."

They all laughed at her modesty.

"Those roots aren't going to dig themselves up," Celeste concluded and turned back toward the gardens.

"You know I love you, right?" Lily asked Kala, putting an arm around her.

"It's one of the few things that keeps me going," Kala replied and put an arm around her too.

2

Soren

Soren looked across the tent at his advisors. Lennox was in the middle of explaining his thoughts about the potential breach in Bayre's security provided by the broken grate on one of its sewer outflow tunnels. Seline was actually concurring with his assessment, which was rare enough that Soren was distracted by it.

"The opening is just too small for a sizable enough force to enter the city," Lennox lamented. "I had a man try to widen the opening, and he sawed at it all day, only to ruin a dozen saws making an incision shallower than his fingernail."

"They're made of hardened steel. I examined them myself. Of course, he failed," Seline chastised him.

Lennox took umbrage at being called out. "Whatever broke the grate in the first place had to have been unnatural," he defended himself.

"On the contrary," Seline countered, "it was probably water and time." Lennox looked at her uncomprehendingly, prompting her to question why she ever thought she could explain anything to the man.

Soren took advantage of the pause in their bickering to tell Seline, "I don't like you putting yourself at risk," referring to her examining the grate within bow range of the city's archers.

"I wasn't at any risk," she countered. "The city's defenders seem loathe to provoke us. They're probably worried it will hasten an attack. Besides, I was just a woman scurrying over the rocks – hardly a threat."

Soren thought to himself, *You're anything but 'just a woman,'* but he kept it to himself.

Discussion of the tunnels seemed to be concluded for the moment, so Seline moved on. "About the amnesty…," she began.

Soren nodded encouragement for her to continue, despite his concerns about Lennox's possible reaction.

"Should we move forward with offering amnesty to the city's fighting men to join us and safe passage out of the city for non-combatants?"

Soren glanced at Lennox and surprised to find him nodding in agreement.

Lennox picked up on Soren's skepticism. "It's a great idea," he offered. "We lure them out, then slaughter them. It will crush the spirit of anyone still in the city." He leaned back, smiling.

"No, we honor the amnesty," Soren explained.

Lennox made a confused face as though he was pained to have to explain the obvious to a child. It pissed Soren off.

"If I don't honor my word, I will spread that my word is worth nothing," Soren elaborated.

"A person's word is worth what people think it's worth," Lennox countered.

Soren's head hurt trying to follow the man's logic, so he gave up trying. "We do it my way," he concluded. Really, it was Seline's way, but Soren preferred his advisors not be at odds, so if taking credit for Seline's idea shielded her from Lennox's ire, it's what Soren would do.

"You're the boss," Lennox conceded, but his tone did not convey enthusiasm.

Soren ignored it. It was just part of dealing with him. "Is there anything else?" he asked his advisors.

Seline piped up. "Just that when we move on, I suggest we concentrate on sacking fishing villages up and down the coast to replenish our stores."

Soren thought about the city they'd recently bypassed for Bayre. It was the seat of the Church, and he hated leaving it standing a moment longer than necessary – the Church had never done him any kindnesses. However, what Seline suggested made sense. "Good thinking," he agreed. "Our main body will move south along the coast, and we'll send some forces north to add to our resupply."

Having addressed all of her concerns, and Lennox appearing to have none, Seline packed up her papers, stepped out, and walked away. Lennox followed suit.

Soren called to his guards. "Prepare my horse," he commanded. One of the men strode off, and Soren turned his attention to putting on his armor. *Must look the part of the conqueror*, he thought disdainfully. Once dressed, he covered up in a cloak, which he'd wear until he arrived at the stables. He would have preferred if his horse was brought to his tent, given that he thought it stupid to continue to obscure where in the camp he resided when it seemed pretty clear that the enemy had figured it out when they'd spirited away Cera. But, protocol was protocol.

Once at the stables, he discarded the cloak and mounted his horse. He trotted toward the city – his soldiers clearing a path. He stopped just short of the range of the archers on the walls and waited a moment for his presence to be noted. He needn't have bothered waiting as they had watched his approach the entire way and were already waiting for him to say what he intended to.

He cleared his throat. "People of Bayre," he called up to the wall loudly, "I am not without mercy. I offer amnesty to any man or woman of fighting age that chooses to join us. Further, I offer safe passage to anyone not of fighting age who chooses to leave the city. In two days, I will pull my forces back from your gates to let anyone coming out do so without fear of imperiling the city. You have two days to decide." He spurred his horse, turned, and cantered back to the stables.

3

Forest

Forest stood in the doorway, staring into the same piercing blue eyes as Soren's. She had no doubt that she'd finally found his mother.

"Your son is alive, ma'am," she told her.

The woman swayed slightly and gripped the doorframe to steady herself. She regained her composure and looked sternly at Forest. "If this is some sick dare that you and your friends…," she began.

"You used to sing to him to sleep, even when he was too old for it," Forest interrupted. "Your husband would stay up with him and point out the constellations. He had a dog…"

The woman's breath caught, and her legs gave out. Forest barely caught her before she fell.

"May I come in?" Forest asked, helping her to stand.

The woman nodded in shock.

Forest stepped into the living room, which lay under a thick layer of clutter, which itself lay under a thick layer of dust.

The woman looked about the room with a touch of shame. "Sorry, I don't get visitors," she apologized. "Please sit down, and I'll make you tea," she added, thinking that the distraction would help her collect her wits.

"Tea would be nice, thank you," Forest replied and moved a pile of clothing off a chair to sit down while the woman hunted for a kettle. She struggled to locate it, her heart and mind both racing. She willed herself to calm down and noticed the kettle in the sink. She filled it with water, carried it to the fireplace, and hung it on a hook, then sat down on the sofa facing Forest, her hands shaking.

"Forgive me if I don't trust that this is real," she began, rubbing her hands to still them.

"I understand," Forest comforted her. "I assure you that it is." Forest placed her own hands in her lap. "Pardon me for not introducing myself. I'm Forest."

"Pleased to meet you, Forest. I'm Petra." She lowered her hands to her sides, then decided to wedge them under her legs. She mustered the courage to ask, "How is my son?"

"He is well," Forest assured her.

Relief flooded through Petra, but doubts nagged her. "How do you know him?" she asked.

"I come from far east of here. That's where I met him."

"How is it that you come to be here, but not him, if you don't mind my asking?"

"Your son couldn't be here because he is preoccupied, but undoubtedly would be if he could. He doesn't know that I'm here. He doesn't even know that it's possible that I could be here." Forest paused, uncertain whether to reveal how it was possible. She decided she should. "I've been shown how to control the airships. Very few people know this even can be done, let alone how."

"So, he didn't send you?" she asked, crestfallen.

"In a way, he did." Forest braced herself and leaned forward. "I need your help."

The kettle began whistling, interrupting her, but Petra seemed not to hear it.

"The kettle, ma'am," Forest pointed out.

"Oh, right," she replied, coming to her senses. She got up and reached to take it off its hook.

"It's hot!" Forest warned her, just in time to stop her from scalding her bare hand on the metal. "Perhaps I should get it," she added, rising and politely shooing Petra back to her seat. Forest picked up a dishtowel and used it to insulate her hand while carrying the kettle to the kitchen. She rummaged around for a couple of cups and located a tin of tea on the counter. She prepared two cups of tea and brought them to the living room, handing one to Petra on a saucer before returning to sit down with the other one.

Petra took the dish, but her trembling hand made the cup rattle, so she put it on the table. "You say you need my help?"

"Yes." She put down her own cup. "Pardon me, but I'll speak frankly." She gauged Petra's readiness before continuing. "Your son is consumed with rage. He feels betrayed by the world."

Tears began to flow down Petra's cheeks, but she nodded for her to continue.

"He leads an army that lays waste to everything and everyone in its path while he tries to assuage his anger." Petra seemed unable to absorb this information, but Forest pressed on regardless. "If you're willing, I'd like your help in convincing him that the world hasn't thrown him aside."

This was too much for Petra, and she stood, unsteadily. "Give me a moment," she said and stumbled through the clutter to the bathroom. She failed to close the door fully, and Forest could see her hunched over the sink sobbing.

Forest shifted uncomfortably in her chair, waiting for her return.

She emerged a few moments later, having dried her tears. "What can I do?" she asked stoically.

"Come with me, and I'll take you to him. Pack lightly, but dress warmly."

Forest warmed her hands by the small flame of the burner that Petra had acquired for their journey by bartering what few possessions she still had. She'd told Forest that she didn't plan on returning home, come what may. She was able to buy provisions that would last most of the way east.

Petra looked across the compartment and examined Forest. "You're skin and bones, girl. Forgive me for not noticing before. I was befuddled. Are you all right?"

"I'm okay, thank you. It took me a long time to find you, and I didn't have much to sustain myself while I searched."

Forest's sorry state compounded the guilt that Petra felt. "I'm sorry about that, but I'm glad you found me in the end." She reached for some hard bread and handed it to Forest. "You should eat something."

Forest politely refused. "We should conserve what we have. It's a long journey."

Petra was silent for a while as she sat thinking. "At my house, you said that my son feels thrown away. How can he feel that way, knowing how much his father and I love him?"

Forest debated softening what she said, but decided ultimately that Petra needed to understand her son fully if she was going to reach him. "He thinks you abandoned him," she said finally.

The blunt statement stabbed Petra through the heart, and she sat silently for a long while before replying. "My son's name was chosen by secret lottery when the airship came. Armed guards came to our house and took him to the holding cells. When his father came home and discovered that he'd been taken, he concocted an ill-conceived plan to rescue him. Apparently, that's pretty common, and because it was anticipated, he was easily caught and imprisoned. I was arrested too, under suspicion of aiding him, and we were both still in jail when our son was escorted to the airship and sent away. We were released immediately afterward, but I couldn't forgive my husband, and he couldn't forgive himself. We separated, and he took to drinking. He drank himself to death within a few moons. Soren's dog sat on the stoop, waiting for him to return. He waited year after year until one day he was just gone, and I was alone. I thought about my son every moment of every day. We never abandoned him."

Forest mulled it over. She'd too easily accepted Soren's view because she felt abandoned by her own mother, but in truth, it was Petra that had been abandoned, being left behind by her son, her husband, even her son's pet. Forest wondered if Lily felt abandoned by her. She hadn't spent much time with her sister since their father's death, and then she'd left her in Bayre to ride north with her adopted family, Jarom and Nara. She'd deserted them too, as well as Addis, who'd be nothing but kind to her after their rough introduction. *Am I becoming my mother?* she wondered and vowed to make family a priority when she returned to Bayre, if the world allowed it.

"Where did the airship take him?" Petra asked, interrupting Forest's thoughts.

"A hard place in the far north. He survived it, but I think it changed him, fed his anger, and solidified his resolve."

"He always was a sensitive child. The world isn't fair," Petra responded, more to herself than to Forest.

Forest looked over their supplies. "We should land so I can hunt for food to last us the rest of our trip," she said. "We'll stop at my village. I know where to find game."

Petra wrapped herself tightly in blankets and closed her eyes.

As the airship landed, Forest stood at the door and warned Petra, "Brace yourself. I expect my village won't be in great shape." Forest herself hadn't seen it since she'd fled and wasn't prepared for the quiet as she stepped out of the ship. She'd readied herself for the ruin, but not the silence. When she closed her eyes, it was as though her village had never been. She opened them to the remains of familiar structures, but it felt ghostly.

Petra exited the ship behind her and stepped around her to survey the village. "My son did this?" she asked, shocked.

"His army, yes."

Petra was paralyzed. "Why?"

"Anger. Loss."

"We can't stay here," Petra said, agitated. "I have to go to him. I have to stop this."

"We have to eat," Forest reminded her. "I'll hunt, and we'll leave as quickly as we can. Can you start a fire?"

Petra wavered but accepted that she had to defer to Forest's judgment. "Yes – I think so. I'll try."

Forest stepped back into the ship and grabbed her bow and a quiver of arrows. It felt odd in her hand, as though she had somehow traveled back in time. She shook off the feeling and headed toward the woods.

It was near dark when she returned, but she could see from the treeline that Petra had been successful in getting a fire going. Forest shifted the game to her other shoulder and trudged toward the fire. Getting closer, she didn't see Petra, so she called out, "I'm back. Hunting was good. We'll be out of here in no time."

"Forest," Petra called back, forcing Forest to seek out her voice. Forest spotted her, knife at her throat, with a shifty-looking man standing behind her.

"You're not going anywhere," he said.

4

Kala

The day on which Soren had promised Bayre immunity for deserters arrived, and people began congregating in the streets, waking Kala with the unusual sound of activity in a city that had been eerily quiet for moons. *Today would be a day of tough decisions for many people,* she reckoned. She looked at the leathers at the foot of her bed but opted instead to dress casually – she didn't want to be recognized as the de facto symbol of Bayre's defense. *Let people decide their fate without my interference,* she thought. She didn't bother checking the kitchens for food, knowing the cupboards had been bare for days, and just slipped out the temple gates into the gathering crowd. She kept her head down and moved with it toward the city's gate.

Skinny children and gaunt elderly shuffled past her, straining to carry what they could in bundles in their arms and packs on their backs. They looked exhausted, hungry, desperate, and ready to take their chances in the terrifyingly unfamiliar world outside the city. Kala understood the preference of many to face death moving forward, rather than waiting for it to come to them.

Men and women of fighting-age also moved with the crowd, keeping their heads down in shame. They'd chosen survival, even if it meant becoming the enemy of their neighbors, friends, and family. Kala acknowledged their numbers dispiritedly but did not judge them.

Families argued. A young mother pleaded with her son not to leave. He pulled away in his ill-fitting armor and as she begged him to come back. Kala passed a woman trying to convince her elderly parents to join her. They held hands and steadfastly refused. "This is our home. If we're to die, we'll die here," they told her. Kala hurried past, feeling like an intruder.

From up ahead, she began to hear demands of, "Open the gate!" and the number of voices calling for it grew steadily. The gate guards drew their weapons and took up defensive positions as the crowd edged forward. The citizens gripped their own weapons, and tensions grew. A stone was thrown that bounced off a guard's armor. *This is what Soren wants*, Kala thought angrily, *for us to fight each other and save him the trouble.*

One of the city's Councilors stepped between the crowd and the guards, trying to re-establish order. "You can't trust the amnesty," she told them. "You're safer inside the city."

"We'll take our chances," a woman declared, clutching a child to her breast.

"It's better than starving," a man beside her added.

A lookout from the wall interrupted the proceedings by reporting that Soren's army was moving back.

The crowd stilled. "Soren is honoring his word," a man cried out, which emboldened the mob.

Kala never doubted that Soren would keep his promise. *So long as it advances his agenda, why wouldn't he?* she thought.

Chants of, "Open the gates!" resumed and grew in volume.

The Councilor deflated and waved everyone silent. "You have the right to leave if you wish," she conceded and turned to the guards. "Open the gate," she ordered, loud enough for everyone to hear, then added quietly so that only they could hear, "but be prepared to close it quickly."

The evacuees began to queue up, no longer anxious to leave but resigned to their need to. Deserting fighters embarrassedly avoided looking the guards in the eye.

Two strong men approached an enormous wheel around which heavy chains were wrapped. They began to turn it and the chains went taut as the wheel spun and the gate began to open. They continued their labor until the gate had opened the width of two people, then stopped and stood ready to close it upon receiving the order to do so.

Kala left her hiding place in a doorway and strode up the stairs to the ramparts. Looking down from the wall, she could see that Soren's forces had indeed moved back and created a corridor that would let people pass unimpeded toward the south. The old, the young, and the sick exited the gate and moved hesitantly toward the corridor.

Deserting fighters were directed to a second line that advanced directly toward the opposing army, terrified that it was all a ruse and that it would surge forward at any moment. They edged forward cautiously, hands in the air. Their weapons were confiscated, and they were absorbed into the enemy lines. Kala couldn't make out what became of them afterward.

Kala turned her attention back to the line of people heading south. It stretched as far as she could see, and it seemed like an eternity before its tail end came into view. She watched until it became apparent that no more stragglers would join it. She estimated that two-thirds of the city's population had left. The corridor of safe passage closed behind the last of the evacuees, leaving an unbroken front of soldiers facing the city.

The mighty wheels began to spin again, the chains pulled back, and the gates closed with a finality that made it clear that those who remained were now truly on their own.

Days went by, and Kala's continued her routine of patrolling the ramparts, keeping an eye on Soren's army, swollen now with the recent desertions. Her stomach clenched. It had been some time since she last had something to eat. *If they're waiting for us to starve to death, they won't have to wait much longer,* she thought despondently.

Horn began to blare, followed by shouting. "We're under attack – from the sea!"

This caught Kala wholly off-guard, and she cast a last look down at Soren's army before sprinting along the wall toward its seaward side. As she neared it, she spotted an armada of varying-size ships emerging from a fog bank and heading toward the city's sea gate, spears bristling from the bow of the lead ship. Kala skidded to a halt, pulled out her swords, and prepared herself for the assault that had finally come.

Soldiers of Soren's army began edging gingerly over the rocks to join the coastal attack, shielding themselves from the archers on the walls. The lead ship came alongside the pier at speed and sailors swung down onto it to secure the vessel. Ramps were dropped to bridge the gap, and spear-wielding men and women streamed off the ship. Two women led the charge toward the city. The color of their paths seemed all wrong to Kala, prompting her to look closer. *That looks like Dhara and Kaia*, she thought. *By the gods, it is!* As she realized this, Soren's soldiers drew their weapons and charged at them.

"Open the gate!" Kala shouted to the guards below. "They're on our side!"

Kala sprinted down the stairs, taking them five at a time. She raced out the stairwell toward the men guarding the gate. "Open the gate," she ordered again. "They're friendly."

They looked at each other uncertainly, sending Kala into a rage. "Open that gate, or I will flay ever gods-damn one of you and open it myself!" she bellowed and stepped closer, swords drawn.

The fire in her eyes changed their minds, and they turned and began opening the gates, which had opened no more than a crack before Kala squeezed through to join her friends. Soren's forces had already engaged the spear-wielding vanguard, and Dhara's people formed a human wall, holding them back while sailors bounded off the ship carrying sacks of grain and other supplies to the city's open gate.

"Hold them back!" Dhara shouted and stabbed at a soldier, forcing him to back up. The front row of Dhara's people knelt, spears out, and were joined by two more rows of spear-wielding men and women, who formed a wall that prevented the soldiers from accessing the pier. A provisioning line formed behind them and goods were rushed into the city. The guards at the gate took them, shouted for help, and the sailors sprinted back for more.

Dhara's people successfully held Soren's forces back until soldiers carrying larger shields began to replace those who were less well equipped to face spears, and they began to push forward again. Kala spun around at the clash of steel and raced to reinforce the defenses opposite Dhara and Kaia. Soldiers had formed a wedge of shields and were trying to break through the barrier of spears. Kala threw herself at the wall of shields, climbing them, and attacking the soldiers from above. It was enough to break their formation, and the line of spears reformed.

The sound of intense fighting behind her had Kala rushing to reinforce the defenses further down the pier. She roved along its length, engaging Soren's soldiers wherever the line of spears broke, and she beat back the soldiers until the line could reform. Kala heard Dhara's voice shouting a steady stream of commands above the din, but she was too busy engaging the enemy to spare a glance at how she fared.

Any ship that could squeeze a place against the pier docked and began unloading supplies that were quickly whisked inside the gates. Soren's archers began peppering the ships from the shore until the city's archers along the ramparts returned suppressing fire.

Despite the valiant defense by Dhara's people, the battle for the pier was slowly being lost to Soren's more experienced fighters. They pressed inexorably inward. Kala flew along the line, a whirlwind of steel. No matter where she pushed back, breaches formed elsewhere. They were steadily being overwhelmed.

Kala stumbled over one of the many bodies that littered the pier, righted herself, and paused to catch her breath. A soldier lunged at her, swinging his axe down on her. She raised her swords to absorb the blow, but another sword parried it first. Kala swiveled around to see Brother Grey standing behind her.

"What did I miss?" he asked, as he disarmed the man and ran him through. Before Kala could reply, he spun off to engage another pair of soldiers that had broken through to the pier. Kala turned and raced to fill another breach. Together, they kept the defenses from shattering beneath the onslaught of Soren's forces, but it was only a matter of time before they did.

A lookout from the wall above shouted, "Pirates!" The sailors ferrying goods into the city didn't even blink, so Kala paid the news no mind and kept up her attack.

"They're attacking the rear of Soren's army," the lookout reported.

The attacking soldiers wavered at the news and were pushed back a step or two before they realized that there was nothing they could do about their flank and resumed pressing forward. The defenses began to crumble, and the last of the ships broke off, some still unable to unload their cargo.

Dhara recognized that they were could not last and shouted, "Fall back to the city!" Her people began to retreat. Those that got separated from the main body and were quickly cut down, but most stayed together and reinforced each other. They slowly collapsed back to the gate.

One of Dhara's companions lunged forward to protect a friend and fell herself. Kala leaped to their aid and found herself outside the circle of spears that was receding to the gate. She whirled and slashed, parried and dodged, and barely kept herself alive. She spared a glance backward and was relieved to see the pair rejoin the formation of spears. The distraction cost her, however, as she slipped on a pool of blood and fell. She rolled over in time to see a spear whistle over her and impale a soldier striking downward at her. Dhara hauled Kala to her feet. She and Kaia had left the protection of the formation to retrieve her. They were joined by Grey and together, the four of them

24

fought ferociously to make it back to the gate. Defenders on the wall heaved stones down on the advancing soldiers, buying Kala, Grey, Dhara, and Kaia the briefest of windows to squeeze through the gate before it slammed shut behind them.

Kala collapsed to her knees, utterly spent, her swords falling from her leaden arms.

"I'm sorry," Brother Grey apologized to her.

"What for?" she asked him wearily.

"For losing track of you. It won't happen again."

"You were defending the city. That's more important," she assured him.

"No, it's not," he replied flatly, helping her stand.

"Are you okay?" a familiar voice inquired, prompting her to look up in time to see Calix rush forward to examine Dhara's wounds. She protested but didn't stop him.

Shock and relief flooded through Kala. *Calix is alive?!* she thought and would have burst into tears if she were she not so emotionally spent.

Grey retrieved her swords for her, wiped them off, and handed them to her when a second familiar voice called to her, "Kala?" She scanned the courtyard for its source, her gaze finally settling on Skye. He was standing in front of her, still holding a lamb that he'd just carried through the gate. He transferred it into the arms of the woman beside him, never taking his eyes off Kala. He walked to her and enveloped her in an embrace. She buried her head into his chest, and he held her tightly, unwilling to ever let go again.

She looked up into his eyes. "How?" she asked.

"We found allies," he laughed.

"I noticed – but how?"

"Well, first, I found a navy, and they agreed to help, but they weren't fighters, so we found the pirates, and Hawke convinced them to help us, then..."

"Hawke. Where is he?" Kala interrupted, noticing his absence and looking about for him anxiously.

"He was on a pirate ship, helping coordinate their attack. They did what they do best," he chuckled. "They stole a good portion of Soren's supplies."

"Uh oh," Kala observed.

"What do you mean, 'uh oh'?" he asked. "We restocked the city's supplies and pilfered Soren's. What's the problem?"

"The problem is… you just reversed the siege."

Skye didn't grasp the implication.

"You just forced Soren's hand."

5

Soren

Soren was livid. "What just happened?" he demanded to know.

Lennox and Seline sat across from him. "The city had allies," Seline replied, stating the obvious.

"How did we not account for that possibility?" Soren asked.

"Every settlement we've come across has acted in isolation. We've never seen them coordinate before," Seline explained.

"How are they coordinating?" he asked.

Seline thought for a moment. "People once communicated using birds," she replied.

Lennox scoffed, but one look from Soren shut him up and had him resume his strategy of keeping his head down.

"It could be airships too," Seline speculated.

Soren reddened in anger and gripped the table forcefully.

Seline readied herself for him to flip it, but he restrained himself. "What's the impact of this attack?" he asked.

"Our losses were minimal, but the city has been resupplied, while our own stores have been seriously reduced," she replied.

"The upshot being?"

Seline winced to deliver the news. "The city can probably now outlast our siege."

Soren swept the papers off the table. "I'm done waiting for the siege to deliver us the city. It's time we act," he declared, slamming his fist into the table.

"I have an idea," Lennox said tentatively.

Seline and Soren turned to face him. "It is?" Soren asked impatiently.

"We agreed that the tunnels below the city were too small to allow a sizable force into the city… but we don't need to take the city – we just need to sabotage the gates. Then, our forces outside it will have free access."

"And why didn't you suggest this before?"

"The reward only now justifies the risk."

"It'd be a suicide mission," Soren pointed out.

"Not a problem," Lennox replied coldly.

Soren didn't like Lennox's methods, but he was willing to overlook them when they got results. "How exactly do you propose we sabotage the gate?"

Seline was sure Lennox had no idea or was about to propose something inadequate to the task, so she jumped in. "I may have just the thing," she replied. One look at Lennox confirmed that he was relieved that she had an answer, so she pressed on. "Based on conversations I've had with our alchemists, and the ingredients I've collected as we've traveled, I think I have everything I need to make an explosive. It'll be crude, but it would be enough to render the gate mechanism inoperable."

"Like fireworks?" Soren asked skeptically.

"Yes, just more powerful."

"Then, why sneak in at all?" Soren asked. "Why not just blow the gate from the outside?"

"It wouldn't be that powerful," Seline had to admit, "but I could make something strong enough to destroy the mechanism that holds the gates closed."

Soren mulled this over and began to look slightly less apt to murder someone. "Make it happen!" he barked. "Dismissed."

Seline and Lennox filed out – Seline to check her notes and supplies, and Lennox to recruit a team of saboteurs. Soren stayed in his tent and brooded. What he was most unhappy about, having had his nose bloodied twice now, was the possibility that his army might start viewing him as fallible. *That would not do*, he concluded. *The city needs to be crushed and fast.*

Seline walked back to her tent and greeted her assistant as she entered. "Where are we with the black powder?"

Her assistant waved at a tabletop filled by ruined tins. "Further," she reported. "I've tried different ratios of the ingredients, and I think I've found one that explodes more than it burns, unlike like our earlier trials." She handed Seline a tiny urn that had been blown apart from within. "The bat guano is by far the most important ingredient."

Seline turned the remains of the urn over in her hand. "Excellent," she said. "How long would it take us to produce enough to do some real damage?"

Her assistant thought for a moment. "Do you want it to work well, or do you want it quickly?"

"Judging by Soren's mood, I'd say 'quickly.'"

"One day then, but we'll need help."

"We have an entire army."

"They're dolts," her assistant countered.

"Perhaps some of our captives might have the necessary skill."

"That's more likely."

"I'll talk to the commander and see who he'll give me." Her assistant nodded and got back to work, while Seline left to secure help. She returned shortly with twenty captives that had experience as tradespersons, along with a few soldiers to keep an eye on them. Seline put several to work collecting crystals from vats of bat guano that were soaking in urine, some to scraping sulfur from stone, and others to grinding charcoal into a fine powder. Seline and her assistant reserved the task of combining the ingredients for themselves. Her tent smelled like hell, but she made steady progress. By midday, the following day, they had worked without ceasing until they had produced enough explosive powder to do the job. Seline delivered it to Soren and returned to her tent to rest, despite the foul smells pervading it.

Randl met with his team of thirty soldiers, hand-picked by Lennox for the mission of disabling the city's gates. Randl didn't know what Lennox had promised the others but surmised that they all had their pressure points. His was his young daughter, who needed constant care to ensure that her lungs did not fill with fluid and drown her. Lennox had promised him all the help he could ever need to care for her if he would lead this mission. With one look at his daughter's labored breathing, he agreed without reservation.

Lennox had produced a detailed map of the city based on accounts sourced from the city's deserters and cross-referenced using multiple sources to confirm its accuracy. He'd had to kill a few people whose memories were weak or whose information he didn't trust. He was sure that some lied outright to protect loved ones in the city, and he respected them all the more for it, even as he killed them.

Lennox had provided Randl with the satchel of powder that Seline had produced and relayed to him her exhortation that it be kept dry. Randl reread her instructions for igniting it. He was to plunge a lit torch into it and run like hell. He couldn't fathom how that would do anything, but he'd long suspected that Seline was a witch, and trusted that her concoction would have the desired effect.

Randl and his men dressed entirely in black, smeared their hands and faces with soot, and blackened their blades with paint. Randl had trouble seeing them when darkness descended, so he was confident in their ability to pass unseen by the guards on the wall. It was also a moderately cloudy night, so if they timed things right, they should be able to slip into the tunnels unobserved.

Lennox poked his head into the tent and informed them, "It's time."

Randl nodded and led his men out of the tent and along the shoreline toward the sewer outflow that had a damaged grate. The moon would occasionally poke through the clouds, and his team would freeze and blend into the rocks. He could hear formations of soldiers moving about in the camp, intended to hold the attention of the guards on the wall. No alarm was sounded, which he took to indicate that his party was succeeding in the first step of their mission. They reached the grate, and one-by-one, they squeezed through it.

The men moved through the tunnels, occasionally climbing up shafts to confirm where they were in the city and descending again to report to Randl. They finally found a shaft that Randl was pretty sure came up near the city gates. They queued up beneath it, the strongest of them first, and Randl last. Randl had them wait until the city guards would be deep into their shift and consequently most tired, but not yet perking up at the prospect of being relieved. *It's time*, he thought and tapped the man in front of him to signal that it was time to move out. The signal traveled along the line and the men began to climb the ladder.

At the top of the ladder, the man at the lead peered through the grate. He saw no one and heard nothing. He braced himself and pushed with all of his strength against the grate. It held for a moment, then lifted with a scraping sound. He paused and waited to see if the sound had given them away, and when it appeared that it hadn't, he lifted it slowly and pushed it out of the way. He pulled his blackened sword from its sheath and tapped the man's shoulder beneath him. He waited a moment for the signal to pass along the line, then climbed out to the street above. No one saw him, and he peeled off and pressed himself against a wall deep in the shadows. The second man emerged and did similarly. Ten men successfully exited the shaft before a shout rang out. The men fanned out to provide cover while the remaining twenty men rushed out of the hole.

City guards began shouting, "They're in the city!" but they were confused as to how it was possible, where else they might be, and what to do about it.

Randl emerged last, surrounded by fierce fighting. His party appeared to have the upper hand, and the fighting moved toward the gate. Randl clutched his satchel and followed his men, hiding in the shadows.

His men fought their way to the gate and began battling the guards there, even as more defenders streamed down off the walls. Four of his men dropped their weapons, ducked past their comrades, and grabbed hold of the enormous wheel that controlled the gates. They strained and began to open them.

"The gate!" the guards yelled. "They're opening the gate!"

Randl looked around quickly. A third of his party had fallen, and the remainder were locked in combat with a number of guards that seemed to grow by the moment. *Now or never*, he concluded. He clutched the satchel tight against his body and burst from his hiding place toward the wheel that opened and closed the gate. The bodies of the four men who had opened it were peppered with arrows and lay motionless on the ground. He dodged past the fighting. An arrow buried itself into his side, and he stumbled but kept running. He slid under a blade as one of his men threw himself on it to buy Randl passage. A second arrow struck him in the shoulder, and he lost feeling in his left arm.

He slid along the ground, past a pair of men who were covered in blood, but still fighting. He grabbed a fallen torch and raced toward the gate mechanism. He leaped over the bodies at its base, sliding the satchel off his shoulder and hitching it against one of the wheel's handles. Four more arrows bit into his back, and he slumped down the wall. He rolled to face forward, spitting blood as he raised the torch in his faltering grip. *For my daughter*, he declared and plunged it into the satchel.

The blast shook the city. A guard, who had rushed to join the melee, only to be blown backward off his feet, picked himself up off the ground, ears ringing. As the smoke cleared, and his wits returned, he found himself looking through the ruined gate at the fires of the army camped outside it.

6

Forest

Forest laid the brace of fowl gently on the ground, not wanting to spook the man that held a blade against Petra's throat. Petra was terrified, so Forest tried to keep him calm. She slowly raised her hands back into the air to show that they were empty.

"We don't want any trouble," she told him.

"Well, you've found it anyway," he replied sharply and pushed Petra forward a pace. He whistled, and several more men emerged from behind buildings. They were dirty and thin and had a feral look about them. They surrounded Forest as she stood motionless. She mentally took stock of where her knives were on her body and which of the men looked the most menacing, but she stayed still for Petra's sake.

"Looks like you're making us dinner," the man said to Forest, gesturing to the birds on the ground, "but put your knife on the ground first."

"If you want me to make you dinner, I'll need it," she replied curtly.

The man looked back and forth between his comrades, but a last hungry look at the birds convinced him to relent. "Okay, but try anything, and I'll slit her throat."

No need to be so gods-damn graphic about it, Forest thought angrily, seeing the terror in Petra's eyes. "I won't," was all she said, knelt down, picked up a bird, and began plucking it. Forest looked up after a moment to see the men still standing around her, watching her warily. "This would go a lot faster with some help," she told them.

The leader motioned to two of his men, who stepped toward Forest. She tossed each of them a bird without looking up to see what they did with it. *If they want to eat, they'll figure it out*, she thought ruefully. She finished with her first bird and picked up another, hazarding a glance at the two men who were still struggling with the ones she'd given them. She sighed. "Hold it upside down," she told them. "Pull downwards. Not too many feathers at a time," she corrected one of them. "You'll tear the skin." They appeared to comply with her advice, so she turned her attention back to her own bird. Finishing up, she rose slowly to her feet to stretch her muscles. "I don't suppose any of you know how to build a spit?" she asked those around her to blank stares. "Great," she muttered. "I need to fetch some branches," she informed the supposed leader.

"Callum, keep an eye on her, and..." he began.

"Yes, yes," Forest interrupted before he could threaten Petra's life again. "I'm not going to try anything." She turned and headed toward the woods, with the man she assumed was Callum following behind. She foraged about for what she needed to make a pair of spits on which she intended to roast the birds. She returned to find that the leader had bound Petra's wrists and ankles, and she sat by the fire, eyeing the men nervously, who watched her as hungrily as they did the birds.

Forest could not let this stand. She stood with her armful of branches and faced the leader. "I have terms," she told him bluntly.

"You're not in a position to negotiate," he told her smugly.

She looked over the sorry state of his men. "I sure as hell am. You lot seem to struggle with feeding yourselves. Me, I know these woods like the back of my hand. If you want me to provide for you, I will, but I have one condition – no one touches her," she said, pointing at Petra. "If anyone does, you can gods-damn starve."

"You'll starve with us," he threatened.

"I'm prepared for that, but I'm guessing that you're tired of starving."

The man looked angry and desperate to find some way to reassert his authority over her, but Forest stood resolutely, and he could see in her eyes that she would not be cowed. He looked over at the man nearest Petra. "Leave her alone," he barked, choosing instead to assert his dominance over his men.

Forest assumed she'd only bought Petra, and likely herself, a temporary reprieve, but resumed assembling the spits and roasting the fowl. The men salivated as the birds cooked, and Forest had to shoo them away to keep them from tearing into the birds before they were fully cooked. *That's all I need*, she thought. *They get sick from their own stupidity and blame me.* She announced when they were ready, and was rewarded with having her hands and feet bound like Petra, before the men devoured their dinner, leaving nothing for her or Petra. Forest's stomach rumbled, but she'd been hungrier before, and pushed the hunger down deep inside along with her anger.

The leader looked up, wiping grease off his chin onto his sleeve, and waved a leg of grouse at the airship. "What's with that? Why is it just sitting there?"

"It probably needs a passenger before it'll leave," Forest said, in part truthfully.

"It's not tied down," the man observed, suspicious. "It's just sitting there," he repeated.

"How do I know? Seems cursed to me," Forest replied.

The man shuddered involuntarily, then feigned that he'd lost interest and resumed eating.

Forest shifted closer to Petra. "I'll get us out of this," she whispered. "I just need to figure out how."

"Thank you," Petra whispered back.

"We're not out of here yet," Forest replied.

"I meant for before. Thank you."

Forest patted her leg with her bound hands. "We'll see our way through this," she assured her.

The leader woke in the morning to find Forest sitting, still bound, staring at him. He glanced at the man assigned to keep watch over her in the night, who was snoring loudly nearby. The leader rose and kicked him awake, gesturing angrily at Forest.

The man sheepishly resumed keeping watch, despite how obviously unnecessary it was – she hadn't done anything when she was unobserved, so why would she now? Further, the leader had her bow and knife stashed somewhere.

"I assume you want breakfast," she said to the leader.

He licked his lips despite himself. "Of course. Get to it."

She held out her hands, reminding him that she needed her restraints removed first.

The man gestured to her 'guard' to remove them.

Forest got up and stretched. She held out her hand, "My knife?" she asked.

The man retrieved it and handed it to her.

"My bow?" she asked.

He looked annoyed. "Do you need it?"

"I hope not, but you never know. The woods are a dangerous place."

He retrieved it reluctantly and gave it to her.

She strapped it to her back and turned to Petra. "I won't be long," she told her, but loud enough for everyone to hear. She headed back out into the woods, shadowed wearily by the man assigned to keep an eye on her.

She started by looking for the nest of the birds she'd killed the day before, to see if she could find eggs. She found the nest, but scavengers had devoured the eggs overnight – bits of shell lay strewn about. She sighed and began looking for mushrooms and other edible plants. She gathered them in a makeshift basket that she fashioned from her cloak. She returned to the village with a cloak full of food before the sun had been too long in the sky.

"Do you have a large bowl?" she asked, and someone fetched her one. She placed the produce wrapped in her cloak down near the fire. "Get that going again," she ordered a man lying nearby. She ignored his foul response and crossed her arms, delaying preparing the meal until he knuckled under. The leader glared at him, and he shot her a look of murder in turn before grumbling and restarting the fire.

Having won that contest of wills, Forest turned her attention back to making breakfast. She looked about the village until she spied an unburned plank that she could use as a cutting board. She returned with it and began preparing an enormous salad. Forest cooked the mushrooms and added them to the bowl. It was pretty obvious when she'd added the last of her ingredients as the men watched her anxiously. She pushed the full bowl toward the nearest man.

The leader stopped him before he could serve himself. He looked warily at Forest. "You eat some first."

"She'll eat some," Forest replied, gesturing to Petra.

"You both will," the man decided.

Thank the gods he's an idiot, Forest thought and prepared two tiny portions for herself and Petra.

The man looked over the bowls and added a mushroom and some berries to each, ensuring that they contained some of everything that Forest had brought back.

Forest and Petra ate their breakfast under the watchful eye of the leader. Once they'd finished, he gave the go-ahead to his men to serve themselves. The salad was gone in an instant, and the men did not look as though their hunger was even remotely sated.

"I need to relieve myself," Forest announced.

The leader looked up, annoyed. "Why didn't you do it when you were in the woods?" he demanded.

"I didn't need to, then," she replied.

He rolled his eyes. "Callum, watch her – closely," he ordered, intending to unnerve her.

Forest just got up and marched toward the trees. Callum scrambled to catch up to her. She entered the forest and looked around.

"What the hell are you looking for?" he asked.

"You ever wipe your ass with poison oak?" she asked him back. He shut up, and she found a bush that afforded her a little privacy. "Turn around," she demanded.

"I'm not allowed," he replied.

"Well, I can't go with you staring at me," she countered.

He sighed and spun around slowly.

Forest finished up and marched past him. "I need to hunt," she told him. "I assume you'll want to get permission," she added and headed back toward the village.

Arriving, she grabbed her bow and secured her quiver to her back while Callum spoke with the leader. Callum returned, looking glum that he'd been assigned to shadow her.

"Let's go," she told him and headed briskly back into the woods. She led him to a stream and filled her waterskin. "We're hunting rabbit, and their skittish, so keep silent," she told him as she got up. She led him around the woods for a while, and eventually back to the stream.

"This isn't working," she told him, knowing full well that his stomach rumbled. "You make enough noise to wake the dead. You stay here."

He looked unwilling.

"I'm not going to doing anything. You still have Petra."

He looked at her blankly.

"Your *other* hostage," she reminded him.

Understanding sparked in his dim eyes, and she did her best to suppress rolling her own. He nodded grudgingly and sat down with his back to a tree.

Forest gestured to a nearby berry bush as she walked away. "Do *not* eat those," she warned him, even though she knew full well that they weren't poisonous.

A long while later, she returned to find the man staring off into the woods, bored out of his mind. She walked up to him, moving as silently as she always did in the woods, and he didn't notice her approach. She stood, looking down on him, then finally reached up and snapped a twig.

Callum looked up at the noise and nearly jumped out of his skin when he saw her hovering over top of him.

"Relax," she told him. "At least nothing ate you while I was gone."

He looked around fearfully and scrambled to his feet to move closer to her.

She handed him the brace of rabbits she carried. "You carry it," she ordered him. "I'm exhausted." She headed back to the village, with Callum hurrying behind her.

"Anyone ever skin a rabbit?" she asked on her return. No one volunteered. "For the gods' sake," she muttered and began preparing them herself. It took a long time, and it was starting to grow dark before she'd finished. The men were ravenous. She placed the rabbits' organs on stones by the fire to get them cooking. "You can eat those while the rabbits are cooking," she told them. She pulled her pack to her and pulled out some herbs and flowers that she'd collected. She cut some up and stuffed them inside the first rabbit.

"What are you doing?" the leader demanded to know.

"Seasoning them," she replied impatiently. She stuffed the leaf of an herb in her mouth and began chewing it. She handed him a flower, which he sniffed cautiously.

"Smells sweet," he told her, handing it back.

"That's the point," she replied and got back to work. She let the men know when the organs were ready to eat, and they consumed them greedily. She placed the rabbits on the spits. She dropped the smallest one and cursed. She picked it up and wiped the dirt off it.

"That one's yours," the leader declared, and his men laughed.

At least I get to eat something, she thought and finished skewering the remaining rabbits.

She announced when they were done, and the leader reminded her magnanimously which rabbit was hers. She grumbled, but removed it from the spit and carried it over to Petra. It was difficult to divide in two with bound hands, but she did her best and handed Petra the larger half.

"You should take this one," Petra told her, but Forest politely refused and began eating her portion.

Having watched her begin eating, the leader signaled his men that they could do the same. They tore into their dinner like savages.

Forest was disgusted by their lack of manners and looked away before resuming eating. It was well after dark by the time dinner was finished. The men crowded around the fire, so she and Petra lay down a short distance away, under the watchful eye of the leader.

"This relationship is working out well," he announced. Forest rolled away from him as her response and moved closer to Petra so that they could keep each other warm.

Forest waited until she heard snoring from the men around the fire before rolling back over to face the man assigned to watch her and Petra. As she guessed, he too was sleeping soundly, slumped over on his side. Forest reached down and quietly pulled a knife from her boot, giving silent thanks to Kala for showing her how to conceal it. She spun it around in her hand and awkwardly sawed at her restraints until she cut through them. She reached down and removed her leg restraints. She put a finger to Petra's lips and woke her gently.

"We're leaving," she whispered, and quietly tried to untie her restraints. Finding it difficult, she gave up and just cut them. "Go to the ship," she told her and handed her pack to her to carry. "There are nuts and berries inside. We should be fine for the remainder of the trip."

Forest stepped gingerly toward the fire, which was burning low, no one being awake to tend to it. She looked to the treeline and saw the reflection of several sets of eyes peering back at her. She hurriedly stepped over the bodies of the men she'd drugged, the rabbit that she'd intentionally dropped being the only one that she didn't stuff with the narcotic flowers. Forest retrieved her bow, quiver, and knife, and stepped back toward the fire. She memorized the position of the men around it and quietly overturned a bucket of water into the firepit. The fire guttered out. *Your turn to contend with beasts*, she thought and tiptoed by moonlight toward the airship.

7

Cera

The mood in the great room was upbeat for the first time in several moons. It was well past midnight, but no one could sleep. Even the children in Celeste's care wandered in and out, not that she had ever enforced a strict bedtime. Skye and Calix had dragged chairs around the fireplace, and everyone sat talking and laughing.

Skye had prepared dinner with simple ingredients, but an elaborate preparation that exceeded his mastery. He did succeed in not burning it, however, and everyone raved about his cooking. "It's easy to please the starving," he joked. Lily and Celeste sang while they helped him wash dishes, trying without success to coax him into joining in. Skye had to threaten Kala with tying her to her chair if she tried to get up one more time to help. "Sit down and enjoy yourself. Let us take care of you for a change," he told her. She sat back and basked in the warmth of her friends.

Cera and Lily fawned over Calix, newly returned from near death. He joked that having Dhara's blood coursing through his veins gave him superpowers. Cera ran her fingers through his hair to confirm tactilely that he was really there. He feigned annoyance, but he was just as happy to be back among them as they were that he was. Eventually, he fled to the kitchens for an apple and returned with one for Dhara too – clearly just a pretext to sit beside her. Kaia noticed Kala's amazement and nodded knowingly in her direction. When pressed, Dhara swore that there was nothing between them, but Kaia saw the closeness that she permitted him but no one else, *ever*.

Skye declared the clean-up complete, put down his towel, and returned to the great room. He threw a log on the fire and plopped down beside Kala, pulling her onto his lap. He regaled everyone about his time among the pirates, during which he constantly feared for his life, but came to see that many of them had kind souls, despite their rough edges. Hawke wasn't around to corroborate Skye's stories, and Kala found herself missing him.

Kaia told everyone about how she'd snuck back into her village, hailed an airship, then went in search of transport north for those who had fled her village and those that Dhara and their newly-discovered brother liberated. She couldn't figure out how to make the airship go where she wanted and wound up bouncing around settlements along the coast. She finally landed at a port town and bumped into Skye, walking down the middle of the street. Once she's explained to him what they needed, he convinced a flotilla to head south to the river's mouth and ferry her people north as they arrived there by canoe. When they heard about the dire situation in Bayre, they retasked their makeshift navy with a resupply mission.

Skye about to describe it when an enormous explosion rocked the building. The high-set windows burst inward, and shards of glass rained across the room. Kala leaped off of Skye's lap, checked rapidly to make sure that no one was injured, then bolted to the temple gates. Brother Grey arrived just as she was hauling them open. A glance told her that he had no more idea than she did of what just happened. Frightened people ran past, and Kala heard them say, "The gate is open. The enemy is already in the city." She cursed herself for not being appropriately dressed for battle.

She grabbed Grey by the arm. "Get Celeste and the children out of the city through the tunnels."

"My place is at your side, protecting you," he protested.

"Can you please just protect my heart instead?"

A battle waged behind his eyes, but he relented. "As you wish."

She hugged him, despite his uncomfortableness. "Thank you!" she exclaimed and spun around to go fetch her weapons. Dhara and Kaia raced into the courtyard, with Calix, Lily, Cera, and Celeste hot on their heels, followed by Petr pushing Twill in his wheelchair.

Kala stopped and addressed Celeste, "Get the children. Go with Grey. He'll get you out of here. Petr, bring Twill."

"We're staying," Petr told her.

Celeste started to protest, but Twill stopped her by saying, "I know I'm not much help staying to fight, but I'd only slow you down fleeing."

Petr stepped forward and placed a hand on Twill's shoulder. "I'll look after him," he said.

Celeste stepped between them and embraced them.

Kala turned to Lily and Cera. "You're going with them," she told them and waved off Lily's protest. "Do as I say, dammit it. Celeste is going to need help with the children."

Lily looked torn, but Cera acquiesced and intervened with her. "It's okay," she told her. "It's only temporary," she lied.

Kala turned to Dhara and Kaia, and told them, "The gate is breached. We need to close it." Calix took a step closer to Dhara, clearly not leaving her side.

Skye skidded into the courtyard carrying Kala's leathers and weapons.

She took them, thanking him with a look. "War is upon us again," she told him.

Standing in the alleyway, Grey strained but succeeded in pulling the grate free. He slid it aside, and Celeste handed him the torch. He swung himself onto the ladder and began the descent to the tunnels. "Stay close," he told the group. Celeste shepherded the children down one by one after him, then waited for Lily and Cera to join them before following herself. Grey waited for them to assemble at the base of the shaft before leading them off down a tunnel, reminding them to stay silent.

They followed him through the crisscrossing tunnels as he navigated toward the exit that would take them outside the city's walls. At the last interchange, he stopped them. "Hold hands," he told everyone. "We go the rest of the way in the dark." He confirmed that all the children had joined hands, forming a chain bookended by Cera and Celeste. "When we exit, if it's safe to do so," he qualified, "stay together and stay behind me. If anything happens to me – run away from the city. Scatter. Do not stay together. Follow the coastline south. Do you understand?" The children nodded bravely, so he put down the torch, took Cera's hand, and guided them the last of the way to the exit in darkness.

He halted at the wine-covered opening and listened intently. The sounds of battle from inside the city masked any that might be nearer. He brushed the vines aside and peered outside. By the faint moonlight and the light of sporadically placed campfires, he could see that the fields were largely deserted of soldiers, but not entirely. *We can't wait,* he decided and squeezed Cera's hand to warn her that he was dropping it. He pulled out his sword and dagger, stepped out of the tunnel, and made his way quietly toward the nearest soldier. He flipped his dagger into a throwing position and hurled it at the man. The soldier gripped the pommel sticking out of his chest, but fell to the ground without raising an alarm.

Grey motioned for Cera to guide the children out of the tunnel and directed them to head toward the woods. Satisfied that she understood, he turned to stalk a second soldier. The soldier noticed his approach but didn't register that he wasn't an ally until Grey's thrown sword hit him full in the chest. A third soldier witnessed the assault and shouted to his compatriots. Grey pulled his sword free and called to Cera, "Run for the trees! Hide there." He turned to face a dozen soldiers approaching him. They fanned out, but Grey backed up to stay between them and the fleeing children, buying them as much time as he could.

Cera led the way, running toward the distant trees. She tripped and fell frequently, but picked herself up and made sure the children followed. It was hard to see them all in the dark, but she trusted that Lily and Celeste would pick up any stragglers. The enemy campfires receded, their light too far away to see by, but also too far away for anyone to see them she hoped.

She slowed as she approached the treeline and struggled to see the children that she hoped had followed her. She snagged a young boy who almost ran past her, then hazarded a low call to a girl she spotted off to her left. Slowly, they reassembled as a group. Celeste arrived with a pair of the youngest children and checked to see if anyone was missing. She quickly determined that everyone was there, except one. "Anya is missing," she reported. "Children, stay with Lily while Cera and I look for her." The children gathered around Lily. "I'll go right, and you go left," she suggested to Cera, who nodded and headed off.

Cera and Celeste risked calling quietly to Anya, hoping that she could hear them without alerting any of Soren's scouts to their location. Cera ventured as far as she could before fearing that she would be unable to find her way back, then turned and did her best to retrace her steps. It took Lily spotting her moving past and calling to her for her to rejoin them. "No luck," she reported, but added to bolster the children's spirits, "Celeste must have found her by now."

After what felt like an eternity, Lily asked Cera, "How much longer should we wait?"

"Just a little longer," Cera replied, worrying for Celeste.

A moment later, Celeste emerged, carrying Anya. Cera gestured for her to transfer the girl to her.

"She twisted her ankle but didn't want to call out to tell us," Celeste informed them, and handed Anya to Cera. Celeste double-checked that all the children were still there and signaled that it was okay to proceed. They entered the trees, pushing branches aside, careful not to let them snap back into the face of the person behind them. Cera found a dense thicket for them to hide in until either Grey rejoined them or it grew light enough to see by. She steered the children into it and motioned for them to sit down. They huddled together in the dark, waiting. Cera felt the ground around her and gathered a few stones that would have to suffice as weapons. She held Lily's hand and prayed silently for those who had stayed behind in Bayre.

After a while, a rustling roused Cera to alertness. She reached for Lily and tapped her arm to warn her that someone or something was coming. She picked up her collection of rocks and transferred one to her throwing hand. She listened intently for the rustling to resume so that she could get a sense of its direction. It returned, closer now, and she could tell that it was approaching them. She reached back and launched a rapid volley of rocks into the darkness.

"Oww," Grey announced as he poked his head into the thicket, protecting it from further assault with his upraised hands. "Please stop."

Cera jumped up. "I'm *so* sorry," she gushed, noticing the blood on him.

He looked down at himself. "You didn't do this," he assured her. "Although you did land a nice throw," he added, rubbing his temple. "Well done."

Cera was mortified.

He reassured her, "Seriously, it's okay." He looked at the sky. "Dawn isn't far off. We should get moving."

Celeste organized the children and had them follow Grey while she, Lily, and Cera took up the rear. Light seeped into the sky as they walked into the increasingly inhospitable territory.

"I don't like it here," Anya said, saying aloud what they were all thinking.

"I think we're not supposed to," Grey replied gently and lead them deeper into it. They arrived at the structure that resembled a dead spider, and the children grew increasingly uneasy. Celeste had to pick

Anya up and carry her. Lily and Cera held hands with other unsettled children.

Grey used his amulet to call an airship. One landed, and he opened the door for everyone to board.

He took Cera aside and handed her the amulet. "I've dialed it to the port town that Skye tells us is sympathetic to our plight. Just press the center button once you're on board, and it'll take you there."

"You're not coming with us?" Cera more stated than asked.

Grey nodded. "I've already strayed too far off my path. It's time for me to return to it."

Cera hugged him. "You're a good man Grey. The world could use more like you."

"Gods' speed," he replied and waited to ensure that the ship launched successfully before turning and heading back toward Bayre.

8

Kala

Kala made her way through the streets, swords in hand, ready to engage the enemy. *Where are they?* she wondered. Dhara, Kaia, and Calix followed. They turned the corner into the ruined courtyard in front of the city gates. Bodies lay all about, but what struck Kala more was that she could see through the gates to the fires of the enemy outside.

Guards rushed into the courtyard and joined her. One pointed to the open grate in an adjacent alley. "They came from the tunnels," he concluded.

What have I done? thought Kala, remembering sending Lily, Cera, Celeste, and the children down into the tunnels. She decided that she just had to trust in Grey and put it out of her mind.

"Post a guard at all the openings," she ordered the man, pointing with her sword at the open shaft as she strode past it on her way to the gate. The left door was hanging open at an odd angle, the control mechanism utterly destroyed. Kala looked at the army through the open space. *At least it's a narrow opening to defend*, she thought, knowing that it wouldn't matter much against such numbers in the long run.

The city guard began to fill the courtyard. "What are they waiting for?" a man asked nervously. In answer, Soren's army roared and charged.

"Spears and shields to the gate!" Kala yelled. She sheathed her swords and raced up the stairwell to the ramparts, where she picked up a spare bow and a fistful of arrows from a nearby hopper. "Concentrate fire at the entrance," she told the archers. "Make every arrow count." She lined up a shot and waited for the man to get within range. Her arrow caught him in the neck, and he fell, but two more leaped over him. *There are so many*, she thought as she fired another arrow, then another, and another until she lost count. Every one of the city's archers vied for a place along the parapet and reigned death down on the advancing army, but it didn't seem to dent their numbers. Soren's archers began firing up at the wall, reducing the rate at which the city's archers could fire. Several men around Kala fell off the wall to their deaths.

She hazarded a glance down at the gate. The spears formed a dense pincushion, on which many of Soren's soldiers were impaled as they were pushed forward by the men behind them. The weight of the onslaught was pushing the spears back, however. She wondered if Dhara and Kaia were among them. She could tell that they wouldn't hold the soldiers back for long. She dropped the bow and tore back down the stairs to the courtyard. She pushed through to the front row of guards who waited for the inevitable breach of the wall of spears. She pulled out her swords and readied herself.

Despite their best efforts, the spears were pushed back through the opening and into the courtyard. A barbarian vaulted over them directly into Kala. She redirected his momentum and dispatched him with a slash between the joints of his armor. She turned to face the next man as they began streaming through the gates.

Hawke stood impatiently on the deck of the pirate ship. After their raid on Soren's flank, they'd rendezvoused with the ships that had resupplied Bayre and transferred the supplies they'd stolen to them. The evacuees from Bayre had been spotted on the coast, and the mission of the makeshift navy changed to transporting them to the relative safety of the coastal communities along with provisions to help feed them. Once Hawke's ship had transferred the spoils of the raid, it turned and sailed with haste back toward Bayre. It floated off the coast with the rest of the pirate fleet waiting for an opportune moment to reengage the enemy.

Dawn began to break, and the lookout shouted down from the mast, "There's fighting at Bayre."

Hawke turned to see how the Pirate Lord would react, but he was already barking commands to unfurl the sails and close the distance to the coast. The other ships took their cue from the lead ship and the fleet made for Bayre. Every sail filled with wind, but it felt to Hawke as though they still approached far too slowly. His hands subconsciously moved between his weapons, checking and rechecking their placement. The Pirate Lord came up beside him and laid a hand on his shoulder.

"Waiting is always the hardest thing to do," he commiserated.

A lookout atop the city walls spotted their approach and called down to have the sea gate opened for them. It stood open as they approached the pier, an invitation to battle and most likely death.

"Into the breach," the Pirate Lord told Hawke and turned to face his men. "Anyone fancy a fight?" he shouted, and they roared in answer. He turned back to Hawke, smiling. "They're not a sentimental bunch and not much into speeches." The ship pulled alongside the pier as frightened citizens poured out the gates, fleeing the fighting. The Pirate Lord turned to his Captain and told him, "Once we're off, take as many people as you can away from this place. I don't think we'll be back." The Captain nodded gravely.

The pirates swung down on ropes, and Hawke joined them in charging into the city.

Kala held the courtyard, but her energy was flagging, while every enemy soldier that stepped through the gates was fresh. She made peace with the fact that her strength would eventually fail her, but until that moment, she'd stand her ground and fight. She'd seen Dhara and Kaia leading her people in holding the exits to the courtyard to keep the enemy from spreading out into the city, and Kala prayed that they were still alive. The thought distracted her, and she was pummeled by a mace. She staggered back, pain exploding through her right arm. She lifted her sword feebly to parry the next blow, but it didn't come – a dagger sailed over her shoulder instead and embedded itself in her assailant's eye.

Hawke strode forward and helped her up. "Miss me?" he winked, then turned to fend off another attacker. She joined him as the wave of pirates entered the square and engaged the enemy. They were less well armed but more surefooted as they stepped over the thick carpet of bodies, and they matched Soren's barbarians in ferocity. The tide shifted slightly, and even though Kala knew it would be short-lived, she relished it.

Horns blared outside the gates, and Kala wondered what new threat they signified.

The scout rode north at breakneck speed, his mount laboring. "It's okay, girl," he encouraged it, "you can do this." He broke onto open ground and sped toward Addis, who was moving south with the riders that he'd mustered. Spying Addis, the scout rode straight for him and pulled up in front of him.

"We're too late, my lord... the city is already under attack," he reported.

Addis raised his hand and signaled the charge. He spurred his horse, and it shot forward like lightning, his host following closely. They flew across the fields, and as they neared the city, they could make out the sounds of fighting. Cresting the final rise, Addis took stock of the massive army surrounding the city. He could see them funneling slowly toward the open gate. *We're not too late*, he thought, *they still hold the gate*.

"To the gate!" he yelled, spurring his horse. His riders caught up to him, and together, they crashed into the left flank of Soren's forces along the city wall. Horns blared.

Kala could tell that something had shifted outside the gate when the enemy stopped pouring in. She dispatched the man she was fighting and looked around. Hawke was off to her right, and she caught a glimpse of Dhara, bloody but still standing, but she didn't see Kaia. Dhara was surrounded by the remaining defenders, who had held out valiantly, but of which precious few remained.

Kala stepped toward the gate, Hawke joined her, and the rest followed. They climbed over the pile of bodies that clogged it and blocked their view. Kala emerged to see a ring of armed riders facing Soren's army. It was but a momentary pause while the army regrouped to adjust its tactics to this new development. Kala took stock – Bayre's defenders had dwindled to perhaps a hundred and fifty, a mix of city guards, Dhara's people, and pirates. The addition of five hundred cavalry elevated their numbers, but they still faced an army that still looked to number close to ten thousand. It seemed to be their final stand, but Kala contented herself that it would be on open ground, rather than hemmed in by the tiny courtyard.

A young man around Forest's age rode over to her, acknowledging her as the de facto leader of the defenders. "Addis, at your service, miss," he introduced himself.

"Addis, thank you for your support," she replied.

"I wish I could do more," he said regretfully and returned to his place among his riders.

An airship sailed overhead. *Celeste, you fool!* Kala grimaced, but it was too late to do anything about her misguided decision to return to Bayre, undoubtedly on a mission to rescue Twill and Petr, knowing her. Kala turned to face the army and prepared herself, stoking the fire that burned in her veins.

A general at the front of Soren's army began to bang her sword against her shield. Several soldiers deep within their ranks returned the call. Soon the entire army was banging their shields in anticipation of the order to charge.

Kala squared herself against the general. Something about her seemed familiar, and it took a moment for Kala to register that it was Brinn, leader of the warrior priestesses. She winked at Kala and glanced subtly over her shoulder. Kala looked past her to see Soren's standard flying at the rear of the army and instantly grasped what she was trying to tell her.

"Addis," Kala called. "Can you drive a wedge toward the rear of Soren's army?"

"It would be my pleasure to try," he replied.

"Great. You'll know when," she told him and readied herself.

Brinn stopped hammering her shield and raised her sword to signal the army, which went silent as they waited. She turned to face them and brought down her sword, slaying the man to her right. All hell broke loose.

Addis order the charge and his riders surged forward toward where Brinn had stood a moment before, but somehow melted away. The flanking cavalry wheeled behind him and formed a phalanx that charged the line of soldiers, crashing into it like a tidal wave. The ranks split apart, and Kala raced toward the breach. Hawke and Dhara followed, as did the other defenders, rallying to make their final attack.

Kala raced past horsemen that pushed soldiers out of her way, slashing at the ones that got through as she ran. Brinn's warriors faded in and out of the opposing army, cutting down a foe, then disappearing as quickly as they appeared. Together they fought to open the corridor that Kala surged down. Brinn herself slew the last two men standing between Kala and the circle of guards that surrounded Soren. Kala broke through and stood, panting, facing Soren himself.

"My Scourge," he acknowledged and signaled a horn blast that temporarily halted his men fighting. "You have my attention."

9

Forest

Forest and Petra drifted over the army surrounding Bayre. Forest peered out the window. *My gods*, she thought, *there are so many of them.* The ship spun in the wind, and she saw a small force of riders charge into the front lines of the vast army. *Addis!* She knew it had to be his people, and she worried about him. *Hold on*, she prayed. *I'm coming.* The ship descended maddeningly slowly, and Forest nearly exploded with pent-up energy.

Petra looked out the window at the force arrayed around the city. "That's my son's army?" she asked herself. "What have you done, Sorrie?"

The airship passed over the city's walls and dropped to the port inside. The airfield was still littered with crates, but terrified townsfolk had rearranged them into a defensive barrier. Forest's ship headed toward a pad inside the circle that had been cleared of crates. She opened the door before the ship even landed and jumped out as soon as it was low enough. She hit the ground, absorbing the shock with her knees, the impact jarring her teeth. As the ship moored itself, she reached up to help Petra out the door. She turned and came face-to-face with the throng of frightened townsfolk. She spotted the exit to the airfield and pulled Petra toward it. The mass of people blocked their way and wouldn't let them leave.

"Get us out of here," a woman begged, looking from Forest to the airship she'd just disembarked.

"We don't have time for this," Forest replied and tried to take a step toward the exit.

The crowd edged forward, tightening its circle around her.

Forest grabbed Petra's hand and slipped her other inside her tunic. She felt for the amulet against her skin, grasped it, spun its dial slightly, and pushed the center button. She looked over to the airship that had just come unmoored. "I think it's leaving," she observed loudly.

In its desperation, the crowd forgot all about Forest and Petra and rushed toward the ship. Forest shielded Petra from the surging mob and pulled her toward the exit. They scrambled over the pile of crates, exited the airfield, and rushed through the deserted streets toward the distant sound of battle. The sound echoed off buildings, and Forest struggled not to run in circles. She ran in the opposite direction of anyone she came across, hoping that they were fleeing the fighting. Gradually, the streets emptied, and a horn blast silenced the sound of battle. Forest despaired that whatever was happening, she was missing it, and all her efforts were in vain. She continued to run down a main street and came to a screeching halt when she spied the open gate down a side street. Bodies clogged the square before it. Petra had almost caught up to her, so Forest locked eyes on her to keep her from turning her head.

"Brace yourself," she commanded Petra. "It isn't pretty." She gripped her hand tightly and turned toward the gate.

Petra's eyes widened in horror as she realized what she saw. "Sorrie, what have you done?" she repeated. Forest had to pull her along. Crows already hopped among the dead as Forest lead Petra through the first of the bodies. Petra froze, paled, and threw up.

Forest supported her while she retched and helped her back to her feet when she was done. "If we're to prevent more of this, we have to get moving," she told her, holding her by the shoulders and staring into her eyes.

Petra nodded weakly and let herself be led toward the gate. Once in the courtyard, the only way out the gate was to climb over the mountain of bodies. Petra was terrified to touch them, and Forest had to help hold her steady as they climbed. Petra shook like a leaf but did her best to hold down the nausea that pushed up within her. Forest led

57

her down the hill of bodies on the far side of the gate. The army before them stood facing the opposite direction and disregarded them.

Forest placed an arm around Petra and guided her toward the army. "Out of my way," she demanded of the soldiers barring her path. They looked uncertain but yielded as Forest pushed through them. "Excuse me," "Coming through," "Step aside please," Forest kept up until she pushed through the final row of soldiers to see Kala standing before Soren.

"You can't win like this," Kala told him.

"I appear to be doing just that," Soren replied, surveying the scale of his army.

"Which is why you don't notice that your strings are being pulled."

Soren bristled. "No one pulls my strings."

"Maybe a better way to say it is that you're playing your role flawlessly in a play as old as time. My role is to stop you, but I've failed to live up to that assignment. The plan was for us to annihilate each other, but not before we burn the world to the ground."

"And whose plan is this?" he asked skeptically.

"The Ancients and their servants, who encourage us to believe the lie that we have free will, and all the while consign us to a life of brutal stasis. I, for one, refuse to live that life."

"You would have me believe that ghosts are orchestrating all of this?"

"Yes, although those 'ghosts' are very much active in the world. They keep us down out of fear that we'll jeopardize their existence."

"I don't believe in ghosts," he replied dismissively.

"You should. You've marched through the ruins of their great cities, and if you think they're dead and gone, who do you think keeps the airships flying? Do you think any of us living has that level of skill?"

At the mention of the airships, a look of doubt crossed his face for the first time. "And if you fail to oppose me, who will stop me?"

"If you and I fail to destroy the world, it will fall to the Ancients' servants to complete the task."

"And where are these fearsome servants?"

"Everywhere. They hide in plain sight, wearing the mask of the Church of Death."

Soren laughed. "They're as good as ghosts themselves. We've seen no trace of them. Everywhere we go, they've vanished before we arrive."

"Your true enemy stays one step ahead of you, and this fills you with confidence?" Kala asked. She could tell by the look on Soren's face that he didn't appreciate being insulted before his followers, but she was too weary to care. "I know you could choose not to believe me and continue obliterating everyone that you think opposes you until the world is yours? Do you think the people who built those mighty cities so long ago and still keep us enslaved will just let you have the world? You know in your core that greater forces than you and I operate in the shadows."

"And you think that *you* can triumph over those forces?" Soren challenged haughtily.

"Probably not," Kala admitted, "but I know that we stand a better chance trying together than we do at each other's throats. It's time to stop playing their game. It's time to put an end to the bloodshed."

"Listen to her, Sorrie," a voice declared from behind Kala.

Soren clenched his fists, enraged at being mocked. "Only my mother called me that," he growled.

"I still do," Petra replied, emerging from the ranks of his army.

Soren looked her over. "My mother is dead," he declared.

"I am not," she replied.

"Well, she's dead to me."

"I'm sorry for everything that's happened to you."

"I'll tell you what happened," he raged, ignoring the thousands that surrounded them. "You abandoned me."

"I did no such thing," Petra defended herself. "I've hoped ever moment of my ruined life that I would find you again."

"You let me go."

"I was kept from you."

"You and father didn't even raise a finger..."

If Petra had been standing closer, she would have slapped her son. Her eyes spat fire. "Do *not* speak ill of your father. He died a broken man when you were taken from us. He tried to get you back, and we were imprisoned for it. We never loved you with anything less than our whole being."

Kala could see the emotions warring behind Soren's eyes. She stepped forward. "You want to overthrow the system that causes such pain. I do too. I'm not your enemy. We're not your enemy. The system is, and I know who is behind it." She looked at Forest, standing behind Petra. "A ghost once told me that no amount of vengeance will ever staunch the pain. Join me, and together we'll face our true enemy. Together we'll put an end to pain."

Kala took a tentative step toward Soren, and his personal guard raised their weapons. He waved them to stand down and moved to stand before her. His blue eyes burned into hers. "You know where to find them?" he asked.

"I do," she confirmed.

"I will have my vengeance?" he asked.

"And you will have my aid," she replied and held out her hand.

He stared at it, considering, then took it.

A flock of birds took wing, almost symbolically. Seline watched them rise. *Birds*, she thought. "Stop them!" she shouted urgently, interrupting the proceedings and pointing frantically at the birds.

Soren's archers released a volley into the air, knocking many of the birds from the sky. When the last arrow fell back to earth, a single bird remained flying away. Seline watched it. "I fear that our common enemy will soon know we've allied."

"Who released those birds?" Soren demanded.

"Lennox," a guard replied, pointing to the man lurking in the background.

Soren motioned for his guards to capture him and haul him forward.

"It makes no difference what you do," Lennox spat, ceasing to struggle, "she'll kill you all."

10

Priestess

The Priestess rolled over in her bed for the millionth time. Her head ached, and she couldn't sleep. She mulled over the vision that the Ancients had implanted in her head. It was a baby again, but this time, it was crying. The baby cried constantly in her mind, impossible to ignore. She didn't know why she knew that the baby was a girl, but she knew. She couldn't fathom what the Ancients wanted to tell her through the baby, and she was tired of trying to figure it out.

She swung her feet off the bed and sat up, contemplating getting up for a glass of water. Eventually, moving seemed more appealing than continuing to sit still, and she rose to walk to the pitcher on her dresser. It was still dark, but even in perfect darkness, she knew where everything in her room lay. She reached for the glass that she knew would be there and poured herself a drink.

Her days were as fatiguing as her sleepless nights. She was called upon endlessly to brief the Church Council and consult with the other Oracles. She had to defend the Church's actions or inaction in the face of the conflict that was sweeping the continent. She sighed and proceeded to wash and dress. Though it was still not quite dawn, she made her way to the auditorium, took her customary seat, and waited for the day to begin anew.

She called a novice to bring her some fruit for breakfast. "Thank you, Novice Frey," she told him when he returned with it, pleased with herself to have remembered the name of even the youngest recruit.

As the sun rose, people gradually filed into the room. The elders came in individually and sat down at their places at the head table. The audience filtered in, and eventually, the two other Oracles took their seats on either side of her.

The Council's chairwoman surveyed the room and deciding that all of the key people were in attendance, called the meeting to order. "What is the news from Bayre?" the crone asked, as she did every day.

"Soren continues his siege, but the resupply of the city and the raid on him have weakened his ability to see the siege through successfully. I believe he will be forced to adopt a different strategy."

"And what will that strategy be?" the crone pressed.

"That remains to be seen," the Priestess responded.

The crone's annoyance at her Oracle's lack of prescience was clear to all present.

The Priestess hid her anger behind a veil of calm and clenched and unclenched her fists below the table.

"And our 'supposed' champion is still in the city?" the crone asked.

"From what we know, yes."

"But that accomplishes her nothing, sitting there on her hands," the old woman complained, challenging the Priestess's faith in her once more.

"She has orchestrated allies, which the resupply of the city and the raid on Soren demonstrate. The Ancients have faith in her resourcefulness. Who are we to second-guess them?"

"The Ancients? How do we know what they believe or don't believe? We are misplacing our faith. It seems pretty clear that the girl will fail in countering Soren, and we should prepare ourselves for that inevitability."

The Priestess did not appreciate her or the Ancients being doubted, but she stopped listening when a squawk caught her attention. She looked out the window and spied the blackbird sitting in the tree outside the window, a single silver band around its right leg. Her spy within Soren's army was informing her that the unthinkable had just happened – far from failing, the girl had succeeded in swaying Soren to her side. She sat up straighter.

"I agree," she announced suddenly.

The Council Chair was unprepared for the Priestess's capitulation. She paused, forgetting what she was in the middle of saying.

The Priestess pressed on. "It is wise to prepare ourselves for the possibility of our Champion's failure, even if she ultimately succeeds."

The crone stared at her blankly, waiting for her to elaborate.

"Our city is next in Soren's sights. He may even have already dispatched forces in our direction while his main body lays siege to Bayre. The gods know he has the numbers to spare." The Priestess could feel the unease she was stoking and seized the opportunity to make her suggestion. "Perhaps it's time to relocate the Council and the Oracles to the safety of the Fortress in the Wastes."

The room erupted into debate while the Priestess leaned back in her chair and allowed it to rage. She knew which way it would settle out – she simply needed it to be the Council's decision, and before official word returned from Bayre of what had just transpired there.

The Council discussed the matter among themselves before the chairwoman stood and announced that they would indeed decamp to the Fortress.

"Shall I organize transport for the Council, and we can reconvene this meeting once everyone has settled in at the Wastes?" the Priestess asked.

"That would be acceptable," the Chair replied dismissively.

"I will make it happen, then," the Priestess replied deferentially and stepped out of the auditorium to make the arrangements while the Council wrapped up its discussion and left to collect their belongings.

The Priestess met the Council and the two other Oracles at the airfield. She had summoned an airship large enough to accommodate the entire Council, their principal retainers, and the Oracles. She also had guards bring the Ancient's crystal from the catacombs and ready it for transport. It sat in a large chest, surrounded by members of the Church's elite guard.

"Would you prefer to travel with the Ancients?" The Priestess asked, gesturing to the chest and its guards, knowing full-well that it would make the space aboard the ship terribly cramped, "Or, would you prefer if I were to bring it up in the next ship?"

The Council Chair took one look at the burly guards escorting the crystal and chose to have it travel separately. The Priestess also knew that she was not well-liked among the Council, and if accompanying the crystal gave them an excuse not to travel with her as well, they'd seize it.

"Bring it with you in the next ship," The chairwoman decided.

"As you wish," the Priestess replied. "I will finalize the logistical arrangements and join you shortly." She gestured for the guards to wait with the crystal for the time being. "I have sent ahead word of your arrival, and your accommodations at the Fortress are being prepared for you."

The Chair ignored her and boarded the ship, followed by the remainder of the Council and the Oracles.

"Safe travels," the Priestess wished them as the door closed, and the airship began to rise. As it moved away, she ordered the guards to take the crystal back to the catacombs. "We won't be moving it immediately," she informed them offhandedly.

The members of the Council looked out the ship's windows at the frigid wasteland surrounding the Fortress. The wind blew columns of snow into the sky, and the cold penetrated the ship, making its occupants pull their jackets tighter against their bodies. Another airship drifted by, already having dropped off the advance party.

The ship descended and moored itself. The Council braced themselves for the cold while an attendant opened the door and stood aside as a blast of frigid air entered the cabin. The party hurriedly exited the ship and trudged through the snow toward the Fortress, the only feature in the otherwise bleak landscape. The cold assaulted them, and they did their best to move quickly.

The first of them hurried up the long walkway that led to the thick wooden doors and banged on them to announce their arrival, even before the rest of the party had joined her. There was no immediate answer, but this was not unusual, so she banged again and waited. The remainder of the party assembled around her and huddled, shivering while they waited for the door to open. It did not. The cold began to sink its teeth deeper into their flesh. Fear began to rise in them as they beat on the doors in unison and yelled loudly to attract the attention of the guards inside.

"We'd better return to the ship," The chairwoman suggested, her teeth chattering, and the party hurried down the ramp and back into the howling wind. Arriving at the base of the ramp, they could see clear to the horizon, with no airship in sight. It had deposited them and left immediately. Panic set in as they raced back up the ramp and resumed banging on the door with hands that they increasingly could not feel.

The Priestess boarded the airship with hand-picked members of her personal guard and headed to the Fortress in the Wastes. She flipped up her hood, pulled on her fur-lined mitts, and readied herself for the cold journey.

After the long voyage, the ship landed gently, despite being buffeted by intense winds. The Priestess stepped out and began the short hike from the landing pad to the Fortress. She ignored the numbing cold as she traversed the distance. She walked up the ramp toward the doors. Huddled against them were the bodies of the Council and the Oracles, their faces frozen in anguish.

She leaned over them and knocked a coded knock. The doors immediately swung inward and admitted her entrance. The remainder of her personal guard greeted her as she stepped inside. She turned to her travel companions. "Dispose of the bodies," she instructed them. They nodded and began ferrying them out onto the tundra for the bears or whatever else prowled the Wastes.

She pulled the key to the Vaults from beneath her tunic and gestured for her guards to follow her. "We have a weapon to collect," she said to herself.

11

Kala

Soren turned his attention from Kala to his mother. It was plain that he didn't yet know how he felt about their reunion. He ordered one of his guards to escort her to his tent, telling her that they'd talk later. The guard nodded and moved to collect Petra.

Soren finally registered Forest standing beside his mother. "You," he said, pointing at her. "We will have words." Two guards moved toward her, pointlessly, given that she was already surrounded by his army.

"I'd be delighted," Forest quipped and strode confidently toward the two men. She spared a glance at Kala. "Good to see you," she called, walking past with her escorts.

Soren turned to one of his generals and instructed her, "Cease hostilities and have the wounded seen to." He turned back to Kala. "We have much to discuss." He waved her toward his tent, where he typically conducted meetings, then remembered that he'd sent his mother there. He ordered his guards to move his council table from his tent to an adjacent one.

Kala took advantage of the delay to request a waterskin and discretely wipe the blood from her hands and face.

With his new council tent set up, Soren invited her in and summoned Seline to join them. Seline's eyes belied her razor-sharp mind, and Kala could tell that Soren was using her to verify the plausibility of her claims. Soren's other advisor, the man who had been revealed to be a spy, Lennox, had been arrested and held under guard with strict orders from Soren that he be gagged so as not to weasel his way out of captivity with appeals to his guards' baser interests.

Soren waved his personal guards outside the tent and sat down to speak with Kala and Seline alone.

Kala watched his guards station themselves outside the tent and noticing that she hadn't been relieved of her weapons, marveled at how cavalier Soren was with his life. It was true that she'd not killed him the last time she was alone with him, but she decided to take it as a token of trust.

"Tell me more about this 'true enemy' that you say threatens us," he began.

Kala explained, as best she could, the existence of the Ancients and their reasons for wanting to keep the people of the world stagnant or in conflict. Seline took it all in, and while it seemed to Kala's own ears to sound far-fetched, Seline let her continue and reserved judgment. Kala explained the self-appointed role of the Church in furthering the inferred wishes of the Ancients, and described her interactions with the Priestess.

Soren leaned back and absorbed all that Kala said. When she was done, he leaned forward. "So the Ancients keep us down so that we never grow to threaten them?" he asked.

"In part," Kala agreed, "but also to protect us from ourselves. By keeping us stagnant, we won't destroy ourselves completely through run-away conflict or by stripping bare the world of its resources. I don't agree that it's their decision to make, but I understand it."

Soren mulled it over. "I still don't understand why they'd create a system whereby young people are forcibly moved about against their will."

He's fixated on the airships, she thought. It was clear that it was still very personal to him. "I've wondered that myself, but I don't know either," Kala had to admit.

Seline chimed in. "Based on what you've told us, I have a theory."

Soren nodded for her to continue.

"I think that the airships' primary purpose is to allow communities to exist in isolation while sharing resources without actual contact. That helps keep society stagnant. Further, the ships consume few resources themselves, so this allows this to be sustainable indefinitely. However, stagnancy can lead to apathy, which could erode society over time. I think the airships require the occasional transfer of youth simply to insert an element of disruption."

"Why young people?" Soren asked.

"The emotional pain it causes. It's a pretty creative way of maximizing disruption with the least possible effort," Seline concluded dispassionately.

Soren hid his balled-up fists under the table. "It's an evil system," he concluded.

"I never said it wasn't," Seline countered, "simply that it's effective."

Soren considered everything he'd been told. "I need to think about this. We'll meet again tomorrow at midday to discuss what we do next."

Kala could tell that she had been excused and exited the tent. Hawke was waiting for her outside. She gave him a hug, which he accepted readily. "I'm glad you're alive," she told him unguardedly.

"I'm hard to kill," he quipped, but they both knew it was fortunate that any of them had survived the day.

She released him from the hug and looked toward the city, but was hesitant to leave without Forest.

Soren stepped out of the tent, asking a guard, "The girl?" and being directed toward a nearby tent that was under guard. He noticed Kala follow his eye to the tent and assured her, "No harm will come to her. Go see to your people."

If Kala objected, it would signal that she didn't trust him, so had no choice but to head back to Bayre. His soldiers eyed her warily as she did, her reputation preceding her. She could feel the blood of their comrades still on her. A truce had been declared, but no one yet celebrated it – it was still too fresh and too tentative. Several men sat sharpening their blades, assuming that any respite would be short-lived.

While she didn't really feel in personal danger, she was comforted by Hawke's presence. As the adrenaline wore off, she realized just how emotionally and physically spent she was and placed an arm on his shoulder to support her as they walked.

"So you're a pirate now," she joked.

"*Honorary* pirate," he corrected, but a cloud passed across his face. He'd seen many of them meet their end today – they'd known they likely wouldn't survive, but it didn't stop them from coming to the aid of a city full of strangers. Hawke and Kala walked the rest of the way in silence, contemplating the dead.

Wounded soldiers were carried past them on stretchers, groaning, many of whom would not recover from their injuries. *This is not a victory*, Kala thought. They approached the gate to find the dead there being claimed by their kin and colleagues so that the funeral traditions of their people could be applied, be it burial or burning. Despite having been the defender, Kala felt personally responsible for an untold number of those deaths and slipped quickly through the gate.

Skye was waiting for her in the courtyard and swept her into his arms. "I was worried about you, alone in Soren's camp."

"I wasn't alone," she replied, nodding toward Hawke.

"I envy your ability to waltz through an enemy army," Skye said to Hawke.

"Brighten up," Hawke replied, patting his shoulder, "your girl is returned to you in one piece." He spotted the Pirate Lord and excused himself to go assist with his dead.

"Get me away from all this," Kala requested, anxious to distance herself from the dead.

"Of course," Skye replied and led her back to the temple.

"Are Dhara and Kaia…?" she dared to ask.

"They're okay. They're really banged up, but they'll pull through."

Kala said nothing, but Skye felt her relief as palpably as if she had. Walking back through the temple gates, she spotted Twill conversing with Petr and walked over to hug them both.

"You're still on guard?" she laughed at Twill.

"I take my job very seriously," he replied but looked around sadly. "It's not the same here without Celeste. I hope she's okay."

"She is," Grey replied, walking through the gate.

Kala spun around at the sound of his voice.

"They all are," he corrected himself. "Celeste, Lily, Cera, and the children all got away safely."

"How can I ever thank you?" Kala asked him earnestly.

"Continuing not to die seems like a good start," he replied, looking her over. "How exactly is it that Bayre is not overrun?"

"I convinced Soren that we're better allies than enemies."

"Allies against the Priestess?"

"Yes."

"Wise. You know that she won't stand for it, though. She'll decide that she needs to take matters into her own hands in extinguishing us all."

"I know, and that has me terrified. Soren is a threat that you can see coming. The Priestess is a threat that we likely won't."

"Surely, we have time to enjoy our reprieve," Skye cut in.

"Probably," Grey replied, "but she has eyes and ears everywhere. The respite will be short."

Kala told him about Soren's man, Lennox, and his birds.

Grey nodded his understanding. "Signal birds. I've heard the Priestess speak of them."

"I need to get cleaned up," Kala declared. "I'll meet you both back in the great room for dinner?"

"Dinner, right, damn… I should do something about that," Skye agreed and rushed off.

"You've got yourself a good man there," Grey confided in Kala as they watched Skye disappear into the building.

"I know it," she replied wistfully and headed inside to find a bath.

Soren pulled back the tent flap to find Forest sitting alone, an untouched tray of fruit beside her. She began to stand, but he waved her back down, taking a seat opposite and examining her.

"You have a penchant for turning up unexpectedly," he told her.

"I go where I'm needed... and sometimes where I'm told, apparently," she replied, although not with rancor.

"My mother was your idea?" he asked.

"It was," she admitted, reluctantly.

"Clever trick," he congratulated her.

"It wasn't a trick," Forest replied indignantly. "She is the origin of your pain and only she can end it."

"I'm not in pain," he defended. "I came to terms about her a long time ago."

"Bullshit," Forest countered. "This war of yours says otherwise." She softened her tone. "You once told me that I don't know pain because I was never ripped from my family... well, I've had family ripped from me. I know what it's like to lose a mother. Not a day goes by that I don't want her back. You can tell herself that she means nothing to you, but you're lying to yourself."

Soren mulled this over in silence, grabbing a pear from the tray and examining it.

"I'm sorry for being so blunt. I know it's not my place. It's just that I've spent time with Petra. She's wonderful, and she yearns for you as much as I know you do for her. And if you pardon my asking, why are you in here talking to me and not in there talking to her?"

"Stalling, it seems," he admitted, putting the pear down.

"Go to her," Forest urged kindly.

"You're a remarkable girl, Forest," Soren told her, rising. He walked to the entrance and turned before leaving. "I just wanted to say, 'thank you.'" He got the guards' attention. "Escort her back," he told them and went to see his mother.

Kala emerged from a long soak in the tub, put on fresh clothes, and went in search of her friends. She stumbled across Forest. "Thank the gods, you're okay," Kala greeted her, relieved beyond measure.

"Where are Lily and Cera?" Forest asked, worried.

"No one told you? I'm sorry," Kala replied. "I had Grey spirit them out through the tunnels with Celeste and the children and put them on an airship out of here. Grey assures me that they're safe."

Forest relaxed visibly.

Kala put a hand on her shoulder. "That was an amazing thing you did, finding Soren's mother. I'm not sure he would have listened to me without her prompting."

"It was a gamble, but I am glad it paid off. Petra is sweet too. She deserves her son back."

"That's why you're my conscience," Kala replied, mostly to herself. "You're thin as a rail," she observed, pointing out how Forest's clothes hung loosely on her.

Forest looked herself over. "I haven't eaten much the past few moons," she admitted.

"We must remedy that immediately," Kala declared and made to escort her to the kitchens.

"Can I steal her for a moment first?" a voice inquired.

Kala turned to see the young horse lord, propped up by a deeply-tanned older man.

"Addis!" Forest exclaimed, her eyes giving away her happiness at seeing him alive.

"I was told I could find you here," he replied, wincing at the pain in his side.

"I'll leave you two," Kala informed them and headed back toward the great room.

Forest didn't notice her retreat. "Are you okay?" she asked Addis.

"It seems that I ran across a man whose mace was weightier than me," he replied, favoring his left side.

"How's your horse," Forest asked worriedly.

"I should have known you'd be more concerned about my steed than me," he joked.

"Addis?!"

"He's fine. He's in the stables getting brushed to calm him."

"Thank the gods," Forest concluded, relieved. "And for the record, I am concerned about you... just more so about your horse."

Addis smiled broadly. "I am happy to see you. I wasn't sure I'd see you after you flew away on me."

"I told you I would," she replied.

"This is war," he countered. "People say things."

"I mean what I say," she stopped him. "And I'm happy to see you too. I saw you charge the enemy, and I was certain I'd lost you."

Addis didn't miss the sincerity of her concern. "Getting knocked off my horse probably helped my longevity," he admitted. "My people protected me." He paused to consider those he'd lost. "Do you think it's still worthy of a song?"

"More like an epic poem."

"Oh gods – I hate poetry. Can't it just be a song? A short one, at least?"

"Okay. Short, but epic." She reached out and took his hand. "Want to come with me and find something to eat. I'm famished."

"I'd love to, but Jon will need to help me get there," he said, gesturing to his cousin, who was helping prop him up.

"Nonsense. I've got you," she said, shifting to take his weight. She slid her arm around his waist to support him. "Is this alright?" she asked.

"More than alright," he replied. "Jon, I'll call for you if I need you."

"As you wish, my lord," his cousin replied and ducked out.

"My lord?" Forest giggled.

"Hey – I'm important," he defended himself lightheartedly.

"Sure you are," she teased and guided him toward the kitchens.

The smell of something savory had caught Kala's attention, and she had also followed it to the kitchens.

Skye noticed her enter and waved her over. "I made an everything-that-fits-in-the-pot stew. Probably not my finest creation, but Calix swore it was alright."

Calix! Kala remembered and turned to seek him out and see how he was doing.

"Whoa, whoa… not so fast. Eat first. Calix isn't going anywhere."

Kala sighed and sat down while Skye ladled her a bowl of stew and handed her a tiny container of salt. "If it isn't to your taste," he explained.

"I'm sure it's fine. Thanks for looking after me." She put down her spoon and picked up his hand. "Seriously, only my grandfather ever did, and he's not here." She wiped the corner of her eye, and Skye bent down and kissed her cheek.

"I made biscuits," he declared to cheer her up and turned to pull them out of the oven. "That should make up for the stew," he added and watched her eat.

"Stop it," she complained.

"What?"

"Stop watching me eat."

"Sorry. I can't help myself. This morning, I wasn't sure I'd get to again."

"Okay. I'll let it go this once." She finished her stew, and as Skye promised, she had a second biscuit, the first having been so tasty.

She sighed contentedly and picked up her dishes to carry them to the sink.

"Not on your life," Skye told her, took them from her, and placed them in the sink. "I'll get to those later," he declared. "I'm sure there are people who want to see you." He took her hand and walked with her to the great room, passing Forest and Addis on the way.

The great room was lit by the fire in the hearth, torches along the wall, and candles on tables. It was bright and cheerful. Kala made a beeline for Calix, who was sitting with Dhara and Kaia. Dhara had an arm in a sling, and Kaia was bandaged all over.

She hugged Calix but noted that he was dressed for travel. "What's with the outfit?" she asked.

"I was just waiting to see you before heading out to bring back Lily, Cera, and Celeste."

"I'm glad you waited. It's good to see you," she replied, gazing at him until he squirmed under the attention. "Go tell them we're okay, but tell them too that Bayre might still be in danger, and maybe they might want to wait a bit before returning."

"But you've brokered a truce with Soren."

"Yes, but I think that may bring a more dangerous threat down on us. We'll have to see."

"If you think so," he replied and made to leave.

"Surely it can wait until morning?" she begged.

"I wouldn't want them to worry about how we fared a moment longer than they have to," he replied.

"You're right, of course. I'll just have to enjoy your company later."

Calix left after excusing himself to Dhara and Kaia.

Kala turned to them and gestured toward their bandages. "You look a little worse for wear," she observed.

"You should have seen the other guy," Dhara replied, smirking.

"I'm sure you unleashed unholy terror on them all," Kala admitted.

"Damn right," Kaia agreed.

Kala bent down and pulled them both into an embrace. Surprisingly, they didn't resist her. "I'm so glad you're on our side," she said and released them. She sat down on a loveseat across from them, and Skye squeezed in beside her.

She looked around the room. Forest was talking with her reunited uncle and cousin, Jarom and Nara, but sat with Addis closely beside her.

"I think there's something there," Skye whispered.

"Shush. Don't jinx it," Kala whispered back. "I'm happy for her. She's always giving of herself. She deserves to get something back." Kala watched them surreptitiously, noting how the young lord laughed at her jokes and was not afraid to touch her. "There's definitely something there," she agreed.

Hawke was missing, but he was probably in his room pining for Emilie. Kala made a mental note to check on him later.

Grey walked in with Brinn, and Kala waved them over to adjacent seats. Kala got up to introduce Skye to Brinn and vice versa, telling him, "Skye, this is Brinn. I don't think you've met. Brinn is the leader of an order of warrior priestesses."

"Leader is an overstatement," Brinn deflected humbly.

"Thank you for the path you cleared to Soren," Kala told her. "We wouldn't be here if it weren't for you and your people."

"That could be said about a great many people, none more than you," Brinn countered, "but you're welcome. I wish more of us could be here, but I sent them home to prepare for the coming conflict."

"So you think the Priestess… Winter," Kala corrected herself, "will try to finish what Soren started."

"Without doubt," Brinn replied.

Skye was struck with a realization, and turned to Kala, "Brinn's people are the ones referred to in the book you got Eden to copy, right?"

"Yes," Kala confirmed.

"And you think the Priestess will learn of their involvement today?"

"Most likely."

"So she'll figure out that you stole her book. Eden's in danger. Kala, what have you done?"

12

Eden

Tallie sat at her desk, reviewing manuscripts she'd found in the deepest vaults. Being the head librarian gave her unequaled access to the archives, even to documents that the Church had forgotten existed. The events, people, and places recounted in the oldest books and scrolls had long since faded from memory, but themes recurred. What worried her were the apocalyptic cycles that were so frequently alluded to. From what she pieced together, the slate of the world was overdue to be wiped clean.

Her thoughts were interrupted by the tinkling of a bell she'd recently installed at the entrance to the library. She peeked around the corner of her doorway into a mirror she'd also newly installed and had angled toward the entrance. Two armed monks had come in and were looking about. *She knows*, she thought and her heart began to race. She heard one of her acolytes approach the monks and tell them what she'd been instructed to, that the head librarian was among the stacks verifying the filing. She heard them move off in the direction they were pointed and seized the opportunity to move to the filing room behind her tiny office.

She grabbed the packs that she kept ready, pulled a torch from the wall, threw a hidden switch that opened a wall panel leading to lower levels, slipped in, and closed the panel behind her. She moved through the winding tunnels past storage rooms and other rarely-accessed chambers. She'd explored them in her youth, but her dire situation had prompted her to refamiliarize herself with them. She stopped at an intersection and tried to recall the route. *Keep calm*, she told herself and chose the left doorway. She and Eden were in mortal danger now that the Priestess had likely discovered their involvement in the theft and forgery of a forbidden book.

She hoped that because Eden could always be easily found in her room, that they'd come for her first and not Eden. If she was wrong, she was rushing to her death. Tallie came to the end of the tunnel and placed the torch in a holder on the wall. She looked about for the lever that operated the hidden door. She was beginning to worry that she might have taken a wrong turn when she felt it in the shadowed recess. She turned it, and the stone groaned as the catch holding it in place withdrew. She pushed open a section of the wall that pivoted smoothly despite its weight. She stepped into the narrow space and pulled the section of wall back into place, which in turn released the catch that held the exterior exit of the antechamber closed. It opened incrementally, and Tallie found the crack from the exterior light peeking through it. She opened it just wide enough to squeeze through with her packs and closed it behind her.

Tallie stood, back to the stone wall, in a deserted courtyard behind the library building. She felt vulnerable outdoors, having spent most of her life in the confines of the library. She looked around for any sign that she'd been seen, but she was mercifully alone. She pulled her hood up and hurried toward the building in which Eden lived, praying that her luck would hold. She slowed to a purposeful walk as she emerged onto the pathway that connected the adjoining buildings. She did her best to appear as though she was simply running an errand until she ducked into Eden's building. She didn't hear any voices or footsteps, so she raced up the stairs to the third floor, on which she'd find Eden's room.

She stood in the stairwell, trying to slow her breathing and calm her racing heart. Accepting that she couldn't risk waiting any longer, she stepped into the hallway, having left the packs in the stairwell. She rounded the corner into a corridor that was empty except for the guard standing outside Eden's door. Nothing seemed amiss, so she walked toward him.

"Evening," she said to the guard. "I have the pigment Eden requested, but it seems dried out," she added, faking disappointment. She reached into her pouch and pulled out a handful of powder. "See," she said and held it out to him. He turned toward her, annoyed to be drawn into such a disinteresting matter, and looked in her open palm. She waited until he exhaled, then blew the powder in his face as he inhaled, stepping back quickly.

His eyes went wide with surprise, then anger, then shock when he realized that his throat was constricting. He fought for breath, braced himself on the doorframe, wavered, and fell over unconscious.

It worked, Tallie thought, amazed at her luck. *Thank the gods for obscure herbology texts.* She stepped over his body and shoved open Eden's door, surprising her. "Come with me now! Bring nothing. Hurry!" she ordered her.

Eden immediately grasped what had brought Tallie to her room and jumped up to join her in the hallway. She stepped over the guard's body.

"What did you do to him?" she asked.

"Nothing permanent," Tallie replied, hurrying around the corner to the stairwell. She slung a pack over her shoulder and handed the other to Eden. When they heard a door open two floors below, Tallie shepherded Eden up a story, and they crouched against the wall, out of sight of the landing below. Two monks climbed the stairs and exited on the third floor. Tallie pulled Eden to her feet and rushed her as quietly as she could down the stairs to the main floor.

She peeked out into the courtyard and spied several monks standing around. Tallie pulled Eden deeper inside the building. "We can't go this way," she told her. "Is there another way out?"

"This is the only exit, but we could climb out a window at the back of the building," Eden suggested.

"Lead the way," Tallie replied.

Eden guided them down the hallway, as they heard footsteps hurrying down the stairwell. Eden tried a few doors until she found one that was open and stepped inside, closing it quietly behind them. She rushed to the window, opened it, and looked out. The rear of the building appeared deserted, so she crawled out, falling into the bushes below the window. She got up and took Tallie's pack so that she could crawl out. Tallie had more difficulty leveraging herself out the window, but Eden helped her, and soon, they were both standing behind the bushes with their backs pressed up against the building.

"What now?" Eden asked.

"I'm not really sure. I just know that we need to get away from this place," Tallie replied.

"The gates out of the city are guarded, and if they're looking for us, we should avoid them."

"I was hoping we could hide out in the levels under the library, but now I think that wouldn't be safe. Do you know anywhere else we could go?"

Eden thought and thought, but she'd spent almost her entire life locked away in the temple, so it was all she knew. *That's it!* she thought as inspiration struck. *Almost my entire life.*

"I have an idea," Eden announced. "I grew up in the city, not the temple. On a whim a few years back, I went past where I used to live and found it deserted. We could try there."

"Won't they think of that?"

"I was collected at such a young age, and from school, so I don't think they kept track of where I lived or even cared."

"Sounds like our best option. Lead the way."

They followed the wall that encircled the temple grounds to an opening out to the broader city, then they took side streets until they arrived at the neighborhood where Eden had lived as a young child. The dwellings were not well maintained and signaled the relative poverty of their inhabitants.

Looking out from an alleyway, Tallie asked, "Which house was yours?"

"Third from the end," Eden replied, indicating a fairly dilapidated dwelling with boarded-up windows.

"Looks unoccupied to me," Tallie agreed but was concerned about the people in the streets. "I don't think we should be seen – someone could report us."

"So, we stay in this alley all day?" Eden asked.

"I feel too exposed here. Let's wait in the orchards. At this point in the season, no one should be there."

Eden agreed, and they headed there to spend the remainder of the day hiding among the trees. They made it to the orchard without incident and moved deeper into it until they felt that they couldn't be spotted. Tallie put her back up against an apple tree and Eden sat down, leaning back against the trunk of the adjacent tree. She nervously plucked blades of grasses to pass the time. She turned to ask Tallie, "Be honest with me – we can't spend the rest of our lives hiding. Are we doomed?"

"Not necessarily," Tallie reassured her. "The world is being reshaped, even while we're sitting here. We need to cling to the hope that a way out of this mess will present itself. We just have to be patient." Eden knew that Tallie was just trying to make her feel better, but it did, and she was thankful for her.

When darkness began to fall, they headed back to Eden's former home. The street was empty, and they were emboldened to cross it briskly to her house. They turned the doorknob, finding it unlocked. Tallie pulled the door open, and they quickly slipped inside. Tallie stood in the doorway and used the last light of day to see as she rummaged through her pack for a candle. Finding one, she closed the door and lit the candle. The rooms were empty, but it was mercifully clean – just dusty. It was depressing, but they felt safe for the moment.

Eden plopped down on the floor, leaned against the wall, and pulled her knees to her chest. Tallie sat down beside her and put her arm around her. "We're going to be okay," she assured her.

Looking around at the empty house, Tallie asked, "What became of your parents?"

"I don't really know," Eden replied. "I was taken to the temple as a young girl. After that, I never saw them again. I tell myself that they were probably better off without me and moved out of this place," she said, gesturing to the cramped space that surrounded them.

"Oh, child," Tallie replied. "I'm sure nothing could be further from the truth. It must have broken their hearts."

Eden said nothing, and Tallie moved closer to comfort her. They fell asleep that way.

Tallie woke Eden before dawn. "If we're going to hide out here, we need supplies, but we can't move around the city looking as we do, so we're going to have to get some things now."

Eden got up stiffly from where she'd slept on the hard plaster floor. "Okay."

They opened the door, peered out to confirm that no one was about, and slipped out into the street.

"Our first order of business," Tallie said, "is to find clothes that don't mark us as coming from the temple. Even from a distance, you look like an acolyte."

They moved around the streets, looking in yards until they found clothes hanging on a line. Tallie pointed out an outfit that looked like it would fit Eden.

"I feel guilty stealing," Eden confessed.

"It beats dying," Tallie countered and snuck into the yard. She quickly grabbed what they needed and clipped a coin to the line with a clothespin. They raced away, fearful of getting caught. No one raised an alarm, however, and they made their way back quickly. Tallie peeked out at their hideout from the opposite alleyway and froze when she saw a pair of monks moving down the street toward them. "Move back," she whispered to Eden and pushed her back around the corner to hide in a doorway. She put a finger to her lips to let her know that they needed to be silent and waited.

The monks passed by the alley, so after a short while, Tallie peeked back out and down the street. The monks had gone, so they slipped across the street and into their dwelling. Eden's heart thudded in her chest.

"I'm not sure I can do this," she declared.

"You've done great so far," Tallie replied. "Keep calm, and you'll be fine."

Eden was unconvinced, but she accepted that she didn't have much choice in the matter if they were going to survive. She changed her clothes, folded her old outfit, and placed it against the wall. *At least it will make a good pillow*, she thought. She stared at the pile of clothes for a moment longer. "I don't think I can remember wearing anything other than the clothes the Church provided me with," she observed wistfully.

"I guess this is the start of a new you," Tallie responded, judging that Eden's new outfit suited her, and truth be told, flattered her more than her temple garb.

"What are we going to do about food?" Eden asked, her stomach already rumbling.

"We're going to have to buy it," Tallie replied. Before Eden could point out that she had no coin, Tallie added, "I raided the library' coffers before we left. We have plenty of funds. Unfortunately, we can only buy food during the day, so it necessitates braving daylight."

This made Eden nervous, but she accepted the necessity. "I guess I should go find something for our breakfast."

"That would be wonderful," Tallie replied, handing her some coins, "but I think it would be best to wait until a few more people are about, so you stand out less. Step out when there's no one out front, and on your way back, walk past if there is anyone around that could see you enter. While you're out, I'll try to come up with a more complete shopping list of other things we need."

Eden waited for the sun to rise higher, and while she waited, she tried to talk herself into feeling more confident, with limited success. When it seemed late enough, she and Tallie listened at the door until they heard nothing, then cracked it open and peeked out. When they didn't see anyone, Eden stepped out quickly and began walking toward the nearest market. Every time she spotted monks in the distance, she'd move perpendicularly to them as casually as she could. She was sweating with nerves by the time she arrived at the market. She chose vendors along the perimeter of the market and tried to minimize the time she spent browsing. She avoided eye contact and didn't talk much with the salespeople. She did her best to be as unmemorable as possible.

As she headed home with a bundle of food in her arms, she couldn't shake the feeling of being watched. She couldn't tell if she actually was being watched or if it was just paranoia, but it made her walk more briskly. She had to pass by her door twice before she circled back and found the street empty. She walked as though she was simply passing by, then ducked into her old house at the last moment.

Tallie looked up from a book. "You're back. Well done." She got up and stretched out her stiff muscles. They ate sparingly and spent the rest of the day holed up, Tallie reading and Eden pacing.

Over the following days, they repeated their routine and Eden would often bring home some surprise that eased their existence, be it a small chair or a handful of candles. She came to enjoy the freedom of her sorties, having spent much of her life cooped up in her room in the temple. Some days, she'd stray from her errands and explore the city, ever wary of the monks that patrolled widely. Eden could never shake the feeling of being watched, and she had many close calls, whereby she narrowly avoided walking past monks that could easily have been out looking for her.

Tallie spent her days reviewing the documents that she'd taken from the archives, thinking that they might contain useful information, even though much of it she couldn't understand.

Eden felt bad that Tallie spent so much time cooped up in their drab dwelling, so she decided to paint a mural for her on its walls. She went to the market and took the risk of frequenting one of the paint vendors from whom she used to buy hard-to-get colors. The old woman eyed her with vague recognition but sold her the supplies without saying anything. She returned home and set about sketching an outline, a project that she worked on late into the night.

The next morning, she got up early and headed back to the market with a more mundane list of foods to purchase. The number of monks in the streets was much higher than usual, and she struggled to keep out of sight of them. Eventually, she abandoned her errand altogether and hurried home.

"Something is going on," she reported to Tallie, closing the door behind her. "There are monks everywhere."

They spent the rest of the day worrying, so much so that Eden couldn't concentrate on her mural. That evening, their worst fears were confirmed when they heard a soft rap on their door. Tallie shushed Eden, and they stayed still, hoping that whoever was at their door would move on. The doorknob started to turn, and Tallie exhaled the last of her hope. The door swung inwards, and Skye stepped in cautiously.

"Skye?" Eden asked, shocked.

"Eden?" Skye replied, then confirming that it was her added, "Thank the gods you're okay," took a last look outside, and closed the door behind him.

Eden noticed that Tallie was still on edge. "It's okay, Tallie, this is Skye… he's a friend of Kala's."

The tension left Tallie's body, but she remained shaken by the stress of Skye's unexpected arrival. All she could do was raise a hand by way of acknowledgment.

"Tallie," Skye said, recognizing the name, "Kala sends her regards." He didn't dwell on pleasantries, however. "We have to get out of here. I sort of announced my presence by landing an airship. The monks know someone has come to town – they just don't know who or why, but they're out looking for me. Plus, I've been scouring this neighborhood all day looking for you, and I don't think that will escape notice. The sooner we get out of here, the better."

Tallie and Eden wasted no time in gathering their more critical belongings. Skye looked out the door and spotted a couple of monks talking to a woman up the street.

"We've got to go, now!" he said and stepped into the street. Tallie and Eden followed him. They bowed their heads and moved off in the direction opposite the monks, trying not to draw attention to themselves. At the first cross street, they moved laterally to get out of the monks' line of sight. They kept moving, not trusting that they'd escaped detection.

"I'm a little disoriented," Skye admitted. "Can either of you guide us closer to the airfield?"

"I know how to get there. It's near the temple grounds," Eden replied, thankful for her explorations of the city, and took the lead. Her frequent forays had increased her confidence, and she was successful at keeping them from being discovered as they moved within sight of a moored airship.

They ducked down behind the row of bushes that ringed the airfield. Skye felt inside his tunic to confirm that he still had his amulet. "We're going to have to steal an airship," he informed them. "I think they'll be ready if one lands unannounced, but one that's already here might warrant less scrutiny."

He peeked over the bushes to examine the airship on the ground. Monks moved about the airfield, but none too close to the ship. *Thank the gods*, he thought, but his blood froze when he spotted a regal-looking woman in flowing robes talking to a small group of monks. *The Priestess. Damn*, he thought and ducked back down behind the bushes. He hazarded another look and judged that he, Eden, and Tallie were closer to the ship than the monks and the Priestess.

"We're going have to make a run for it," he told them. "Do you think you can do that?"

Eden and Tallie nodded nervously.

"Okay. Start by walking toward the ship casually, as though we have a reason for being here, but as soon as we're noticed, run for it as fast as you can. Skye noticed the heavy pack that Tallie carried protectively. "I can carry that, if you like," he told her.

Tallie looked at it possessively but handed it over.

"Okay," Skye announced, slinging it on his back. "Let's do this." He stood up and slipped through the bushes. Eden and Tallie followed him closely. They walked nonchalantly but purposefully toward the airship. Skye kept an eye on the nearest monks. They'd made it about a quarter of the way when a monk noticed them and looked them over more closely, trying to puzzle out who they were and what they were doing on the airfield.

"Run!" Skye yelled and raced toward the ship to open the door for Tallie and Eden. Shouts rang out across the field, and he braced himself to be struck by a weapon but made it to the airship intact. The door was already open, and he waved Eden and Tallie through it, jumping in after them. He slammed the door closed and pressed the button on his amulet, releasing the ship from its mooring.

A row of archers notched arrows and aimed at the airship. Skye locked eyes with the Priestess. She raised a hand to stop the archers from firing, never taking her eyes off Skye. Chills ran down his spine as he could see the machinations taking form in her cold eyes. He slumped down in the ship, knowing that he'd only escaped the frying pan by stepping into the fire.

13

Kala

Kala and Soren spent the day finalizing plans for his assault on the Church. He was impatient to get the army underway, while she was apprehensive, knowing how formidable an adversary the Priestess was. Kala walked back from Soren's camp, hoping to spend a final night with her friends before joining the march. *The army moves slowly. Skye can always catch up when he returns*, she thought hopefully. She was still angry with him for going off half-cocked on a mission to save Eden, without a plan or help. That was a sure way to get oneself killed. She understood that he felt a responsibility to Eden and a desire to right his mistreatment of her, but while getting oneself killed in the process of righting a wrong was noble, it wouldn't actually help the person wronged. She already felt terrible for the danger she'd put Eden in, felt worse because of her inability to go herself, and the more she thought about Skye putting himself in danger in her stead, the fouler her mood became.

Unbeknownst to her, Skye had already returned earlier in the day and brought Eden and Tallie to the temple. Eden had been dumbstruck by the scale of the city. Tallie had to tug her along when she'd stop to stare in wonder at some magnificent building. When they finally made it to the temple gates, Eden and Tallie quailed at the prospect of entering a Church facility, but Skye assured them that the monks had deserted Bayre long ago and hadn't returned. They were still nervous as they walked through the gates.

"Let me find us something to eat," he suggested. It had been a long trip in the airship, and they were all famished. Walking through the great room, Skye spotted Hawke talking with the Pirate Lord. "Why don't you wait here while I scrounge up something?" He suggested to Eden and Tallie and walked them over to Hawke.

"Eden, Tallie, this is Hawke, and…" Skye stumbled in his introductions.

"Eryl," the Pirate Lord finished for him, rose, and bowed low. "Ladies."

"Pirate Lord Eryl," Skye mused. "That's a swashbuckling-sounding name if I've ever heard one."

"I do come from a long line of pirates," Eryl replied, "and my father named me."

"You sail the sea?" Eden asked, curious, while Skye wandered off to the kitchens.

"That's a big part of being a pirate," Eryl laughed.

"As far south as the Thousand Islands?" she asked.

"Yes, have you?" Eryl responded, intrigued by her knowledge of them.

"No," Eden sighed. "Until today, I'd never been anywhere but my city, but I've often dreamt that I have. I imagine the first rays of the rising sun striking the tips of the coastal mountains as it rises from the ocean."

"It is a sight to behold, alright," Eryl agreed. "Perhaps I can show it to you someday."

"Really?" Eden asked skeptically, bruised enough by the world to know that people often made promises they had no intention of keeping.

"I promise," Eryl replied, placing his hand dramatically over his heart. "On my honor."

"Whatever that's worth," Hawke chimed in good-naturedly, slapping Eryl's back.

"Sadly, true," Eryl conceded.

"Well, I'll hold you to it," Eden said.

"It would be my pleasure," Eryl added, as Skye re-emerged with a plate of fruit, cheese, and some meats.

"Nothing elaborate," Skye apologized, "but the cheese is tasty."

Hawke and Eryl rose to excuse themselves. Eryl bowed low to the ladies, and they left.

"He's such a gentleman," Eden noted.

"He does make quite the impression," Tallie agreed. "But, I think you made as much of an impression on him as he did on you."

Eden went beet red and picked up a piece of fruit to hide her embarrassment.

Skye desperately wanted to apologize to Eden, but he still hadn't had a moment in private to do so. Tallie could tell that they had unfinished business but also hadn't anywhere to go to leave them alone. She shifted uncomfortably in her chair, watching them avoid prolonged eye contact.

Tallie faked a yawn. "I'm exhausted. I slept terribly on the airship," she lied. In truth, she'd never slept better than since Skye had rescued them from their hideout. "Is there somewhere I could rest?"

"Of course," Skye replied. "I haven't seen Celeste around, but I can find you a room. This place is huge."

"That's great," Eden chimed in, "I'm beat too," not picking up on Tallie's intention of leaving them alone, or perhaps doing so and just not wanting to have an awkward conversation with Skye.

Skye stood. "Just let me put the remains of the cheese away, and I'll show you to your rooms." He returned a moment later and guided them to the wing of the building that housed the residences. He walked past a row of rooms that looked occupied, as well as some he wasn't sure about. "To be safe, let's move you a little further down the hall," he suggested.

Arriving at the first room that was clearly unclaimed, Tallie slipped past Eden, bumping her slightly with her bags and apologizing.

"Thank you for everything," she said to Skye and closed the door quickly, leaving Skye alone with Eden for the first time. He led her to the next open room.

"Eden," he began.

"Don't," she stopped him. "I was a foolish girl. It was nothing more."

"That's not true. You're a wonderful girl."

"That always ends with 'but,'" she replied ruefully.

"But," Skye conceded, "I was not so wonderful back."

"It's okay."

"No, it's not. Can you ever forgive me?"

"You saved my life. How can I not?"

"Because the one does not excuse the other."

"I'm trying." She struggled with what she wanted to say. "I was young and naïve, so it's still a bit raw. But I can tell you're a good person, so yes, I forgive you. Give me enough time, and I'll probably come to feel that way too." It was clear there was nothing more to say. "I think I should rest," she said, stepping back into the room.

"Of course. Thank you," he said earnestly and stepped back into the hall as the door closed. *If I'm forgiven, why do I still feel like a jerk?* he wondered, and headed back toward the great room.

He almost walked right into Kala as they rounded the same corner, both lost in thought. She wanted to embrace him, her relief at seeing him alive was so palpable, but he'd startled her, so they stood apart uncertainly.

Kala recovered more quickly than he did. "You're back," she noted awkwardly. She hesitated to ask if he'd been successful in his mission out of fear of confirming that her actions had indeed killed her friend.

Picking up on her uncomfortableness, Skye quickly assured her, "Eden and Tallie are resting. They're safe."

Kala's knees buckled ever so slightly with relief. "Thank the gods," she declared. "And thank the gods you're okay. Please, never do that again."

"Do what? Rescue someone?"

"No, of course not. Don't rush off on your own again without help?"

"Can't I be the hero for once?" he asked angrily. "Why does it always have to be you?"

"That's not what I meant. First of all, I'm not trying to be a hero. I do what I do because I have to, not because I want to. Second, of course you can be a hero. I'm just saying that it's dangerous out there." She thought of the Priestess and shuddered.

"You don't think I can look after myself?"

"That's not what I'm saying. It's dangerous for all of us. Look, I get that Eden is important to you."

"It's not about me or her, or me and her. We put her in danger – we had a responsibility to get her out of it."

"Are you sure it had nothing to do with you feeling guilty for using her?"

Skye bristled at being reminded of his past misdeeds. He felt the need to lash out. "Are you saying that she's expendable? Acceptable losses in the fight for a greater good?" Even as he said it, he knew his words wounded her deeply.

"The good of the world *does* not, and *can*not ever outweigh the good of the individual."

The hurt in her eyes made him feel awful. *It's true – I am a jerk*, he thought. "I thought you'd be happy to see me – happy that Eden and Tallie are safe," he said bitterly.

"I am. This is coming out all wrong," she replied, frustrated.

Skye felt emotionally drained and defeated. "I'm tired," he declared and stalked off, leaving Kala shivering in the aftermath of their first fight.

What the hell just happened? she wondered. *I didn't mean any of that the way he took it.* Her desire to chase after him warred with the need to give him space. Her pride broke the tie, and she slunk off to find an unclaimed bed of her own.

The next morning, she waited in her room until she figured that Skye had probably already had breakfast before venturing down for a cup of kai. She peeked into the kitchens and didn't see or hear him, so she risked entering and poured herself a cup. Poking her head into the great room, she spied Tallie sitting alone.

"Tallie," she called, waving over.

Tallie looked up and gestured for her to join her.

"I'm so sorry I turned your life upside down," Kala apologized.

"It's all for the greater good," Tallie replied, echoing Skye's words and making her wince. "We need to talk," she added, growing serious.

"Okay," Kala replied, putting down her mug.

Tallie turned and pulled her bulging pack over to her. She opened it and lifted out an enormous pile of books and scrolls. "I brought everything I could find about the history of world conflict, even things I didn't know existed until I went hunting. Did you know that this is not the first time the world has gone to war?"

Kala remembered the Priestess telling her that this was a cycle that had repeated for eons. "Yes."

"Did you know that the Church has intervened in the past to tip the scales or complete the destruction?"

"Yes."

"Do you know just how fearsome the weapons are at the Church's disposal?"

"No, although I can imagine."

"I don't think you *can* imagine. I fear that the end of the conventional war has only hastened darker times."

"Soren should be warned," Kala concluded, even though she knew that she'd told him as much before, just without any proof to back up her concerns. She got up.

"Before you go," Tallie stopped her by holding her wrist. "I also brought all the books about airships that you once asked for, plus a few more that I found. They're all quite technical, so I don't know how to interpret them.

"I know someone who might be able to." Kala took the heavy pack from Tallie and guided her out of the great room and into the city. As they walked toward the city gates, Kala asked, "Where's Eden? I'd like to say hi."

"Probably flirting with her beau," Tallie replied offhandedly, and Kala didn't ask any more questions.

Arriving at the gates, Kala called up to the scaffolding, "Seline, are you up there?"

Seline popped her head over the lip of the top level. "I'm here. What's up?"

"Can you come down a moment?" Kala asked. "It looks safer than us coming up."

"I'll be right down," Seline replied and disappeared from sight. A moment later, she stepped off the ladder and came over. She looked back up at the scaffolding. "Nice of Soren to lend me to the city to fix the gates I blew up. I sure outdid myself," she said absentmindedly, wiping dirt across her forehead.

"Thanks for coming down," Kala said and introduced Tallie. "Seline, this is Tallie. She's the Church's head librarian."

Seline looked at her appreciatively, wiped her hand on her trousers, and held it out to her, "Pleased to meet you. The stories you could tell…"

Tallie shook her hand. "They all read like nightmares these days."

"Sign of the times," Seline shrugged.

"Seline," Kala began, "Tallie brought with her from the Church archives technical documents about the airships that I thought you might be able to decipher."

"And it's not even my birthday," Seline replied with relish. "Let's have a look."

Tallie looked hesitantly at Seline's dirty hands.

"I won't touch them," she assured her. "Just show them to me."

Tallie pulled them out and cataloged each one for her.

"That's brilliant. I'll look them over when I'm done here for the day."

"Where should I put them?" Tallie asked, possessive of her treasures.

"There's a locking cabinet in the gatehouse," Seline replied. "I'll show you." She led them over, and they deposited the relevant books inside. "I promise I'll wash before I touch them," she assured a worried Tallie.

"We won't keep you," Kala told Seline, and she and Tallie bid her good luck with her repairs. They wandered back to the temple, where Tallie excused herself. Kala spotted Lily and Cera, newly retrieved by Calix, and walked over to say hi.

"Morning," Lily greeted her.

"I'm not so sure it still is," Kala ribbed her.

"Well, morning is a vile time anyway, so good riddance to it if it isn't," Lily replied.

Kala spotted her long-abandoned kai, picked up the cup, and took a sip.

"Eww," said Cera, "that's cold."

Kala shrugged and took another sip.

Cera shook her head, as Lily chimed in, "I convinced Forest to stay here a while and not march out with you and Soren. She needs to rest and recover from the past few moons. Besides, Nara and Jarom are around here somewhere, and it's nice not to have family scattered to the four winds." Too late, she realized that Kala's grandfather was still unaccounted for, having fled before Soren's attack. "I'm sorry," she apologized, admonishing herself for her stupidity.

"It's okay," Kala replied, despite constantly worrying about her grandfather. "Calix and Dhara are going to go search for them. His dad is out there too, and Dhara's sister's daughter."

"I doubt he'll be able to keep up with her, wounded or not," Lily said.

"I think they're cute together," Cera added.

"Cute like a chipmunk and a wolverine," Kala laughed.

"Don't let her hear you say they look cute," Lily warned her. "She'll bite your head off."

"I guess we don't want to jinx it either," Cera agreed.

"Is Kaia going with them too?" Kala asked. "She looked pretty injured the last time I saw her."

"No, she's in no condition," Cera replied.

"I guess it'll just be me heading off with Soren," Kala concluded, partly with relief for her friends' safety, and partly with sadness at being separated from them again.

"At least you'll have Skye for company," Lily comforted her.

"I'm not so sure," Kala admitted. "We had a fight."

"You poor thing," Lily consoled her.

"Everybody fights," Cera assured her. "I'm sure it'll blow over."

"I hope so," Kala replied. "I should find him and apologize. I said a lot of things that came out horribly wrong."

"Good luck," Lily encouraged her, reaching for Cera's hand. "We're rooting for you."

"Thanks," Kala replied and went off in search of Skye.

———————————

Skye was similarly looking for Kala, equally eager to set things right between them. He poked his head into the room they'd been sharing before he left to rescue Eden.

"Hello, Skye," a silky voice called from a chair hidden in the shadow of the bright sunlight streaming through the window.

Skye craned his neck to see who hailed him. As his eyes adjusted, he took in the Priestess sitting calmly in the gloom. He froze. She put down the book that she'd been leafing through, Kala's journal, and lifted a glass of water to her lips to take a slow drink.

"You're looking well," she said, putting down her glass, and taking him in. "So is Evelyn, by the way," she added.

Skye's blood ran cold. "Keep my mother out of this," he said defiantly.

"I'd like to," she replied earnestly. "I really would. In fact, I have a proposal for you that would guarantee her safety." She drummed her nails on the cover of Kala's journal to stretch out the tension.

Skye waited for the hammer to fall.

"Break up with Kala, and I'll let Evelyn live."

Skye stared at her dumbstruck.

"It's such a small thing, and no one gets hurt."

"Skye?" Kala called from the hallway. "Are you in there?"

Skye froze again, caught between the two most fearsome predators he knew.

The Priestess raised an eyebrow, challenging him to do something. She reached for the glass of water and, with a single finger, tipped it over onto Kala's journal.

"Skye?" Kala called again, closer.

Skye wheeled around to warn her. "Kala!" he called to her.

She stepped through the doorway a moment later.

Skye spun around to see how the Priestess would react, but the chair by the window was empty – the drapes stirring in the breeze.

Kala followed his eyes to the chair and spotted her journal on the bedside table, dripping water.

"Skye, what the hell?" she couldn't help but say and stepped around him to rescue it. She held it up in the light of the window to survey the damage.

"I need some air," Skye said and stepped out of the room in a fog.

Kala collapsed into the chair, cradling her journal. *Why does it smell like perfume in here?* she wondered.

14

Soren

Soren rode, surrounded by his army, with Petra at his side. She wasn't very comfortable in the saddle, but she suffered through it to spend time with her son. As they made their way over the countryside, they spoke of places he'd seen and people he'd come to know. She soaked it all in, new life breathing into her with every passing day.

Kala rode near the back of the advancing army, in part to give Soren and Petra privacy, but also to defer to his leadership. Skye joined her, but they'd spoken little to each other since his return, and it was as if he carried a heavy weight that he refused to share – Kala could only watch him helplessly.

Grey and Hawke opted to accompany Kala as well, and while Grey could be bland, she appreciated his company, and even more so Hawke's, with whom she felt an easy camaraderie. She could tell that this bothered Skye but decided he'd just have to be an adult about it.

The days wore on, but they made good progress, and before long, they approached the city that was the seat of the Church's power – the city that the Priestess called home. Soren's army crested a rise, and it came into view. Just past the vineyards, the city was ringed with a low stone wall, but nothing as impressive as Bayre's. Soren had long-since decided there would be no siege, only an attack to rid the world of a cancer as he'd put it, *and perhaps exorcise his demons*, Kala thought. Soren arranged his fiercest warriors along the front lines, comprised mostly of barbarian tribes from the north. His archers marched closely behind, followed by the remainder of his soldiers and the supporting forces.

As the army advanced onto the plains that surrounded the city, Soren rode to its front and sent Petra to the rear. Kala stayed at the back as well, waiting to be summoned to the front. She was in no hurry to face the Priestess, despite something deep within telling her that they were locked in a gravitational spiral that drew them inexorably closer. The army spread out as it advanced, resembling a river overflowing its banks.

Despite her position at the rear, from her vantage point in the saddle, Kala could see over the heads of the soldiers right to the city. Monks stood sentry on its walls, and in the middle of them was a robed woman that Kala could tell from the cold she radiated had to be the Priestess. Kala sat up straighter in the saddle and looked to her colleagues on either side of her. Grey stared wistfully at the Priestess, and Kala recalled that they had a history that he'd never divulged. Hawke sat relaxed, simply awaiting battle. Kala looked around for Skye and spotted him frozen in his saddle, eyes fixed on the Priestess. He turned his horse and trotted further toward the rear.

A solitary airship rose out of the city and drifted low over the wall toward the army. Just seeing it incensed Soren, and he spurred his horse toward it. "Archers!" he ordered, and a thousand men and women notched an arrow and waited for the ship to move closer.

Something about this is wrong, Kala thought and looked back to the Priestess on the wall. Kala swore that she looked right at her before stepping out of sight. All the monks soon joined her in disappearing from the wall. It stood empty, and Soren didn't notice, fixated as he was on the airship.

"No!" yelled Kala at the same instant that Soren yelled, "Fire!" and a hail of arrows arced up into the sky toward the ship. Collectively, they shredded its fabric, and it rapidly descended toward the front ranks of the army. Soren himself raised his sword and charged it.

"Get down!" Kala yelled, grabbing Grey's and Hawke's sleeves and yanking them off their saddles as she dove for the ground. A flash blinded her just before a ferocious wall of air pushed her into the ground and knocked her horse off its legs. It was silent for a moment, despite her ears ringing, then falling debris began to pelt her. She rose to her knees, only to be knocked off of them by a second blast of air racing back toward the city.

Kala looked about frantically and spotted Grey patting out the fire that had ignited his cloak. She checked herself over to ensure that she wasn't on fire herself. She glanced the other way to see Hawke lying still. She crawled over to him, her head pounding the whole way. She was relieved to find him breathing, just knocked out by flying debris. She checked him over for visible injuries and found none.

Kala rose to her feet and immediately fell over, struggling with her balance. She tried again and barely succeeded in remaining standing. She gazed toward the city – the army that had stood between her and it was simply gone. An enormous crater squatted in its place. Around it, the ground was littered with bodies. Flames had engulfed anything combustible. It was a hellscape.

She moved from body to body, assessing their wounds. Most were dead or injured too badly to recover, but for the few that could be saved, she did her best. She screamed for aid as she staunched the flow of blood where she could and said comforting words where she couldn't. She looked up to see a wall of airships rising into the sky over the city. She prepared herself for a barrage, but they drifted up and away to the north. She couldn't even waste time cursing them – the lives of so many hung precariously in the balance.

She worked deep into the night, saving anyone she could. She carried them to hastily-erected hospital tents at the rear of what had once been a formidable army. By morning, she was beyond exhaustion. Despite her best efforts and those of many, the dead vastly outnumbered the living.

As dawn illuminated the horrors of the field, she caught a glimpse of Petra, kneeling at the bottom of the crater, sobbing. Her heart went out to her, having lost her son again after so short a reunion, and in so horrific a manner.

She turned away and spotted Skye walking toward her. *Thank the gods*, she thought. He was as covered in blood as she, but she still tried to wipe her face clean of it as he drew closer. He stopped just out of her reach, shoulders slumping.

"I can't do this," he told her, a tortured look in his eyes.

"Don't," she implored him, realizing he was breaking up with her. "I need you," she begged.

"Goodbye," he replied and strode away.

Kala's heart imploded.

PART II
THE WASTES

15

Kala

Kala reeled as though punched in the gut. *This isn't happening*, she thought as Skye walked away. *Turn around*, she begged wordlessly as he drew further and further away. Her heart pleaded with her to call to him, but she was so breathless that all she could manage was to croak, "Please," before he disappeared from sight. Her knees buckled, she swayed and fell to her knees.

The sights and sounds of the surrounding carnage assaulted her – the screaming, the wounded, the blood. *This is just a nightmare*, she tried to convince herself, *I only need to wake up*. She pinched herself and screamed, but nothing changed – no one even looked at her. Her breathing became shallower, the air knocked from her lungs, and she grew panicked. *I can't be here*, she decided and turned toward the city.

She walked in a daze toward the distant walls, skirting the crater without really noticing it. She registered the smell of charcoal and sulfur as she traversed the uneven ground, tripping over remnants of armor that stuck haphazardly out of the earth. She felt ephemeral, her very existence negated.

She entered the city's open gates. Citizens peeked furtively out their windows, terrified that the survivors' wrath would fall on them. Kala saw a woman quail at the sight of her and duck into a building, yelling, "Death stalks the streets – stay inside!" Kala was too numb to notice that it was her that the woman referred to. She was drawn to the temple at the center of the city and walked onto its grounds unopposed, the monks having deserted it. Dust blew across the courtyard in tiny tornadoes.

She found herself walking up the steps of the cathedral and pushing open its doors. The dim interior wrapped around her like gauze, and she walked toward the statue of the Goddess of Death that faced the pews. She stopped in front of it and stared at it. *It's not enough for you that I swell your ranks?* she thought bitterly. *It's not enough that you've robbed me of my soul, now you steal my heart? I'll be dead soon enough, why do you want me dead inside first?* The statue stared back mockingly. "Bitch," Kala muttered.

Someone cleared his throat behind her, announcing that she was not alone. She turned to see Grey sitting in the front pew.

"Something upsetting you?" he asked.

"Nothing I feel like talking about," she replied testily, walking over and collapsing down beside him. "Why are *you* here?" she asked.

He exhaled heavily before replying. "I was just thinking that this isn't the church I joined," he sighed.

"The Church worships death," Kala responded incredulously and perhaps a little more accusatorily than she'd intended. "What did you expect?"

He wasn't offended. "You might not believe it, but we actually celebrated life. Death was just the culmination of a cycle that begat more life – a perfect, unending circle."

She leaned back, feeling jaded. "Life only looks perfect from a distance. Up close, it's messy."

Grey was quiet for a while, contemplating the light filtering through the stained glass set high overhead. "She can be quiet convincing," he said, half to himself.

Kala surmised that he was referring to the Priestess. "Intimidating would be more apt," she corrected.

"She's not all bad," he replied.

"I'll just have to take your word for it on that," Kala replied skeptically, accepting that he and the Priestess had had some type of relationship.

"You two are a lot alike," he said, which appalled Kala, so he quickly explained, "You both exude passion – the difference is that you have no personal agenda."

Kala recalled the Priestess telling her that people loved her enough to die for her. *Skye wasn't among them*, she thought crossly, but couldn't bring herself to blame him.

"Ever feel like your heart's been ripped out?" Grey asked, interrupting her thoughts.

Her chest tightened. "I think I can relate," she replied and placed a hand sympathetically on his.

He hung his head, and they sat in shared misery while the shifting shadows marked the passage of time. Eventually, he sighed, rose, and made his way out of the cathedral, leaving Kala alone with her pain.

Without Skye's emotional support to cow them, her demons swirled inside her unchecked. She wrestled with feelings of self-doubt, inadequacy, and failure. A thousand regrets cut her until her heart bled itself dry. Eventually, she too rose, cast a last dirty look at the statue of the Goddess, and exited as well.

The bright light outside made her wince. She looked around the temple grounds, which now seemed both familiar and strange. She wandered between the buildings. The dining hall was eerily silent, in stark contrast to her memory of it as a hub of activity. She exited out its far side, passing doorways to empty classrooms and the auditorium. She imagined the debates about whether to let the world live another day, take another breath.

On a whim, she grabbed a torch, hunted around for the means to light it, and finally finding one, carried it down into the catacombs. She searched for the room in which the crystal housing the Ancients resided and finally identified it by its stone bench. The spot where the crystal had been was vacant, but she sat down anyway and stared at it. *How dare the Ancients pass judgment on her and her friends, deeming them unworthy of living. More life coursed through her veins than the cold crystal, regardless of however many souls resided within it.*

She left the room but found herself twisted around as she headed back to the surface. She stumbled into what she surmised had been the armory, judging by the row and after row of empty racks that looked to have once stored weapons of all sorts. Curiosity made her enter the cavernous room. It was so large that the torchlight didn't penetrate very far into it. She moved between the racks, thinking about the size of an army that would require so many weapons. It made the remnants of the forces that she was allied with seem puny in comparison, particularly now that Soren's army had been decimated. Hopelessness gnawed at her and chased her from the room.

Emerging at last from the temple's sublevels, something drew her toward the Priestess's quarters. *Maybe I'll find answers there*, she thought and made her way down the empty hallways to its open door. She entered to find the room vacant, but tidy – the bed was made, the dresser drawers closed, and the papers on the desk neatly stacked. The order of the room contrasted starkly to the chaos she felt inside.

She sat on the bed and glanced about. Beneath the bedside table, she spotted a single book, which she bent down and pulled out. It was the forgery that she and Grey had orchestrated, left to mock her. She threw it across the room, making a terrible crash, and eliciting a faint yelp from inside the closet. She pulled out a dagger and stalked forward, raising it as she yanked the door open.

The tip of her blade wavered a hair's breadth from Frey's heart. It wasn't recognition that had stayed her hand; rather, it was his terror. His eyes were wide with panic, then wider still when he recognized her. He nearly collapsed with relief. "Kala?" he asked, looking uncertainly at the dagger poised over his heart.

"Frey?" she replied distantly. "What are you doing here?"

"The dagger," he prompted, still looking down at its cruel tip.

She looked down at her hand, which didn't fully register as her own, and noticed the dagger. "Sorry," she muttered and re-sheathed it.

He relaxed. "I wanted to become an assassin like you," he laughed. "Some assassin," he added ruefully, "hiding in a closet."

"Assassin's hide – there's nothing wrong with that," she assured him and helped him out of the closet.

"Don't patronize me," he protested but accepted her help. She could tell that despite his bravado, he was still terrified.

She pulled him into a hug, and his entire body shook.

"I was so afraid when I saw the army marching on the city," he sobbed.

"It's okay," she comforted him.

He slowly regained his composure.

"The army is no more," she told him.

He looked confused. "Are you in league with the Priestess?"

"Hell no," Kala responded, offended. "She left and took her monks with her."

Frey calmed. "I know where she went," he said.

16

Priestess

The Priestess looked down at the plains surrounding her mountain fortress. They were filled with tents that housed the monks and priestesses that she had relocated to the ruins. The barren plains stretched out into the distance, featureless save for the remains of the Ancients' buildings that jutted haphazardly out of the ground. She smiled to think that the world was oblivious to the hive of activity going on here. She surveyed the practice fields where row after row of monks drilled with weapons. Deep in the mountain, her assassins prepared in their own way to be unleashed on the world. Generations had spent their entire lives training to fight on a day that only came around once an eon, and she presided over that day. She stood tall beneath the mantle of responsibility. *No one else has the resolve to do what needs be done*, she concluded, turned, and walked back into the cavernous room.

She wound her way past her personal guard, who had taken up stations about the throne room. She had handpicked them for their skill and their loyalty. Brother Grey's image flickered in her mind, and she felt a twinge of sadness at his absence before tamping it down.

She turned to the captain of her guard. "Brother Rapir, what is the status of the relocation?"

"The bulk of our forces are set up on the plain. We have sufficient supplies to support us here for three moons. The Fortress on the Wastes is secure with a skeleton force guarding it. If need be, we could relocate a sizable number of people there. The crystal has been installed in the keep, as per your orders. The library has been moved into storage deep in mountain caves kept dry by fires maintained by acolytes."

Everything is as it should be, she thought. "Thank you," she replied.

She made her way to the circular stairwell that led up to the keep where the crystal had been placed. She readied herself for the draining task of communing with the Ancients. She stepped past the last torch that lit the stairwell and climbed the rest of the way in darkness. Muscle memory made her stop at the top stair and reach for where she'd find the pull that opened the door. She wrapped her fingers around the iron ring and drew it toward her. The door swung wide, and she stepped into the room. The twinkling light of the crystal reflected off the stone walls and provided just enough light for her to locate the stone bench that sat before it. She pushed aside her trailing robes and sat down on the cold, hard seat.

She closed her eyes and emptied her mind. The visions came quickly, as though the Ancients had been waiting for her. She found herself standing at a crossroads, an imaginary wind blowing her hair out of her face. She looked over her shoulder at the path behind her, which terminated at a chasm, the ruins of a bridge dangling into its depths. Returning the way she'd come was clearly not an option. She turned around and examined the three paths that diverged from the intersection in front of her. She stared down each, her inner eye carrying her along it.

The path to her left began pleasantly enough. Birds sang as she soared past flowers, but the landscape gradually blighted until it was a wasteland. The land itself was toxic – nothing lived. Her spirit recoiled at the emptiness and fled back into itself. She found herself back at the crossroads looking down the second path. It, too, seemed appealing as she began to move down it, the wind warm against her skin. Gradually, the wind grew hotter and hotter until the land was aflame. Corpses dotted the landscape, a veritable land of the dead. Her spirit once again quailed and retreated, until she was back facing the third and final path. It was dark and foreboding, and she edged forward cautiously, advancing under a close canopy of trees, their branches scratching at her. She emerged at last into an open field, where the clouds parted, and the sun shone brilliantly across a verdant land. Her spirit basked in the warmth.

Her mouth felt dry, and the sensation brought her crashing back into her physical body. Her back was stiff, and her muscles ached. She'd been in the dark tower for a very long time. She rose slowly, her body protesting. Pain shot up her legs, and she gritted her teeth until it passed. She moved slowly toward the exit and descended the stairs, bracing herself against the wall for support. She passed through the throne room, where her guards stood mute as she headed to her quarters. Her captain would command an acolyte to bring her something to eat and drink. She looked out past the throne room into the depths of night. *The Ancients held me in their thrall for a considerable time*, she thought.

She opened the door to her room and collapsed onto the bed. A small fire was going in the hearth, and assorted fruit had already been left for her on the bedside table. She lacked the strength to reach for it and simply lay still. The visions continued to swirl about in her head. One thing was clear – the Ancients demanded that she take the difficult path.

She awoke to sunlight filtering down the hallway, announcing that the day had arrived. An acolyte had kept the fire going while she slept, given how cold the drafty mountain fortress could become. She felt more rested than she had in days, despite having fallen asleep on top of her bed fully clothed. She got up, ate a few figs, freshened up, and changed her clothes. She made her way out into the throne room to find her guards awaiting instructions.

She waved them to be patient – she'd give them orders soon enough. For now, she wanted to address her forces. She stepped out onto the ledge toward the path that wound down to the plains below. Her guard inferred her intentions, joined her, two in front and two behind, and together they began the descent. The steps were cut directly into the mountainside, and she navigated them carefully as any misstep would prove fatal. She could just have easily taken an airship down to the plains, but what type of message would that send? *Perhaps I'll return that way*, she thought, thankful to some distant predecessor that had engineered the transport of a landing pad up the treacherous slope. How that miraculous feat had been accomplished was now lost to the fog of time.

By midday, the slope grew less steep, and the descent easier. Soon after, she walked out into the camp. Her trek had been noted long ago by the monks, priestesses, and acolytes in the plains, who now waited patiently for her in fields ringed by the remains of mammoth structures dating from the age of the Ancients. She walked through them and stepped onto a stage that elevated her to where all could see her and stood facing them.

She cleared her throat. "Long have we waited and watched, entrusted with the care of the world," she began with conviction. "Our day has come at last," she announced, her voice rising. She paused to look into the sea of eyes before continuing. "The peoples of our world strain against their constraints. If left unchecked, they will expand until the world tears itself apart or consumes itself, like a snake eating its tail. We are all that stands against its self-destruction." She let the words hang in the air and began again in more measured tones. "We alone recognize the danger of want. We understand the need to surrender the desires of the moment to the needs of the future, the individual for the whole." She pointed to them. "The Ancients have revealed our path to be righteous, but it will be difficult. What you are called to do will test you; it will take strength, but I know that it is in you. You are the sword of the Goddess, and with it, She will clear away the growth that chokes our world and return it to a paradise."

She continued in honeyed tones, "When our work is done, we will stand in the garden, hand in hand, and we will lay down our weapons and rebuild a perfect world, one without want." She looked out over the faces of men and women long denied families, and dangled permission to love in front of them as a powerful incentive. Hunger for it burned in many eyes.

"Prepare yourselves for what must come. The Goddess will call each of you soon." She descended the stage into the crowd, placing her hand encouragingly on many shoulders, touching foreheads. She made her way through the throng slowly, but she soaked in its energy and knew that they would do whatever she asked of them.

She spent the remainder of the day moving about the camp. She ate alongside her people and slept in a cot in the barracks surrounded by them. She was one of them, and they were an extension of her.

On the morning of the next day, she began the exhausting climb back up the mountain. It was arduous but symbolic of the challenge she called her forces to share. She steadied herself with her hands as she climbed, noting the sunlight glinting off minerals in the rocks and lost herself in its beauty, despite the burning she felt in her legs. A thousand sets of eyes tracked her progress up the mountain, so she resolved not to rest for even a moment and pressed on.

Arriving at last at the fortress atop the mountain, the captain of her guard held out his hand and helped her up to the ledge that overlooked the plains.

"Thank you, Brother Rapir," she said, accepting his help. She stood on tired legs, looking out over the land. "Go to the Wastes," she said to the air, her captain knowing it was he whom she addressed. "Fetch the most virulent plague and unleash it on Bayre."

He turned on his heel and exited the room to perform her bidding.

17

Dhara

Calix and Dhara returned to the town from which his father, her sister's daughter, and the other evacuees had fled. It was the logical place to start their search for them. Their airship touched down just outside the town walls, and they stepped out warily. Despite fire damage visible across large swaths of buildings, the town looked largely intact. Movement caught their eye through the breached gates, but it disappeared again quickly.

"Should we check the town?" Calix asked.

"If you'd just been chased from this place by Soren's army, would you return to it?" Dhara countered.

"Probably not," Calix replied.

"So we won't waste time looking there, then. Besides, we don't know if any of Soren's forces stayed behind, and if they did, it's unlikely that they know we're allied now. Best not to push our luck."

Calix pointed out that remnants of the refugee camp seemed intact, despite the sack of the town.

"That's worth checking out," Dhara decided, although she was really just curious to see how her temporary home had fared during the invasion – she didn't actually expect to find that the evacuees had returned there. They walked over, staying vigilant. Much of it was trampled or looted. From memory, Dhara found her tent – one of the few that still stood, despite the canvas having been slashed in places. She was somehow offended that her tent had not been looted.

"Morons," she muttered. "This is a perfectly good tent."

Calix wisely kept his mouth shut while she sifted through what few of her possessions still lay strewn about.

Dhara bent down and picked up a muddied shirt that had belonged to her sister Zara. She gripped it tightly before throwing it back on the ground. "Nothing here," she declared and pushed through a slit in the canvas wall.

Calix followed her out and began moving toward the part of the camp where he and his father had resided. Those sections had fared worse during the invasion, and nothing meaningful was left of them.

"It doesn't look like anyone came back," he concluded, surveying the camp. He looked back at the town and worried that they had perhaps tarried longer than they should have. "We should get going," he suggested as Dhara joined him.

"Agreed," she replied, shifting the weight of her pack and holding her spear like a walking stick, but still at the ready if needed. She scanned the distant treeline. "I recall correctly, they headed in that direction," she said, pointing to a break in the trees, between which her memory could visualize the train of evacuees passing.

"Looks about right," he concurred and began walking towards where she'd pointed. He cast a last look over his shoulder at the open fields before they entered the trees. Despite all he'd been through, he still wasn't comfortable in the woods.

Dhara stepped past him and took the lead, being the more experienced tracker, more at home among the trees, and seemingly uncaring about danger at even the most harrowing of times.

Calix sighed inwardly and took his place beside her as she led them forward and paused occasionally to examine tracks and broken branches. Faint signs of passage still survived, and Dhara proved adept at ferreting them out. She scanned the forest from the perspective of which way would most appeal to a frightened collection of people carrying or pulling heavy loads. Despite losing the trail repeatedly, she continued to find it again by following her intuition. Calix simply followed alongside and marveled at her skill.

Night began to fall and sensing Calix's unease, Dhara started looking for a safe place to bed down for the night, or at least as safe as could be achieved in the hostile wilderness. She settled on a stand of dense trees that would form the equivalent of a wall at their backs. They'd only have to worry about predators approaching from one side. She pointed it out to Calix, and together they began collecting wood for a fire.

They sat by the fire that they built, sharing rations, and enjoying each other's company. Calix looked out into the dark and shuddered to think of his father out here in these woods, too, without someone as formidable as Dhara at his side. He uttered a silent prayer for his safety. Dhara arranged the logs on the fire so that it would last a good while into the night and began preparing a place to sleep.

Calix looked about for a spot of his own, glancing up at every noise the forest made.

Sensing his unease, Dhara patted the ground beside her. "Come here," she said. "It isn't like we haven't shared a bed."

Calix moved closer, somewhat embarrassed, but happy to have her close. She turned onto her side, and he lay down along her back.

She waited a moment, sighed, and reached behind her to lift his arm and place it around her. "Better," she murmured and closed her eyes.

Calix let himself relax and fell asleep quickly, feeling surprisingly safe at her side. He woke in the morning to find that she'd woken periodically in the night to keep the fire going, and sat nearby watching him sleep. He immediately felt guilty. "Not much of a woodsman, am I?" he admitted.

"And you snore," she added.

"I do?" he asked, worried.

"No. I'm just kidding – but you're cute when you sleep."

He blushed and sat up. "We should get going, I guess," he said, changing the subject awkwardly.

"That we should," she agreed and began putting out the fire.

He moved to help, following her lead. "I guess we can't just leave it?" he asked.

She just shook her head and muttered, "Not a woodsman, no."

They broke camp and ate a light breakfast as they walked, mainly in silence that was only broken when Calix would ask Dhara whether she thought that they were still on the evacuees' trail. They continued on in this way for several days, winding their way south.

Calix began to feel more comfortable in the woods and was congratulating himself about it when a mountain lion stepped out from behind a tree in front of them. Calix froze.

"Dhara," he cautioned.

"I see it," she said, and stood taller, holding her arms out to look larger.

"What do we do?" Calix asked.

"Try not to look like lunch," she suggested, then realizing he had no idea how to do that, added, "Do your best to look threatening, but don't make any sudden movements."

The mountain lion sniffed the air and eyed them warily.

"It's more scared of us than we are of it, right?" Calix asked.

"Oh no, it wants to eat you… it's just sizing up its chances against the two of us."

Calix swallowed hard and slowly reached to draw his sword.

Dhara lifted the tip of her spear to point toward the animal. "Okay," she concluded, "This is either happening, or it isn't," she said and began moving slowly toward the cat. Calix followed suit.

The cat curled its lip, tensed to spring, then bolted back into the trees.

Calix's released the breath he was holding, and his entire body relaxed.

Dhara simply watched the spot where the cat had retreated. "Keep wary, in case it's simply circling round to catch us off guard from another angle."

Calix spent the rest of the day on pins and needles. "Do you think my father's party had to contend with predators like that?" he asked.

"Probably not, given their numbers," she replied. "That would have scared away lesser predators, but attracted greater ones."

Calix didn't want to think about what might prowl the woods that was a greater threat. "You'd probably have been happier if Kaia were here," he admitted.

"Sure, we'd do each other's hair at night."

"Really?"

"Of course not, you idiot. But, she's handy with a spear."

Calix resumed his silence and vigilance.

A day went by with no signs of the evacuees' passage, and Calix began to worry that they'd lost the trail completely.

"No point in backtracking," Dhara pointed out, "unless we head all the way back to town. Might as well keep heading south. The lay of the land should guide us the same way it would them," she reassured him.

They continued on for another day until Dhara stopped suddenly. Calix froze, and his hand went to the hilt of his sword.

"That print looks fresh," she said, gesturing to a divot in the earth. "*Really* fresh," she clarified.

Calix couldn't see how it looked any different than anything else they'd seen, so he took her word for it. "Friend or foe?" he asked.

"I don't know," she replied. "Human, though," she added and looked about. She found another print and began heading in the direction that they appeared to have come from. She found increasing signs of passage until they stepped through a dense thicket to see a moss-covered wall of old timber in the near distance. "That's curious," she observed, "And not new."

They moved closer and noticed faint tendrils of smoke drifting up over the wall. They stopped in front of it and looked down its length. It curved into the distance, surrounding some type of old settlement hidden here in the woods.

"I'm not walking around this," she muttered and raised her voice to call, "Hello?" loudly over the wall. She shrugged at Calix and waited for some type of response.

A head popped over the wall and looked down at them. "Hello?" it called back.

"Oriel?" Calix asked.

"Calix?" Oriel confirmed.

"Thank the gods we found you!" Calix replied.

"Can you let us in?" Dhara interrupted, impatiently.

"Of course. I'm just a little shocked is all," Oriel replied. "Move along the wall to your left, and I'll meet you at the gate."

Calix and Dhara heard excited shouting from the other side of the wall. The gate burst open ahead, and a ragtag group of children peeked around it. Calix's father, Emrys, pushed past them and stood in disbelief as his son walked up.

"Hi, Dad," Calix greeted him casually as though bumping into each other in the middle of the forest happened all the time.

Emrys swept him into a hug, and despite looking emaciated, surprised Calix by how tightly he held him. "Come inside quickly," Emrys said, releasing him, "Before the monster returns."

18

Kala

Kala spent the day helping move those wounded by the detonating airship into the city and into buildings that had been converted into hospitals. No one had much skill with medicine beyond battlefield medicine, so those with more grievous injuries succumbed to them, and the number of dead grew steadily.

A young woman who Kala thought of as a nurse because she had taken charge of triaging the wounded asked to speak to her in private. In an otherwise deserted corridor, she whispered, "There are many here for whom there is nothing that can be done, and they suffer greatly."

Kala waited for her to finish her thought, but the woman waited instead for Kala to make the inference. "You think that they should be put out of their misery?" Kala asked, shocked.

"It would be a kindness," she replied but didn't give Kala time to respond, having said what she needed to say and hurrying back to her charges.

Kala stood in the corridor listening to the screams reverberate through the building and knew that the woman was right. She chafed under her reputation as Angel of Death, but that did not mean she wouldn't do what she recognized needed to be done.

Kala stormed out of the hospital toward the dining hall, where people congregated when they needed a break, even if they weren't eating. She entered the hall and stood in the doorway, taking stock of the men and women sitting there. Whether it was her reputation or the dark cloud that swirled around her, the room fell silent.

"Who knows the most people here?" she asked loudly. Vague as her question was, her tone demanded an answer, and a few hands rose timidly. "You, you and you," she said, pointing to three candidates,

"Come with me." She turned and retreated into the hall. Her three conscripts rose from their seats and followed her.

"I need something done, and I need it done discretely," she began and waited for them to signal their understanding. "I need someone who knows poisons, and I don't have the time to find them myself." She paused to allow them to process this. "I want you to find me that person and send them to me in the cathedral." She hated that this meant she would have to waste time there waiting, time that could be better spent in the infirmary, but she did not want people connecting the threads. "Understood?" she asked, by way of dismissal. The three of them nodded and scooted away. To their credit, at least, Kala had observed the wheels turning behind their eyes before they fled her presence. She stepped back into the dining hall, just long enough to grab a roll from one of their abandoned plates, and stalked off toward the cathedral.

Passing through the courtyard, she was rewarded with a rare sighting of Skye as he carried a body to a series of shallow graves that she surmised from the dirt covering him that he had dug. She could tell from a distance how emotionally anguishing the task was for him, and her heart was moved to go to him, but pride and hurt prevented her. With an effort, she pried her eyes from him and continued to the cathedral.

She entered and was struck by the quiet. She had grown so accustomed to the cries of the anguished that her mind struggled to adjust to their absence. She sat in a pew at the back, as far from the statute of the Goddess that so offended her. A wave of exhaustion overtook her, and she closed her eyes for the briefest of moments, slumping over, fast asleep.

She was awoken to the query of, "Miss… miss..." She opened an eye and saw an old man and a young woman standing before her, clearly too afraid to rouse her by touching her. She cringed to think how long they might have been trying to wake her – every part of her felt leaden and gauzy. She willed herself into consciousness and sat up.

"You are well versed with poisons?" she asked, not wasting time on introductions.

"I am," the old man replied without elaboration.

Kala turned to the young woman.

"My father was a healer," she replied by way of explanation. "I used to help him mix medicines. I remember his warnings." She looked uncertain that this would be sufficient, but Kala nodded to allay her fears.

"I need a poison that can be easily administered, one that kills relatively quickly, but without causing suffering," she informed them. "And I need a lot, and I need it now. I'm sure you can surmise why. Can you do this?"

"Aye," the man agreed.

"I can help," the woman added.

"Excellent," Kala concluded. "You can work here, and you can conscript anyone and anything you need to make this happen quickly. If anyone questions you, tell them to come see me." The look in her eye told them that no one would question them at the mention of her name, and they knew it too.

The man turned to the woman and rhymed off, "Hemlock, nightshade, and snakeroot. You know what they look like and where to find them?"

She nodded.

"Okay. You get them, and I'll get ready here," he ordered her.

Kala could tell that her presence was no longer necessary and returned to the infirmary. The nurse looked over at her from across the room expectantly, and Kala nodded in reply. The woman looked relieved and returned to caring for the woman grimacing in the cot before her.

Kala spent the day doing whatever was asked of her, some part of her hoping that any life she helped save would help rebalance the cosmic scales, despite the voice in her head telling her that the scales were tilted so heavily by the death wrought at her hands that she could toil the rest of her life and never right them.

Late that night, the young woman from the cathedral brought her the first patch of poison. "They told me that I could find you here," she said uncomfortably.

"They were right," Kala replied wearily.

The woman handed her a vial. "It doesn't look like much, but just a few drops will do the job." She gave Kala an eyedropper and turned to go.

Kala stopped her with a hand on her shoulder. "Thank you," she said. Nothing else seemed apt, so she left it at that.

The woman nodded knowingly. "I'll bring you more later," she said and took her leave.

Kala walked over to the nurse, holding the vial at her side. The woman held out her hand hesitantly. Kala pulled a spool of ribbon from her pocket and placed it in the woman's hand instead. She looked at it questioningly. "Mark the patients," Kala told her, "then go back to doing what you do, and I'll do what I do."

Relief washed across the nurse's face as she clutched the spool of ribbon to her chest, spared a task that would have haunted her for the rest of her days.

Kala spent the night sitting with the marked patients, administering a few drops, and holding their hands while they crossed over to a better place, or so she wished. They were the hardest deaths she'd ever caused, and she cried her eyes dry.

———————————————

Kala tracked down Grey and Hawke and let them know that she planned on returning to Bayre. "We've been away too long. Bayre needs to be warned about what the Church is capable of," she told them. "I should probably let Skye know too," she added, mostly to herself.

"I think he left already," Grey informed her.

Not even a goodbye, Kala thought bitterly.

Hawke noted the cloud pass across her face and tried to dispel it by saying, "I'm sure he was just thinking what you're thinking and sought to warn Bayre as quickly as possible."

Kala wasn't sure she cared anymore, so she just nodded noncommittally.

"I'm glad we're headed back," Hawke continued, trying to lighten the mood. "I have a surprise for you."

Kala looked at him warily.

"The good kind," he added quickly, "but you'll have to wait until Bayre for it."

Kala was not a fan of games, but she could tell what he was trying to do and forced a smile. "It had *better* be the good kind," she warned him.

"The best," he promised.

She shook her head. "Grey, can you hail an airship, and we'll meet back here as soon as we've gathered whatever we care to bring?"

He nodded and headed off toward the airfield. Kala and Hawke split up to collect their things, and they all met back shortly after that. The ship was waiting. They boarded and departed.

"I brought fruit and cheese," Hawke suggested.

"Not right now," Kala deferred. "But, I could use a distraction. Are you up for some close-quarters sparring?"

"In an airship?" Hawke asked her back, skeptically.

"It's about as close-quarters as you can get."

"If you want to, then okay," he agreed.

Grey just leaned in closer to the wall, shook his head, and tried to stay out of their way.

Hawke started tentatively, to Kala's annoyance. "Are we going to do this?" she asked him testily.

"Okay, okay… I was just warming up," he lied and jabbed without warning, grazing her temple as she barely dodged the blow.

"That's more like it," she said, rubbing her temple.

Try as she might, she was too distracted to see the path of combat clearly, and his punches kept landing, to his chagrin.

"It's okay," she told him, swallowing a trickle of blood.

Hawke cared deeply enough to give her what she wanted, despite his discomfort, so he didn't pull any punches. *If she wants to get beat up to feel something, who am I to judge?* he thought.

She eventually raised a hand to signal an end and slumped down to sit on the floor, cradling her bruised ribs. "Just like old times," she chuckled and winced through the pain that her laughter caused her.

"Kala…," Hawke began.

"Don't," she stopped him. "Thank you. I needed that."

Grey said nothing but clearly disapproved.

It felt as though the airship took forever to complete the trip, but Kala felt in better spirits when it landed.

She stepped out of the ship to find the landing pad ringed with a low iron wall angled up and back.

"What the hell?" she muttered as Grey and Hawke stepped out behind her.

A pair of eyes peeked through a slit in the wall at the sound of her voice. A lanky youth wearing an oversized helmet popped up from behind it. "It's just her!" he called loudly over his shoulder. "Sorry, I didn't mean 'just,' I meant…" he apologized awkwardly.

"What's this?" Hawke asked, stepping forward and pointing to the ring of iron.

"Hmm? Oh, that," the youth acknowledged. "A fellow came in an airship a few days back and told us about airship bombs. That Seline woman had us build this. I'm on duty," he said proudly.

Hawke turned to Kala. "I told you Skye had a reason for hurrying back."

"Skye… yeah, that was his name," the youth chimed in, but everyone ignored him.

Kala puzzled over how they'd made the airship land in the center of the ringed pad when the port was filled with landing pads. She looked over the wall. "They blocked all the other landing pads," she observed, impressed.

"Seline told us to do that too," the youth added, but shut up when he noticed that no one was paying attention to him. He tipped a chair back upright and sat down sullenly.

"Keep up the good work," Hawke encouraged him, and the youth brightened slightly.

"My surprise?" Kala reminded Hawke.

"I didn't forget. Tomorrow morning," he replied.

She was discouraged to have to wait longer, but she nodded, and they leaped over the low wall and made to leave the airfield.

"You can't go anywhere," the youth informed them. "Seline says…"

"I say they're fine," Seline called, hurrying over.

The youth went back to being sullen.

"Good to see you back," Seline greeted them. "Tell me everything. Skye's already given me an idea of what happened."

"Can I tell you over a cup of kai?" Kala asked. "I feel like hell after that flight."

"Of course. I'll meet you back at the temple once you've freshened up."

Kala smiled gratefully, and the four of them parted. She made her way back to her room at the temple. Lily greeted her at the gate, squealed, and pulled up short just before enveloping her in a hug.

"Oh my gods, you look like hell, and smell worse," she declared.

"You do realize that not everyone says what they're thinking," Kala chided her, but smiled.

"I can see why Skye told me to prepare a bath for you… oh, and a cup of kai," she added, handing her a warm mug. "What's with him?" she added. "He's mopey as hell, and he could just as easily have brought you the kai himself," she muttered.

"I wish I knew," Kala replied and began to tear up.

"Oh, honey," Lily said and pulled her into a hug.

"I thought I smelled," Kala blubbered.

"You do," Lily agreed, rubbing her back.

Kala laughed through her tears and melted into Lily's comforting embrace.

Lily squeezed her and released her. "Now we both need baths," she declared, and led Kala to her room, shooing away anyone who peeked out to see who had arrived.

Lily deposited Kala in her bath and carried her leathers out of the room, muttering something about incinerating them.

The warmth of the water seeped into Kala's bones, and she felt better – better for being back with friends. *I just need to adjust to a new world, a world without Skye*, she told herself, and the thought brought fresh tears. She remembered her promise to meet Seline and pried herself out of the bath, dressed, and went off in search of her.

Seline was waiting patiently in a chair in the great room. Across the room, Lily, Cera, and Forest positively vibrated with excitement to see Kala. "I'll be with you in a moment," she called over to them, pacifying them to some degree. Lily grabbed Cera and Forest and led them toward the kitchens. Kala sat down across from Seline.

"Tell me everything about our new enemy," Seline began, getting straight to the point.

"It's a her, and a what," Kala began. "I fear that the Church is our new enemy, and it's lead by a woman simply called the Priestess. She, or they, or both, believe that every few millennia, the world's populace

132

needs to be cut back before it grows enough that it risks destroying itself or the world."

"Makes sense," Seline replied.

Kala was shocked.

"I didn't say I agree, just that it makes sense."

Kala carried on, increasingly unsure of who's side Seline was on. "The Church has access to terrible weapons, such as the one that was used to decimate Soren's army."

"We'll need to destroy those weapons, then," Seline concluded.

"We don't have weapons like that to counter them," Kala replied.

"Then we'll just have to work with what we've got," Seline replied unperturbed.

"I wish I had your confidence," Kala said wistfully.

"It's just pragmatism," Seline replied, but the blast of a distant horn interrupted them, and she got up.

"What's that?" Kala asked.

"An airship, that's all. I'm just going to check it out. Can we talk more tomorrow, maybe around midday?"

"It's a date," Kala replied lightheartedly, but Seline simply nodded and hurried out. Kala got up and walked into the kitchens.

"We're not done yet," Lily despaired, seeing Kala enter. She put the tray of uncooked rolls over a fire that Forest had gotten going, judging from the soot on her face.

Kala walked over and gave each of them a kiss on the cheek, being careful to wipe the soot off Forest's first.

"I heard you broke up with Skye," Cera said, patting Kala's arm sympathetically.

"Yes, although he broke up with me," Kala corrected her.

"So why is *he* so depressed?" Lily asked.

"That's so wrong," Cera added.

"Thanks," Kala replied.

"No, I meant something about this is off," Cera clarified.

Kala shrugged. She'd felt too hurt to guess at Skye's motivation, but hearing Cera say it did make her wonder. *Perhaps I'll demand that he explain himself,* she thought but doubted she'd feel emotionally strong enough to do that for a while. She decided instead to change the subject. "Rolls?" she asked.

"Yes!" Lily confirmed, rubbing her hands together. "There's leftover soup. I'm a baker, not a cook," she pointed out.

"Hot rolls with soup sounds divine," Kala assured her. When the rolls were ready, they ate and chatted late into the night.

Kala woke early and searched for Hawke's room to claim her surprise. She knocked and heard nothing in response, so she swung open the door, flooding the room with light.

Hawke groaned from under a pile of blankets. "I said this morning, not dawn," he complained.

"Get up, sleepyhead," she cajoled him. "I'll meet you in the great room." He rolled over and buried his head, but she trusted him to get up, so she left him be.

Entering the great room, humming on her way to the kitchens, she stumbled into Skye as he was walking out of with a cup of kai. He froze, surprised. He looked like he hadn't slept well in days, in contrast to Kala feeling perky for the first time in several moons. He opened his mouth to say something but changed his mind when the words wouldn't come. He put his cup of kai down and headed back to his bedroom.

She watched him go longingly, then picked up his abandoned cup. "Finders, keepers," she proclaimed and plopped down onto the sofa with it.

Hawke emerged soon after, still looking bleary-eyed.

Kala put the cup down. "So?" she asked excitedly, trying to banish Skye from her thoughts.

"Follow me," he directed her and headed toward the door.

She threw him an apple, which he caught by sheer reflex and began munching. "Thanks," he said, between bites.

"Never say I don't have your back," she replied.

"You're in a better mood," he observed. "Maybe you don't need your surprise."

"You promised – now you deliver," she commanded, poking his arm.

"Yes, ma'am," he conceded, blinked himself further awake and led on. He guided her to a nearby schoolyard that was empty at this early hour.

"What did you want to show me?" she asked, unclear as to why they were there.

"Patience. It's you who wanted to come at this ungodly time, not me."

She pouted and waited. School children began to arrive in small numbers.

"Not everyone fled the city," he explained, answering her unspoken question.

"There," he said, pointing out a small cluster of children.

Kala couldn't figure out what he wanted her to see, but one of the girls looked vaguely familiar.

"Who's the one in the middle?" she asked.

"I wasn't sure you wanted this chapter re-opened," he hedged.

"You're not answering my question."

"Remember the gambler that Baron made you fight?"

She cringed at the memory, but the girl's face swam into view in her mind's eye, albeit younger. "His daughter?" she asked, incredulously.

"Yes, that's her." He looked through the fence at her. "Her name is Zoe. Marija thought she ran away, but I smuggled her out and placed her with Emilie's family's friends. I wasn't sure she got out of the city before Soren attacked it, but she did, and she wound up here."

Kala stared at her through the fence. "I always thought...," she began, then pushed the nightmares away. A small weight lifted off her chest. She spun and hugged Hawke tightly. "Hawke, I love you," she declared.

The sound of someone clearing his throat made her look back up the street from where they'd come. Skye stood there, looking shocked. "I...," he started. "...never mind," he said brusquely and turned to walk away.

"Skye," Kala called after him, but Hawke stopped her from rushing after him.

"You don't have to explain yourself to him. He knows. Just give him time to process. He'll come back."

She sighed and watched Skye walk away, then spared a final look through the fence at the shadow of her past. "Thank you for my surprise," she concluded and squeezed Hawke's arm.

They walked back together, and Kala decided she would set things right with Skye the first chance she got, but only after she gave him space a little longer.

"Can I ask you for a favor?" she asked Hawke as they approached the temple grounds.

"Ask away."

"Can you go check on Skye's mother, Evelyn? Something's going on with Skye, and she's his pressure point."

Hawke looked torn. "Not that I wouldn't do anything for you, and I'd appreciate seeing Emilie while I'm there, but we sent both of them there to sit out the war. I promised Emilie I'd come back to her when we'd made the world a better place, and it sure doesn't feel better yet."

"I know. That's why it's a favor. I'm sure you'll get there and back in no time, having missed nothing in your absence."

He sighed. "Okay, but just because it's you asking."

"Have I told you lately how much I love you?"

He rolled his eyes, but said goodbye and went off to prepare for the trip.

Kala found Seline waiting for her on her return to the temple. "I'm not late, am I?" Kala asked.

"No, I'm early. I felt it couldn't wait to learn more about this Priestess woman."

Kala sat down. "How'd it go with the airship?"

"It was empty, but that of itself is suspicious, and that's why I'm here now."

A young woman raced into the room. "They're dead!" she informed Seline breathlessly.

"Who's dead?"

"The guards that searched the ship. Every one of them."

19

Dhara

"What do you mean by 'monster'?" Calix asked Emrys, knowing that his father wasn't prone to exaggeration or overreaction.

Emrys shepherded them inside the gates as he responded, "There's something out there stalking us, and it's gotten some of us too." He looked nervously through the gate before motioning for it to be closed and barred.

"We've caught glimpses of it and heard its cries," he continued, shuddering. "It isn't natural, whatever it is, but it doesn't seem to bother us inside our walls. But, we can't stay cooped up in here forever, or we'll starve, and it's when we head out to hunt or forage that it strikes. We've lost four good men and women to it."

"So, we're not in any immediate danger?" Dhara asked.

"Not inside our walls, I don't think," Emrys replied.

Dhara relaxed her grip on her spear. "Okay, I'm going to go look for Nina."

"Your sister's daughter, right?" Emrys asked.

"Right."

"The children are probably over near…" he began but stopped when a huge group of children came roaring around a building in the direction he was pointing.

Dhara strode toward the children, and Calix watched as she picked up Nina and threw her high in the air. She hugged her and put her back down, kneeling to explain why her mother wasn't with them.

Emrys followed Calix's eyes, "So, Dhara?" he probed.

Calix made a face that said, "Don't make a deal out of it, dad."

Emrys didn't pursue it. "You're here," he declared, "and you're alive," he observed, recalling that they'd parted ways just as Calix and his friends were preparing to make a stand against Soren's forces.

"By various miracles, yes, I'm alive. There is much news to tell about what's happened since you led these people to safety."

Emrys tensed slightly at the mention of 'safety,' taking responsibility for their predicament with the monster, the way he did everything.

Calix ignored his father's reaction. "What is this place?" he asked, watching Dhara walk over to the mossy village wall to check its condition with her knife, a horde of children following her.

"We stumbled on it as we headed south. The thing in the woods had begun stalking us, and we took refuge within. We've been here ever since." He looked around and added, "It's very old," stating the obvious, "and falling apart... but it's been home for the past few moons."

Dhara walked up with Nina in tow. "If your monster has any strength at all, it's not the wall that's keeping it out. I'm surprised it's still standing," she reported.

"I doubt our numbers are a deterrent either," Emrys added. He glanced at Nina, debated keeping the next bit to himself, but decided there was no point in shielding her from what she already knew. "The thing attacked a hunting party a while back and killed two hunters before the others escaped. The next morning, we could see from the wall that it had hung one of the bodies high in a tree. A few days later, it was gone." He shuddered at the memory.

"This place isn't safe," Calix concluded but tried not to sound like he was accusing his father of poor judgment.

"The whole world seemed a dangerous place," Emrys justified, "and we had nowhere else to go."

"It's better now... the world," Calix explained. "Kala convinced Soren to stop his attack, with help from Forest."

Emrys raised an eyebrow. "That sounds like quite the story."

"It is," Calix replied. "I'll tell it to you on our way out of here. We need to get everyone to prepare to leave."

"And go where?" Emrys asked.

"The nearest airship beacon. We'll get you out of here and to Bayre."

"It'll be dangerous traveling through the woods, but better than staying and getting picked off slowly," he agreed. "But, enough of the day is gone that we can't do much until tomorrow. We'll prepare tonight and leave at first light. How many days travel will it be?"

"About two and a half," Dhara replied, consulting the journal that Kala had lent her. Calix was amazed that she had any idea at all of where they were after so many days of moving through a forest that looked endlessly the same.

"Two nights," Emrys noted, worrying about their vulnerability in the open.

"If we push hard, we could make it in two days," Dhara countered, "but many of those here don't seem like they'd be up to it."

"I guess we'll just have to do what we can and see," Emrys concluded. "I'll ensure that everyone gets organized to leave, then we can meet again for dinner, or at least what passes for dinner here," he admitted, slightly embarrassedly.

"That would be great," Calix assured him.

Dhara pointed out a little girl who had been hovering expectantly and asked Emrys, "Who's she?"

"Pippi," Emrys answered, and noting her expectant look too, added, "I think she was hoping Lily was with you. She really connected with her back at the refugee camp," he said, looking for confirmation from Calix that Lily was okay before continuing.

"Lily is doing well," Calix answered his unspoken question.

Emrys nodded his thanks and turned to Pippi. "Come with me, honey, and let's get organized. We're going on another journey... to see Lily."

Pippi's brightened at the prospect and let herself be led off.

Oriel rushed up and slapped Calix on the back. "Gods-damn it man, it's good to see you," he said in greeting.

Calix pulled him into a stiff hug, uncharacteristic of him, but fitting the moment. "You too," he replied. "How's Allie?" he asked, hoping for the best, but being prepared for the worse if need be.

"She's well," Oriel assured him. "Hating every moment of this place, mind you, but well otherwise," he said, smiling. "I heard we're returning to civilization tomorrow. She'll be thrilled."

Calix clapped him on the back as he rushed off to give Allie the good news. Calix called after him, "Where can I find Kala's grandfather?"

Oriel turned and called back, "At the school," then recalled that would mean nothing to Calix, and waved vaguely toward a cluster of buildings. "That way," he said and disappeared.

Dhara was left with Calix. She looked down at the sword at his belt. "Be ready to use that thing," she said, turned, and continued her exploration of the village, with Nina as her guide.

Calix headed in the direction that Oriel had instructed him, but had to look inside several buildings before he found the one that served as the school. Poking his head in the door, he spotted Kala's grandfather scrubbing a wall that he used as a makeshift chalkboard. Calix cleared his throat, and Kala's grandfather turned and froze when he saw him.

"Kala misses you," Calix said, to assure him that she was okay.

Kala's grandfather shuddered involuntarily with relief. "Thank you for looking after her," he said.

Calix laughed heartily. "Hardly. She looks after us."

"That's my Kala," he replied, smiling.

"We're leaving this place tomorrow morning. Kala brokered a truce. Soren is no longer a threat." Calix looked around the classroom that Kala's grandfather had organized during their time in the village. "Do you need any help gathering your things?" he asked.

"No, thank you. There's nothing here of value." He glanced down at the cloth in his hand and placed it carefully down on the board that he used as a desk. "Thank you for letting me know that Kala's okay," he said earnestly.

"You're welcome – it's the least I could do," he replied. "If you're okay here, I'll head back to see if I can help my father."

Kala's grandfather waved him away, and Calix hunted down Emrys to see how he could be useful. His father gave him a list of errands, and he spent the rest of the day running them.

As the sun began to set, a large fire was set in the village center, and torches were lit along the wall. People began to assemble around the fire, and the evening's meager meal was distributed. Dhara and Calix declined their portion, taking in the sorry state of those around them, although everyone's spirits were buoyed by the prospect of leaving the village.

Dhara and Calix were waved over by Fayre to sit near her and at the center of those assembled. Calix and Dhara sat down, and Nina made herself comfortable in Dhara's lap. Calix noted that Fayre looked older than he remembered and surmised that her time since fleeing Soren must have weighed heavily on her. He greeted her warmly, and she smiled broadly in response, taking him in and telling him, "Emrys raised a fine young man."

Calix blushed and Dhara smiled at his uncomfortableness. The children were fascinated by her, unaccustomed as they were to warriors. Dhara bore their attention well, although she would rather have escaped it.

Fayre asked them the questions that everyone had on their minds, starting with what had happened since they parted ways, "How did you survive Soren's attack?"

"We defended well," Calix began, then qualified as he looked to Dhara appreciatively, "...the warriors among us anyway." Dhara snorted, and he continued, "We were overwhelmed, and Kala was challenged to duel their champion in order to broker the terms of our surrender."

The children hushed expectantly at the mention of Kala's name.

"She relieved him of his head," Calix continued, but the children interrupted him with their excited applause. Calix was a taken off guard, forgetting how used to Kala's superhuman feats he had become.

"And they just let you go?" Fayre asked incredulously.

Calix nodded, but clarified, "On the condition that we leave Cera with them." The silence that followed the collective gasp was deafening, and several children teared up, remembered their beloved teacher. The smallest girl began to cry.

"She's fine," Calix added quickly. "We stole her back." The children's relief was palpable.

"How?" Fayre asked.

"Kala," Calix replied and chuckled to see a little boy pump his fist. He felt obligated to stoke her legend and added, "She snuck into the enemy camp and, surrounded by ten thousand soldiers, snuck Cera out."

"And it's safe to return?" Fayre asked.

"A truce has been brokered. Soren has accepted to ally with us."

Fayre looked confused. "Ally against whom?" she asked.

"The Church. It's a long story, but Kala believes that it will take it upon itself to complete what Soren started. She and Soren aim to stop it."

Fayre digested it all. "A lot happens in a few moons," she concluded.

"You can say that again," Calix agreed.

Dhara wanted more information about the monster, but glancing at all the young faces, she had the presence of mind not to start that discussion. She didn't need to, as an unnatural cry from outside the village walls silenced everyone.

"Was that…?" Calix began, and his father nodded in response as several men and women rose from their places by the fire and took up spots at elevated platforms along the wall.

"We're safe," Emrys assured him. "It's never attacked us inside the village. It doesn't need to as we have to come out to it regularly."

Dhara gestured questioningly at the guards along the wall.

"We still don't take chances," Emrys replied to her unvoiced observation.

"Can we help?" she asked, gesturing to Calix and herself.

"Thank you, but we have a well-established rotation. Get your rest. You'll want all of your wits tomorrow to lead us out of this place."

Dhara started to object, but Emrys waved her down. "Seriously, get some sleep."

She nodded and got up to find a spot to bed down for the night, patting Nina goodnight on her head. Dhara took a step, then turned to Calix, "Coming?"

Calix went as red as a beet, but rose bashfully and followed after her, while his father smiled at his awkwardness.

"I didn't see that coming," he admitted to Fayre, who smiled back.

Dhara woke before dawn and got Calix up to prepare to leave. People were already milling about the village. After gathering her things, she announced to him, "Let's go."

He nodded and followed her to the village gates. Oriel and several guards held torches and waved Dhara and Calix over. They waited until Emrys and Fayre completed their headcount and confirmed that everyone was assembled. They had divided up the remaining food into packs to eliminate the need for carts. They were prepared to travel light, and hopefully, fast. Anything that was not absolutely necessary was left behind. Everyone waited expectantly for Dhara to give the word for the gates to be opened.

She signaled her readiness, and the gates were pushed outward. Oriel and a colleague stepped out and confirmed that the way was clear.

"We head northeast," Dhara informed everyone and led the way into the forest. Oriel and Calix joined her near the front but gave her space and quiet to divine the route. Emrys and Fayre escorted the main body, still comprised mostly of children and the elderly. The few remaining hunters took up the rear and glanced nervously over their shoulders as they advanced.

A bone-chilling cry came from the village behind them, and everyone shuddered and sped up as much as they could.

Dhara did her best to balance keeping them moving with respecting the need of the frailer members of the party to rest. They took frequent, short breaks, but otherwise kept up as quick a pace as they could.

After midday, a guard at the rear called up to the front, "Something's following us." Breaks stopped being an option, so they pressed on a little slower while they readied themselves for the possibility of an attack. The day wore on, but no attack came. They continued as late into the day as they could until the descending dark forced them to stop in their tracks. At the last possible moment, they hunkered down for the night, not even in a clearing, just when it grew too dark to continue. Everyone forded out in pairs and braved the forest to collect wood that they used to build five small fires arranged in a rough ring around them. They huddled close, more for comfort than safety. Despite their exhaustion, few people slept. Grunts and howls came from all directions through the night.

They broke camp hurriedly before dawn and resumed their trek. Dhara reckoned that they had made good enough time the first day that it was possible that they could make it to their destination before nightfall. The stronger among them helped the weaker, even if it meant compromising the security of their perimeter. It was unspoken but accepted that speed was the only real security they had, and even that wasn't much. Calix carried a young girl in his arms for most of the day, passing her to his father only when his arms throbbed with prolonged exertion.

The ground became rockier, and the trees thinned out. More and more often, there were reports of movement in the forest behind them or around them. Dhara told Oriel and Calix to keep an eye out for a rock formation that Kala described as a dead spider on its back. "It can't be far," she concluded, and they kept their eyes peeled.

They began to feel a creeping unease. "This is good," Dhara announced, to their confusion. "I've felt this before. It means we're close." She didn't need to tell them to look harder. The sun was beginning to set, and they knew in their bones that the night would not pass uneventfully if they failed to find their destination.

They rounded a low hill, and Oriel pointed out what appeared to be the possible rock formation in the distance. Dhara squinted to discern it better. She agreed that it looked promising, and they altered course to head toward it. As they neared it, she could tell by its creepy shape and the unease that it evoked that they had found what they were looking for.

"Hurry," she called over her shoulder and pointed where to go. She turned and made her way in the opposite direction.

"Where are you going?" Calix asked.

"I'm not needed to lead anymore," she replied. "I'm going to protect our flank."

"I'll go with you," he offered.

She gave him a withering look, as though she thought he was being an idiot. "First, you know what to do when we get to the circle of rocks. Besides me, no one else does. Second, you can't even lift your arms. Do you think you could swing a sword?"

He had to admit that she was right on both counts and watched her disappear toward the back of the chain of people following them. He turned reluctantly and hurried back to Oriel's side. As they neared the circle of stones, he called to all who were close enough to hear, "Look for spherical stones, even if they're buried. Roll them up against the pillar on the east edge of the circle of pillars." He turned to Oriel, "Help them figure out which way is east," but added, "Kala says it's pretty easy to figure out which is the right pillar. She says it'll probably be on its own."

Calix spotted several stones poking out of the earth. "There," he pointed out, and again, "There," at another. Oriel singled out the correct pillar and waved people towards where he stood. Children struggled to free the stones from the earth.

"Dig them out," Calix instructed and helped with one. He called over to Oriel, who had Allie replace him at the pillar and was helping roll a boulder toward it, "When an airship lands, get people onboard, then roll a stone away from the pillar to release it."

"No ropes?" Oriel called back.

"No ropes," Calix confirmed.

"Okay, got it."

Satisfied, Calix got up and pushed through the throng toward where he'd seen Dhara head. He flexed his sore muscles and recognized that he was next to useless at the moment, but he refused to leave Dhara. He heard someone shout from behind him, "A ship," and he thanked the gods that they would soon be safely out of here.

He pushed through to the rear of the procession only to see Dhara standing motionless, spear held forward. He looked over her shoulder to the ragged line of trees. Emerging from them was a creature the height of two men. It seemed vaguely human but misshapen and baleful. Its skin had a sickly yellow sheen, its eyes were narrow slits, and its arms ended in vicious claws. The mere sight of it chilled Calix's blood. It bellowed a tortured sound that unfroze Calix. He drew his sword in a spurt of adrenaline and rushed to Dhara's side.

She registered his approach. "Get out of here," she commanded.

"Not happening," he replied.

She exhaled in frustration, but couldn't spare any further attention for him, and she braced herself as the creature advanced in long, uneven strides.

"Come and get it," she taunted it.

Its eye slits narrowed further, and it raised its claws as it lurched forward.

"Stay away from it," she hissed at Calix and surged toward to meet the creature. It swiped at her, but its claws found empty air as she slid past it. She regained her footing faster than it turned, and she thrust her spear at its back. The tip of her spear struck firmly but didn't pierce its skin.

The creature spun and batted her flying. She landed hard on her side and winced as she staggered to her feet, leaning on her spear for support.

Calix yelled at the monster, and it turned to face him in a moment of indecision.

Dhara profited from its distraction to close the distance and prod it again with her spear.

It spun, annoyed, and clawed at her.

She was ready for it, ducked under its reach, and speared upward at the creature's face. The tip of her spear slid along its iron-hard skin and grazed its right eye.

The creature roared and swatted angrily at her spear, slashing it in two with its claws.

"Run, Calix!" Dhara yelled. He hesitated. "Now, damn it!" she demanded. The creature turned its attention on Calix, and she tapped it on the arm with the half of the spear that she still held. "I'm still here," she reminded it. It turned back to face her, and she bolted for the trees.

The last thing Calix saw before turning for the airship was the monster smash through the trees after her.

20

Hawke

The entire city of Bayre was in lockdown, waiting to see if the plague that had come in the airship would spread. The city was untraversable, and the airfield even further off-limits, not that any sane person would go anywhere near it. Hawke asked Grey if he could smuggle him out through the tunnels for his mission to check on Skye's mother. They were walking through the great room on their way out of the temple when Jarom spied them.

"Where are you two gentlemen off to?" he called from the sofa.

"On a mission," Hawke replied obliquely.

"Sounds like fun, and I'm bored. Want company?"

Hawke was about to refuse, just to be on his way, when he thought, *Why the hell not?* "Sure," he replied. "How long will it take you to get ready?"

Jarom reached around the back of the sofa and hauled out his pack. "I'm ready."

Hawke looked at him suspiciously.

"Did I mention how bored I am?"

Hawke relaxed and waved him along. "Is it in you to be quiet while we sneak out of the city?"

"Quiet like a mouse, or quiet like a man punched in the throat for asking me if I can be quiet?"

"Like a mouse," Hawke replied, rolling his eyes.

"Sure, but I could always do either," he joked.

Grey shushed them and led them out into the dark streets. They crept along in the shadows in search of an unguarded grate to the tunnels below the city. Seline had ordered the grates watched as an extra precaution against intruders, but the city folk didn't know all of them the way Grey seemed to. Jarom was much quieter for a large man than Hawke had given him credit for, so he vowed, while not to apologize, to at least not doubt him in the future.

Grey led them down a narrow alleyway, unlit by any window, with only moonlight illumining their surroundings. He stopped and bent down to brush the gravel off of a sheet of wood. Uncovering a corner of it, he lifted it and slid it aside to reveal a grate hidden below. He leaned it up against the wall while Hawke raised an eyebrow at him. "Always have a backup plan," Grey whispered, shrugging. "Care to help me lift this thing?"

Jarom stepped forward, lifted the grate easily, and placed it down far enough aside to allow them to slide past and down the shaft.

Grey descended first, followed by Hawke, and Jarom last, who slid the grate closed behind them. Once together in the tunnels, Grey picked up a stone and tapped it against the wall. "Follow the sound," he told them. "Voices carry down here." He headed out, tapping the wall every few moments to allow Hawke and Jarom to follow him. He led them through the labyrinth tunnels to the exit, bid them farewell, and headed quickly back into the city.

"You know where to go from here?" Jarom asked.

"Kala and Grey gave me directions. It shouldn't be difficult to find the airship landing pad outside the city." He headed off and, true to his word, located it without difficulty. He hailed an airship, and it also arrived quickly.

"Did I mention that I snore?" Jarom announced, boarding the ship.

"Am I going to regret allowing you to come along?" Hawke asked.

"Probably," Jarom replied, smiling and placed his pack down as a pillow. He was asleep before the ship even rose above the clouds.

Hawke thanked the gods that Jarom turned out to be kidding about snoring, and he fell asleep too.

After many days, the airship finally drifted down to land in the dead of night outside a seaside village across the continent. Hawke and Jarom exited quickly and hid behind some bushes, while Hawke sent the ship away. They waited a while to see if anyone would come to investigate, but no one did.

"I know somewhere we can stay," Hawke said, and got up. He led Jarom to a small cottage and climbed the steps onto the porch, but reconsidered knocking. "I don't feel right about waking Edith. Are you okay if we sleep on the porch until first light?"

"I've slept in worst places," Jarom replied and made himself comfortable.

At dawn, Hawke got up and knocked on the window in the door. Not long after, Edith peeking through the curtain in her nightclothes. She recognized Hawke and opened the door.

"Kala's friend, Hawke, right?" she asked, dredging her memory.

"That's right. And this is Jarom," he replied, introducing his companion.

"Pleased to meet you," Edith replied. "Care for some tea? I was just about to put some on."

"Tea would be lovely," Jarom replied.

"Thank goodness it was you at my door and not one of those dreadful monks," Edith muttered as she moved into the kitchen.

"Monks?" Hawke asked.

"Oh yes, they're all over the place. Creepy fellows."

"Damn it," Hawke declared. "We should have brought Grey."

"Language," Edith scolded.

"We are *not* going back for him," Jarom said firmly.

"Sorry," Hawke apologized to Edith, then turned to Jarom. "Of course not. It just would have been handy to have his take on the monks."

"What's to know? They're armed, and as Edith points out, they're creepy."

Hawke began to regret bringing Jarom again. "We need to scout the town, but its small enough that everyone will know we're not from here," he thought out loud.

"I have an idea," Edith chimed in.

They turned to look at her.

"Go fishing."

Hawke was beginning to wonder if everyone was insane.

Edith clarified, "Fishermen all wear identical-looking rain suits with a large cowl. You could walk to the docks without drawing attention to yourselves. Then, you can loiter off the coast near the village, and no one would think twice about it. When you return, you can hang any fish that you catch on the drying racks on the hill overlooking the village. It has a commanding view."

"You're brilliant, Edith," Jarom exclaimed warmly.

She blushed. "It's actually not that creative considering this is a fishing village. I'll ask my neighbor if you can spend the day with him on his boat, after tea mind you. He'll have rain gear for you, considering he's near your size, Jarom, although he's more portly than burly, and his nephew is about your size, Hawke. If you're here to stick it to the monks, pardon the expression, he'll be only too happy to help."

"That would be wonderful," Jarom replied.

"But first, we're having tea."

They drank tea around Edith's tiny table, and she filled them in on what she knew about Evelyn, Emilie, Amber, and even Ashlynn, Skye's former girlfriend... which seemed to be everything. There were evidently no secrets in so small and gossipy a village. When they each had had a couple of cups of tea, and Edith judged it late enough to politely call on her neighbor, she headed out and returned carrying two slickers.

"Ernest is happy to oblige. He's waiting for you. Just get changed first and head over there when you think it a good time.

"No time like the present," Hawke replied. They got dressed and presented themselves to Edith.

"You look like proper fishermen," she gushed and bade them happy spying.

They walked down the hill to Ernest's cottage. He looked up from rethreading a net and rose to shake their hands and introduce himself. The three of them headed toward the docks.

"Is Evelyn's on the way?" Jarom asked.

"Aye," Ernest replied. "She's a looker," he added appreciatively.

Hawke smiled and concentrated on studying the placement of the monks through the town. Edith was right that he and Jarom were virtually invisible dressed as fishermen. Hawke noted two monks stationed outside Evelyn's door, and several more pairs patrolling the town.

They made it to the docks and boarded Ernest's tiny fishing boat. Hawke was expecting something a bit bigger, but it did the trick. They spent much of the remainder of the day fishing near the shoreline and surreptitiously tracking the monks' movements. Jarom looked increasingly green as the day wore on, and the little boat bobbed up and down in the waves.

"I think I've figured out their routine," Hawke declared, concluding their day on the water, which pleased Jarom greatly. "They patrol in a rotating cloverleaf centered on Evelyn's place, relieving the pair guarding her place. I'm guessing they keep that up nonstop, given their numbers. I've seen two shift changes that align with dividing the day into thirds."

"Plus the two men on the roofs," Jarom added, impressing Hawke that he'd spotted them, given how well hidden they were. "It'll be a tough nut to crack."

They decided to return to town and dry the fish they'd caught, despite Jarom and Hawke combinedly catching only two to Ernest's twelve. Ernest handed them each three of his to carry. "You'll never pass as proper fishermen carrying a single fish back after an entire day on the water," he explained.

They spent a while longer sitting on the hill, filleting and hanging their fish while reinforcing the observations they'd made from the water. Jarom got on well with Ernest, and soon, Ernest was trying to set him up with a cousin of his who was also single. Jarom humored him, making the day pass pleasantly enough for a stakeout.

Hawke was distracted from his surveillance, as he kept hoping to catch a glimpse of Emilie. He debated seeking her out, but he knew that it would be risky, and it would be a thousand times harder to leave again, having seen her. He wasn't sure she would even permit him to leave her a second time, and he was here to fulfill his promise to Kala, not assuage his lovesick heart.

They arrived back at Edith's late in the day and ravenous. She had predicted as much and had a feast ready for them. Jarom almost shed a tear, he was so grateful. They discussed what they'd found during the day.

"It's pretty clear that Evelyn is their reason for being here. We're not going to be able to just walk up and escort her out of here. We could wait for her to run an errand, but they would certainly be tailing her, so that's not an answer. They're stationed out front of her cottage, but they most assuredly have tripwires or worse set up at any other entrance or exit to the cottage. Worse, one of the rooftop scouts seems to be positioned to keep an eye on the guards at her door, so we can't just dispatch them. The other scout seems to have a general eye on the town, and both the rooftop guards are within sight of each other. They know what they're doing," Hawke concluded.

"We can't just dispatch them one or two at a time either as that would get noticed quickly. It's a puzzle," Jarom agreed.

"It's not just getting to her that I'm concerned about. It's getting us all out of here. Anything out of order and they'll send someone to stop us from leaving by airship, and if we try to get out of here any other way, they're sure to be able to chase us down faster than we can flee." Hawke had a headache from trying to figure it out. "I'm going to sleep on it," he decided in the end, and begged off early, while Jarom stayed up and visited with Edith.

Hawke bolted upright in the middle of the night, the outline of a plan occurring to him. He got up and started making a list of what they'd need. When Jarom and Edith woke, he filled them in on the plan. They each agreed to their part and got busy.

It began with Edith spending the day in the village running errands until she spied Evelyn running one of her own, shadowed by a pair of monks. Edith made sure that she bumped into her at the bakery.

"Hi Evelyn, my granddaughter Kala sends her love," she said in greeting.

Evelyn froze for the briefest of moments before recovering and responding casually, "How sweet. Give her a kiss for me."

"I'll bring her by some evening. Ta ta," she called as she exited.

Meanwhile, Hawke borrowed some tools from Ernest. "I might not be able to get these back to you," he felt compelled to admit.

"That's okay. I'm sure you'll put them to good use."

Hawke thanked him and waited for dark to head into the village. He prayed that the monks would stay true to their routine as he navigated the streets in a dance that kept him out of sight of their patrols and the rooftop scouts. He waited in an alleyway for the guards at Evelyn's door to change. The pair that had just been relieved circled her cottage, examining it thoroughly, then headed out on patrol. Hawke had a narrow window of time. He climbed the ladder he'd been lugging around up to the roof of the cottage adjacent to Evelyn's, then pulled it up after him. He swung its end across the alley, straining his muscles to counterbalance its weight as the other end landed on her cottage. He scrambled across and pulled the ladder after him. It made a faint scraping sound as it slid over the lip of the roof, and Hawke held his breath, waiting to see if a monk would investigate. None did, so he pulled a prybar from his pack and began pulling off shingles, then the boards underneath them. He worked as quickly as he dared while trying not to make any noise. He was sweating by the time he'd created a decent size hole in the roof. He peeked in, and Evelyn waved up at him. He put a finger to his lips to warn her, knowing it was unnecessary, but feeling compelled to. She nodded and put a finger to her lips to signal that she understood.

Hawke pulled the ladder to him and slid it through the opening in the roof. Evelyn steadied the end as it landed on the floor. She wasted no time in climbing up it. Hawke helped her through the hole and pulled the ladder up. Evelyn balanced unsteadily on the roof while he swung the ladder's end across the alley. His strength was flagging, and it made a small tap as it connected with the opposite roof, but he knew that their time was nearly up and crawled quickly across without waiting to see if the sound had been heard. He held it steady while Evelyn followed him across. A shingle slipped from where he'd laid it aside, and it slid down the roof to balance precariously over the edge. Hawke cursed silently, as it teetered but didn't fall. It moved at the slightest gust of wind, so he knew he couldn't risk moving the ladder for fear of causing the shingle to fall. Instead, he shimmied across the roof, staying low, and gestured for Evelyn to follow him. Hawke swung over the far lip of the roof and let himself fall. His legs absorbed the shock, and he made little noise. He gestured for Evelyn to follow suit. She looked uncertain for a moment, but a glance over her shoulder convinced her that she had no choice. She swung over and dangled long enough to say a quick prayer and let go. Hawke caught her with a grunt, and the two of them collapsed into the ground, making enough noise that Hawke was sure it would warrant investigation by the monks.

He rose quickly, helped Evelyn up, and pulled her with him as he ran toward the docks. They'd crossed less than two streets before a call went up behind them, signaling that the ladder had been discovered. He did some quick calculations to figure where each of the patrols would be and raced in as straight a line as he could and still avoid them. He had no idea what protocol the monks would follow, now that they knew that an escape attempt was in progress, but he doubted it would be to his advantage.

He threw caution to the wind when they made it to the docks and hurried Evelyn into an old rowboat that Ernest had offered him. Hawke heard shouts and footfalls behind them as he threw off the rope securing the boat to the dock, and pushed off with all his strength. He began rowing toward the sea with short, powerful strokes. Facing shore, he saw the shadows of six monks appear on the docks, and they were quickly joined by six more. The moonlight glinted off their blades before they turned to look about for boats of their own. Hawke would have desperately liked to have sabotaged all of the remaining boats, but he couldn't do that given that their owners relied on them to feed their families. Instead, Jarom had tied the ropes that secured them in intricate knots to slow the monks down, although the monks just sliced through the rope, hopped in the boats, and pushed out to sea.

Before long, five boats chased Hawke's, and he judged that the monks were closing the distance. Hawke steered to follow the coast south, even though it allowed his pursuers to cut the angle and move closer. The monks were almost close enough to use missile weapons when Hawke spied an airship drifting low toward the sea. He dug his oars into the water and raced to intercept it.

The ship's door opened, and Jarom stuck his head out. He spun the dial on Hawke's amulet as he'd been shown to make the airship oscillate between two trajectories. He threw down the rope ladder that he and Ernest had spent the day knotting. He cursed his lack of fine control over the airship, and worse, the ship rose slightly with every passing moment, and the rope began to rise out of the water.

The monks figured out the plan and rowed harder to bring themselves closer. Hawke altered course to bring his skiff under the path of the airship. When he judged it close enough, he dropped the oars, and one fell into the water. *Damn it*, he thought, *no second chances now*. He got up and helped lift Evelyn up to the ladder. "Climb," he instructed her, giving her a boost. Splashes behind him signaled that the monks had finally closed within missile range. The airship rose higher, and Hawke tensed his legs and leaped for the rope's trailing end. He snagged it with his left hand and scrambled to grab on with his right as the ladder twisted and swung. A thrown dagger grazed his leg as he struggled to climb after Evelyn. Jarom braced his feet against the door frame and strained to reel in the ladder.

Hawke paid no mind to the monks below as he climbed for his life. The rope swung wildly, and he spared a look down at the great distance to the water below. A fall from this height would be fatal, and he gripped the rungs tighter. His hand finally grazed the metal of the airship's underbelly, and Jarom's hand wrapped around his and lifted him into the ship. Hawke lay panting as Jarom pulled in the remainder of the ladder and slammed the door closed.

Hawke sat up in time to be grappled in a teary hug by Emilie. Amber waved hello from over her shoulder.

"Couldn't very well leave them behind," Jarom snorted, sitting down and shaking out his tired biceps.

"Thank you," Emilie, Amber, and Evelyn said in unison and laughed.

21

Kala

The unleashing of plague on Bayre was sobering. It reminded Kala that the Priestess's goal was nothing short of reducing the population of the world so drastically that it would take millennia to rebuild it. No one would be spared – not the young or old, kind or wise – no one.

Seline rushed to the airfield to assess if the disease could be contained there, or if it had already spread. Kala followed along, feeling powerless against this type of threat. Seline ordered a guard to tell the Council to place the city in lock-down to prevent the spread of the plague. The man hesitated until Kala took a step toward him, and he quailed and rushed off.

Nearing the airfield, Seline cut left and headed off at an angle.

"It's the other way," Kala pointed out.

"We don't want to arrive downwind," Seline explained, not slowing.

Kala hadn't even noticed that there was a breeze, let alone from which direction it was blowing. *By the gods, Seline's mind works quickly.* She vowed to shut up and not question her again. They continued threading through the streets, Kala bullying anyone they came across back indoors until they arrived at the fence ringing the airfield. It was eerily quiet – there was no movement inside the fence. They spotted a few bodies lying haphazardly about the yard. The recently arrived airship still sat inside Seline's blast ring.

"Not how I planned on doing it," Seline said to herself, surveying the yard.

Kala remembered that Seline was once Soren's lieutenant and ruthlessly efficient when she set her mind to a task, even if that task were the destruction of a city.

Seline turned to Kala. "First, we need to make sure that nothing and no one comes in or out of the airfield, carrying the disease into the wider city. Second, we need to make sure that no one enters the city without first being checked for disease. I'll arrange for the first; you arrange for the second."

Kala nodded and left to hunt down the Captain of the Guard. Seline headed over to a party of worried-looking guards standing nearby and organized a perimeter.

Kala ensured that the guards stationed at the two gates understood Seline's protocols and had additional guards stationed at the grates to the sewers. She made her way back to the temple later that evening. The city's inhabitants were confined to their homes by decree of the city council, so the city was as still as a graveyard. Kala noticed that many homes had prayers to the Goddess of Death affixed to their doors, beseeching Her to spare them. She mentioned it to Grey when she got back to the temple.

"Doesn't it seem ironic to you that the citizens of Bayre seem more religious than the Church?" she asked him.

"People get religious when they're scared," he countered. "What matters is what kind of person you are when you're not scared. Besides, I don't think the Goddess cares as much about prayers as She does about actions."

"Like trying to exterminate an entire city?"

"I have a hard time believing the Goddess wants that," he replied but was quiet for a moment. "This is just her first attempt," he mused, referring to the Priestess.

Kala sighed and sat down. "What other tricks does she have up her sleeve?"

"She has an army of monks and an order of assassins, and ancient weapons like the one she used on Soren's army, but disease is her most potent weapon against a city like Bayre. She'll keep trying until it works."

Kala mulled it over. "We have to prevent her access to her store of diseases," she concluded.

"Easier said than done. They're in an impenetrable fortress hidden in the high wastes. *I* don't even know where it is, and I was the one she most trusted." Annoyance creased his forehead.

"I know someone who might know," Kala replied. Grey looked skeptical, but she called across the room, "Celeste, can you find Frey and send him over?"

Celeste signaled that she would and headed off toward the personal quarters.

While they waited, Kala looked around the great room at her friends milling about. It usually would have cheered her to be surrounded by them, but now it worried her that they were all in the Priestess's sights. She didn't see Skye but didn't have time to dwell on it before Lily walked over with a plate of food.

"You missed dinner," she said, handing her the plate. "It's cold, but I don't think it'll suffer for it," she apologized.

Kala was chewing on a carrot when Frey entered and came straight over. She put down her dinner. "Hi, Frey. You told me that you know where the fortress in the wastes is?"

Frey nodded but said, "Not exactly." Kala looked confused at the contradiction, so he hastily clarified, "She once got me to fetch cold-weather gear from her room and meet her at the airship. Before she departed, I saw her pull out one of those amulet things and fiddle with the dial. She was preoccupied, so I don't think she saw me watching her."

Kala pulled out her amulet and handed it to him. "Can you show me?"

Frey took it, pressed the middle button, and adjusted the dials before releasing the middle button. "I think that's it," he concluded and handed it back.

"Are you sure she held the button while she adjusted the dials? You don't normally do that."

"I remember thinking it was odd that she used two hands. She usually doesn't."

"Gods-bless your powers of observations."

"Truth be told, it's just that old habits die hard. Part of me was thinking of stealing the amulet because it looked valuable, but she's way too scary to mess with."

"Gods-bless your thieving nature, then," she corrected herself and rubbed his head good-naturedly. She turned to Grey. "That's one problem solved."

"We just have the 'impenetrable' problem to puzzle out," he replied.

"We need Seline for that," she concluded. "There's no puzzle she can't solve." She turned to Frey. "Could you do me the favor of finding Seline and asking her to come here?"

"No one is supposed to be moving around the city," he pointed out.

"Tell them it's official business."

"Only if I need to. I'll just be sneaky."

"My little assassin," Kala teased, and he departed.

Kala was busy assembling what she'd need for a trip to the high north when Frey poked his head in the door.

"She's here," he informed her.

"Thanks, Frey," she replied and left packing until later. She returned to the great room and spotted Seline talking with Grey. They turned when she walked over.

"Has Grey filled you in on our mission?" she asked.

"He has." Seline paused for a moment. "It's extremely cold where we're going, right?" she asked.

"Yes," Kala apologized.

"Excellent," she replied, the wheels of her mind already turning.

Kala was getting used to Seline's eccentricity, so she shrugged it off. "I can find cold-weather gear for you, if you want to collect what you think we'll need to breach the fortress."

"That would be greatly appreciated," Seline responded. "I have no clothes to speak of."

Kala believed it. "Can we meet back here first thing in the morning?"

Grey and Seline agreed, and they separated.

It wasn't easy for Kala to find appropriate clothing for their journey, especially in a city in lock-down, but she managed. Forest had lent her a set of furs and the small heater that Petra had given her. The mention of Soren's mother saddened Kala as she remembered that the last sight she'd had of her was her kneeling in the crater where her son had been obliterated.

Kala was able to eke out a little sleep before dawn but rose early to not keep her party waiting in case they arrived first. She waited in the great room, and they both arrived shortly after her. Grey had scrounged up gear for himself somehow, and Seline carried a small pack and dragged a sledgehammer. Grey took the sledgehammer from her, regarding it quizzically. Seline smiled her thanks at being relieved of the burden.

"Do you have everything?" Kala asked them.

"As long as you have clothes to keep me from freezing to death, I'm good," Seline replied. Grey simply nodded.

"Okay, let's go," Kala concluded.

They made their way through the deserted city to the gate. The smell of smoke was heavy in the air.

"Sanitizing the airfield," Seline explained as they walked out the temple gate and Grey guided them to the tunnels and out them to the landing pad outside the city. They hailed an airship and began their journey north.

It grew so cold in the ship that their teeth chattered, despite the warm clothes they wore. They could tell that it went beyond the high altitude – they were also well north and getting closer to their destination.

The ship began its descent and deposited them on the wind-swept tundra. It was brutally cold.

"We have very little time to do whatever we're going to do here," Grey reminded them, stating the obvious.

"We're not going to need much," Seline replied as they trudged away from the airship toward the fortress. They left the ship where it was for their return journey.

"Won't someone see it?" Kala asked.

"No," Seline replied. "No one in their right mind would be outside in a place like this, and I doubt they'd have windows anywhere except the roof."

"Strange place for windows," Grey muttered.

"People like light," she explained.

They could tell as they approached it, that there was no easy way into the fortress. The walls were an untold thickness of ice frozen as hard as rock. There was a long ramp up to the door, but it would hardly be opened to anyone who came knocking. Seline patted the fortress wall with her mitt as she looked up it.

"We need a way onto the roof," she observed.

"Let's see if there are drifts on the windward side of the building," Grey said over the gusting wind.

They walked around the building, bracing themselves as they left its sheltered side, and on the opposite side, they did find drifts they could use to climb to the roof. They trudged up, lugging their gear and slipping backward repeatedly, but eventually gaining the roof. The wind cut through their clothing, and they resisted the urge to drop everything and head back to the airship.

Seline walked up to a skylight and peered down at it. Grey joined her and examined it discouragedly, noticing the thickness of the glass.

"It's all good," Seline assured him, "but we need a windbreak. I can't work in this wind."

"I'll see what I can do," Grey replied, and began pushing loose snow over to the window and tamping it down so it wouldn't blow away in the stiff wind. A low wall sheltering the window from the wind began to take form. Kala and Seline helped him, mostly to keep warm by moving, but no matter how hard they labored, it didn't seem to warm them. It did, however, keep their minds off of the cold, even if just a little. Before long, the wall that they constructed deflected the wind somewhat away from the glass. Seline pulled off her pack and took out a pouch of clumpy white paste that she spread in a thick line across the window. She then pulled out the tiny heater that Forest had loaned them and lit it in the lee of the wall. The flame caught but radiated the feeblest amount of heat.

"Look away," she instructed them, and once she'd confirmed that they had, smashed the heater against the glass beside the line of paste, causing a small fireball, then a flash of brilliance as the paste caught fire and burned with the intensity of the sun. "The sledgehammer," she prompted Grey. He pulled it over to her, but she shook her head. "Can you do the honors?" she asked.

He nodded, lifted the sledgehammer, closing his eyes against the glare of the burning paste, and swung it down hard. The glass cracked at the impact. He lifted the sledgehammer and swung it down again, causing the glass to shatter and rain down into the corridor below.

Seline would have congratulated herself had she been warm enough to do so.

Grey pulled a rope out of his pack, tied it around the sledgehammer as best he could in his mitts given the stiffness of the rope. He buried the hammer in the snowbank they'd built and tamped snow down on top of it. "We'll just have to hope it holds," he said and picked up the free end. He dropped it down the open skylight. "I'll go first," he declared, and walked backward toward the opening, holding the rope. He swung into it and hung precariously for a brief moment before sliding down to land hard on the floor, his hands too cold to grip the rope well. He had at least slowed his descent enough to not break his legs, but barely.

Kala went next and fared similarly, except that Grey helped cushion her landing. Seline went last, and the two of them helped her land safely. It was less cold inside the building, but certainly not warm. Kala looked at the glass on the ground. "Think they heard that?" she asked.

"Most assuredly," Grey replied and pulled a pair of daggers from his belt. He shook his arms to warm them. Kala followed suit and readied herself. A couple of guards rushed around the corner and Grey and Kala felled them with poorly thrown daggers, but sufficient to the task.

"Now what?" Kala asked, pulling her daggers from one of the bodies.

"Now we take control of the facility," Grey replied casually, retrieving his daggers as well. They moved through the facility, which was mostly empty, dispatching the few guards that they encountered. They rounded a corner to find a gnome-like man standing before the gigantic doors to the entrance and holding a torch over a trough of black powder.

"Stop," Seline warned him.

"You'll never take this place," he declared. "The vaults are impenetrable."

"Just like the building?" Kala taunted before she could stop herself.

The man closed his eyes in silent prayer and dropped the torch onto the powder. A trail of flame sped down the corridor behind him.

"Shit," declared Kala. "Run!" She raced to the heavy door, wrenched it open, and darted through. She slowed to let Grey and Seline catch her, and together they hurried down the ramp, every step an eternity.

They had barely made it to the bottom when the building erupted in a massive fireball. Kala shoved her companions out of its way as the blast funneled down the ramp, lifting her off her feet, and depositing her in a broken heap a great distance away.

She lay on her back, contemplating the starry sky. She couldn't feel any part of her body, but at least she didn't feel cold as the life seeped out of her. A single tear rolled down her cheek.

I tried. I'm tired. I'm ready, she told the Goddess as She lifted her off the ground and cradled her in Her warmth.

22

Skye

Skye tossed and turned in his bed, haunted by the shock and pain in Kala's eyes when he broke up with her. It gutted him utterly. She was such a pure soul. She gave of herself without ever asking anything in return. The very least she deserved was someone who supported her, and he couldn't even be that.

He kept replaying his decision, trying to convince himself that he'd made the right one. The Priestess has made him chose between his relationship with Kala and his mother's life. Kala was strong – she was the gods-damned Chosen One as far as many people were concerned – she could hold her own. His mother, on the other hand, had no such skills. She was defenseless, she was an innocent, and she was his responsibility. The choice was obvious. So why did every part of him scream that it was the wrong one?

He didn't have the courage to face Kala or the strength to be around her and not go to her. He watched her from afar instead. He watched her care for Soren's wounded to assuage her own hurt. He watched her put several of them out of their misery, and he knew her well enough to know the toll that would take on her – and still, he kept his distance. He even returned to Bayre before she did because it hurt too much to watch her any longer.

Then she returned, and his resolve wavered. When he stumbled into her the next morning, it took all of his will not to reach for her. It was only the realization that she deserved better that gave him the strength to walk away. Stewing in his room, however, he decided that she needed to know that the break-up had nothing to do with her and everything to do with him. It was cliché, but he was overcome with the need to let her know.

He followed after her when she left the temple with Hawke. He had to hunt around to find them but spotted her eventually outside a nearby school. He approached slowly, debating what he would say when he got there. Indecision slowed his pace, and when he finally got close enough to announce himself, she turned and hugged Hawke with a joy that he hadn't seen her express in moons. He knew instantly that he'd made a mistake – she'd moved on already; she wasn't as tortured as he felt. The rehearsed words died in his throat, and he choked. She turned at the sound and locked eyes with him – those beautiful eyes. They destroyed him.

He escaped as quickly as he could but had no time to dwell on it when plague descended on Bayre, and the city went into a panic. Were it not for Seline's protocols at the airfield, the plague would have killed everyone in the city. People locked themselves in their homes and shunned all contact with others. Skye already felt dead inside, so fear of actual death didn't deter him. He sought out Seline and asked to be put to work, whatever the risk. She tasked him and a few other brave souls with sterilizing the airfield with fire. The other volunteers were mostly old people who already felt close to death or those who felt they'd cheated death once and lived beyond their appointed day.

He and the other volunteers wrapped themselves in bandages that they replaced regularly and breathed through thick cotton cloth that they'd fashioned as masks.

Skye looked around the airfield, trying to decide where the priorities lay. He decided to tackle the airship first to postpone having to deal with the bodies. Skye asked two of the volunteers to help him, while the others acquired the necessary supplies. He learned later that the names of the pair assisting him were Jovan and Tilda. When they first started, no one expected to live long enough for names to matter, but a camaraderie slowly crept in, displacing the hollowness Skye felt inside.

The three of them started by tossing combustibles inside the airship through its open door. They tried not to get too close. When they deemed the amount sufficient, Skye crept forward with a lit torch and tossed it inside. It didn't take long for the oil-soaked rags to ignite and grow into an inferno inside the ship. The ship strained against its mooring in the powerful updraft until the fabric of the balloon ruptured and deflated in a burning mess.

While the airship burned, Skye and his companions took the opportunity to gingerly change the bandages covering their hands. That accomplished, they turned their attention to the barracks where most of the dead would be found. Skye originally planned on extracting the bodies but decided instead that burning the building to the ground with the bodies inside was the more practical strategy. They couldn't avoid entering the barracks to properly set the fire, however, so they carried the materials inside. The corpses inside confirmed that the afflicted had died terrible deaths. Skye kept his eyes off them as he placed oil-soaked wood and rags around the building. It took the remainder of the day to prepare it, and his clothes were soaked through with sweat by the time he judged the building ready. He wanted to be sure that the building burned thoroughly, so he volunteered to enter it and ignite the fire, starting from the back of it. Skye carried a lit torch inside, hopeful that errant sparks wouldn't set the room ablaze prematurely. He made it to the far corner and ignited a pile of wood. He needn't have worried about the fire spreading evenly as the flame leaped from pile to pile faster than he could retreat from the room. He barely made it out before the fire engulfed the interior. He stood panting outside the building and resisted the urge to tear the cloth from his mouth so he could gulp in air more freely.

Their next tasks were the bodies lying around the yard, and then the yard itself. They burned the corpses where they lay and tried to avoid walking through the smoke. They had to stay alert because the winds changed frequently. After a while, it became an automatic reflex, and they moved in unison, like a zombie dance troupe. For the ground, they tied branches to long poles to create brooms, then set them afire and dragged them along the ground to scorch anything on its surface. It took days to torch the entire field. They ate and drank little, fearful of removing the cloths from their faces and taking anything into their bodies. When they slept, which wasn't often, they slept in a tiny corner of the yard.

Skye lost the ability to think – his movements became robotic. He grew short of breath, paused his work along the fire line, and sat down for a short break. He tried to call for help, but his lips were cracked and dry, and no sound came. He slumped over and passed out, the flames licking his skin.

———————————————

Skye woke in a bed, the world around him hazy and only coming slowly into focus. He beheld a vision of his mother sitting on the edge of his bed and assumed that it meant he'd failed to protect her, and now the plague had taken him to join her in the afterlife. He began to cry.

"I'm sorry I let you down," he wept.

She took his hand with a look of concern. "You've never done anything of the sort," she rebuked him kindly.

He looked around. Heaven appeared to be a little more disorderly than he'd imagined. "What is this place?" he asked.

"Quarantine," she replied.

Skye dropped her hand, remembering too late the danger he placed her in. He withdrew as far from her as his bed would allow. "You can't be here," he told her.

"On the contrary," she replied. "Once you're in here, you're not going anywhere until your cleared." She shrugged as though it wasn't her choice to have entered quarantine to be with him. "Tilda says you're the bravest boy she knows."

"Tilda?" Skye asked, his head swimming for context.

Evelyn nodded toward the woman in the bed across from him. She smiled, and Skye recognized her from the airfield.

"Jovan didn't make it," she told him sadly, referring to the third member of their party. "We think it was a heart attack, not plague, though," she added.

"And us?" he dared to ask.

"The nurse thinks we're suffering from exhaustion, not plague," Tilda assured him. "They're just being cautious," she added.

It suddenly occurred to Skye that his mother couldn't possibly be there – she was across the continent. *Am I hallucinating?* he thought, rubbing his eyes. "How did you get here?" he asked suspiciously, fearful of dispelling the dream.

"Kala sent Hawke and Jarom to rescue me, and rescue me they did," she replied, smiling broadly.

Kala, thought Skye. *What have I done?*

"How is your girlfriend?" Evelyn asked.

"I don't know," he replied anxiously and started to get up. "I need to see her."

Evelyn stopped him from getting up. "Plague or no, the nurse said you need to rest."

"I've made a terrible mistake," he admitted and told his mother everything.

"She'll understand," she comforted him.

"She shouldn't have to," he replied despondently. *Kala never stopped looking out for him, even when he didn't deserve it. He desperately needed to make it up to her.* He chafed at his confinement.

———————————————

Skye and his mother were let out of quarantine a couple of days later. Skye felt better rested than he had in moons, but he was anxious to see Kala.

Evelyn stopped him before he could rush off, sitting him down on a bench, and holding his hands in hers. "It's time I released you," she told him.

He stared back uncomprehendingly.

"You've always looked after me, and I love you for that," she told him, "but, it's time you look after yourself. Follow your heart. I'll be okay." She stood and guided him to his feet, placing her hand on his shoulder. "Go find her, and never let anything stand between the two of you again, including me. Okay?"

"Okay," he agreed, liberated but somehow saddened. "I love you," he told her, kissed her cheek, and hurried off to find Kala.

He spotted Lily as he entered the temple.

"Hi, Lily. Do you know where I can find Kala?" he asked.

"You're out of quarantine – thank goodness. She went off with Grey and Seline to take out the Priestess's weapons store."

"Alone?" Skye asked, incredulous.

"No, with Grey and Seline," she repeated.

"I mean, only the three of them?"

"Apparently, it's some type of fortress that an army wouldn't be helpful against," Lily replied, repeating the speculation she'd heard.

"How long has she been gone?"

"Several days."

"When is she due back?"

"I don't know. How long does it take to infiltrate and incapacitate a fortress?"

Skye couldn't stand the thought of Kala in harm's way with things left between them the way they were. He thanked Lily and rushed out to find Seline, completely forgetting that Lily had just told him that she was with Kala.

"I'm glad you're more yourself," Lily called after him, shaking her head.

He searched for Seline everywhere, including at the airfield, which was still sealed off. He finally spotted Forest at the market.

"Forest!" he called to get her attention.

"Hi, Skye," she replied as he walked up. "I heard you helped sterilize the airfield."

"That's what I've wanted to ask you about. If airships can't use it, how are people getting in and out of Bayre?"

"They're not, really."

"Then how did Kala leave?"

"I guess she used the airship landing site outside the city."

"Thanks. I'll check it out. How do I get to it?"

"Just go to the city's land gate. The way from there should be decently obvious."

"Thanks again," He called and left to gather his things. If Kala was going to return there, then that's where he'd be when she did.

The Council had commissioned a temporary camp at the landing site outside its walls where newcomers could be quarantined before they entered the city. Skye moved there and awaited Kala's return.

Several days later, a string of airships drifted into view from the south. *Kala's party wouldn't have needed more than one ship*, he thought, but still hoped it was her. He walked to the landing pad and waited eagerly. The first ship landed, and Fayre stepped out.

"Fayre?" he greeted her incredulously. "You're back."

"Thanks to Dhara and Calix," she replied happily, then turned to help others out of the ship.

Skye guided the disembarking people to the camp and sent word back to the city that more food would be needed, particularly given how emaciated everyone looked. He returned in time to help with the next ship. Kaia's daughter, Nina, exited with several other children in Emrys's care. Skye thought it odd that Dhara wasn't with her niece, and Calix wasn't with his father.

"Where are Calix and Dhara?" he asked Emrys.

"Right behind us, probably," Emrys replied and helped guide the children to the camp.

Two more airships landed, and Dhara and Calix weren't in either of them. Word of a monster spread through the camp, and Skye began to worry for them.

Lily and Cera arrived from the city with the wagons of food and other supplies. They found Skye standing alone on the landing pad, staring at the sky.

Cera left Lily with the wagons and walked over to Skye. "What's up?" she asked.

"Calix and Dhara didn't come back with the others," he told her. He didn't want to worry them with talk of a monster, so he didn't bring it up. "They were probably just taking up the rear, and their ship caught unfavorable winds," he added but didn't believe it.

Cera returned to help Lily distribute the food, and chatted happily with Kala's grandfather, letting him know that Kala was away, but hopefully returning soon… all the while glancing at the skies, hopeful to see an airship.

Emrys emerged with a little girl in tow. She clung to his leg until she noticed Lily. Her eyes went wide, and she hurled herself at her. "Lily!" she exclaimed.

"Hi there, darling," Lily replied, picking her up and hugging her.

"My hair's a mess," she admitted guiltily, lifting a tangled strand to show her.

"I'm sure there's a brush around here somewhere," Lily assured her, and the girl brightened.

Emrys stood with his mouth open.

"What is it?" Cera asked him.

"Pippi hasn't said a word since she lost her mother fleeing the village." He continued to stare. "Not one word," he repeated to himself, shaking his head in amazement.

Lily looked up at the darkening skies. "I think we're staying here tonight," she told Cera.

"There's lots of space," Skye added, having given up on waiting for another airship. "We'll find you somewhere to sleep."

"Thanks, but not before we do something about this hair," Lily said, tickling the girl's cheek with the ends of it and making her giggle.

Skye started a fire, impressing everyone with his growing repertoire of skills, and they heated water to wash Pippi's hair. They sat around the fire, chatting about everything other than Dhara, Calix, and Kala. It was bad luck to jinx them with their worry.

"Someone should go tell Kaia that her daughter is back," Cera noted.

"We're sort of stuck here, as per Seline's rules," Skye pointed out.

"She'll get word, I'm sure," Lily added.

Right on cue, Kaia raced up. "Where's Nina?" she asked breathlessly.

"I'll show you," Skye replied, getting up to guide her. They returned a moment later with Nina on Kaia's hip.

"Where's my sister?" Kaia asked.

"She's fighting the monster," Nina guessed.

"What monster, honey?" Kaia asked.

"*The* monster," Nina replied, frustrated with her mother's lack of understanding.

"I'm sure she's fine," Skye interjected. "It's Dhara, after all."

They sat back down around the fire and Nina filled them on their trek through the forest, the refuge they found, and the monster that terrorized them. They listened raptly while praying for Dhara and Calix's safe return. Nina and Pippi eventually fell asleep in Kaia and Lily's laps respectively, exhausted from their recent trials.

Skye spotted a patch of dark occluding the stars. He tracked it long enough to be sure it wasn't a cloud before pointing it out.

"There's an airship coming," he announced.

Lily and Kaia looked down at the sleeping girls.

"You've got time to put them to bed," Skye informed them. "Go on. We'll wait."

Lily rose with Cera's help and Kaia with Skye's. They carried Pippi and Nina to a tent with several empty cots and laid them down without waking them and hurried back to meet the airship. Cera passed each of them a lit torch, and they walked to the landing pad just as the ship touched down. They watched expectantly as the door opened, and Calix stepped out.

"Calix, thank the gods," Lily and Cera announced in unison and crushed him in a hug.

"Dhara?" they asked.

"Right here," she announced wearily, limping through the doorway.

"Your leg!" Lily exclaimed.

"It didn't seem to bother me when I was running for my life," she shrugged. She noted Lily and Cera embracing Calix. "No love for me?" she kidded.

The girls pushed Calix aside playfully and hugged her instead.

"I was just joking," she protested, then noticed her sister and waved her over to join them.

"You have to stop making me worry," Kaia rebuked her sister, her voice full of barely-contained emotion.

Dhara detached herself and limped over to her sister.

"Let me help you," Calix offered, but Dhara shooed him away.

Dhara took Kaia by the shoulders and pulled her into an embrace. "I'll see what I can do," she whispered and held her tightly.

Kaia sighed and pivoted to prop up her sister.

Dhara allowed herself to be guided to the fireside. "So," she began as they sat down, "do you believe in monsters?"

———————————

Everyone relocated back to Bayre in a few days except Skye, who stayed behind to maintain his vigil for Kala. A few days later, he was rewarded by the sight of a lone airship drifting in from the north. He hurried to meet it as it landed, and the door swung open, but no one exited.

"Some help?" Grey called from within, emerging a moment later carrying an unconscious and severely injured Seline.

Skye rushed to his side, yelling to one of the junior guards, "Fetch a nurse – hurry!" The young man sprinted toward Bayre.

Skye took half of Seline's weight and helped carry her clear of the ship. He couldn't help himself and looked over his shoulder expectantly at its open door.

"Sorry Skye, she's not with us," Grey informed him. "I looked everywhere before I left. She's gone."

23

Kala

Kala's eyes fluttered open. She was surrounded by soft white light. Her vision cleared and she saw a kindly old woman seated across from her, hands folded in her lap.

"I'm not dead," Kala concluded.

The woman shook her head slowly, although whether in agreement or contradiction was unclear.

"This doesn't look like hell," Kala observed.

"You're too hard on yourself," the woman replied in a gentle voice.

"So, I am dead?"

"You were."

"Am I now?"

"No, we brought you back. Your work here isn't done." Her expression was serious, but her eyes remained serene.

"Who are you?"

"We are Illusaq, and I am Siku."

"Where are we?"

"You're in our home."

Kala waited for more information.

The woman smiled. "It is under the ice, near the heat of the world."

Kala noticed that she couldn't move her body.

The woman reassured her, "Your body is healing. We've fixed the damage done to it, but it needs rest." She rose gracefully from her chair and approached Kala's side. She lit a shard of wood using a candle and placed it in a bowl of herbs. A tendril of sweet-smelling smoke wafted upward. "We'll talk again," she said.

Kala's eyes closed, and she floated away.

She woke sometime later feeling refreshed. She cautiously moved a finger and was surprised that it wasn't accompanied by pain. She performed a thorough inventory of her body and concluded that she was none the worse for wear, despite the impact of the blast. She attempted to rise and found that control of her body had been returned to her. She swung her legs over the padded table on which she lay, sat up, and looked around. The room was large, and on closer inspection appeared to be carved straight out of the ice, although she didn't feel particularly cold, despite the light clothing that she'd been dressed in.

She looked down at her feet and noticed that she was wearing light sandals. *I guess they don't object to my moving around*, she assumed. She slid off the table, readying herself for some discomfort from supporting her weight, but was surprised again to find herself feeling rejuvenated instead. She walked over to the wall and placed her hand against it. It registered as cold, but not uncomfortably so. She held her hand against it a moment longer, then lifted it away to reveal a faint sheen of moisture that refroze as she watched.

She turned and spied a doorway that opened into a cavernous space. She walked toward it and stepped through, finding herself on a balcony overlooking a gentle slope. The gigantic cavern was oddly bright, despite having no specific light source. Buildings dotted the cavern floor. People moved about in the distance, including a group of children playing lower down the slope. Kala watched them for a moment. They played with a joyfulness that had been robbed from the children of Kala's world. It made her sad.

She looked around and noticed Siku sitting in a chair, watching the children play. An empty chair sat beside hers, and she gestured to Kala to join her.

Kala walked over and sat down in the comfortable chair. "Thank you for healing me," she said.

"We healed your body. You still have to heal your spirit."

"My spirit needs healing?" Kala asked.

The woman said nothing because she didn't need to. Kala knew it to be true – she just didn't want it to be.

"How do I heal it?"

"It's a journey," Siku replied. "The first step is embracing yourself."

Kala was silent. She thought of all the terrible things she'd done. *You are what you do*, she concluded ruefully.

"There is darkness in you, yes," the woman replied to Kala's thoughts, "but it's in all of us, just as there is light. You fear that the darkness holds sway."

Kala didn't just fear that it was possible – she knew it in her core to be true. She was the Angel of Death.

Siku sighed. "You'll never be whole until you accept that you can choose to follow the light or the dark, or both, or that there is no light or dark, just you."

That's not helpful, Kala thought.

"It's a journey," the woman replied.

Kala watched the children. They seemed utterly innocent – not a shred of darkness in them. She felt like the foreigner she was in this land.

"I can't stay?" she asked.

"Would you, even if you could?" Siku replied.

Kala knew the answer. Her friends needed her, and even if she abhorred the responsibility, she felt it. "When do I leave?"

"That is your choice. You're welcome to stay as long as you like."

Kala felt the tug of the outside world and knew she would not stay long.

"Where should I go?" she asked, expecting an equally vague answer. Siku surprised her.

"South, to the ruins beneath the water. You'll find answers there."

"I don't know where that is."

"We'll lend you a guide." She whistled a note that sounded like music. A moment later, an enormous white dire wolf padded up and nuzzled Siku's hand. "You were wearing her cousin's fur when we found you," she said to Kala.

Kala felt terrible. "Does that offend her?"

"No. She says that you have her cousin's spirit, so it's fitting."

"You can talk to the wolves?"

"In a manner," she replied.

Kala steeled herself up. "I should go."

"I know," Siku replied, and pointed to a neat pile of Kala's possessions. "The furs are singed, but we've warmed your body from within, so the cold shouldn't bother you."

Kala got up. "How can I repay you?"

"Heal," she replied, then rose herself.

Kala scooped up her possessions and returned inside to change. She emerged a moment later, dressed for her journey.

"I'll walk you out," Siku said. She waved goodbye to the children, who waved back and resumed their play. She guided Kala along the edge of the cavern, the wolf padding along behind them. She stopped at a tunnel carved through the ice that led upward to the surface. A sled sat off to the side. Siku secured a harness to the wolf and turned to Kala. "This is where I leave you."

Kala walked toward the sled but stopped midway, a million questions on her mind. "Who are you?" she asked, settling on one.

"We fled here during the last apocalypse and have lived here in hiding ever since."

Kala would have to content herself with that for now. She positioned her feet on the sled's rails and gripped the handle. "Thank you again," she said.

Siku smiled warmly, then whistled, and the wolf shot forward, carrying Kala back to the world.

24

Priestess

The Priestess shifted on the throne that she guessed had been carved from the rock to serve a distant predecessor. She chided herself for allowing her mind to wander and think about the past when matters in the present were far more pressing. She focused her attention on the report that her scout was relaying.

"The Fortress is in ruins. The blast caused enough damage that the ceiling collapsed. It will take a very long time to dig it out, let alone rebuild it," he reported.

"The vaults are unreachable?" she asked for confirmation.

"They're on the lowest level, so they're completely unreachable. We will not have access to the Ancients' weapons for the duration of the campaign."

The Priestess mulled this over. The Ancients' weapons sped up the process, but success wasn't dependent on them. She still had a formidable arsenal without them. She was more interested in better understanding her opponents. "What could be ascertained about the attacking force?"

"Almost nothing, Priestess," he replied, fearful of disappointing her. "The state of the Fortress leaves no clues, and the blowing snow covered any prints that may have told us their number. However, a large force would not have helped them. It isn't by force that the Fortress can be breached. They engineered themselves a way in. The destruction of the facility was a defensive measure, so the force must have been sufficient, however, to convince the defenders that loss was inevitable. My guess is that the attack was carried out by a small but very capable group."

She inventoried her mind for a probable list. *Kala*, she thought. *She's usually at the center of everything, and she has the skill to overcome the guards. She doesn't, however, possess the expertise to gain entry, so who would that leave? Soren's engineer, Seline, most likely - she's a bright woman.* They would have known about the existence of the Fortress from her former consort, Brother Grey, but not its location. She doubted that they figured it out on their own – someone told them.

"Who all knows its location?" she asked the scout.

"No one outside this room," he replied.

She sighed, doubting that was true, given the undisputed loyalty of those present.

"Is there anything else you can think of that you haven't told me?" she asked.

"I have told you everything I know," he replied.

Her hurled dagger pierced his eye, and he collapsed. "Pity," she muttered, "It might have kept you alive longer." At least there was now one less person who knew the location of the Fortress.

Her Captain waved to one of her guards to remove the body and cleaned up the blood.

"I'm going to consult the Ancients," she announced and rose to climb the stair to the keep. As she ascended in darkness, she pondered the failure in Bayre. From what her scouts had told her, the airship carrying the virus had landed successfully. However, several days later, life was still very much in evidence within the city, and eventually dense smoke rose from the airfield, indicating that they were sterilizing it. They had either been outrageously lucky or unpredictably smart. She'd have to speak with her chief assassin and have Seline put down, she concluded, assuming the latter.

She opened the door to the room in the keep that housed the crystal and sat on the bench facing it. It took longer than usual to clear her mind, despite the insistent tug of the Ancients on it. When she finally was ready for the visions, they were vivid. She found herself staring at an image of a dagger on a table in a dark room. The blade glinted in faint light, but moonlight or candlelight, she couldn't tell. Feelings of insistence and foreboding swirled in and out of her mind, vying for dominance. When the Ancients released her, she fell crashing back into her body. While she'd communed for the better part of the day, it was still unusual in its brevity. The Ancients wanted something done swiftly, she concluded.

She rose from her seat and stretched her back. She walked to the door and descended to the throne room.

"Summon the Head of the Dark Order, and tell her to ready her men," she ordered her Captain. "I will speak with her after a brief rest."

She retired to her chambers and lay down to recover a measure of energy while her order was carried out. She rose near dusk and returned to the throne room, where Amara stood waiting. The Priestess sat down and got right to the point.

"It's time. Send your assassins to cleanse the smaller communities. You know your craft, so I leave you the discretion to plan it accordingly."

Amara nodded. She had waited her entire life for this mission, as had many who had come before her.

"Call as many ships as are necessary, Brother Rapir," she ordered her Captain.

Amara was about to take her leave when the Priestess motioned for her to wait a moment. "I have another task for you. There is a woman named Seline. She is most likely in Bayre. She is an engineer and an obstacle in our way. Kindly remove her."

"I will see to it myself," Amara agreed. "And if I have the opportunity to dispatch the girl, Kala?"

"Leave her. You would not survive her," the Priestess replied dismissively.

Amara bristled at what she took to be as an insult to her abilities, but seeing that the Priestess had nothing else to say to her, she nodded brusquely and left.

Rapir similarly took his leave to organize the requisite number of airships to carry the assassins across the continent.

The Priestess rose and walked to the balcony. She watched as one thousand assassins, dressed in various shades of black, left the mountain through hidden tunnels and marched toward the camp on the plains. It was as if night flowed out of the mountain and crept onto the plain. Even her most skilled fighters gave them a wide berth. They queued up in groups before the airship landing pads and awaited to be carried to their victims.

25

Forest

Seline lay in a hospital bed recovering from the injuries that she'd sustained from the blast that destroyed the Fortress in the Wastes. Her body ached all over, but she was alive, thanks to Kala shoving her out of the way of the brunt of the explosion. She was thirsty, so she groped for the bell that had been left near her hand. The pain was excruciating, but she needed water. She grasped the bell, but let the pain subside before ringing it softly.

Surprising her, Forest walked into the room instead of the nurse. "What can I get you?" she asked.

"Water," she replied, her voice raspy from disuse and dehydration.

Forest returned with a waterskin that she used to drip water into Seline's mouth.

"Better," Seline thanked her when she'd had enough.

Forest put down the skin and took a seat beside the bed.

"Why are you here?" Seline asked, not wanting to sound rude or ungrateful.

"I was hoping to talk," Forest replied.

"About what?"

"About everything, but starting with the airships."

Seline made an expression that told her to go on.

"I heard that you destroyed the Priestess's weapons store in the north," she began.

"More like they destroyed it themselves to keep it out of our hands," Seline corrected her.

"That's one threat neutralized then, but it seems to me that the Priestess has many more. For example, she seems to have a more advanced command of the airships than we do, and she uses them as weapons."

"That's a fair assessment."

"I was thinking that we need to either reduce her control over them or increase our own."

"How do you propose we do that?"

"I don't know, which is why I've come to you." Before Seline could respond that she knew nothing more than Forest did, Forest continued, "I've been to the island base from which the airships operate."

Hearing this intriguing news, Seline tried to sit up, but the pain prevented her, and she settled back down, grimacing.

Forest waited until Seline got comfortable before continuing. "It's a deserted island. Kala and Skye found it," she added, not wanting to steal the credit. "We think that it's technology from the era of the Ancients that still functions."

"I highly doubt that anything could still function after all that time," Seline countered.

"The spiders seem to keep things running."

"Spiders?"

"Nasty looking metal things," Forest replied, shuddering.

"Okay, this I have to see."

"I thought you might say that. I can take you there when you're feeling up to it."

"Forget feeling up to it – let's go now."

Forest looked skeptical, given Seline's failure at sitting up.

"It's a fair distance, right?" Seline asked.

"Yes."

"Fine. I'll recuperate on the way. Just get someone to carry me to the ship."

"We can do that, but rest at least a day more while I make arrangements."

Seline was unhappy about the wait but realized that she wasn't in a position to push matters.

The next day, Forest had an airship ready and four guards to transport Seline, who was still in her hospital bed. She had a pile of blankets, a small heater, and more than enough food and water for the two-way journey. Seline had asked someone to fetch Tallie's books about the airships, and they were stored aboard as well.

On the flight to the island, Forest helped nurse Seline back to health, and re-explained numerous times every detail she recalled about the island, from the airship fields, to what Seline concluded were the repair facilities, to the map room. When they finally neared the island, Seline was still fairly weak, but she could at least get out of bed and move about the ship without too much pain, which her curiosity overrode anyway.

When the ship landed, Seline spent the first half day navigating the landing fields, categorizing the different types of airships, and trying to decipher the markings on the landing pads. They retired for the first night back inside the ship that they had come in. Seline was exhausted, but happy.

On the second day, they made the arduous trek up the volcano to the fissure through which they gained access to the caldera and the rooms within. Seline had to sit down on the ledge for a long while to recover from the climb before feeling up to continuing on. Squeezing through the fissure, Seline caught sight of her first spider.

"Fascinating," she declared as it watched her with its unblinking black eyes. She moved forward and bent down to pick it up.

"Seline!" Forest warned her, but the spider skittered backward out of her reach.

Seline ignored Forest and tried harder to catch it. She wound up chasing it as quickly as her stiff body would allow, but ultimately to no avail as the creature always proved marginally faster than her. Forest just watched in awe. *Trust Seline to frighten the spiders*, she thought. Seline gave up chasing the spider and began to explore the caldera. There were numerous rooms off of it, and she took her time to explore each one thoroughly. While the spiders unnerved Forest, Seline seemed oblivious to their watchful eyes once she realized that she couldn't catch one.

Seline spent a fair bit of time watching the spiders build or repair airships in the enormous room that seemed dedicated to that purpose.

"I think the Ancients built the spiders to keep infrastructure like the airships running after they disappeared," she concluded.

"Built? You mean they're not alive?" Forest asked.

"I guess it depends on how you define 'alive.' There's no doubt that they're aware of their surroundings and that they communicate with each other, but are they self-aware? That's hard to tell without more observation."

"Can we observe them later?" Forest replied, disliking the idea of spending any more time among the creatures than was strictly necessary.

"It's not our priority right now, so yes, we can leave that until later."

Forest was relieved until Seline decided to explore beyond the repair room. She walked purposefully across it to its far end and began examining the tunnels that the spiders entered and exited. The spiders seemed to object to this because they positioned themselves to block her way, but were forced to yield when Seline took it as another opportunity to try to pick one up. Ultimately, Seline won the contest in that the spiders retreated, but Forest shuddered at the potential ramifications of pissing off a host of metallic spiders.

Most of the tunnels were sized for spiders, not people, so Seline had to crawl on her hands and knees to explore them. They connected to a series of rooms that contained piping that was larger around than a person was tall.

"What do you think the pipes are for?" Forest asked.

"I haven't figured that out yet," Seline responded and continued to trace their length until it she realized that it wasn't yielding any further clues. The ground rumbled and vibrated slightly beneath their feet.

"I don't feel comfortable being this far underground," Forest said. "Can we head back to the rooms closer to the surface?"

Seline wasn't making much progress at unraveling the purpose of the piping, so she consented, and they retraced their steps. When they finally arrived at the map room, Seline was captivated.

"This clearly was built for someone to take stock of the state of the world. Who, for what purpose, and what happened to them?" she thought out loud. She picked an amulet from the collection on the wall.

Forest noted that the ones that she had taken on her earlier visit had been replaced, presumably by the spiders or someone or something that they had not yet encountered.

Seline played with the dial on the amulet, and the light illuminated the various gemstones on the floor that marked the location of settlements.

"That black one is my village," Forest pointed out, but realizing that meant little to Seline added, "and that red one is Bayre."

Seline didn't acknowledge what Forest said, and continued her experimentation. "There are two sets of settings," she noted. "One is for locations where people live or until recently lived, and another for locations not marked on the map, like the Fortress in the Wastes. There are several hidden sites, but I have no idea where they are or what they're for. If there's a logic to the settings, however, there must be something in the northern plains. Apart from that, your guess is as good as mine."

A spider entered the room and began replacing a blue gemstone with a red one.

"Didn't Kala say that red signified that the location was under threat?" Seline asked Forest for confirmation as she studied the spider.

"That was her guess, yes," Forest confirmed.

A second spider entered and began switching another stone to red. Then another, then another. Soon the spiders were teeming in the room, and a red circle spread out from the northern plains.

"That looks bad," Forest stated the obvious. "We have to figure out the airships fast. The only way that threat is expanding so rapidly is if it's carried by airship."

"I need to consult Tallie's books," Seline decided and turned to head back to the caldera where they'd left their possession before they went exploring, once they'd concluded that the spiders showed no interest in their things. The ground rumbled and shook again.

"I don't like that," Forest said to herself, not recalling the volcano being this active the last time she was on the island.

They returned to the caldera, and Seline pulled the books about the airships out of her pack and began sifting through them. Forest wandered around bored, occasionally stooping to pick up a stone to see if she could throw it into a distant crevasse. Soon even this game lost its appeal. It suddenly struck her that they were alone in the caldera. They were never alone – there were always spiders coming and going. She headed to the repair room and peeked in. The unfinished airships remained, but the spiders were nowhere to be seen. *This is not good*, she thought and raced back to Seline.

"The spiders are gone!" she called to Seline as she re-emerged into the open space of the caldera. "We should get out of here." The ground began to shake in earnest, almost as if to prove Forest's point.

Seline got up quickly and stuffed the books back into her pack. Forest joined her, and the two of them sprinted for the fissure through which they'd entered. The ground trembled beneath their feet as they pulled themselves through the narrow opening. Forest was overcome with fear of being crushed between the rock walls. She never felt a greater sense of relief than when she squeezed out the opposite end. She looked up to see smoke and ash rising from inside the caldera.

"We have to run," she told Seline, grabbing the heavy pack from her, and racing down the mountainside, sliding down long patches of loose rock. They fell repeatedly, and their skin was badly abraded, but they didn't slow down. They were half-way down the mountainside when the airships began to lift off en masse.

No, no, no, thought Forest, *don't go!*

Flakes of hot ash began to fall around them as they reached the plain. Forest hazarded a look over her shoulder to confirm that Seline had kept up with her, and beheld a towering plume of ash rising from the caldera. They didn't have much time to get off the island before they'd be covered by it.

By the time they arrived at the airship fields, they were empty, every ship drifting away.

"We need our ship," Forest shouted to Seline over the rumbling. "It has our food and water." She ran to approximately where she thought their ship had been situated, but every landing spot looked the same.

Seline used her foot to scrape the ash off the markings on the pads and tried to recall her earlier observations. *What's the pattern?* she racked her brain.

"What are we looking for?" Forest asked, spying the ash cloud rolling down the mountain after them.

"It's too hard to describe," Seline complained and kept looking.

Forest tried to stay ahead of her and brush off the plates before Seline got to them, but Seline kept angling off in different directions if a symbol looked vaguely familiar. The cloud kept getting closer.

"I think this is it," Seline declared and fished out her amulet frantically. She pressed the center button, and a lone ship broke off from the mass of others, drifting back toward them. The front edge of the ash cloud reached them as the airship neared. They pulled their arms in, but its heat seared their skin regardless.

It was hard to see through the ash as the ship landed, but Forest heard the familiar thud as it made landfall. Forest felt along its side for the opening housing the wheel that opened the door. Forest found it, spun the wheel, and pulled the door open. She and Seline jumped in, escaping the burning ash. Seline pressed the button on her amulet and dialed it to the setting for what she judged to be the nearest hidden location. She released it, and the ship was jerked violently by the hot wind as it was released from its mooring. Forest and Seline were thrown across the tiny cabin, their supplies raining down on them. They tried to stay low as the ship rocked back and forth in the tumultuous air currents. It was blown a fair distance east before it rose far enough to start moving west on high altitude winds.

"We're heading back toward the volcano," Forest observed and did her best to brace herself.

As the airship neared the ash plume, it was thrown about like a toy. Forest and Seline were tossed from one side of the cabin to the other. Forest's head slammed in the wall, and everything went dark.

26

Kala

Kala flew across the Wastes on the sled pulled by the great white wolf. The wind whipped her face, but she didn't feel the cold thanks to whatever the Illusaq had done to her body. They traveled for the entirety of the first day, then slept that night curled together for warmth. At first light, they were off again. The wolf had an innate sense of direction and peering over her shoulder, Kala confirmed her suspicion that the wolf didn't deviate a hair from the path it took. The tracks made by the sled's runners stretched out into the distance, utterly straight.

The wolf raced across a frozen lake, extending its claws for additional traction. In the distance, Kala saw a party of ice-fishers that they would pass closely by, if the wolf's path stayed true. As the wolf loomed closer and was spotted, the fisherfolk scattered in terror. A moment later, Kala roared past their camp, waving sheepishly at the men and women who turned to face her. A young girl waved back, and Kala was sure this would be talked about for generations.

The wolf crossed the lake and resumed pulling the sled through fields of snow. The snow grew patchy and eventually gave way to barren ground. The wolf stopped and motioned for Kala to remove its harness. They abandoned the sled.

"I guess we're on foot from here," she concluded.

The wolf shook its head and knelt beside her, indicating that she should mount it. It was the size of a small horse, so she did as she was suggested to do. The wolf rose and broke back into a run. It was possessed of unnatural endurance and only stopped when darkness fell.

They continued on until they arrived at the shore of a shallow lake. The water was utterly still, and Kala could see the bottom for a considerable distance from shore. The wolf knelt to let her off its back, and she could tell that this was the end of their journey together. She nuzzled its neck and hugged it.

"Thank you," she whispered in its ear.

It leaned in closer in response. When Kala released it, it nodded to a pile of rocks that looked to have been pushed together by a glacier that had long ago advanced, then receded.

Kala could tell that this was where she was supposed to go. She removed everything she didn't need and placed them in a neat pile. She decided to leave her swords but bring her daggers. She put her lightened pack on her back, having kept only her waterskin, food, and a few other supplies. Kala saluted the wolf a final time. It dipped its head in response, and she turned and walked toward the rocks. There was no clear path through them, they were so jumbled, so she simply followed her instincts. She had to remove her pack to squeeze through several narrow openings, but never reached an impasse that required her to retrace her steps. She wondered which of the gods guided her.

Kala came at last to a solid wall of stone that the glacier had pushed the boulders up against. She decided to follow along it to the right. Crawling over a boulder, she put out her hand for support but found empty air instead. She forced her way sideways until she recognized the space as an entrance into the wall. *Found it*, she thought. It took some exploration to find an angle at which she could enter the passage, given that its entrance was packed with rocks. Descending the pile of stones that clogged the opening, she finally found herself on level ground. The faintest hint of light trickled through the pile of boulders outside, but she would soon leave it behind as she moved deeper into the tunnel.

She pulled out her flint and secured it around her waist for easy access, figuring she could try to see by the sparks it would cast. In the meantime, she had to accept moving blindly. She re-secured her pack and headed off. The tunnel angled downward slightly, putting her quickly below the level of the lake that she judged to now be under.

She shuddered at the thought of all that water over her head, but shook it off and continued moving forward slowly in the dark.

She took a cautious step forward and found herself at the top of a flight of stairs. She took out her flint and struck it to see if she could see how deep the stairs went, but the light didn't penetrate far. She put her flint away and began descending. After what she judged to be the equivalent of many stories of buildings that she was familiar with, she began to step on rubble and found that the stairwell's roof had partially collapsed, and the rock was slightly damp. *Not liking this*, she thought, but she was committed to proceed. She scrambled over the loose rock to the other side of the cave-in. The walls and floor of the tunnel ceased to be smooth and regular, and she couldn't tell whether she still followed the original tunnel or some more natural channel that had formed later.

The walls and ceiling closed in on her until the only way forward was to crawl. Kala began to wonder whether she could even turn around if she wanted to or whether she would end up dying deep underground, wedged tightly in a narrow fissure. She banished the thought.

She found it easier to loop her pack around her foot and drag it with her, rather than pulling it by hand. The downward slope leveled off, and she groped along, moving near horizontally. Her hand splashed in a puddle, which alarmed her initially, but the walls were dry to the touch, so she continued, wading through puddles that increasingly filled the tunnel. She had to twist onto her back several times to keep her face in the air pockets along the roof of the tunnel. Finally, even that gave way to a completely water-filled tunnel.

This could just be a stretch, not the end, she thought. She took a deep breath and edged forward, clawing along the roof of the tunnel. Her hand broke the surface of the water, and she surged up to breathe in the tiny air-filled space. Several more times, she had to fully submerge herself and just hope that there would eventually be air. *The gods could not have led me this so far, only to abandon me now,* she thought. She took another deep breath and pushed off underwater again. She felt along the ceiling but found no pockets of air. She was beginning to panic and question if she could retreat before her breath ran out when she saw a faint glow ahead. *If it's moss, I assume it's not growing underwater,* she thought and dragged herself forward frantically. Her lungs threatened to explode as she released their last bubble of air, just as her head broke through the surface. She gulped in air and took several moments to realize that she was in a pool in a large cavern, dimly lit by patches of moss, growing up its walls.

She swam forward toward the shore and dragged herself up onto it. She lay panting for a while before standing and taking in her surroundings. It looked like the remains of one of the Ancients' structures – there were intermittently flat stretches of wall, floor, or ceiling. She considered rummaging through her pack to see what had survived the trek underwater and what hadn't but decided that was a depressing task that she'd face later.

A red sparkle caught her attention in her peripheral vision. She walked around several piles of rocks to find one of the Ancient's crystals sitting on a pedestal, twinkling with internal light. *I guess this is where I find my answers,* she thought. She wasn't sure how to converse with the crystal, or even what she wanted to know. She approached it cautiously and placed her hands on it. She felt the gentle tug on her mind that she'd felt before, but this time instead of running from it, she opened herself to it.

Pictures began to form in her mind. She saw people who didn't look dissimilar to those she knew. She watched them discard their bodies as they stepped through a crystal doorway into a hall of lights. *The Ancients,* she thought. *I know who you are. What do you want?* she asked in her mind. The image shifted to a garden. Songbirds sang pleasing songs, and the blossoms smelled exquisite. Then the smell of smoke stung her nostrils, and the garden combusted in flame. Before her panic could register, the fire extinguished itself and flowers pushed up out of the ash until the garden was restored. The cycle repeated several times.

You want me to let the world burn? she asked. The scene went dark, and the garden formed around her once more. This time the crystal was in its center. She waited, but the cycle of fire didn't come. Instead, the sun warmed her face, and the breeze stroked her cheek. This garden persisted. *Not all of you think the world should be destroyed*, she guessed. The sun warmed her face more strongly. *I assume that's a yes*, she thought.

Some distant part of her called to her to return to her body. She found her senses return gradually and realized that she'd slumped over the crystal. Embarrassed, she pulled herself off of it, but her muscles were stiff from disuse. Her stomach screamed its hunger, and her dry lips indicated her thirst. She pulled her waterskin out of her pack and took a deep draught. She pulled out the remains of her food and discarded what was ruined and ate a little of what wasn't.

She looked at the crystal. "What do you want from me?" she asked. The crystal beckoned to her in answer. "I'm not spending another day draped over you," she concluded and moved closer to judge its weight. It was surprisingly not as heavy as she imagined. "Brace yourselves," she said to it and hefted it to the ground. "Don't worry, I'll put you back later," she assured it, part of her wondering if she was insane to be talking to a cube of glowing crystal. Kala lay down beside it and placed her palm against its surface. No visions came, and fatigue overcame her, so she drifted off to sleep. She couldn't tell whether she dreamed or had more visions, because when she woke, she couldn't recall either.

She sat up and took better stock of her surroundings. She heard a fish swimming in the pool and strained her eyes until she caught a trace of its pale white body. *Wait a moment*, she thought, *I shouldn't be able to hear or see that*. She bolted upright faster than she thought she would and was thrown momentarily off balance until she stabilized herself. "What did you do to me?" she demanded to know from the crystal. It barely twinkled. Whatever its energy source, it seemed momentarily spent. "I'm not a pet project. I'm not a toy!" she yelled at it. It didn't even flash in response. She picked it up and returned it to its pedestal, realizing only after the fact how much lighter it felt the second time she lifted it.

She paced around the cavern, trying to recall her dreams – hoping for some real answers but finding none. Part of her told her that she needed to get back to her friends, that she'd been away too long already. "Whose fault is that?" she cursed the crystal. She scooped up her pack, which was now completely dry, further evidence of the passage of time. She pulled out fruit that had rotted during her long sleep. The jerky at least still seemed edible, so she chewed on some while making up her mind about what to do next. She decided that she needed to get back to Bayre. She looked at the pool, and the path back to the surface became clear in her mind, despite her having fumbled along it in absolute darkness on the way here. She gave up questioning the changes she felt and dove into the water.

What felt like mere moments later, she had traversed the underwater tunnels, climbed back to the surface, and squeezed through the pile of jumbled rocks to emerge into the sunlight. The wolf was lying down nearby and sniffed the air suspiciously when she emerged. "Not you too," she thought out loud. It padded over and nuzzled her. "Thank you for not thinking I'm a freak," she said, rubbing its fur.

She looked around. "Do you know where I can find an airship around here?"

The wolf turned and began walking toward the shoreline. It entered the water and waded out into the shallow lake. Kala collected her belongings and followed the wolf until it simply stopped and stared at her. She looked down at the ground under the water and saw that she was standing on a submerged stone dais. *Do these things still work underwater?* she thought and pulled out her amulet. She pressed it and waited. Sure enough, an airship drifted in eventually. It even knew enough to hover above the water, although it moved around a fair bit. *How do you know to do that?* she wondered. She gave the wolf a final scratch behind its ears and boarded the ship.

"Thank Siku for everything," she called as the ship drifted higher.

The wolf dipped its head and padded back toward the shore.

Kala sat down and felt her body humming beneath her skin. *How am I going to live with myself like this?* she thought.

As the airship drifted closer to Bayre, Kala looked out the window to see if everything seemed in order in the city. She'd been gone so long that she worried that the Priestess might have succeeded in a second attack. She spied movement in the streets, however, and concluded that it seemed to have survived so far, and hopefully with it, her friends.

The ship bypassed the city heading toward the landing site outside its walls. As it neared the ground, Kala spied the cluster of tents that housed new arrivals until they were permitted to enter the city. In an adjacent field, rocks had been arranged to spell out, "Welcome Home!" When the ship landed, and she stepped out, Skye stood facing her expectantly.

"You're alive!" he said, overcome with joy.

"Grey and Seline?" she asked nervously, unable to contain her worry.

"Hmm? Oh, they came back, without you, mind you, which was why we were all worried," Skye replied, rambling.

"Skye, slow down. They're okay?"

"Sorry, I'm just excited to see you. They were in rough shape, Seline especially, but she recovered enough to head out again with Forest. Grey's in the city, I imagine. He'll be happy to see you. He's all gruff and unreadable, but I could tell he was worried," Skye replied, still rambling.

A weight lifted off Kala's chest. "Thank the gods."

"I never gave up hope," he told her earnestly.

"Skye…" she began, but he interrupted her.

"I'm *so* sorry. I let you down, and I'm sorry."

"I understand," she replied kindly, but emotionally drained.

"Can you forgive me?" he risked asking.

"Give me some time," she told him. "When we broke up, I didn't like how I felt." Skye tried to apologize again, but she stopped him. "What I mean is that I didn't like how it made me feel about *myself*. No offense, but I don't want to need you to feel human."

Skye deflated. "I guess I shouldn't have hoped for anything different. I was an ass."

"You sure get a lot of practice at it," she chuckled.

"I do," he agreed dispiritedly.

Kala pulled him into a loose hug. "It *is* good to see you."

He hugged her back, careful not to overstep the bounds she'd placed on their intimacy. "Evelyn is well, by the way. Thank you for that."

"Thank Hawke. I just pushed him in her direction."

"I did. He's kind of annoyed at how often I thank him, actually."

Kala laughed. "He would be."

"Brace yourself for what I'm about to ask. I know it might be too soon…"

Kala wrinkled her nose and tensed up.

"My mom will want you to come to dinner the moment she hears you're back."

Kala relaxed. "That I can do."

"Tonight?"

"Really, Skye? She needs some warning."

"Okay. Tomorrow then."

Kala sighed. "It's a date."

Skye brightened. "She'll be excited to have me back too."

"Have *you* back?"

"Yes, I've been living here waiting for you. I don't see her as much as I should."

"So you're compensating for being a bad boyfriend by being a bad son."

"Let's just say that I like to spread the misery around."

"That you do," she laughed. "I'll walk you home," she offered. "Unless I'm supposed to stay here a while first."

"You've returned from the dead. I think that gets you a pass. Besides, no one here would dare to ask you to. Your eyes have that glinty look you get before you eviscerate someone." She narrowed her eyes at that, but he held out his hand tentatively, and she took it. They held hands as they walked toward Bayre.

Passing the field with the rocks, Kala asked, "Was that your sign?"

"You saw it?" Skye asked, brightening. "Did you like it?"

"It was sweet," she admitted.

"No one really accepted that you were dead, but you do make a habit of disappearing," Skye noted. "Cera floated the idea of putting up 'Have you seen this girl?' posters around the city."

Kala laughed, "I'm not a lost cat."

They walked on in comfortable silence. The longer she was around him, the more she felt herself, and the more conflicted she became over whether that was a good thing or a bad thing.

Skye stopped, and it took her a moment to realize that they'd arrived at his house. "This is it," he declared, gesturing toward the door."

"Until tomorrow then," she replied and leaned in to give him a chaste kiss on the cheek.

Skye's heart went through his chest as he watched her walk away.

Kala heard him call, "Mother, I'm home," practically singing. She smiled and shook her head. *Skye*.

She made her way back to the temple, but somehow word had arrived before her that she was back. Lily, Cera, and Celeste were at the door, with her grandfather, Calix, Hawke, and Grey standing behind. Tears were streaming down Lily's face.

"I thought you'd be happy to see me," Kala pointed out.

"I am," Lily blubbered and hugged her fiercely. Cera joined in, and Kala squeezed a hand through to pull Calix in as well. They hugged until tears streamed down everyone's faces, even stoic Calix.

Kala released them and turned to face her grandfather. "Skye neglected to mention that you were back," she said, wiping away tears.

"You've grown," he replied, looking her over.

"It's only been a few moons," she countered.

"And still, you're all grown up. I'm so proud of you." He beamed, and they hugged.

She looked around. "Where's Dhara? And Kaia?"

"Probably chasing monsters," Calix replied. "Seriously."

Kala filed that away for future elaboration. She hugged everyone except Grey, who nodded at her respectfully. She wouldn't have it and hugged him anyway, much to his chagrin. He tolerated it though and even patted her on the back. "You have some explaining to do," he said.

"Can't a girl have some mystery?" she chided him.

"You're nothing but."

"A tale for another day," she replied.

They walked into the great room together, everyone talking over each other to bring Kala up to speed on what she'd missed. Celeste tugged on her sleeve. "There's someone who's been waiting for you," she said and gestured to a young man sitting alone across the room.

"Give me a moment, guys," Kala requested, detached herself from the group, and walked over.

He stood up at her approach and took off his cap. "Ma'am."

"My gods – I'm not *that* old. Relax. You're Torin's nephew, right?" She searched her memory for a name.

"That's right, ma'am," he started, then cringed at his gaffe. He worried that he wasn't making a good first impression. "I'm Cade."

"Pleased to meet you again, Cade. Sit," she ordered to get him to relax. "What can I do for you?"

"I'd like to be your retainer."

Kala was a bit shocked at the request.

Cade barreled on, "All my life, I've been a screw-up. I watched my uncle die protecting me, but I've done nothing with my life since to justify his sacrifice. You, on the other hand, do everything. Please let me serve you so I can feel like my life has some purpose."

He looked at her so earnestly that Kala couldn't refuse him out of hand, no matter how insane his request sounded. "I've been told that I live at the center of the storm," she warned him. "What you're asking will probably get you killed. Are you sure?"

"I'm sure," he replied, barely stopping himself before adding 'ma'am.'

"Okay. We'll give it a try. Be here at dawn, and we'll see what there might be for you to do."

"Thank you," he beamed, rose and hurried out.

Kala returned to her friends and pleaded amnesia about what happened in the Wastes. She felt it was her responsibility to protect the Illusaq. Her friends didn't buy it for a moment, but they didn't press her on it.

Emilie entered and sat down beside Hawke on the loveseat near the fire, curling her legs underneath her, and snuggling into him.

"Emilie's here?" Kala observed.

"Jarom and Hawke brought her back with Skye's mother, and Amber. It wasn't safe to leave them in Edith's village," Cera explained.

"Amber's here too, then?" Kala asked, looking around for her.

"Yes," Lily confirmed. "She's probably in her room."

"Do you mind if I go say, 'hi'?" Kala asked her friends for permission.

"Of course not. We're sort of monopolizing you," Cera replied, albeit reluctantly.

Kala said her goodnights to everyone and went off to find Amber's room. She almost passed it but caught a glimpse of her sitting on her bed through the open doorway. She stopped and knocked lightly to get her attention.

Amber looked up, smiled broadly, and rose to meet Kala in a hug.

"Why didn't you come out to the great room?" Kala asked.

"I did, but I saw you with your friends, and I didn't want to intrude," Amber replied shyly.

"You're my friend," Kala confirmed.

"Not like them."

"That's true," Kala agreed and took Amber's hands in hers. "They've been my friends for a long time – through the good times and the bad times."

Amber nodded dispiritedly.

Kala tightened her grip on Amber's hands. "You've been my friend through the *really* bad times."

"Don't you want to forget those times?"

"Them, yes… you, no. You were the only thing that stood between me and the darkness."

"You rescued me," Amber reminded her.

"And you rescued me," Kala countered. "And for that, we need to celebrate." Kala spotted Frey walking past and called to him, "Frey!"

He poked his head in the doorway.

"Can you do me a favor?" she asked him.

"Anything."

"Can you scrounge up a bottle of wine?"

"Of course. The good stuff, or the *really* good stuff that Celeste hides for special occasions?"

"Well, this is a special occasion."

"Done," he agreed and darted away.

"Won't your friends miss you?"

"They can live without me for one more night. Besides, there are things I can tell you that I can't tell them."

Frey returned with a bottle of wine and a couple of glasses and left with a conspiratorial wink.

"Assassins' secret," Kala called after him as he closed the door behind himself.

They stayed up late talking about the horrors that Kala had seen on the battlefield and after, her indecision about Skye, and the unsettling changes that the Ancients had made to her body. Amber listened, laughed and commiserated, and Kala felt like a thousand tiny weights were lifted off her. As dawn approached, she just crawled into bed beside Amber and fell asleep.

It was with great effort that Kala rose early enough to honor her promise to meet Cade. She was beginning to regret it, but only because sleeping longer seemed so appealing. She snuck out without waking Amber and returned to her room to get changed. She ambled toward the kitchens hoping to grab a cup of kai before Cade arrived in order to wake up a bit more thoroughly.

Walking through the great room, her senses told her something was amiss, and she was immediately on high alert.

"Aren't you the early bird," a cold voice teased from a chair near the fireplace.

Kala turned to see the Priestess sitting back, legs crossed, hands in her lap.

"Come join me," she said, gesturing to the seat across from her. "I have a proposition for you."

Kala walked slowly to the offered chair and sat down cautiously.

"Your propositions are poison," Kala countered.

The Priestess ignored her, studying her movements. "You seem… more," she observed, using 'more' holistically. She raised an eyebrow. "Interesting."

Kala tensed. "Get to the point. You said you have a proposal."

The Priestess made a face that said she was disappointed in Kala's lack of patience, then started by saying, "You're friends don't have to die." She let that hang in the air a moment before continuing, "You can't protect them from what is coming. The mere fact that I'm here should be proof enough of that. I could just as easily have brought the plague with me and left it in your quaint little kitchen."

"We destroyed your weapon stores."

"Do you really think I don't have more?"

"Do you?"

"I'll never tell," she replied, smiling. She leaned forward slightly. "You can't win, but that doesn't mean you have to lose. I'm prepared to let you round up all of those who you care about and relocate to a quiet corner of the world to sit out the apocalypse." She leaned back. "Surely, that sounds appealing after everything you've seen and been through."

"It does sound appealing, I have to admit, but I don't trust you."

The Priestess looked innocent and hurt, which Kala thought was rich, knowing what a viper she was.

"More importantly, someone has to stand up for everyone else."

The Priestess looked disappointed in Kala. "And you think that someone is you? You're just a child and a foolish one at that. Don't play at being noble. You and I both know the real you – who you are – what you are. You're a weapon, a finely crafted weapon, but in the end, that's all you are. Nothing else suits you, and you will fail at trying to be anything that you're not."

The Priestess's words stabbed deep into Kala's heart and resonated with her insecurities. "Are we done here?" she said to mask her uncertainty.

The Priestess's response was interrupted by Cade's arrival. He could tell right away that something was off about the Priestess, even though he didn't know who she was.

"Is everything okay?" he asked, placing his hand on the pommel of a sword that he'd scrounged up.

"How adorable," The Priestess purred and rose slowly from her seat.

Kala rose and moved to stand between her and Cade.

Grey took the opportunity to step out of the shadows and place his dagger against the Priestess's throat.

She didn't move a muscle or seem the least bit concerned. She slowly raised her hand to his and trailed her nails along the skin of the arm that held the dagger. "I've missed you," she said coyly.

Kala noticed the thin trail of blood her razor-sharp nails left in their wake but didn't have time to call out a warning before the Priestess dropped her arm and her cloak fluttered to the ground, empty. Grey dropped his dagger and clutched his throat to stop the bleeding from where she'd slashed it.

"Grey!" Kala exclaimed with worry and surged forward. She tore an arm off of her blouse and fashioned it as a bandage around his neck. In the instant it took, she concluded that the wound was not deep enough to be fatal, and wondered if the Priestess was capable of sentimentality.

Cade drew his sword, although he held it awkwardly. "Should I go after her?" he asked.

"No. Let her go," Kala responded, very much doubting that he could find her if she didn't want to be found, and not wanting his death on her conscience if she did.

Kala helped Grey sit, and he replaced her hand with his own in providing pressure against his throat. "I guess we're not getting back together," he joked, careful not to aggravate the wound.

Kala laughed, but the Priestess's words kept playing over and over in her mind – "You can't win."

PART IIII
COGADH

27

Kala

Kala left Grey's room in the infirmary, lost in thought, and almost bumped into Cade standing just outside the door. "Gods, Cade, you don't have to go everywhere I go," she said, trying not to sound annoyed, but not entirely succeeding given how upset she was with herself for not warning Grey in time to protect him.

Cade looked apologetic. "Is he going to be okay?" he asked uncertainly, gesturing toward Grey's room.

"It looks like it," she replied, relaxing somewhat.

"There was a lot of blood," Cade countered, uncertainly.

"Neck wounds are like that," she assured him. "Now, seriously – go home. I'll call you when I need you."

"Of course. I was just waiting to remind you about dinner at Skye's mother's tonight. He came by."

"Damn, I forgot about that," Kala admitted.

"That's what I'm here for," Cade replied, brightening.

"Thanks. I need to clean up." She turned to go but stopped herself. "There is something you can do for me," she decided.

Cade looked eager to be useful.

"Can you round up the following people for a meeting at the temple tomorrow: Hawke, Dhara, Kaia, Jarom, and Calix?"

"I can do that," he replied.

"Are you going to remember all that?" she asked.

"Not a chance," he replied, and pulled out a tiny notebook, scribbling down the names and repeating them back to her.

"Excellent. Thank you. Oh, and one more thing… when you're done, see if you can find a woman named Brinn in the city, and ask her to come meet with me? She won't be easy to find. I have a hunch that if you go by the brothels – *they're* not hard to find – and ask for her, you might find someone who can steer you in the right direction. Her people have a penchant for hiding in plain sight."

"I can try," he agreed, a bit apprehensive about combing the brothels, but if this is what she wanted him to do... "Have a nice night," he wished her and hurried away.

Kala headed back to her room, wondering what in the world she was going to wear tonight. She had nothing that wasn't fairly form-fitting or a bit too dressy for dinner with Skye's mom. She cursed her lack of wardrobe and headed to Cera's room for help.

Cera was ecstatic to be enlisted. She rummaged through her closet, examining the options. *Someone's clearly found time to shop*, Kala thought. Cera held out two skirts. "Too much leg," she concluded and discarded one. "Not enough leg," she concluded, rejecting the other, and turned to look for more options. She eventually settled on a skirt that hung to the knee. "A good compromise," she declared to herself. "We'll have to pin it to fit. You're not expecting to take it off tonight, are you?"

"Cera! Of course not. It's dinner... with Skye's mom!"

"Just checking." She rooted around for a sleeveless top, then procured a silk belt that tied in a loose bow.

"A bow?!" Kala rebelled, feeling it looked a little too girly for her.

"It completes the outfit," Cera replied, standing firm.

Kala threw up her hands, accepting that she this was the price of asking for Cera's help. She let Cera finish dressing her, brush out her hair, and apply some subtle makeup. When she was done, Kala looked herself over in the mirror. She had to admit that she looked good, just not herself. She resisted sighing and hugged Cera. "What would I do without you?"

"Go through life looking like a warrior peasant, and scare all the boys away," Cera concluded and shooed her out the door.

Kala made her way to the house where she'd dropped off Skye the night before, careful not to wobble in the shoes that Cera had procured for her. They were woefully impractical, but they did make her calves look good. She chided herself for caring what Skye might think about her calves and reminded herself that she wasn't trying to get back together – it was just dinner. Lost in her inner debate, she arrived before she knew it, and stood uncertainly staring at the door before taking a deep breath and knocking lightly.

Skye opened the door. "Wow," he exclaimed. "You look great."

"It's all Cera," she replied shyly.

"I'm pretty sure it's all you," he assured her and waved her in.

It smelled delicious inside. Kala had forgotten what a good cook Skye's mother was.

"Come sit by the fire. My mom is just finishing up in the kitchen."

Kala allowed herself to be directed to a pair of comfortable chairs and chose to sit in the one on the left.

Skye joined her. "Cade told me about Grey. How's he doing?"

"He's okay. It was strange. This is going to sound terrible, but there was something intimate about the way Grey stood behind her, dagger, or no dagger… and he was a hair slower than I know him to be in defending himself… and I swear the Priestess held back. She could have killed him, and she didn't. I didn't expect that from her." Kala blushed to realize that she was rambling and sounding a little insane to focus on this aspect of what had just happened.

Evelyn walked in, rescuing her from her embarrassment. "Hi, Kala," she greeted her. "Dinner is ready."

They made their way to the small table in the adjoining room.

"It smells wonderful," Kala told her.

"Considering that you've saved my life twice now, a roast seems like an inadequate repayment," she sighed.

"It was actually Skye the first time, and Hawke the second," Kala deflected.

"And always you at the center of everything," Evelyn countered. "Please, have a seat."

Over dinner, Evelyn recounted the story of her rescue, including crawling through the hole in the roof, running from monks, and climbing a rope to the airship. "I think I had a taste of your life," she admitted to Kala. "I prefer my kitchen, thank you very much," she concluded.

Kala felt the tension seep out of her body as the evening wore on. She watched Skye joke and laugh readily. His hand brushed hers, and a familiar shock traveled up her arm. She withdrew her hand but marveled at how he made her feel. *Surely, this wasn't a bad thing?* she wondered.

Skye got up to wash the dishes and vanished into the kitchen. Evelyn took the opportunity to talk privately with Kala. "Thank you for giving him a second chance, or third maybe. He doesn't always make the right call, but he adores you."

Kala didn't know what to say, plus a lump had formed in her throat. Luckily, Evelyn didn't expect her to say anything in response and just sat back, sipping her tea.

Skye emerged with a pie and served everyone a piece. It was a mixture of sweet and tart, and Kala helped herself to a second piece. When they finished dessert, Evelyn shooed them into the living room, volunteering to clean up the dessert dishes.

Skye and Kala sat by the fire, chatting about life in Bayre. Evelyn brought them each a glass of wine and begged off early to bed. They talked late until Kala remembered the meeting she'd organized for tomorrow. "I should go," she announced, reluctantly.

"I'll walk you back," Skye offered, wanting to prolong the evening. Kala accepted his offer, and they strolled back to the temple. She asked if he could join them in the morning, and he agreed. They stopped at her door, and she turned slowly, placed her hand tentatively on his chest, then changed her mind, curled her fingers behind his neck, and pulled him in for a kiss. His initial shock subsided, and he kissed her back.

She pulled back and thanked him for a lovely evening. He glowed as she watched him walk away. She turned and entered her room, nearly having a heart attack to find Lily and Cera sitting on her bed.

"So?" Cera asked eagerly.

Kala's racing heart slowed. "It was nice," she replied.

"Just nice?" Lily probed.

"Okay… it was more than nice."

The girls shrieked their joy and jumped up to hug her. "They're back together," Cera concluded, dancing around.

Nothing had been declared, but Kala couldn't contradict her, so she just soaked in her friends' happiness for her.

———————————

Cade found it awkward to ask people for directions to a brothel, but he'd given up searching aimlessly, and Kala had entrusted him with this task, so he vowed to stomach his pride and do whatever was necessary to accomplish it. A fairly seedy-looking gentleman pointed him down the street, so he headed off in that direction.

The place didn't look notably different from any other establishment. He walked in, and sure enough, girls were circulating around the room looking for clients. He approached the closest one.

"I'm looking for Brinn," he told her. She shrugged, so he asked the next girl.

"I can be Brinn," she cooed.

"Thank you, but no thank you," he replied and moved off to ask a third girl.

"Forget about her," she told him. "I'm far more inventive."

Gods, he thought, *this is not going to be easy.*

He repeated this process at four more brothels and discouragedly entered a fifth. The second girl he asked about Brinn, asked, "Why?" back. No one else had asked 'why?' – they just assumed that Brinn was his favorite girl.

"It's personal," he replied cagily.

"It always is," she sighed. "I know Brinn. I can take you to her."

"Are you sure?" he asked, tired of an evening of games.

She just beckoned with her finger, and the fact that she wasn't trying to be the least bit coy lead him to trust her, so he followed. She led him down a flight of stairs, also unusual in a brothel, and through a doorway. He entered, and she threw him against a stack of barrels, dagger under his chin.

"I asked why?" she repeated coolly.

Kala had gone to sleep content but woke sobered by the task of organizing a resistance to the Priestess. She splashed water on her face, got dressed, and headed to the great room.

Calix, Jarom, and Hawke were already there. She walked up to Hawke, who offered her his cup of kai.

"Pried yourself away from Emilie, I see," she noted, taking the cup.

"Reluctantly," he admitted.

"I don't think I properly thanked you for rescuing Skye's mother."

"Believe me; he has," Skye replied.

Kala laughed. "Well, thank you anyway."

"All in a day's work."

"Not the way she tells it."

Skye entered and took a seat beside Jarom. Dhara and Kaia wandered in, looking sleepy as hell, and collapsed onto a sofa.

"It's too early," Dhara complained.

"Looks like everyone's here," Kala concluded.

"Almost," Grey said quietly from the doorway.

"Grey, what in the world are you doing here? You need to rest," she scolded him.

He just shrugged to save his voice and wedged himself in beside a sprawling Dhara.

Kala turned to face those assembled. "Morning, everyone," she started. "I'll get right to the point – we're back where we were several moons ago – up against a threat much greater than us. The Priestess has called all the Church to her. That will be a sizable force. Worse, the monks have trained from a young age to fight. Is that a fair assessment, Grey?"

He nodded, so she continued. "We need to raise an army again. Soren's army has been decimated, but we can start there. Rumor is that some of his forces still march west, but we have no idea where they might be. We also have allies among the plains horsemen – thank you, Jarom, and Forest if she were here; the pirates – thank you, Hawke and Skye; Dhara's people – thank you, Dhara, Kaia and Calix; and Brinn's people – thank you, Grey. Plus, there's what's left of the defenders of Bayre. That doesn't make for much of an army, but it's what we've got. We should split up and reassemble our army. Thoughts?"

"I'll go talk to Addis," Jarom volunteered. "Some of his people are still camped near the city – he may be among them. Forest has more sway with him than I do, but she's not here."

"That's great, Jarom. See if they can raise more fighters too."

He nodded, and Hawke piped in, "Eryl returned to his people, but I can go see who he might be able to lend us." Kala nodded her approval, so that was settled.

"I'll talk to my brother," Dhara offered. "Most of our people have headed north to settle, but we might be able to call some back to join us."

"I'll help round them up," Kaia added.

"They're pretty beat up, but I can go see how much of Soren's army remains in fighting shape," Skye suggested.

"Excellent," Kala acknowledged. "I may join you in that."

"I'll see how many fighters Bayre will give us," Calix suggested.

"Remind them that if we don't succeed, it will have been pointless to have held people back to defend Bayre – it will fall," Kala told him. She turned to Grey. "Brinn's people?"

"Will be where they need to be," Brinn declared, walking into the room, followed by Cade, who looked moderately terrorized.

"Brinn, thank you for joining us. You can be hard to find."

"This one managed," she replied, gesturing to Cade.

"Where should we ask everyone to assemble? Here at Bayre?" Skye asked.

"No," Brinn cut in. "I know a place. Our people call it Cogadh. It means 'the place for fighting.' If I know of it, you can be sure that the Priestess does too," she said. She gave everyone instructions on how to get there.

"It's settled then," Kala concluded. "Get what you need, and for those of us traveling, we'll meet at the airship port outside the city. We'll meet again at Cogadh."

28

Forest

Forest awoke with a splitting headache. It took her a moment to realize that she was lying on the floor of an airship that was going gods-know where and had been traveling there for gods-know how long. She looked down to see a hand across her at an angle that told her it wasn't hers. It took her another moment to remember that it was Seline's.

"Seline?" she called, shaking her hand gently, anxious to know that she was still alive.

Seline groaned.

"Thank goodness, you're alive," she said, breathing a sigh of relief.

"Calling how I feel 'alive' might be an exaggeration," Seline replied, rolling slowly onto her back. "What happened?"

"The volcano happened."

"Right – not something I should be forgetting." Seline pushed herself into a sitting position. The room around them was in complete disarray. She pulled out an apple that was pushing into her spine and held it out to Forest, "Hungry?"

"Chewing would hurt too much," Forest replied, declining the offered fruit.

Seline took a bite instead and looked around. Pages were strewn about. "Tallie is going to kill me," she winced and started gathering the closest of them up.

"Where are we going?" Forest asked.

"Somewhere important," Seline replied, "but apart from that, your guess is as good as mine."

"It could just as easily be somewhere that has ceased being important eons ago."

"That's true, yes."

Forest checked herself over to make sure she had no broken bones. She seemed to pass inspection. "I hate to be drifting aimlessly while the Priestess is on the offensive," she said, recalling the spread of red gems across the map room floor. "I'd feel better about stopping in Bayre first to warn everyone, then continuing our exploration."

Seline looked pained at having to decide.

"We could play rock-knife-hand?" Forest suggested.

"No need," Seline sighed. "You're right." She pulled out her amulet and spun the dial to the setting for Bayre and pressed the center button.

Forest got up and began tidying the room, while Seline finished her apple, core and all.

"Eww," Forest observed.

"No waste," Seline replied, defending her approach to eating apples.

Forest looked out the window. "We're over land, drifting west or northwest. Bayre's on the coast. We're not heading to Bayre."

Seline pulled the amulet back out and dialed Bayre in again, exaggerating her movements. "There," she concluded. "Any change?"

"These things are dreadfully slow to change course," Forest complained, waiting while she stared out the window. After a while, she concluded that nothing had changed – they were still drifting west/northwest, and definitely not east back toward the coast. "It's broken," she concluded.

"The amulet or the airship?" Seline asked.

"Who knows? I just hope we're actually heading somewhere, rather than just drifting."

"There is no point in thinking too much about it. We'll know soon enough when we either land, or we don't."

Forest peered out the window and provided periodic updates about their surroundings as Seline spent her time pouring over the reassembled books about the airships.

"I think we're descending," Forest finally reported. "The ground seems closer."

Seline put down her book and stood to stretch. "Thank goodness, we're not going to just float around forever."

"I think we're somewhere in the northern forests," Forest concluded.

Seline peeked over her shoulder. "Does that bowl-shaped feature look strange to you?" she asked.

"In what way?"

"It's too regular. Calderas and craters aren't that even. It's not naturally occurring."

"It's enormous. That can't possibly have been built by people."

"Agreed, but the Ancients, on the other hand…" She paused, movement catching her eye. "What's that? Are those people?"

Forest followed her gaze. "I don't think so, although they look kind of human, just bigger." Whatever the things were, they noticed the approaching airship and began moving toward where it was going to land.

"Damn," Forest exclaimed. "Land, damn it," she ordered the ship. "Those things look scary as hell. I don't want to be there when they arrive."

The ship seemed to take its sweet time, but when it finally landed, they were ready and bolted out the door, hurrying to the cover of nearby trees. Just a moment later, three creatures twice the height of the tallest person Forest had ever seen emerged from the brush and quickly closed the distance to the airship. They peered inside it, knocked it around, and howled.

"I think they're upset that their snack didn't get delivered the way they hoped it would," Forest whispered, shuddering.

"I want to explore that dish-thing," Seline whispered back.

"Why?"

"I saw something like it in one of Tallie's books. I want a closer look."

"Okay, but only because that's better than staying here."

They crept through the brush, hoping there weren't more of those creatures prowling about. They emerged onto the lip of the giant bowl. It spanned the distance all the way to the distant hills.

"See that tower in the center?" Seline pointed it out.

"Yes. I didn't see it from the air."

"We were over top of it. It stands out better from the side. That's where I want to go."

"Why?"

"Something I read, but I need the walk to mull it over."

Forest had no better idea of where to go, so she acquiesced. Seline was so consumed by her thoughts that Forest had to intervene repeatedly to keep her from walking into trees and off ledges. It was getting tiring. *This had better be worth it*, she thought.

It was late in the day when they finally arrived. The tower was made of the strange material used by the Ancients that seemed to outlast even the land itself. It stood tall and had no visible opening, even after they walked all the way around it, looking for one.

Forest found signs of broken branches high off the ground. "Those creatures have been here," she declared and looked for Seline to warn her, but she was nowhere to be seen. *Damn, Seline, now is not a good time to disappear.* Forest found her at the tower with her hand on its cool surface.

"It's a signal tower," she informed Forest when she walked up.

"Like for signal fires."

"Something like that."

"Then why put it in the bottom of a valley instead of on top of a mountain."

"A good question. I don't know, but it gives me an idea. One of Tallie's books mentioned something about signaling the airships, another talked about a high-altitude protocol, and another had an explicit warning about never doing what we're about to do."

That didn't sound particularly safe to Forest. "And what's it going to accomplish?"

"If it works, it's going to send the airships – all of them – high into the sky, really high, to wait out a surface-level cataclysm."

"And that's helpful, how?"

"They'll go high enough to be inhospitable to life."

"How inhospitable?"

"Fatally, if the warning in the book is accurate."

"So, if the Priestess is using the airships, anyone in one wouldn't survive?"

"That's the idea."

"And if our friends are using one, same thing?"

Seline nodded gravely.

"Can we take the chance?"

"Can we not? You saw what I saw in the map room."

"I don't want to kill a friend."

"A lot more people are going to die if we don't risk it."

Forest knew she was right, but it didn't make it any easier. She struggled with Seline's cold calculus. "Okay," she decided. "Let's just hope that none of our friends are on their way anywhere. What do we do?"

"There's a code we have to assemble with signal stones. Ten to be precise."

"Gods-damn. I haven't seen any, let alone that many."

"We'd better start looking."

Forest and Seline hunted around and found a few that they excavated and placed in the required pattern against the signal tower, as indicated by Tallie's book. Forest spotted more and more signs that the creatures frequented this place, and that leant an urgency to their hunt. She kept the information to herself, so as not to distract Seline.

They were missing just one last stone when it grew too dark to search further.

"This can't wait," Seline concluded, helping Forest push the ninth stone into place. "We need torches to search for a tenth stone."

"Those things will see them," Forest warned her.

"I know," Seline responded and started piling wood to make a fire.

Gods-damn, Forest thought, *in for a copper, in for a crown*. She began helping build a fire, and they had torches lit in no time, but it was followed by the sound of something crashing through the brush in the distance. "Hurry!" she told Seline unnecessarily as they hunted around for a tenth stone.

The crashing sound was getting closer when Seline called out, "Over here!"

Forest rushed to her side to find her feverishly digging a stone out of the overgrowth. Forest knelt and started helping her. Seline stood up, grabbed the torch that she had propped up, and carried it over to the other nine stones, where she propped it up again and rushed back. They got on their knees and started pushing the stone toward the torch that marked the way. Forest's blood ran cold as the sound of the approaching creatures seemed almost upon them.

The tenth stone made a 'tock' sound as it bumped into the ninth. "That's it." Seline declared. "Let's go!"

Forest grabbed Seline's hand, and they held each other in a death grip as they ran through the dark, as terrified of becoming separated as caught.

Roars split the night as the creatures arrived at the torches, but failed to find prey. Seline stumbled at the sound, but Forest hauled her back to her feet. Branches clawing at their faces as they ran, but they held on to each other tightly. They ran into a neck-level branch that took them clean off their feet. They lay on the ground rubbing their necks with their free hands, trying to catch their breath.

They heard the creatures smash trees into splinters in their rage, and Seline feared that they would disturb their carefully-laid stones. The woods went eerily silent as the creatures listened for signs of their prey. Forest and Seline lay as still as they could, willing their hearts to stop racing and slowing their breathing. The woods stayed silent, so they continued to lay there. Forest listened for hints that the creatures had moved on, but the woods stayed deathly silent, so they lay there until dawn.

When the first light of day bloomed in the sky, enough for Forest to see her surroundings by, she tapped Seline's arm and motioned for her to stay silent but follow her lead. She got to her feet slowly, meticulously careful to remain silent. Forest helped Seline to her feet. A bone cracked in Seline's ankle as she put weight on her foot, and they froze. There was no immediate consequence, so Forest began tiptoeing away from the tower. She couldn't see it through the trees, but as long as she moved up the gentle sloped formed by the enormous bowl, they knew that they were moving away from it.

They succeeded in moving a fair distance without stepping on any twigs or rustling any branches, and eventually, the sounds of the forest resumed around them. While Seline couldn't hear the difference, Forest breathed a sigh of relief and began to walk a little faster and with a little less caution.

Eventually, they rose above the lip of the bowl and looked back toward the tower. They couldn't see its base, just its tip.

"Do you think it worked?" asked Forest.

"We could circle back to where the ship landed and see if it's gone," Seline suggested.

"I am not spending a moment here longer than I need to," Forest replied, and Seline didn't object. They'd both found the previous night terrifying and were eager to put it behind them.

"We'll just have to hope that it worked," Seline concluded.

And that none of our friends were in an airship if it did, Forest thought. It was damned-if-you-do, damned-if-you-don't. She pushed the thought out of her mind. "I say we head south toward the open plains – that's the land of Addis's people. We might find someone sympathetic to us."

Seline nodded wearily as the adrenaline drained out of her body, and she felt her fatigue and each of her injuries.

Forest glanced at the position of the sun. "This way," she concluded and led Seline south.

29

Priestess

The Priestess pulled the book from her personal library. It was the oldest book in her collection, although she recently had it recopied. She regretted the necessity of killing the priestesses that had accomplished the task, but it was necessary – the content of the book was too dangerous to be known by anyone but her. It contained excerpts of the diaries of several of her predecessors who ruled over earlier apocalypses stretching back over the eons – their challenges, their strategies, and their successes.

Deep in the book, there was an allusion to a dangerous gambit that a predecessor had used in desperation. The Priestess didn't feel desperate, but she'd suffered enough setbacks that she decided to leave no option unused. She locked the book back up and rose to consult the Ancients a final time before her journey.

She made her way to the keep and sat before the crystal. She explained her strategy to it, even though she doubted it was necessary to use words – the Ancients could plumb her thoughts, but explaining it helped her think it through more fully. She opened up her mind, and the visions assaulted her. They began with a woman in the midst of a painful birth. The Priestess felt cramps wrack her body as the vision morphed to reveal the birth of a deformed child. There was something scary and unnatural about it. She saw glimpses of a knife, but the visions ended with the child killing its mother with it, not the other way around. The Priestess slammed back into her body, and she threw up. Her body heaved, and she doubled over from the memory of the cramps she'd felt.

She rose and limped down the stairs to the throne room. Traversing the room, she ordered her Captain to have the keep cleaned, and proceeded to her room.

She washed the foul taste out of her mouth and collapsed on the bed. The visions seemed to be more of a history lesson than guidance, although maybe they were a warning. They fit with what she knew about the creatures in the wild. They were originally created as the guardians of the crystals. It wasn't hard to find volunteers – not everyone wanted to leave their bodies behind and descend into the crystals – some people were quite attached to them. Instead, they were enhanced to be bigger, stronger, impervious, and self-repairing to the point of immortality. The creatures were faithful servants for a long time, well beyond the collapse of the world after the Descent, but over time, immortality became a curse. The monotony of existence without end slowly drove the creatures insane. They became dangerous to the Ancients, and they were banished. The Ancients relied instead on the self-repairing spiders as their caretakers.

The Priestess lay thinking, *How do you control something insane? But, it had been done before, and she'd be the one to do it again.* She meant to rise and prepare for her journey, but fatigue overcame her, and she fell asleep.

She woke sometime later and made her way to the throne room. Her Captain was on duty.

"Brother Rapir, call an airship. I have a journey to attend to," she informed him.

"We've tried. The ships won't come."

That's something I'll have to look into, but first things first. "Have my horse saddled, then – I don't have far to travel," she ordered him.

"Shall I accompany you?" he asked.

"Not unless you wish to be eaten," she replied. "Just my horse."

"As you wish, Priestess," he replied and left the room. He returned a short while later. "I've had word passed down to the plain to have it done."

"Excellent. Bring the crystal to the stables and meet me there."

He kept his face from betraying his confusion at the unusualness of the request but complied. He met her later at the stables, arriving with the crystal under guard. He secured it onto the back of a second horse and bit back his desire to inquire again if he should accompany her – she would not take kindly to having her decisions questioned. Instead, he simply informed her, "Everything is ready, Priestess."

"Thank you, Brother Rapir," she replied and swung fluidly into the saddle. "While I'm gone, which will be several days, ready the army for battle." She spurred her steed, pulling along the second horse on which the crystal was secured under a blanket. She headed north out of camp.

She rode for several days as the land around her became increasingly rough and bouldered. *An apt home*, she thought, as she steered her horse into a narrow canyon. She rode through the twisting ravine until it ended in a large circular space, with caves set in its walls. Bones littered the ground, and the horses' hooves crushed them into a fine powder. The horses grew skittish, so she calmed them as best she could and stepped down from her mount. She soothed the second horse while she unsecured the crystal and lifted it, still wrapped in its blanket, off its back. She carried it to the center of the circular space and set it down.

"Beowl!" she called loudly, the name sounding as twisted as the creature she called. She waited and called again. An enormous creature dragged itself from the depths of the ground and out the entrance of the cave in front of her. It towered above her. More of the creatures emerged from their caves and surrounded her.

The horses whinnied in terror and reared, but the Priestess ignored them. She took the creature that first appeared to be Beowl, even if that meant it had been alive for an eternity. It narrowed the slits of its eyes and advanced menacingly.

She pulled the blanket off the crystal, and the creatures froze in their tracks. Several howled as if burned. The lead creature simply stared at her.

"Beowl," she began, fixing her eyes on those of the creature that stared down at her, "the Ancients need you once more."

Several creatures stamped their feet as though restrained by invisible leashes.

"The little people grow in number. They will continue to grow until they choke the world. Then they will come for you and your kind. They will hunt you."

The creature snorted, the first sign of any recognition that it understood what she was saying.

"You know how powerful the Ancients became. You know the little people can become a threat, even to you. The Ancients call upon you to wipe the world clean of them. Rally your kind."

The creature snorted a final time and headed back into its cave, while its brethren tore the horses to shreds.

30

Forest

Forest and Seline continued south, using the sun as a guide. Seline was a hardier travel companion than Forest assumed she would be. She was cognizant of the dangers of the wilds and did her best to pass without undue noise, although she was less attentive as she grew tired over the course of a day. But, she tried, and Forest appreciated it. Forest took it upon herself to keep Seline alive at all costs, given what an asset she had proved to be in the fight for survival against the designs of the Church.

The scrub forest gave way to rolling plains, and they felt less vulnerable with the longer sightlines. They even chanced speaking when something occurred to them to talk about. Forest found that Seline had deep insight about pretty well every topic she broached. She began testing her by starting conversations about the most random things. Seline always had an opinion.

They crested what felt like the millionth hill when Forest spotted riders on horseback in the distance. "I'm going to try and get their attention, if that's alright with you," she confirmed with Seline.

Seline was too weary of walking to object. Even a swift death at the hands of plains bandits was beginning to seem preferable to death by monotony.

Forest cupped her hands to her mouth and called loudly to the riders. Her voice cracked initially, unaccustomed to being raised. She tried again and succeeded in being louder, she thought. The riders didn't seem to notice them despite her calls, but they turned at some point and began riding toward them. Forest and Seline were so tired of walking that they just sat down cross-legged and waited for them to arrive.

The riders slowed as they neared and approached cautiously. Forest understood their uncertainty, considering that they were inexplicably in the middle of nowhere, and not dressed as the people of the plains typically were.

"Are you witches?" the leader asked, slowing to a halt at what he judged to be a safe distance.

Forest couldn't help but laugh, holding onto Seline's arm. "Her, maybe… me, no."

The riders put their hands to their swords.

"I'm kidding," Forest clarified. "Is humor absent in these lands? Of course, we're not witches."

"You have a smell on you that unnerves the horses," the man explained.

"I'd say it was the smell of a ten-day walk, but it could be the smell of the creatures that chased us – the height of two men – hopefully, you have no idea what I'm talking about."

"How did you survive, then?" he asked warily.

"It was dark, and we hid. Dumb luck is probably the only reason we're alive, or the favor of fickle gods, if you're religious." The man didn't relax his vigilance, so Forest tried a different tack. "Are these the lands of King Temuulen?"

"Of course they are," he replied.

"Good. We're friends of his son, Addis."

"*Prince* Addis?" he clarified.

"I imagine so, given that the king is his father, but I just know him as Addis."

"I could kill you right now for your disrespect."

"*Prince* Addis would be most displeased by that."

"Perhaps we should ask him then."

"By the gods, by all means, ask him… wait, what? Is he with you?"

"Of course not, he's in the city."

"Then, by all means, take us to him."

"We will, but not before you wash that stink off you."

"Don't you think we would if we could?"

"There's a stream over the hill," he gestured.

"Great, just give us some privacy," she requested. "…So we can do our witchcraft in peace," she added under her breath.

Seline and Forest emerged a short time later, soaking wet, but cleaner than they'd been in days.

"Better," the man snorted and gestured at two riderless mounts.

Forest restrained herself from kissing him, she was so happy to be off her feet. Even Seline, who wasn't prone to shows of emotion, looked relieved beyond measure. They mounted, and the party headed out.

"I will take you to Prince Addis, and if it turns out that you're lying, I will personally drag you behind my horse."

And if I'm not, can I drag you behind mine? she thought but didn't say it, not wanting to antagonize him further.

Forest noticed him eyeing her as she rode. "Yes?" she asked, prompting him to reveal what was on his mind.

"You two don't ride like plainswomen."

"We never said we were. We're from nowhere near here," she said and left it at that. *Let him think we rode here on our brooms*, she scoffed.

After a day and a half's ride, an enormous tent city loomed in the distance.

"Even your capital is movable?" she remarked.

"We're nomads," the leader replied. "It's in our blood."

"Addis… Prince Addis," she corrected herself. "He said that it was not always so."

"That would have had to have been a very long time ago before it was not as it is now," he replied and moved away.

"Chatterbox," Forest joked. Seline, who was riding within earshot, smiled.

They rode into the city, and he guided them toward a tent that was one of a ring that circled the largest one at the center of the city. Forest noted that the rest of his party had split off and he alone escorted them.

Addis burst through the flap of the tent. "Forest, Seline, I didn't believe it when I heard you were found wandering the plains," he greeted them, still disbelieving his eyes.

Their escort looked disappointed that Forest had been proven truthful, but Addis cheered him up by saying, "Khulan, my house is in your debt. Thank you for bringing them to me." There was no greater honor than having a royal in your debt.

Addis helped Forest and then Seline to dismount, while Khulan rode away with his head held high.

"That man thought we were witches," Forest told Addis.

"Don't be hard on him. We're a superstitious people. Gods, it's good to see you. Did you come all this way to see me?"

"Other girls may cross the continent for you – Seline and I were just in the neighborhood."

He laughed. "How unfortunate and fortunate for me then." He noticed their still-wet leathers. I've had baths poured for you both, and dinner prepared for afterward.

"If this is a ploy to get me to say, 'I love you,' it's working," Forest joked and held out her hand. He took it and led her toward a smaller tent, adjacent to his. Seline followed, trying not to look too uncomfortable at their flirting.

"Tell Badma when you're ready for dinner, and she'll escort you to me," he said, leaving them in the care of a kindly-looking middle-aged woman. She waved them toward their baths, which they found to be a perfect temperature, given the warmth of the day. Once they'd changed out of their clothes and settled into their baths, Badma spirited their clothes away to be cleaned. She returned with light linens with fine embroidery that they could wear in the meantime. She lay the neatly-folded clothing at the foot of their baths and stepped out of the tent to wait outside.

"I'm not sure I'm ever getting out of this bath," Forest confided to Seline.

"I was thinking the same thing. It's so conducive to thought."

"That wasn't exactly what I was thinking, but something close."

They relaxed for a while, then when their energy returned, scrubbed the distance they'd trekked off their bodies, rinsed, dried off, and got dressed. Seline's outfit was a light blue and fit loosely and comfortably. Forest's outfit was a deep green, and fit a bit tighter. Forest rolled her eyes as she looked herself over in the mirror. *Boys are all the same*, she thought. She poked her head out of the tent and let Badma know that they were ready. She walked them over to Addis's tent, but there were no signs of dinner.

Forest looked disappointed as Addis rose to greet them.

"My mother forbade you eating here," he explained.

"Oh, is it a girl from the wrong side of the continent thing?"

"On the contrary – she insisted that we all join her and my father for dinner in their tent."

Forest suddenly felt very shy and ill-prepared. She'd never met a king and queen before, and Addis being a prince hardly counted in her opinion. "What do I call them?" she asked.

"Just call my father Kraj, and my mother Raina. They are titles as much as they are names."

"How do I act?"

"Just be yourself."

"I can't. I'm a smart ass."

"Okay, maybe a restrained version of yourself."

Forest was as flustered as Seline was unperturbed.

"You'll be fine," he assured her and offered his arm.

"Is this proper?" she asked, taking it.

"We're not a formal people, Forest – relax."

She relaxed a little, but just a smidgen. Addis led them out of his tent and toward the large one nearby. They passed stone-faced guards that seemed more like statues than people. They entered Addis's parents' tent to an enormous feast laid out. His mother, Raina, rose to greet them.

"Forest dear, Addis has told me so much about you," she beamed.

Forest glanced at a bashful-looking Addis, then couldn't help herself and bowed to his mother. "Pleased to meet you, Raina."

Raina grasped her by the shoulders and looked at her warmly. "And I, you." She looked to Seline. "And I am pleased to make your acquaintance as well, Miss Seline."

"The honor is entirely mine," Seline replied, making Forest feel even less socially savvy by comparison.

"Please come sit by me," Raina suggested and guided them so that Forest sat beside her, with Addis beside her, and Seline beside him. The king sat to Raina's other side. "Please pardon the Kraj not getting up. He's not feeling entirely well."

Forest bowed low before him. "The continent is in debt to your brave riders," she told him.

He smiled and motioned weakly for her to take her seat. He watched with bright eyes but didn't say much as his wife led the conversation.

"What brings you to our fair city?" she asked.

"We started our journey by exploring the airship base to see if we could figure out a way to limit the Priestess's control over them. She's the one who has been trying to usher in the apocalypse."

"My son has told me about her. Go on," Raina informed her.

"Well, then the volcano erupted, and we fled. Then our airship left without us, but we called it back. Then it broke, and we drifted. Then we landed near a tower and tried to use it to make the airships rise high enough to kill the Priestess's forces using them. Then the monsters chased us away. Then one of your people found us wandering the plains trying to get home. And he brought us here," she concluded and took a spoonful of flavorful rice.

No one moved or spoke while she chewed.

"Forest leads an adventurous life," Addis explained to his mother once his shock wore off.

"It sure sounds like it," she agreed. "And it does explain why several airships landed these past few days containing parties of dead monks, frozen solid."

"It worked!" Forest exclaimed excitedly to Seline. "I hope it helped."

Seline nodded her agreement but was content for Forest to remain the object of Raina's attention. She was so warm toward her that Forest didn't quite know how to take it.

They chatted late into the night before Raina declared the dinner over so she could put her husband to bed. Forest gushed her thanks, feeling awkward the whole time.

"That was an unmitigated disaster," she despaired as Addis walked them back to his tent.

"Hardly. My mother likes you," he assured her.

A man rushed up and waved to capture Addis's attention. "An airship just landed," he told him.

"More dead monks?" Addis asked.

The man looked confused, but continued, "No, it's a man and his daughter who say they know you. The man says his name is Jarom."

"Cousin!" Nara shrieked and rushed to hug Forest as they entered Addis's tent.

31

Amara

Amara walked toward the gates of Bayre in a procession of laborers that she'd joined as they headed back from replanting the fields. As they neared the guard, who was checking everyone before allowing them entry, she 'tripped' and pushed a woman into him. By the time they'd recovered their footing, Amara was behind him, and he didn't see her slip through the gate.

She separated from the group by ducking down an alleyway when they turned the other direction. Now on her own, she concentrated on finding the woman that the Priestess wanted eliminated, the woman named Seline. She walked about the town, ensuring to stay unnoticed, and collecting names and facts that she could exploit in her search. By nightfall, Amara had gathered a lot of information and had a plan for how to use it. She found an abandoned apartment, its owners either having fled the city before its siege or dying during in its defense. She closed her eyes and got the sleep she needed to stay sharp the next day.

She woke before dawn and began circulating around the city, asking vague questions, like, "Do you know Seline? I have a message for her from the Council, but I can't find her."

She was first steered toward the repair work at the gates. They were still not completed as complex parts were still being laboriously fabricated, but Seline wasn't there.

"She led the clean-up at the airfield," someone informed her, and she headed there. She covered her face while she looked over the fence at the charred ground and burned-out remains of the buildings surrounding the field. It was clear that this was a dead-end – no one would be found here, certainly not Seline. Perhaps the person had meant the landing port outside the city, the one she had flown over on her approach before landing instead several days walk away.

Leaving the city proved more straightforward than entering it, as the scrutiny of the guards seemed reserved for those returning inside. Amara walked out in the morning with some field hands, then deserted them to head to the airship port. There was only a small number of people there, so anonymity was harder to achieve, but she did her best to be vague and unmemorable in her interactions. No one seemed to know anything. The last person she had to ask was a young guard that she had avoided until then, in case he was more alert to subterfuge than the others had been. She unbuttoned three buttons of her top and walked purposefully over to him, doing her best to look flustered.

"Can you help me?" she asked, moving a hand to her chest, drawing with it the young man's eyes. "My brother had a message… but then the horse kicked him… so he asked me… but I don't know anything…" She clutched the fabric of her blouse in mock frustration, pulling it open a hair wider. "Have you seen Seline?" she concluded.

The man was having trouble thinking. "Seline?" he registered at last. "She came back injured. She's probably at the infirmary," he guessed.

"You're such a dear," she gushed and spun before his eyes could travel back to her face. She sashayed away with an exaggerated swing of her hips. *The only thing that boy will remember is the woman whose name he couldn't muster the courage to ask*, she smirked.

She snuck back into the city suspended beneath a wagon, then rolled away, brushed herself off, and made for the infirmary. She took on the guise of a concerned relative and roamed the building, peeking in each room. She listened in on the nurses' conversations but heard no clues that lead her to believe that Seline was in the building. Tired of waiting, she approached a solitary nurse and said to her, "The Council has a message for Seline. I was told she was here."

"That's odd," she replied. "I spoke with Councilor Kline just yesterday, and the Council knows she's out of the city."

"Never mind, there she is," Amara replied, looking over the woman's shoulder. The nurse turned to follow her gaze, providing the opportunity for Amara to slide a thin blade into the base of her skull. She withdrew it quickly, covering the wound with a cloth to staunch the flow of blood, and caught her as she crumpled. Supporting her weight with one hand around her waist and the other behind her neck, she carried her into a room and lay her on a bed. She grabbed a nearby blanket and tucked her in, making her seem to all intents and purposes to be a sleeping patient. She completed a rapid last search of the building and made her exit before the dead nurse was discovered. She failed to find a trace of Seline.

She gave up on looking for Seline and started tracking down her associates. There seemed to be a collection of them that had taken up residence in the abandoned temple. She waited until dark and scaled the wall to gain entrance. She procured some dried fruit from the kitchens and climbed into the rafters of the great room, where she hid in the shadows and waited for the building's occupants to gather and talk.

Many came and went, but a couple named Lily and Cera proved to be the chattiest, and they spent a fair bit of time talking below. Within a day, Amara had a decent sense of who was who in the building. That evening, Lily made a passing statement about how worried her sister's prolonged absence made her, especially after the airships went haywire for a spell. Amara mentally filed it away and largely disregarded it until Lily added that she didn't know who was looking after whom, Forest or Seline. That caught her attention. She listened with greater interest whenever Lily or Cera was in the great room after that but quickly ascertained that not only did Seline not reside in the building, no one had any idea where she was or how long she'd be away. Amara became frustrated that she was wasting her time here. She waited until deep into the night when the temple was quiet and climbed down from the ceiling.

She prowled the halls until she identified Kala's room from its possessions. It was empty at the moment, Kala also being away on some mission. She sat on her bed and stewed over the Priestess's lack of confidence in her ability to handle Kala. She fingered the vials of poison inside her tunic as she looked around, but withdrew her hand, deciding that only an amateur leaves poison lying about with no knowledge of its consequence. Even if she were to apply it to only Kala's most intimate items, like her hairbrush, it could just as easily kill someone else and alert her intended victim to her presence. No, she'd do what she'd do when she could observe the result, and she hoped to have the chance to watch Kala's life drain out of her eyes and prove the Priestess wrong in doubting her – but tonight was not that night, sadly. She pulled out her blade and debating shredding Kala's pillow, just to release some tension, but she got up and left the room instead.

She walked past Celeste's room, then Eden's, then Amber's. All three of these girls seemed especially dear to Kala, and she gripped her dagger tightly, debating causing her at least some emotional pain in her passing, but something called her instead to Lily and Cera's room. She opened the door slowly and stepped inside. She stood over them as they slept, twisting the dagger's point against her fingertip. The blade glinted in the moonlight shining through the window, and she angled its edge to reflect it across the girls' throats as they slept. She resisted the urge.

I've got a better idea, she thought.

32

Kala

Brinn stood beside Kala on the crumbling ramparts of the castle ruins, and together they surveyed the activity on the plateau below. Brinn's people had entirely relocated there – her village almost completely emptied. Kala asked her why even their children were here.

"This will be the last great battle of this age," she replied. "We will win, or we'll lose, but it is the fight of all of us."

"But the children?" Kala pressed.

"They've been raised to understand combat. The play you saw in the schoolyard moons ago was not a game – it was preparation."

Kala watched Brinn's people in their temporary camp and observed that even the children carried daggers in their belts, though they looked more like short swords on their diminutive forms. It pulled at her heart. "No attempt at subterfuge this time?"

"Their monks are predominantly men, and our fighters are predominantly women. Besides, we move differently than they do." Brinn watched her people with pride and possessiveness but tinged by hints of sadness that Kala only occasionally perceived.

Kala looked out past the encampment of Brinn's people to Addis's camp. He'd ridden hard with a large cohort of his people, and ascended the plateau. To Kala's great joy, Forest and Seline were with them, though Seline arrived behind the main body as she couldn't keep up the pace set by Addis's riders. The plateau was crisscrossed with deep fissures, *caused by the world slowly pulling apart*, Kala thought. The horses had to travel a long zig-zag path to arrive at the assembly point. There were rope bridges across the crevasses, put in place in some former age, but the horses were too skittish to cross them, and the ability of most to support the weight of a horse led by its rider were suspect.

Kala had questioned why not assemble on the open plains where the cavalry had freer mobility, but Brinn told her that this was the ancestral place of battle, not because of mere tradition, but because the fissures could serve as defenses if their forces were positioned well. The ancient fortification atop the plateau, while badly weathered, provided some tactical advantage as well. It didn't fill Kala with confidence that this was the site of the same battle that had played out repeatedly in the past. If the battle needed to be fought again, it meant that it had always been lost. She struggled not to be disheartened.

The horses were penned in temporary enclosures, and Thorvyn helped look after them. He and Nara, along with Forest, Jarom, and the remainder of his family, had taken up staying with Addis's people, so Kala didn't see them as much as she'd have liked.

Hawke returned with Eryl and a host of people who were either under his command or recruited from the coast. Eryl's pirates joked that they were going to start using airships in their shipping raids, but it was just bravado to lighten the tension, and they were housed together with the sailors that they would otherwise be raiding. A lot of drinking seemed to happen in the sector claimed by Eryl's people.

Skye had similarly returned with the remains of Soren's army. Many had departed for their homes before he arrived, but he sent riders after them and begged them to return. Many did so because a return to the misery of their former lives left them wanting more. It wasn't much of a force, but at least many of them had seen combat, or at least were raised in places more accustomed to violence than the rest of the continent.

Fayre and Emrys had been convincing in their petition to Bayre's Council to release as many fighters to them as they could spare. They still needed a sizable force to protect Bayre from the Priestess's possible machinations, but every available fighter was spared, including some of their best – although Kala had a hard time visualizing them up against monks who had been trained from birth to wield a blade.

Bayre's forces existed more to maintain order, rather than to truly be a fighting force. Hawke and Jarom took it upon themselves to work with them as much as they could to prepare them for battle. *At least the city's archers might prove useful*, Kala hoped.

Dhara had returned with her brother and a force of former slaves that had resettled in the north. Almost every able-bodied person had joined them, and Kala was moved beyond words. *The people who had the least always seemed to give the most freely of themselves*, she thought. The forces from Bayre shared their supplies with them, and Calix took it upon himself to ensure that they were decently armed, although they seemed to eschew armor when offered it.

This was it, thought Kala – this was the force they'd mustered. There were perhaps a thousand riders from the plains, almost a thousand from Soren's former army, about five hundred from the coasts, about three hundred from Bayre, another three hundred of Dhara's people, about three hundred of Brinn's people, and perhaps six hundred more that had joined them from the surrounding areas and were interspersed among the others. It was about four thousand total, and they were up against an untold number of monks under the Priestess's command.

"Is this going to be enough?" Kala wondered out loud.

"We've got you," Brinn said, nudging her, and heading down to meet with her people.

"No pressure, or anything," Kala called after her, picking a loose stone off the wall and throwing it deep into the rubble. She sighed and headed back to her tent. At least she'd find friendly faces there. Lily and Cera had insisted on coming and making themselves useful. Emilie had insisted on coming as well, just to be with Hawke – they had the tent adjacent to hers. At least Amber and Eden had respected Kala's wishes and remained in Bayre.

Lily, Cera, and Emilie were sitting around a small fire when Kala walked up, and their sunny disposition helped dispel the cloud that had been following her.

"Hi, Kala," Lily greeted her and patted the empty seat beside her. "Come join us?"

Kala sat down. "What are we talking about?" she asked.

Cera leaned forward, conspiratorially, "We're scheming to engineer a way for Emilie to see Hawke more frequently."

"You're terrible," Kala accused them, but lightheartedly. She would also have liked to have Skye a little more too, but he accepted how busy she was and tried to keep busy himself. He also had his own tent nearby to give Kala her space while they eased back into their rekindled relationship. She sighed, wishing he were there.

"Where is everyone?" Lily asked.

"I saw Hawke training the people from Bayre. Sorry, Emilie," Kala commiserated.

"Apart from that, I assume Forest, Jarom and Nara are with Addis's people. Dhara and Kaia are with their people," she continued.

"Thank goodness, Kaia left Nina in Bayre," Lily interjected. "Her sister must have talked some sense into her."

"I'm not sure about that," Kala replied. "I think they're of a similar mind when it comes to raising children."

"I can't imagine Dhara with children at all," Cera said.

"Poor Calix," she and Lily said at the same time and smiled at each other for thinking the same thing.

"You're thinking *way* too far ahead," Kala replied, implying that their relationship was only developing, but only realizing after she said it that it could also be interpreted as 'they might not survive the upcoming battle.' It put an unintentional damper on the mood, and they all looked at their feet while Cera stirred the fire.

"How's Skye?" Lily asked to relieve the tension.

"I hardly see him, but he's good. Some part of me wants to make him suffer for breaking up with me, but truth be told, I like being back together, so making him suffer will have to wait until later."

"I hear you," Cera joked, prompting a 'hey!' and a smack from Lily.

"Are they going to come?" Emilie asked, her somberness making it clear that she was referring to the Priestess's army.

"Brinn assures me that they will, and Grey agrees with her. Me, I can't see how they won't. We stand in their way. They want us out of it, and here we are, so yes… I think they'll come."

It was not the answer that Emilie was hoping for, so she got up and walked away.

———————————

Kala watched the airships land across the plateau all day. The Priestess had finally come and brought her army. *She took her sweet time*, she thought. *I wonder why.*

Cade hovered nearby, trying his best to be of use to her, but having nothing assigned to him to do. Grey and Hawke reprised their positions flanking Kala, with their self-appointed goal of keeping her alive to the best of their abilities. Skye had kissed Kala goodbye in the morning and hurried off to help distribute food. She hadn't seen him since.

Everyone waited patiently as the storm gathered. They'd chosen their ground and waited for the monks to come to them. Kala felt the darkness stirring in her veins. She dreaded the coming need to give herself over to it. *If and when she did, could she ever reclaim herself afterward?*

By morning the next day, she could see the Priestess's army advancing across the plateau. Row after row of monks closed on them. Kala tried to estimate their numbers and put them at roughly twice those of her side. Worse, if each of them had even a portion of the talent for combat that Grey had, they were even more unmatched. *We have cavalry though*, Kala thought. *That might even things out a bit.* She had to find hope where she could.

Addis's riders were positioned along the sides of their ground forces to avoid interfering with them during the battle. Kala was at the very center of the front lines, and she could see across the plateau from the robed figure leading the opposing force that the Priestess had done the same. They were destined to cross blades, it seemed.

Addis's advisors had selected the location for the battle – the large open stretch of the plateau gave the cavalry the greatest possible room to maneuver. The battlefield was bordered ahead and behind by deep fissures that required the rickety rope bridges to cross. The Priestess's forces would have to cross a set of those bridges to gain the field, and once upon it, the same fissures would separate them from their support lines and form an obstacle at their back.

Despite these disadvantages, the Priestess directed her forces forward. *Perhaps it was overconfidence that she will prevail*, Kala thought, but she knew the Priestess to be coldly calculating and not prone to hubris or misstep. Regardless of the Priestess having limited options, Kala was suspicious that she made no move to mitigate her army's disadvantages.

The monks began crossing the rope bridges and assembling on Kala's side. She expected them to try to cross quickly and put some distance between themselves and the crevasse at their back, but they did neither. They took their time to cross, and once across, they formed up perilously close to the chasm behind them.

"What are they doing?" Hawke thought out loud. "The cavalry can push them back into the crevasse."

"Something isn't right," Grey concluded, but he wasn't sure what it was.

The Priestess's forces simply waited. Silence permeated the field, broken only by the sound of horses' hooves pawing the ground and the occasional whinny.

Addis looked to Kala for some type of confirmation of what to do. She couldn't figure out why they shouldn't attack, although she knew there to be a reason just outside her grasp, so she nodded her assent. Addis gave the signal, and the cavalry charged, with the men and women on foot surging after them.

The monks held their positions, unperturbed by the wave of horses thundering at them. Every second man moved sideways to create breaks in their ranks. It wasn't apparent why, and as Kala ran forward, she thought, *That's the opposite of what they should be doing.* It was too late to stop the charge when a wave of the metallic spiders climbed out of the chasm behind the monks and surged forward through the gaps in their ranks, scurrying forward on their pincer-like legs.

The spiders spooked the horses, which reared and threw their riders if they were unable to control them in the tight confines of their comrades. The horses refused to advance, and the benefit of the cavalry was instantly nullified. Kala's coordinated attack fell into disarray. That prompted the monks to begin their counterattack.

The front lines of Kala's forces crashed into the front lines of the Priestess's. The fighting was intense, and it was immediately clear that Kala's side was outmatched, particularly without the cavalry to balance the scales. Worse, the spiders roamed around the feet of the combatants, stabbing at the feet of Kala's allies with their razor-sharp legs.

This isn't working, Kala concluded, knowing it to be a battle they would quickly lose. She yelled over her shoulder, "Cade, sound the retreat!"

Cade danced away from a spider at his feet, put a horn to his lips, and blew the signal for the retreat. Hearing it, Kala's forces did their best to pull back from the fighting, but the monks would not let them disengage so easily. They began to flee for their lives, while a small number, including Kala, Grey, and Hawke, did their best to slow the monks and cover the retreat. The lucky ones fleeing the front were scooped up by a rider far back enough from the spiders to control their mount, and they raced away from the battle.

Everyone made haste for the rear of the open space and the safety of the far side of the bridges that spanned the crevasses that bordered it. There were too few bridges to accommodate everyone at once, and people had to wait their turn to cross. The horses wouldn't or couldn't cross, so their riders had to dismount and bid their mounts find their own path to safety as they left them behind to cross the bridges.

The monks did not seem to be in any particular hurry and fought cautiously and deliberately as they advanced, pushing Kala and her allies back steadily. Kala did her best to push back, but she and her friends were hopelessly outnumbered, and it was often all she could do to keep herself alive as she backed off the field. She kept retreating until she found herself, Grey and Hawke each defending a bridge while the last of their forces crossed over them hurriedly over them. Each of them was surrounded by multiple assailants, and they grew weary from sustaining such a prolonged defense. Kala held her own. So did Grey, to the best of her reckoning, familiar as he was with the monks training and movements. Hawke was faring the worst, being slashed at mercilessly by the monks that surrounded him. He fought valiantly, but the monks were skilled at attacking in concert, and he struggled.

Kala cursed her inability to go to his aid as she had her own bridge to defend. When the last of her allies made their way across, she backed onto the bridge and kept up a defense as she retreated across it. It was easier to fend off her attackers on the bridge as no more than one could harry her at a time as they pursued her across. As she fought her way backward, she spared a glance left and right to see Grey and Hawke doing the same. Hawke held his side with his free hand, blood soaking his shirt, and labored to edge backward as he kept the monks back.

Arriving at the far side, Kala's friends were ready and hacked at the ropes that secured the bridge to their side of the gorge. The monks on the bridge fled back across, most of them making it before the bridge collapsed into the crevasse, just a few men falling with it to their death.

Kala rushed to Hawke's side, just as he made it across, and his bridge was cut loose. She pushed through the people standing on their side of the chasm looking across to find Hawke slumped against one of the posts to which the bridge had been secured. She quickly assessed his wounds and could tell that they were not the type that a person recovered from. Panic overwhelmed her.

"Get a healer!" she yelled, cradling Hawke in her arms.

He looked at her with fading sight, but recognition jarred him into lucidity. He knotted her sleeve in his hand. "Promise me," he demanded. "Promise me you'll finish what we started – that you'll make the world a better place for my Emilie. I know I won't live to see it."

"Don't talk like that," she chastised him. "You'll be okay."

"Promise me," he repeated, his strength failing.

"I promise," she replied, tears streaming down her face.

He released his grip, and his hand fell across his lap. He closed his eyes, took a shallow breath, and died.

33
Dhara

Kala looked down at Hawke's lifeless body. *No!* she screamed inside and held him tightly to her bosom, rocking back and forth. The fire in her raged until it consumed her, and she gently lowered him to the ground and rose to her feet, glaring across the chasm at the monks who stood impassively on the other side. She drew her sword and pointed it at each of them.

"You want death?" she shouted across. "I'll give you death."

The healer rushed up and prepared to check Hawke over.

"Don't touch him," Kala commanded, inappropriately harsh, but in such a fury that she couldn't think straight.

The healer quailed at her wrath and fled to attend to one of the many other wounded.

Kala looked left and right for a way across the chasm to exact her revenge but found none. The bridges had all been destroyed. She screamed at the heavens in frustration and sheathed her sword.

She knelt and strained to pick up Hawke's body. Its heaviness was incongruous with the lightness he'd always had on his feet. She struggled to shift his weight so that she could carry him and began the long trek back to camp. The destruction of the bridges had only postponed the battle – it would renew in due course.

Emilie is going to be devastated, Kala thought as she trudged forward. Emilie saw her approaching at a distance and recognized immediately what had happened. She was frozen in place, paralyzed by shock. Her shoulders slumped, and she began to cry piteously.

Kala advanced until she stood in front of her, rivulets of tears streaking her own face.

"I'm sorry," was all she could manage to say.

"You were supposed to protect him," Emilie accused her.

"I failed," Kala admitted. "He protected us," she added as a hollow consequence, knowing it would do nothing to assuage Emilie's pain, but needing it to be said to honor Hawke's sacrifice.

Kala stepped past Emilie, brushing through the flap of the tent that Emilie and Hawke shared, and laid him on their bed.

Emilie followed after her and lay down beside his body, sliding her hand into his and crying onto his chest.

Kala stepped out quietly to leave her to her pain.

Seline spotted her from across the camp and moved toward her.

Now is not the time, Kala thought angrily, but part of her knew that she couldn't afford the luxury of grief in the midst of battle – she'd have to bottle it up and deal with it later, just like her anger. She wearily turned toward Seline and met her halfway.

"That was a disaster," Kala informed her, knowing that Seline would surely have already been briefed about what happened.

"We didn't account for the spiders being at the Priestess's command," Seline concluded.

"They're the creatures of the Ancients, and the Priestess does *their* bidding. We *should* have assumed."

"We need a way of neutralizing them like we did with the airships."

"Sure, like if the Ancients were on our side," Kala replied fliply.

"That might work," Seline replied. "Where do we get one of those crystals?"

"I wasn't serious," Kala responded.

"I don't see a better solution," Seline persisted.

"Okay," Kala capitulated. She lacked the emotional energy to resist. "Round everyone up, and we'll figure this out. My tent – as soon as possible."

They separated to go and find everyone. Not long after, Grey, Brinn, Dhara, Jarom, Addis, and Eryl crowded into Kala's tent. Kaia, Calix, Forest, Skye, and Cade hovered outside. Kala opted to move the meeting outside so that everyone could participate.

Kala started things off by saying, "I am glad you're all here – some of us were not so fortunate." Everyone had lost people they cared about, so Kala gave them a moment to remember them before continuing, "Seline has some ideas. I'll let her explain."

"We're at a decided disadvantage with the Priestess having the Ancients on her side. We'll be hard-pressed to beat her so long as that remains the case. I propose that we try to balance things by getting our own Ancients. We need one of those crystals. Kala tells me that there are several spread around the world."

The preposterousness of what she proposed hung in the air.

"I know where one is," Kala volunteered, "but it's deep underground, and I don't think it can be brought to the surface readily."

"Dhara and I know where another one is," Kaia added, "and it wouldn't be too difficult to bring it to the surface."

"What do you think, Dhara?" Seline asked.

"It would by no means be easy, but I think Kaia's right that it could be done," she replied.

"How long would it take?"

"A couple of days to get there, a couple of days there, and a couple to get back. Not too long."

"Do we have that much time?" Calix asked.

"It's hard to know for sure, but I think the monks will have to either march around the crevasse or build new bridges across it, both of which will take time," Seline replied. "Probably, we have time. What we don't have is the option of not trying."

"What do you need to make it happen?" Seline asked Kaia.

"My sister, Jarom, Calix, and a lot of rope," she replied.

"Jarom, Calix – are you willing?" Kala asked.

"Of course we're willing," they responded.

"I never doubted it," Kala clarified. "I'm just sensitive that in venturing off, you'd have to leave people behind that you care about, and I don't ask that lightly of anyone."

"Understood," Jarom replied, "but we wouldn't be doing right by them if we didn't do whatever was in our power to do."

No one thought they had a chance against the Priestess, but they all understood that they had to try.

"Not all of our horses were lost," Addis noted. "I'll have someone ride with you to the airship port and wait there for your return."

"I've never been on one of those animals," Dhara pointed out.

"You'll find it very natural," Forest inserted.

"I'll get rope," Calix offered.

"However much you think would be enough," Kaia pointed out, "get four times more."

"It's settled then," Seline proclaimed, and Dhara, Kaia, Addis, Jarom, and Calix all rushed away to make arrangements. Those who remained began to plan strategy to make sure they survived long enough for the party to have someone to return to.

Dhara, Kaia, Jarom, and Calix rode hard for the nearest airship port, led by one of Addis's people.

"This is so *not* natural," Dhara complained as she struggled to become accustomed to the motion of riding.

They made it to the airship port without coming across any interference and hailed an airship, which landed not long after that. Addis's rider tied the horses to a small tree and told them she'd wait for their return.

They boarded the ship and were aloft and heading south in no time. Kaia suggested that it would be faster if they landed at the village nearer to where they found the demon-crystal, as she called it, rather than her and Dhara's village, but Dhara over-ruled her.

"They tried to kill you," she reminded her. "Plus, they probably hold a grudge against us for killing their priestess."

"What if we tried to land at night and sneak away?"

"We'd still have to sneak back. And, we don't know if the landing pad is unguarded at night. We're better landing somewhere we're familiar with."

Kaia couldn't disagree with her sister, but reminded her, "And you think mother doesn't hold a grudge?"

"Better the devil you know than the devil you don't," Dhara concluded as the final word on the matter.

They drifted for a day and a half on strong winds before beginning their descent.

"At least the Goddess is on our side," Kaia quipped, as she looked out the window at the rising ground. "It looks clear," she announced.

"It's not like mother to leave the landing area unguarded," Dhara replied. "Be ready in case it's a ruse."

"Maybe she gave up guarding it when airships began to land less frequently," Calix suggested.

"Mother gives up nothing," Kaia replied flatly, and Calix shut up.

The ship landed without incident, and Dhara poked her head out the door. "There's no one here," she confirmed, and Kaia, Jarom, and Calix followed her out.

"I knew you'd come back eventually," a haughty voice said from the jungle, preceding the appearance of Dhara and Kaia's mother, followed by eight spear-carrying guards.

"We don't have time for your vendetta, mother," Dhara told her, standing her ground. "We have business here. When we're done, you're welcome to go back to lording over your tiny world, but don't interfere with us."

"Like you interfered with us in freeing the slaves?" her mother spat.

"They freed themselves, which they wouldn't have needed to do if you treated them decently."

"They're slaves," her mother replied. "They deserved to be treated the way they were treated."

"And that's why they're gone," Dhara pointed out. "You're wasting our precious time. If you'll excuse us," she said and started to walk toward the forest path.

"Not so fast," her mother declared, and her guards raised their spears to bar her path.

Dhara gripped her own spear tightly and prepared to fight, but Kaia stepped forward.

"This is important, mother," she pleaded.

"Shut up, you simpering girl," her mother said dismissively and proceeded to ignore her, pointing her spear at Dhara's chest.

Dhara leaned into it defiantly.

"Resist," her mother declared, "and we'll fill your male friends full of holes." She gestured toward Jarom and Calix.

"I'd like to see you try," Dhara dared her.

A spear whistled over Dhara's shoulder, striking her mother in the throat. Her eyes went wide with shock before rolling back, and her body slumped to the ground. Dhara looked over her shoulder to see her sister shrug.

"We don't have time for this shit," Kaia declared and stepped forward to retrieve her spear from her mother's body.

The guards stepped forward, spears at the ready.

"The bitch is dead," Dhara pointed out. "Whatever allegiance you thought you owed her is a moot point now. Now, get out of our way." She shoved their spear points aside with her own.

The women looked unsure, but didn't stop them when Dhara and Kaia pushed past them, Calix and Jarom following.

"Nice outfit," Jarom teased as he passed a girl, prompting her to blush and throw up her hands to defend herself to her peers.

Dhara led them to the canoe launch and was happy to find several newly carved canoes, replacing the ones they'd stolen. A guard stood when they appeared and raised her spear.

"We're just borrowing a couple of these," Dhara told her dismissively. "Stand down." Her confidence made the woman unsure, and Dhara strode past her as if she weren't there. She pulled out a canoe, while Kaia grabbed another.

"Jarom, you're with me," Kaia suggested, and he nodded his agreement.

Calix stepped over to join Dhara in her canoe. Together they launched them and paddled hard downriver.

"Think you can find the tunnel entrance?" Kaia asked her sister.

"I'm pretty sure I can," she replied and began to scan the riverbank once she judged they'd gone far enough. They had to paddle closer to shore for her to get a better look. The jungle had a way of all looking the same. "I think this is it," she declared finally and steered for shore."

"Are you sure?" Kaia asked.

"Nope, but I'm as sure as I can be."

The pulled their canoes onto the shore and hid them.

"It's getting dark," Dhara noted, but if we can find the entrance before it gets completely dark, it won't matter how dark it is outside, we'll be underground anyway."

"Can't argue with that," Kaia replied and stayed back while Dhara searched around for the entrance. Kaia trusted her sister's memory and instincts over her own.

Dhara had to light a torch as it got darker, but she was eventually able to announce, "Found it."

The others joined her at the well-hidden entrance that she'd located through some miracle.

Kaia leaned her spear against the tunnel wall and lit a torch of her own to examine the tunnel. Its walls were damp, and the ceiling looked dangerously close to caving in. "Be careful," she warned everyone. "The ceiling isn't stable."

Jarom was most careful not to bump into the walls, given that he was the largest among them.

"Got the rope?" Kaia asked for confirmation.

"Yup, all four hundred thousand lengths of it, or however much we've got here," Jarom replied, twisting his back carefully to show her.

"Great. I appreciate that it's heavy, but we'll need it," she assured him.

They walked down the tunnel, single-file.

Dhara turned to her sister. "Must have felt good?" she asked, referring to her killing their mother.

"It was liberating," she agreed, and they walked on in silence.

When they got to the central cavern, at last, Kaia gave them instructions. "We're going to secure a rope from one end of the chamber to the other, over top of the crystal. I'll climb out along it, and when I'm over top of it, we'll dip the rope, and I'll grab it. Then you pull me across, and we'll hightail it out of here."

"Why you?" Dhara challenged her.

"I'm the lightest," she countered.

Dhara was unhappy about it, but she had to accept Kaia's logic. "The demon spiders aren't going to take kindly to your stealing their crystal," she reminded her.

"I'm inclined to agree, so let's hope they don't figure out what we're up to until it's too late to stop us, and even then, we'll go as fast as we can. If we can make it back to the river before them, I doubt they can swim."

The plan settled, they entered the cavernous room. The crystal was exactly where they'd last seen it, as were several of the spiders crawling in and out of fissures in the ground around it.

"Now I know where nightmares go when we wake," Calix shuddered as they edged along the ledge that ringed the cavern. Jarom patted him on the back to reassure him.

On the far side, Jarom hammered a stake into the ceiling and secured one end of the rope to it, testing it with his weight. It held.

"I'll stay here," Kaia told them and tied the end of the second rope around her waist.

Jarom unspooled the rope that was tied to the stake as they walked back around the ledge toward the river side. Dhara unspooled the rope that was tied to her sister, and Calix let it out as they carried it back behind Jarom. The rope was heavy, and it dipped into the cavern, despite their best efforts to prevent it, and it passed perilously close over the spiders. The spiders stopped what they were doing to observe them, but didn't interfere. More spiders climbed out of the ground and took up defensive positions around the crystal. Once at the far side, Jarom secured the rope to a second stake. It hung across the cavern, dipping over the crystal in the center. He joined Calix and Dhara in holding the rope that was tied to Kaia.

"We're ready," Dhara called across the cavern.

"Okay. We get one shot at this," Kaia called back. "When I say pull, for the love of the Goddess, pull as though my life depends on it, because I'm pretty sure it does."

She said a silent prayer, looped a strip of leather around the rope, and stepped off the ledge. She slid downwards toward the crystal with increasing speed that she tried to bleed off by twisting the strap around the rope.

The spiders followed her progress with their cold eyes and shifted their positions on the cavern floor, their sharp legs scratching against the stone.

Kaia had only the faint light of the crystal to judge by, but she pulled the leather strap cross-wise to stop herself over top of it, grabbed both ends of the strap in one hand, bent down quickly, and grabbed the crystal with her free arm.

The spiders went berserk and rushed at her.

"Pull!" she yelled, and Jarom, Calix, and Dhara used all of their strength to reel her in as quickly as they could.

A spider jumped off the vacant pedestal and came close enough to slash Kaia's leg. Her blood dripped down onto the spiders racing across the cavern floor to intercept her on the far side.

"Faster!" she called, but they were already pulling as fast as they possibly could. *They're going to catch me*, she thought as she neared the lip of the far ledge. The rope scraped along it as it rose up and over it. Kaia hauled herself up and onto the ledge as the spiders tore up the wall beneath her.

She rose to her feet, despite the pain in her leg and dashed down the tunnel that the others had backed down while pulling her up. The sound of skittering reverberated off the walls behind her. She ran for her life.

Dhara lit a torch when she felt the rope slacken and knew her sister was across. Jarom raced back toward the cavern to meet Kaia halfway.

She tossed him the crystal. "Run!" she yelled. "They're right behind me!"

Together they raced down the tunnel toward the bobbing light of the torch that Dhara carried. The sound of the spiders' legs scraping against stone told them that they were closing the scant distance between them.

Kaia felt a spider brush against her leg as it caught up to her. It ignored her and surged forward toward the crystal that Jarom carried. The spiders were all around her as she ran.

Dhara burst through the vine-covered entrance into the light, followed by Calix and Jarom.

"Dhara!" Kaia called from behind her.

Dhara spun around to see her sister grab the spear that she'd left leaning against the tunnel wall as spiders streamed past her toward the entrance.

"Tell Nina I love her," she said and jammed her spear forcefully into the ceiling.

"No!" yelled Dhara as the tunnel collapsed, spewing a cloud of dust out the entrance.

When it settled, the tunnel was gone, and with it, her sister.

34

Kala

Kala took stock of their situation. They'd lost a tenth of their number in the disastrous first attack, and almost all of the horses. They were still up against an enemy with more than twice their numbers and twice their skill. And, they still didn't have an answer to the spiders. Seline was constantly trying to devise solutions, but she'd just come to Kala to let her know that her small remaining stock of incendiary powder was gone – stolen. All-in-all, it looked pretty bleak. Kala needed a pep talk, so she went in search of Skye.

She found him helping to make arrows by scraping the bark off the branches pulled from the squat trees on the plateau. *They'll never fly true,* Kala observed, but without their steeds, many of Addis's people had taken up archery as their way of fighting. *Perhaps quantity over quality will count for something when it came to a barrage of arrows,* she thought skeptically.

Skye looked up, put down his knife, and flexed his sore hand. "Hi, gorgeous," he said.

"Hi," she replied, sitting down cross-legged across from him. "You've discovered a hidden talent," she added, pointing to his pile of stripped branches.

"About my skill level, too," he smiled. "I missed you at dinner."

"Sorry, Brinn wanted to talk strategy."

"I have something I want to show you back at your tent," he said, rising and extending a hand to help her up.

She took it skeptically, stood, and they walked hand-in-hand to her tent.

He paused outside the flap that covered the door and turned to her. "I hope I'm not overstepping my bounds," he said, drawing back the flap to let her enter.

She stepped in and noted that the interior had been rearranged.

"I moved in... if that's okay with you?" he explained.

She stared at the pair of cots he'd strapped side-by-side to make the semblance of a double bed. "It's more than okay. I've missed you. I've missed us."

She strode across the room and sat down on the bed, patting the spot beside her. "Not terribly comfortable, though," she observed.

"Best I could do," he apologized and sat beside her.

"We'll just have to make do," she smiled and bent in to kiss him.

He kissed her back eagerly, a wave of relief washing over him, followed by an even stronger wave of desire. He twisted toward her and put a hand on her knee. She shifted to give him freer access and began unbuttoning his shirt. He slowly moved his hand up her thigh while she threw his shirt to the floor and placed her hands on his chest.

A shout rang out outside the tent, followed by another, and another.

"What the hell is it this time?" Kala exclaimed, frustrated. She detached herself from Skye, grabbed her swords, and rushed outside while Skye bent to grab his shirt and followed after her. The shouting was coming from the direction of the opposing army. *Have they traversed the crevasse already?* she wondered as she raced toward the yelling. People streamed past her, running in the opposite direction.

She emerged from the camp onto open ground in time to see misshapen creatures climbing up out of the crevasse and onto the field. They stood twice the height of a full-grown man and looked vaguely human, although their skin had a sickly pallor, and their eyes were slits.

Kala looked past them to see the Priestess standing on the other side of the crevasse, her hand on the Ancients' crystal, which rested on a stand beside her.

Damn-it, she thought. *These are the monsters that Dhara and Forest told us about.* Four of the things stood before her, and more were climbing up behind them. Panic gripped the camp, and only a small number of people rushed to join her, rather than away, Skye among them.

265

"Get out of here," Kala ordered him, and he reluctantly backed away. Brinn took his place, and several of her people joined them in facing the creatures. Twelve of them had climbed up from the depths and began to advance.

"We've encountered these things before," Brinn told Kala, drawing a pair of daggers. "Their skin can't be pierced. Concentrate on their eyes, if you can reach them."

Kala drew her swords, tossed the scabbards aside, and readied herself. She opened her inner eye to the path of combat. The creatures' paths appeared as crimson ribbons and intersected her own path at jarring angles. Their paths stretched back so far that Kala's spirit lost itself following them. The paths terminated in tired souls, desperate for release from existence without end. *I'll grant you release,* she promised.

"Kala, did you hear anything I said?" Brinn asked, snapping her back to the here and now.

"Right, eyes... got it," Kala replied as one of the creatures singled her out and surged toward her. It swung a fist down at her, and she rolled out of the way as it pulverized the ground she'd been standing on. She slashed its wrist with all her strength and succeeded only in dulling her blade. *Just checking,* she told herself as the creature swung at her again, and she narrowly avoided having her bones crushed. She danced aside and beckoned to the monster.

"Is that all you've got?" she taunted.

It charged at her, attempting to grab her with both of its taloned hands. She rolled forward under its reach and through its legs, slashing upward with both swords. They only scraped against the armor-like skin between its legs.

Come on! she complained. *How do these things reproduce?* She rose to her feet and turned to face the monster as it turned to face her.

A glance sideways showed Brinn locked in a similar struggle with another of the creatures. It sported one of Brinn's daggers sticking out of the slit of an eye, while it howled its rage and swung wildly at her. She evaded it deftly, but barely, as she sought an opening to loose a second dagger at its other eye.

Okay, thought Kala, *let's do this Brinn's way*. She readied herself as the creature she was fighting rushed her. She dove at it, spun out of the way of its grasping hands, and launched herself at its foreleg. With her enhanced reflexes, she jumped upwards, climbing its torso, careful to avoid its claws. Kala braced her feet against its chest and pushed upwards and outwards, bringing her swords around as she tracked its movements, and stabbed a sword through the slit of each eye.

The creature jerked its head sideways, wrenching the swords from her grip and sending her flying. She tumbled aside as the creature shrieked and collapsed to its knees, bringing its head closer to Kala's level. She stepped forward, grabbed the hilt of each sword, and drove them deeper into its skull. It spasmed, stilled, then fell over motionless.

Kala had to dive away so as not to be crushed by it as it collapsed, and she lost her swords in the process. *Damn-it – I need those*, she cursed. She briefly considered trying to roll the thing over to retrieve them, but a glance to her right showed Brinn struggling with the creature she fought. It must have connected a blow because Brinn clutched her side and moved slower as she evaded it. It had pulled the dagger from its eye but still flailed with less control than the other creatures.

Kala pulled out a pair of daggers and raced in a tight circle around it. She visualized the next few moments of its movements to time hers. She leaped into the air as the creature leaned forward to grab at Brinn. Kala landed on the back of its thigh and ran up its spine while it concentrated on Brinn. It looked over its shoulder at the nuisance on its back as Kala straddled its neck and plunged a dagger through each eye slit. It roared and swatted at her, knocking her flying. She hit the ground hard and lay dazed for a moment, watching the creature claw at its eyes.

She tried to get up and winced at the pain that shot through her. *Great, now I've got broken ribs*, she grimaced and struggled to her feet. She looked around her at the multitude of broken bodies littering the field. Brinn's people were fairly adept at evading the creatures' killing blows, but they were wholly unsuccessful at landing their own, and when they faltered, the monsters tore them apart or crushed them. It sunk in that they weren't going to win this contest. It was a battle of attrition against an impervious foe.

An incongruous sight caught her attention out of the corner of her eye. Emilie was walking slowly but deliberately out of the camp, dressed in a white gown, a bouquet of wildflowers clutched in her hand, looking every part a solemn bride. *She's gone mad*, Kala concluded as Emilie walked straight toward a group of three of the creatures that were distracted by Brinn's people.

"Emilie, get back!" Kala yelled. The muscles of her chest rebelled, and she bent over from the pain of yelling.

Emilie got closer to the creatures, casually leaving a trail of flowers in her wake.

The creatures finally noticed Emilie's approach and momentarily disregarded their quarry as they turned toward her.

Emilie pulled the pouch that she had tied loosely to her belt with ribbon and launched it high into the air, forming a cloud of fine white powder that drifted down like a winter snow squall. As the cloud descended to the ground, she pulled a flint from her pocket and poised to strike it.

"No!" screamed Kala, and ignoring the blinding pain, grabbed Brinn and threw her to the ground.

Emilie struck the flint, and the cloud detonated in a fireball as bright as if the sun had birthed a twin. Everything in its vicinity was obliterated, friend and foe alike.

Kala rolled off Brinn, the leathers on her back smoking. Her head throbbed, her ears rang, and she beheld nothing but after-glare in her eyes. As her eyes accustomed and her head stopped spinning, the true extent of the devastation became apparent. Emilie was no more, and the remains of three creatures lay charred and smoking in a circle around where she'd been. Seven more of the creatures stood staring at their fallen brethren. They were not accustomed to the death of their kind, and it stunned them. An eighth creature rolled around on the ground, clutching its eyes, and the first creature that Kala had engaged lay motionless. No one else remained standing on the field, including everyone who had been locked in battle with the monsters.

"Retreat!" Kala shouted as loudly as her aching sides permitted. She held her arm tight against her ribs and reached down to help Brinn up. Together, they limped off the field. The monsters' attention was held by their disbelief at the loss of four of their number, permitting Kala and Brinn and a few others fortunate enough to survive the blast to escape to the camp. Kala hoped that her friends were among the survivors.

"To the castle?" Brinn suggested, and Kala nodded her agreement, despite it being more of a ruin than anything else. At least it commanded the high ground. They spread the word to anyone they saw, but many had already fled in the direction of the old castle. It was the only formation that stood out on the otherwise featureless plateau.

Kala wished she could stop at her tent to collect some of her possessions, but in the state she was in, she would be lucky to make it to the castle, so she abandoned the idea and shuffled as quickly as she could. The castle was a fair distance, and darkness was beginning to seep into the sky. They'd likely not make it before night, if at all.

The creatures did not immediately pursue them but chose instead to sift through the bodies on the field, dispatching anyone still living.

As darkness descended, torches began to dot the plateau between Kala and the castle mount, and it became clear that it was the place to which her allies were rallying.

269

As Kala neared the castle, Skye rushed up and put an arm around her waist to support her.

"Grey, help Brinn!" Skye called over his shoulder, but Grey was already moving to do just that.

"Thank the gods, you're okay," Skye said to Kala.

"'Okay' might be overstating it," she replied, wincing as he lifted her arm to prop her up under her shoulder, but she could already feel her body knitting itself back together on the inside.

"You're as hot as fire," Skye noted as they moved closer to the stairs that wound up the mountain to the ruin of the castle perched atop it.

"I hadn't noticed," she replied.

"Those things…" he began.

"Are still out there," she interrupted, "and probably hot on our heels. We'd better hurry."

They moved up the narrow stair until they had to pause and press themselves against the rock face as one of Eryl's men descended past them on his way back to the plateau.

"Eryl got his men to rescue what he could from the camp. They're ferrying the last of it now. Apparently, they're quite experienced at decamping in a hurry."

"Thank the gods for Eryl," she said to herself, then asked Skye, "Have you seen any of the others?"

"Just Lily and Cera. They're up at the castle. Lily said she saw Forest join the fight against the monsters. She was near the crevasse, trying to coax one of the things to tumble over. Lily said she couldn't watch, and Cera pulled her away before the explosion. What was that, anyway?"

"That was Emilie – I'll explain later," she replied, too weary for conversation and now consumed with fear that Forest had perished in the explosion. They climbed the rest of the way in silence. They crested the top of the stair to find most of the people from camp milling about.

Emrys was organizing a perimeter of torches around the castle. Kala remembered that he'd said the creatures don't like fire, but she highly doubted it did them much harm. It did, however, give people something to do, and the illusion of control over their lives that they so desperately craved.

"I didn't know Emrys was here," Kala noted, as Skye helped her sit down with her back to a crumbling wall. He sat down beside her, and she leaned into him.

"What do we do now?" he asked.

"I don't know," she admitted and banished all thoughts from her mind. *Let someone else figure a way out of this mess*, she thought, weary of responsibility.

A short time later, Addis and one of his riders crested the stair, supporting someone between them. As they passed a torch, Kala could see that it was Forest that they were helping. She looked gravely hurt, but alive, and perhaps that was the best that could be said about anyone at this point.

"They aren't far behind us," Addis told a colleague. "They move fast."

Kala tried to get up, but her body told her that she needed time to recuperate, and she slumped back down. She'd just have to await the arrival of the creatures, and it would be what it would be once they got here.

"They're climbing up!" a lookout shouted.

Kala held Skye tighter. If this was their last night, she wanted him close.

A troupe of Addis's archers moved to the outer wall and readied themselves. When the first creature closed within range, they fired a volley of flaming arrows down at it.

Kala knew that nothing short of a miraculously lucky shot would do anything to the monsters.

"They don't like the arrows," the lookout shouted. "They're heading back down."

A cheer filled the air as everyone rejoiced that they'd live another night. The tension left Kala's body, and she snuggled in closer to Skye.

He shifted positions to place his pack beneath her head, and they changed from sitting to lying down.

"It's not quite the night I had planned," he complained, trying to make her comfortable on the hard ground.

She just pulled herself in closer and cried silently on his chest until darkness took her.

She woke at first light feeling more refreshed, and something about the sunrise filled her with hope. She tried to get up without disturbing Skye but failed, and he opened an eye as she shifted her weight.

"Go back to sleep," she told him as she got up.

"It's not the same without you," he replied blearily and got up slowly and unsteadily himself.

"I've got to check on Forest," she told him.

"I'll come with you."

The castle grounds were crowded, but Kala made her way toward a group of plains folk, assuming that if that was where Addis was, Forest hopefully would be also. She was right, and Addis looked up at her approach.

"She's still sleeping, but she'll recover," he assured her.

Kala placed a hand on his shoulder. "Thank you for retrieving her."

"I couldn't leave her," he replied, more to himself than to her.

She squeezed his shoulder and walked to the castle wall to look down.

"You're moving better," Skye observed.

"You're right," she remarked and felt her ribs. They tingled, but no longer ached. "I guess I have the Ancients to thank for that," she said under her breath, but if he heard her, Skye didn't seek elaboration.

She peered over the wall to the plateau below. She spotted several of the monsters prowling around and assumed that the ones she couldn't see ringed the castle.

"Looks like we've been treed," she sighed.

"Can't we fight them with fire?" Skye asked, hopefully.

"They don't like it, but I don't think it does them any harm, so no." She made up her mind to do something that had occurred to her in the night. "There's one ally we haven't yet asked for help."

Skye wracked his brain for any stone that they might have left unturned but came up with nothing. *If she wanted to tell him, she'd tell him,* he thought and didn't press for details.

"I'll be back," she promised and kissed him on the cheek before starting toward the stairs.

"Your swords?" he asked, reminding her that she wasn't carrying them and not knowing that they'd been lost on the battlefield.

"I won't need them where I'm going," she replied and began her descent toward the monsters.

35

Kala

Brinn and Grey looked somberly over the castle wall to the plateau below. The Priestess had arrived at last with her army. It camped a fair distance back from the monsters that roamed freely around the base of the rise on which the castle sat. Sunlight glinted off the backs of spiders that waited, utterly still, between the monsters and the monks, occasionally having to skitter aside to avoid being stepped on by one of the monsters. To Brinn and Grey's assessment, the monks were making final preparations to storm the castle, and it wouldn't be long before the assault began.

Preparations to slow the assault had been made atop the castle, but they had limited resources to work with, with the monsters effectively restricting them to the hilltop. Archery batteries were established around the castle, with fires ready to light arrows as needed. Stones were piled that could be thrown down at someone or something climbing up to the castle. There was no wood to construct any battlements beyond that, so the defenders conserved their energy as their food supplies dwindled, and they waited for the final battle to commence. There would be no retreat from their current position. They would win, or they would die.

Down below, the monks began to mobilize.

This is it, Brinn thought, no words passing between her and Grey, none being needed. She nodded goodbye and turned to rejoin her people, still moving stiffly from injuries that hadn't fully healed. Grey moved off to find Lily and Cera. He knew that Kala would want them protected until their last, and if Kala wasn't here to serve, then at least he'd serve her wishes.

An airship grew visible in the distance.

"Ours or theirs?" someone asked, pointing it out.

"It's not going to matter one way or the other," someone replied fatalistically.

"Are you seeing what I'm seeing?" a lookout called out, squinting into the distance.

"We can all see it," one of Eryl's men replied sarcastically.

"Not the airship. That," the lookout corrected him, pointing downward at the horizon, rather than upward at the ship. Everyone who didn't have a battle station moved to see what the man was talking about.

A thin line advanced along the plateau, a mix of mottled browns and greys, intermixed with some jet black and pure white.

"Those are wolves, at least fifty of them," a woman with sharp eyesight declared as the line neared.

"Those aren't wolves," one of Jarom's cousin's corrected her. "Those are dire wolves, and there's someone with them," he added, at the risk of sounding insane.

Kala had found a pack of dire wolves and asked that they call their brethren, hoping that they understood what she asked. She had run or walked back to Cogadh with them for days and was bone-weary as they approached their destination. Kala collapsed periodically and dreamed, or perhaps dreamed while she walked, but her dreams were full of hatred for the monsters, and Kala felt that she dreamed a shared dream with the pack.

The wolves gnashed their teeth as they drew closer to the citadel and the monsters surrounding it. This was a rivalry between apex predators. The growling of the wolves roused Kala to consciousness, and it finally registered that she'd made it back and hopefully done so before it was too late.

The monsters surrounding the base of the castle circled around it until they were clustered together, facing the line of approaching wolves. They stood as still as stone awaiting them.

The jet black wolf to Kala's left looked at her sideways, dipped its head, then lifted it and howled. The other wolves joined in howling until they stopped abruptly and surged forward toward the monsters.

The black wolf ran ahead of the pack and leaped at the closest creature. It swung its taloned hand at the wolf, but the wolf seized its hand in its jaws and bit down. The creature clubbed the side of the wolf, but it held on. The wave of wolves caught up and a grey bit into the creature's free arm, while two browns nipped at its legs. The black wolf braced its hind paws against the creature's abdomen and pulled. It off-balanced the creature, and it stumbled forward to its knees. The wolves pulled it to the ground and gnawed on its arms and legs.

The creature beside it grabbed ahold of a wolf that was locked onto its leg, lifted it high into the air, and slammed it hard to the ground, where it lay still. Three wolves leaped over its prone form and snapped at the creature.

As Kala caught up to the wolves, the battle between them and the monsters was pitched. Wounded and dead wolves lay about, while many of the monsters were pinned to the ground and slowly being torn apart. Kala walked up to a wounded wolf, breathing shallowly, with jagged slashes across its chest. Kala knelt and stroked its neck as it looked up at her with fading sight. The connection she felt caused its pain to incense her, and she rose to her feet, looking about for something she could use as a weapon. There was little on the dusty plateau, save for a spindly tree. She strode over to it and pried a dry branch from its trunk. Holding each end in her hands, she levered it around her foot to break it in two jagged halves. She dropped one and carried the other over to one of the creatures held prone by gnashing wolves. She stepped between the wolves and knelt on the creature's chest. It thrashed and bit at her, but she held on as she lifted the branch over her head and drove it down through the creature's open mouth and the back of its throat. She leaned forward and used her weight to drive it further into its skull. It spasmed a final time and went still. A wolf sniffed it, and confirming its death, spun and joined the pack in attacking another of the creatures that still stood.

Kala rose to her feet and turned to retrieve the other half of the branch. A glint of sunlight caught her eye, and she turned away from the castle mount to see a wave of spiders scurrying rapidly across the ground toward the melee. She dropped the branch and reached around behind her back to draw a pair of daggers. She braced herself for the onslaught, but the spiders streamed around her toward the wolves. She danced out of their way and sought an opening to do something.

The spiders swarmed around the wolves, stabbing at their paws. The wolves had to release their hold on the monsters to avoid them. Six of the creatures were still standing, though seeping dark crimson through numerous wounds.

Kala stomped on a passing spider and held it prone with her foot as it flexed its legs, trying to push her off. She dropped down, spun a dagger around, and smashed its pommel into its singular black eye. A crack appeared across the black circle, so she brought the dagger down again and again until it shattered. She turned the dagger back around and jabbed the tip of her blade through the eye socket and twisted it left and right. The thing squirmed under her and eventually went still. She rose to her feet wearily. *One down, a thousand to go*, she thought deflatedly.

The wolves had been backed against the rising ground of the castle mount and nipped futilely at the spiders. The remaining monsters stood and wavered, but at least didn't press the attack on the beleaguered wolves.

Kala spotted a rapidly approaching dust-devil in the distance. *What now?* she thought with frustration. She stared hard at the horizon until it became clear that it was a small party of riders, driving their steeds hard. Her eyes narrowed again, and she resolved what she saw with greater clarity than she should have been able to. She recognized

Dhara by her outfit, Jarom by his size, and finally, Calix by his short-cropped hair. They were led by Addis's scout. Kaia was nowhere to be seen.

A spider scurried past Kala, and she leaped to grab it, forgetting the distant riders. She turned the thrashing spider over and searched it for a seam that she could stick her dagger into and pry it apart, but couldn't find one. The spider stabbed her hand with one of its pincer-like legs, and Kala gritted her teeth against the pain. She dropped the dagger from her free hand and grabbed the spider with both hands, lifting it off the ground, and smashing it repeatedly against a rock. Its legs flailed, but eventually, it stilled as well. She threw it down and wiped the sweat off her forehead. As soon as she released it, it flipped over and scurried away. *Sneaky bastard*, she cursed as it raced off to join the assault on the wolves.

"Kala!" Dhara called as the riders drew the horses to a halt before her. She spun around at the sound of her name.

Jarom jumped off his horse, cradling a blanket under an arm, and pulling it off to reveal the crystal wrapped in its folds.

Excellent, Kala thought. *Finally, something goes our way.* "Hold that thing high, Jarom," she told him.

While he lifted it over his head in the sunlight, Kala turned and yelled at the mass of spiders, "Hey, you little bastards! Over here!"

One spider had her in its field of vision and observed the crystal. In unison, they all halted their harrying of the wolves and turned slowly to face Kala and her friends and moved forward en masse.

"Shit," exclaimed Dhara. "Are you sure we want their attention?"

"Put it down, Jarom, and pull out your axe," Kala commanded over her shoulder, ignoring Dhara's concerns and keeping an eye on the slowly advancing spiders.

"Back off!" she ordered. "Bother us, and we'll destroy your precious Ancients."

Taking his cue from her, Jarom lifted his axe high over the crystal and held it ready for a downward stroke.

The spiders froze as the word "No!" exploded in Kala's head. She dropped to her knees from the pain, but shook it off and kept her eyes on the spiders. They withdrew a pace.

"That's right, be afraid – you'd bloody well better be afraid!" she yelled at them, rubbing her temple with her wounded hand.

The spiders turned as one and moved off perpendicular to both the castle rock and the Priestess's forces. Their withdrawal signaled that they were staying out of any conflict that imperiled their masters.

The wolves descended from where they'd been backed up by the spiders, licking their wounds and snarling.

"Kala!" Calix warned her as his horse reared, and he was dumped off the back of it. Addis's scout maintained control of her horse, although it backed up from the advancing wolves.

"It's okay," Kala assured them. "They're with us."

Calix rose to his feet, brushing dust off his backside, and he, Dhara, and Jarom moved closer to each other for protection, despite Kala's assurances.

The wolves faced the remaining monsters, growling. The monsters hesitated, then turned and lumbered away. The wolves pursued them, and the melee continued until the creatures that were not dragged down, climbed down into the safety of a crevasse and disappeared.

"Kala," a syrupy voice called out.

Kala and her friends turned at the sound to see the Priestess walking up casually, surrounded by only her personal guard, her army remaining expectantly a short distance off. The hairs on Kala's skin rose, and her senses heightened at the threat.

Jarom lifted his axe, and Dhara raised her spear into a defensive position, and the Priestess's guard did similarly.

"This is between her and me," the Priestess said to them dismissively.

Jarom and Dhara stood their ground, and Calix drew his sword and joined them.

"It's okay," Kala reassured them, placing a hand warmly on Jarom's shoulder, and stepped past them to face the Priestess alone.

The Priestess's guards fanned out to form a semicircle, and she stepped forward nonchalantly until she and Kala faced each other in a rough ring.

The Priestess examined her fingernails, which glinted in the bright light as she ran her thumb along their tips. She looked Kala in the eyes coolly. "Shall we?" she suggested.

"Let's," Kala agreed, accepting the inevitability of the duel that had been building since the moment she'd first laid eyes on the woman. Every sense shouted warning, but she overruled them and pulled out her daggers. Her left hand smarted from where the spider stabbed it, but she disregarded it and stepped sideways, sizing up the Priestess.

The Priestess pulled a fairly utilitarian dagger from a sheath beneath the folds of her robe. She held it loosely in her right hand as she advanced casually toward Kala, her narrowing eyes the only part of her that belied the seriousness of the danger that she posed.

Kala cleared her mind and tried to see down the path of combat. The Priestess telegraphed very little, so the future was hazy, and she didn't see it coming when the Priestess slashed forward. Only her heightened reflexes prevented her from being skewered as she dodged hastily aside. The Priestess slashed lightning quick with a backhand that Kala parried with her own blade. Kala turned her parry into an attack of her own, but her blades merely cut through empty air or the swirling fabric of the Priestess's robes.

Kala parried and thrust but frustratedly realized that she never truly posed a threat to the Priestess. In contrast, every one of the Priestess's attacks came perilously close to ending her. Their movements were too quick and fluid for Kala's friends to see how mismatched the fight was, but she could tell.

"It's a pity really that you never lived up to the Ancients' expectations," the Priestess told her conversationally.

The comment skewered Kala. She never thought she was the prophesied one and the Priestess was proving it. She was going to let everyone down.

The Priestess feinted with her dagger, uncharacteristically easy for Kala to block, prompting alarm bells to ring in her head. The Priestess slashed casually with her free hand, her sharpened nails slicing shallowly across Kala's arm, then stepped back instead of pressing the attack.

Kala readied herself for whatever ruse the Priestess had concocted, but her vision blurred, and her head felt gauzy. She looked from her bloody arm to the Priestess, to see her wiping her nails on her robe.

"We're done here," she told her guards and turned to walk away. Her guards followed her, keeping a wary eye on Kala's friends.

Kala's head felt heavy, and she stumbled forward, the Priestess's back receding from view as she struggled to concentrate.

Calix surged forward and caught Kala before she fell, holding her upright. Dhara took a step after the Priestess, but Calix stopped her.

"Kala needs help," he pointed out. *Revenge can wait.* "Dhara, your grandmother, is she here?"

"She's with the healers, yes," she replied.

"Jarom, help me with Kala," he requested as Kala lost control of her legs. "Dhara, race ahead and get your grandmother. Jarom and I will carry her up." Dhara bolted for the stairs to the castle, and even though it was unnecessary, Calix's worry made him call after her, "Please, hurry!"

"Give her to me," Jarom instructed him and scooped Kala into his arms. "Grab that damn sugar cube," he suggested, gesturing to the forgotten crystal, and began to run toward the stair. Calix retrieved the crystal, rewrapped it in the blanket, and followed after Jarom.

Kala's heightened metabolism warred against the poison coursing through her. Her body temperature raised by at least ten degrees and Jarom felt like he was carrying an inferno up the hill.

Dhara met them with her grandmother at her side as they crested the hill into the ruins of the castle. Jarom held Kala out for the wizened woman's inspection. She put a hand on Kala's cheek. "Safula weed," she murmured, withdrawing her hand. She rooted around in a pouch she carried.

"She's going to die…" she began, pausing to making sure that the bottle she'd fished out was the one she sought – holding it up to the light to read her hand-scrawled label. "…unless she gets this in her quickly," she added, removing the stopper from the container.

Family or no, I'm going to kill that woman, Dhara thought.

Skye raced up, but seeing the healer ministering to Kala, he suppressed his worry and paced.

Kala was unresponsive, so the healer had to pry open her mouth to pour in the thick liquid. She held her mouth closed until Kala swallowed and choked.

"She should be dead," the healer observed. "The fire god has entered her and battles the poison. It's fast-acting, so she shouldn't have even lived long enough to have been brought to me, and my antidote doesn't even exist in this part of the continent. She's charmed."

"She'll be okay?" Skye asked, unable to stay on the sidelines any longer.

"Only if the fire god wins the battle," the healer replied, tied up her pouch, and withdrew.

"There's nothing more you can do for her?" Skye asked, near begging.

"More has been done already than should have been able to have been done," the woman replied, walking away.

Jarom took a step forward, holding Kala out to Skye. "You want to look after her?" he asked needlessly. He intuited that come what may, Skye would want to be the one holding her close.

Skye wiped away a tear of worry and stress, nodded resolutely, and took her from Jarom, thanking him with a nod. He turned and carried her through the crowd that had only a moment earlier been jubilant at the retreat of the monsters and spiders, but now sobered at the cost.

Skye put his back to a wall and slid down into a sitting position, cradling Kala in his arms. Tears came freely, but he didn't care.

"Come on, Kala… you're stronger than this… you're stronger than anything," he pleaded, stroking her hair.

He reached for his waterskin, wet his sleeve, and dabbed her forehead. He held her tight and prayed fervently to the fire god.

36

Skye

Skye held Kala in his arms into the evening, then into the night. Fires sprung up across the castle grounds. People milled about anxiously despite the late hour. It was widely reported that movement in the monks' camp suggested that they had regrouped after the retreat of the spiders and monsters and looked to be preparing to storm the castle at first light. Skye cared about none of that. His entire world lay in his arms, pulse racing, breathing raggedly.

Kala's temperature fell steadily, a sign that Skye took to be the fire in her going out. Her pulse slowed. Her breathing slowed.

"Keep fighting," he demanded, pulling her close into his chest and holding her tightly.

"Can't breathe," a muffled voice informed him.

He pulled back, angled Kala's head back, and stared into her face as her eyes fluttered open.

"Hi," she said.

"Hi," he replied, wiping his cheek.

She reached up weakly and wiped his other cheek, then reached around behind his neck and ushered him lower.

He leaned closer until his lips almost touched hers.

"That's better," she murmured and kissed him softly.

He kissed her back gently. "I thought I'd lost you," he admitted.

"I keep turning up," she smiled.

"Yes, you do that," he laughed.

She looked around at the people surrounding them and sighed.

"We should get back to saving the world," she said sarcastically and pushed herself off the ground. "Oww," she said. "I hurt all over."

Skye helped her up. Calix noticed her moving and ran to tell Lily and Cera that she'd recovered. Forest was still sleeping, so Lily slipped away with Cera and Calix to see Kala.

"Kala!" Lily called as she ran up.

"Shh, Lily," Cera reminded her, mindful of those who still slept nights.

Kala hugged Lily and Cera, and finally, Calix.

"Fifty wolves?" Cera noted incredulously.

Kala smiled, then remembered something. "Kaia?" she asked, turning to Calix.

He just shook his head, not wanting to put the sad news into words.

"Poor Nina," Kala observed.

"Poor Dhara," Lily added. "She's lost both her sisters. I can't imagine what she's going through."

"She's in a dark place," Calix admitted. "She holds the Ancients responsible for Kaia's death. I've had to talk her out of throwing that crystal off the cliff. I've actually hidden it from her."

"I can't blame her," Kala agreed, "but that's not us. We can't become what we're fighting against, no matter how tempting."

"Then keep an eye on her tomorrow when things begin to go badly," Calix told her, accepting that they were out of both time and miracles.

Kala noted how Cera took Lily's hand and held it tight. Skye followed her eye and took her hand in his.

"We've got until tomorrow, then?" Kala asked.

"That's the consensus of Brinn and Grey," Calix confirmed.

"I want to talk to them. Where are they?"

"They're with Jarom and Seline, I think," Calix responded.

"Show me where."

"Sure, they were over by the wall. I'll show you."

Skye released her hand to let her go, but she picked it back up.

"If we just get one night, you're sticking close to me," she told him and pulled him after her.

Walking up to Brinn and Grey, Kala greeted them.

"Good to see you still in the land of the living," Brinn greeted her back.

"Hey, Grey," Kala pointed to her scratched arm and his neck. "We're claw buddies."

Grey's sense of humor hadn't developed enough to make him smile, which made Kala chuckle alone at her joke.

"It's not going to go well for us tomorrow," Brinn said, bringing them back to the conversation they were having before Kala walked up.

"Our only hope is to cut the head off the snake," Grey concluded.

"But," Brinn reminded him, "my spies confirm that the Priestess has left the plateau."

"You have spies on the ground?"

"Not infiltrated, but ranging freely. They saw an airship leave and haven't seen the Priestess or any of her guard since."

"I think I know where she might be," Seline interjected, having stayed silent until now. "When Forest and I were in the map room on the island that the airships come from, we saw a wave of threat sweep the continent, and it radiated outward from a point on the high plain. If I were a betting woman, I'd put coin on that being her lair. I think there's a setting for it on the amulet."

"Even if we wanted to go after her, there's the matter of her army surrounding us," Jarom pointed out.

"We're not completely surrounded," Kala countered. "The army is massed on the stair-side of the mount."

"They'll have lookouts on all sides, keeping an eye out for anyone sneaking off the hill," Grey responded.

"Brinn, can your people on the ground take out the lookouts?" Kala asked.

"They could, yes."

"They'll expect the possibility of that and have some type of rotation," Grey countered.

"Can your people take out anyone who comes to check on them too?" Kala asked.

"Not with any certainty, and it would take every one of my people who still breathe, but it's possible."

"I hate to point this out," Jarom pointed out, "not that I think we shouldn't try this... but even if we succeed in sneaking off the mountain, getting to the Priestess and eliminating her, we couldn't possibly do it in time to stop the assault tomorrow."

"What if there was no one here to attack?" Kala asked.

"You want to sneak everyone off the mountain?" Jarom asked incredulously.

"The only reason we've not tried it yet is that we've got no better place to defend, her army would chase us down, and we'd inevitably have to fight in a less defensible location."

"That's still the case," Brinn agreed, wondering what part of that Kala thought had changed.

"But it would buy us time to get to the Priestess while our forces fled, wouldn't it?" Kala asked.

"If we pulled it off, it would," Brinn replied.

"Someone would have to stay to make it look like we're still here," Jarom pointed out.

"I'll do it," Calix and Skye both announced.

Kala looked at Skye beseechingly.

"We're not fighters like you all are," Skye noted, "but we can still be useful. Besides, it's not suicide – we'd just be the last to leave."

And most at risk if anything doesn't go perfectly, Kala thought, not ready to see Skye take those kinds of risks.

"You throw yourselves into the jaws of the wolf all the time. You can't say we can't do the same," Skye said, his mind made up.

Kala's look told him that she wasn't happy, but she wouldn't fight him on the matter.

"Okay," Jarom concluded. "We have a plan. Who goes after the Priestess?"

"I will, of course," Kala replied, though uncertainty was in her voice.

"It doesn't have to be you," Skye pointed out kindly.

"It does," she replied. "Succeed or fail, I owe it to everyone to try."

"Who do you want with you?" Jarom asked.

"Our chances are higher if we're a small enough party to have some chance at stealth," she began, hedging against any hurt feelings for anyone she didn't ask to join her. *I want Hawke*, she thought, and her eyes watered. "I want you," she said to Jarom, "and Grey, Brinn, Dhara, and Seline."

"I'm not a fighter," Seline pointed out.

"Your mind is one of our sharpest weapons," Kala responded. "Will you join us?"

"Of course, as long as I don't slow you down."

Kala turned to Brinn. "I don't want to pull you away from your people. Are you okay to join us?"

"I serve my people best where I'm most useful," she replied.

"Jarom?" she asked.

"It would be my honor," he replied.

"Can someone find Dhara and ask her?" Kala asked. "I want her too. She's a lion."

"I'll do that," Calix offered and left immediately.

"How much time do you need to organize your people?" Kala asked Brinn.

"It's already begun," she replied. "You don't think my people weren't following our conversation?"

"Spread the word then. We'll meet back here once Calix returns with Dhara."

Everyone split up, and Kala turned to Skye.

"Be safe," she commanded him.

"An army couldn't keep me from you," he assured her, and embraced her, kissing her a final time before their parting. As he rushed off to recruit help keeping up the illusion that the castle remained populated, Kala couldn't help but think that the kiss tasted like goodbye.

Kala turned to see Cade hovering nearby. "Cade, don't let Skye out of your sight. Keep him safe. Understood?"

"As you wish," he replied and hurried after Skye.

Calix made his way up the treacherous stairs to the ruins of the keep that he'd seen Dhara climb earlier that evening. She was kneeling before a small fire that she was feeding with small squares of cloth that she cut from Kaia's clothing. She looked over her shoulder at his approach, cheeks wet with tears. He'd never seen her show emotion this raw before. It took him aback.

"I can't even honor her properly," she despaired, gesturing to the pile of clothing beside her.

He knelt beside her and placed his arm around her shoulder.

She leaned into him, to his surprise. "It's not fair," she said. "She was the best of us. It should have been me."

It was her because she was the best of us, Calix thought but said nothing and only held Dhara tighter.

"Kala wants you. She wants you to join her in taking the fight to the Priestess. What should I tell her?"

"I'll tell her myself," she replied, rising to her feet. "My sister will be avenged." She bent and picked up the pile of neatly folded clothes and hugged it tightly. It broke Calix's heart. She put the clothes down. "Let's go," she said and made her way toward the stairs.

Kala, Grey, Brinn, Jarom, and Seline were waiting when Dhara walked up, spear in hand and war paint on her cheeks.

"Let's do this," she said.

Brinn led them to a spot on the backside of the mountain where ropes had been secured for the steepest portions of the descent. "We go first," she declared, explaining why so many people were hovering nearby waiting. "My people have cleared the way."

Brinn grabbed ahold of the rope, stepped over the lip of the cliff and disappeared. Grey followed her, then Jarom helping Seline, then Dhara, and finally, Kala.

With just the faint light of the crescent moon to see by, the descent was treacherous, and everyone in the party worried for those who would attempt it after them. Kala feared for Lily and Cera, but especially Forest, who was still severely injured. Even Dhara worried for her grandmother.

They reached the ground without incident, and there was no sign of either the Priestess's lookouts or Brinn's spies. Brinn gestured that they head out and started off at a run directly away from the castle mount. The rest of the party followed, maintaining a speed that allowed Seline to keep up. She felt terrible about slowing them down, but Kala demanded that she join them, so she ran as fast as her lungs and legs allowed.

Kala spared a look over her shoulders at the torches moving along the castle walls. *Be safe, Skye,* she wished.

The darkness began to soften with the encroachment of dawn. *That was way too short a night,* Kala fretted, hoping everyone had time to descend the mountain before they were discovered. No horn blasts signaled the result one way or another, but Grey had told her before that the monks communicated far more subtly than that, so it didn't mean anything.

Seline tired quickly, and they slowed. Jarom carried her for a while, to her mortification, but this tired him soon too, so they alternated between her running and being carried, and they did their best to keep up the pace.

Behind them, dust clouds rose around the base of the hill on which the castle sat. "The monks are moving out," Jarom observed and kept an eye on the clouds as they ran. The cloud split in two. "We're being pursued," he concluded, "and so are the others."

Kala took this as good news. If the monks were pursuing the others, that meant that at least some of them got away. She prayed that her friends were among those that did, especially Skye, who she knew would have been last off the mountain.

They approached the airship port to find a troupe of monks guarding it.

"I'll call an airship," Seline declared, knowing that the others would be busy engaging their foes.

Cade had procured a replacement pair of swords for Kala, and she lunged toward a couple of monks with them upraised. Brinn and Grey both singled out an opponent. Jarom followed them, axe raised, heading toward a pair of monks that remained unmatched. A final monk stood atop a spire signaling the host that pursued them with a mirror. Dhara cut his message short with a spear thrown through his chest, but the damage had been done, the message sent. Kala made quick work of the men she faced, as did Grey and Brinn, and even the monks' skill was no match for Jarom's ferocity, and he cleaved them down.

They wiped their blades and looked skyward, then back toward the growing dust cloud. *Gods-damned slow balloons*, Kala thought, clenching and unclenching her fists.

"There," she pointed, her keener sight spotting the airship descending from a great height before the others did. She glanced back at the approaching cloud. *Come on!* she ordered the ship. It grew larger as it neared, but Kala could also start to make out the shapes of individual monks running tirelessly at the forefront of the dust cloud. She looked up at the airship. *It was a gods-damn race*, she thought, praying the ship would win it.

The ship landed before the monks got within missile range, but just. Kala's party rushed aboard and set the ship quickly aloft again. It rose painfully slowly, and Kala could see from the window various hurled weapons strike the airship. As long as they couldn't throw or shoot high enough to hit the skin of the balloon, they'd be fine, Kala concluded. Everyone held their breath as the airship rose, and didn't seem to falter in its ascent. Soon the ground receded, and the monks with it, and everyone sighed their relief and turned their thoughts to the challenge of facing the Priestess in her lair.

Skye looked over his shoulder at the dust cloud that seemed to tower taller every time he looked back. He turned his attention back to helping Dhara's grandmother. She was hardier than she looked, but even still, despite being one of the first ones down the mountain, she'd fallen back as everyone surged away. Skye had caught up to her and ran with her.

She demanded that he leave her, but he steadfastly refused and kept up a string of encouragement.

"Words won't make these old legs run any faster," she chided, but her eyes belied the truth that she appreciated them none-the-less, and he kept them up.

Cade ran with them, woefully out of shape, but helping as much as he could. He glanced nervously backward as he gripped the hilt of his sword.

They caught up to Calix, who was helping Addis with Forest. Forest moved under her own power, but she was weak and straining at the effort. Addis ordered his cousin Jon to leave them.

"My responsibility as leader is to ensure the safety of my people, but my heart prevents me. You will do this in my stead," Addis told Jon.

"My liege," Jon protested.

"If my honor means anything to you, you will serve my wishes," Addis overruled him, and his cousin reluctantly raced off ahead.

Lily refused to leave her sister, and Cera refused to leave Lily, and nothing Forest could say would dissuade them.

Along with a few other wounded, the eight of them were the tail-end of the fleeing group, and it was only a matter of time before the monks caught up to them. Even now, Skye could make out the line of monks closing on them.

Up ahead, one of Brinn's warriors peeled off and turned resolutely, taking it upon herself to slow down the wave of advancing monks. She stood determinedly as Skye passed, and he prayed for her soul. Cade glanced over his shoulder at the tide of monks and slowed, turning to stand beside the young warrior. She handed him her shield, and he nodded his thanks as he sheathed his sword to attach it to his arm. He checked that it was secure, and she squeezed his free hand, then released it so he could redraw his sword.

"Cade," he introduced himself.

"Sapphire," she replied and turned to face the monks.

Together they roared and ran at the front lines, knowing that they would buy little time, but every moment a precious gift. They crashed into the wave of monks.

The monks surged forward again and inexorably drew closer. They drew within bow range, then within spear range. Skye knew that his party was moments away from breathing their last. *Oh well, we tried*, he concluded, but kept moving to delay the inevitable as long as possible.

The dust kicked up by those fleeing in front of him grew thicker, which he took as odd given that he was sure they were falling further behind, rather than catching up. A whistle caught his attention, and he spied a trio of riders racing at him, one holding the reigns of three more horses. Addis's people had found the abandoned herd.

The middle rider, the one guiding the three spare mounts, reared to a stop before them as Jon and Gerald roared past toward the wall of monks.

"For my liege!" Jon yelled as his horse shattered the front lines.

Addis's chest constricted with the pain in his heart, and he gestured for Calix to lift Forest up to the rider.

"I can ride on my own," Forest mumbled and steered Calix toward another of the horses. He helped her into the saddle and climbed up behind her. Skye lifted the healer onto the back of the rider's horse, while Addis helped Lily and Cera onto a horse.

"Hurry, my lord," his rider urged Addis as he climbed onto the third mount and Skye scrambled up behind him.

"I don't know how to ride a horse," Lily worried aloud.

"Learn," the rider ordered her, turned, and spurred her horse. The three other horses followed.

Skye looked over his shoulder at the receding wall of monks. *We're going to live another day*, he thought.

37

Kala

Kala's party's airship landed at the port on the plains surrounding the Priestess's mountain lair. They landed in daylight and were greeted by a garrison of monks. A pitched battle ensued.

I guess surprise was too much to hope for, Kala thought as she cleaved a man in two and dodged the slash of another.

Even Seline got into the battle, throwing rocks at the monks as they fought members of her party. The rocks were utterly ineffectual, but the distraction they provided was many a monk's downfall as they were struck down by Brinn, Grey, Jarom, and Dhara. Eventually, the battle was won, and they found themselves standing over the bodies of the fallen, breathing hard.

"The mountain," Grey pointed out. "That's where she'll be."

They moved cautiously toward it, wary of traps and the possibility of reinforcements for the garrison they'd bested at the port, but they encountered neither. Arriving at the base of the mountain, they located the stairway winding up.

"We'd be way too exposed if we took that," Jarom noted.

"My people would have other ways in and out of a place like this," Brinn added. "I'm sure the Priestess does as well."

They hunted about, but only Grey and Brinn had any idea what a hidden entrance would look like.

"Found something," Brinn declared, and everyone moved to her side. She put her hands under a boulder twice her height and lifted. It swung up and out of the way, revealing a dark tunnel. "It's hinged," she explained and peered in.

The rest of the party joined her.

"My people would also guard every entrance, or at least lay traps, so ready yourselves."

Brinn to took the lead and entered, with Grey slightly behind and abreast, Kala following with Seline at her side, and Jarom and Dhara taking up the rear. Jarom glanced over his shoulder and spied the distant sky filled with airships.

"We're going to have company," he reported, examining the opening.

"No point closing it," Brinn replied to his unspoken question. "They'll know where it is, and leaving it open will give us light for a little while. We're going to find it dark in here quickly enough already."

They advanced cautiously, Brinn at the front.

"Step around that tile," she told them.

Kala examined the non-descript tile, and sure enough, on closer examination, it appeared to be inlaid and therefore suspicious. They gave it a wide berth, wondering what it triggered. It occurred to Kala that she could still see relatively well in the dim, her eyes amplifying even the faintest light.

"Stop," she told Brinn, spotting a tripwire that Brinn couldn't see. "There's a wire just in front of you, about a hand's height off the ground."

Brinn stepped over it, and the others followed suit, guided by Kala.

"I can still see decently well," Kala told Brinn. "Perhaps I should lead."

Brinn acquiesced graciously and traded places with her.

"What am I looking for?" Kala asked her.

"Tripwires, like that one, and anything at all that seems out of place."

"Got it," Kala confirmed and advanced as cautiously as Brinn had, but with less of an idea what she was doing. She spotted a tiny patch of phosphorescent moss and hoped that there'd be more to help her vision, then it clicked in some part of her that she'd never seen a patch of it growing in isolation. She drew her daggers and did a quick

296

assessment of where someone would be hiding if they were watching the moss for an occluding shadow. She rolled forward, letting the daggers fly down an alcove as she passed it. Two crossbow bolts struck the wall above her, while her two daggers stuck in the chests of two men covered head-to-toe in black. Their crossbows clattered to the ground as they fell forward.

"That's going to have been heard," Kala whispered, annoyed at herself for not thinking of a quieter way of dispatching the men. She recovered her daggers.

"I think they know we're here," Brinn cautioned her. "They wouldn't have been waiting in that alcove otherwise."

The faint light of the moss allowed Kala to see a bit further down the tunnel before it became dark enough that even her enhanced vision would fail her. She spotted a patch of ceiling that was darker than the rest and halted the party by tapping each of their shoulders. She moved back to Dhara and put a hand around her spear.

"Can I borrow this?" she whispered.

Dhara nodded, trusting that Kala could see it in the darkness, and released her hold on the spear. Kala took it and advanced quietly toward the patch of dark ceiling. She stayed just back of it and thrust the spear upwards in several quick jabs. The third connected with something, so she drove the spear higher, and an assassin, impaled on it, fell from the recess in the ceiling, writhing briefly until Kala stabbed him through the heart and he stilled instantly.

Kala wiped off the spear and returned it to Dhara. "Thanks," she whispered and signaled the party to continue following her. They continued without further incident until they came to a stair carved into the stone walls of an ancient waterway that had formed naturally in the limestone. They spread out and climbed it single-file, Kala remaining at the head. She spotted flickers of torchlight high above and led them cautiously towards it.

The stairs terminated at an entryway that opened into the room containing the torches. Kala stepped warily into the room.

"I wasn't expecting to see you again, this side of death," the Priestess's cold voice called from the throne across the room. She sat on it, leaning forward, surrounded by her personal guard, including her Captain, Rapir.

"I'd be happy to show you the way there," Kala replied with more bravado than she felt, stepping farther into the room. Her companions followed her, spreading out behind her, only Seline hanging back.

"Brother Grey, your neck seems to have healed nicely," the Priestess observed, looking past Kala.

"Thank you, milady," he replied, his tone neutral.

The Priestess sighed and returned her gaze to Kala. "You're like a bent copper," she declared. "Always the first drawn from your purse, but the last wanted." She paused. "What am I going to do about you?"

"I have some ideas," Kala replied, advancing with her daggers drawn.

"Not so fast," the Priestess cautioned her. "I believe I have something of yours."

Kala froze uncertainly, and the Priestess motioned toward a dark corridor.

Her chief assassin, Amara, stepped out, pulling Kala's friend Amber with her, holding a wicked-looking dagger to her chest.

The Priestess leaned back on her throne. "Now would be the time to put down your weapons," she declared coldly.

Kala hesitated.

"Don't do it," Amber urged her.

"Shut up," Amara ordered and pressed the point of her dagger hard enough against Amber's breast to pierce her skin.

Amber winced, and this was too much for Kala.

"Okay," she said, holding up her hands in surrender and slowly lowering her daggers to the ground.

"Kala," Brinn hissed. "There's nothing you can do for your friend."

Kala knew she was right, but looking into Amber's terrified eyes, she found herself physically incapable of putting her at risk.

"That's a good girl," the Priestess smirked.

"Not for me," Amber protested, and a look of resolution passed across her face that only Kala read.

"Don't…" was all Kala had time to say before Amber drove herself onto Amara's dagger.

"Not her!" Kala howled, bent down, retrieved her daggers, and hurled them with such force that they pinned a stunned Amara to the wall behind her.

Amara's eyes never lost the look of shock as they rolled backward, and she slumped to hang suspended by Kala's daggers.

Released by Amara, Amber dropped to the ground, still clutching the hilt of Amara's dagger in her chest.

Kala rushed to her side and fretted with what to do about the protruding dagger.

Amber took one of Kala's hands in hers to calm her. "It's okay," she reassured her. "I got to matter, and for a time, I got to be happy. Neither of those things was supposed to be mine, except for you." She smiled faintly and squeezed Kala's hand weakly as the Goddess collected her.

"No!!!!!" Kala cried out, the power in her voice reverberating off the walls. She opened her inner eye and desperately searched for traces of Amber's path. She followed them like tendrils of smoke as they descended toward a black sun. Kala's spirit dove toward it until she was bathed in its dark light. All sense of her self burned away as she surrendered the last of her humanity. She gave herself over, mind, body, and soul to the Goddess. In return, She gifted her understanding. Kala wasn't light or dark, she was both.

I am, Kala understood, and in unbearable anguish, she was reborn.

The Priestess witnessed Kala's path disappear utterly, and a look of uncertainty passed over her face that had never resided there before. She rose quickly from her throne and darted out the corridor that Amara had emerged from. Her guards moved to prevent anyone from following her.

Kala opened her eyes and lowered Amber's body gently to the ground. She looked up to see Jarom offering his hand to help her up the way Calix had a hundred times when she was a girl. She took it and rose slowly to her feet.

"She's mine," was all she said.

Jarom nodded and turned to face the Priestess's guard, singling out the largest of them.

"Come here, big boy," he taunted his foe.

Brinn, Grey, and Dhara each selected an opponent of their own.

"Rapir," Grey acknowledged his adversary coolly.

"Grey," Rapir replied, drawing his sword.

Kala rushed at the monks, read their posture, and launched herself off a pillar before using it to alter direction and sail between their swung weapons, rolling to a stop behind them.

"Go on," Jarom urged her. "We'll clean up in here." He turned to his adversary, drew his axe, and strode forward.

Dhara crouched low and channeled every speck of anger, hurt, and sadness at her sisters' passing and flung herself at the man in front of her.

The sounds of battle echoed off the walls of the throne room behind her as Kala strode down the corridor after the Priestess. She emerged into a large room awash in shadows cast by flickering candles placed along the walls.

Kala could see as clearly as if it were day in the dim room.

"The Ancients favor you with their gifts," the Priestess observed, emerging from behind a pillar to step into the center of the room.

"I could do without the Ancients," Kala replied calmly.

The Priestess had abandoned her robes and was dressed in a tight satin dress.

"You can shed your skin, but you're still a snake," Kala told her.

The Priestess drew two daggers from her belt and readied herself. "I've bested you once. I can do it again."

"That was before you crossed a line from which there is no coming back," Kala countered, circling her.

They raised their daggers in readiness, and the Priestess lunged forward with a thrust that Kala easily parried. Kala slashed at the Priestess, but she spun clear of the blow. Kala turned with her and swiped at her exposed back. The Priestess ducked low and swept a leg up at Kala's foreleg, off-balancing her. The Priestess thrust forward, missing wide, but punching Kala in the mouth with a fist wrapped around her second dagger.

Kala reeled and spat blood, but moved quickly to re-engage. The Priestess swiped broadly, and Kala arched her spine to stay narrowly out of her reach. The Priestess followed up with a downward slash that Kala narrowly evaded, although it cut through the leather protecting her shoulder.

"You'll have to do better than that," Kala taunted her, stalking her.

The Priestess rose for another downward stroke, but Kala guided her momentum downward to throw her toward the ground. She dropped the dagger in her right hand and grabbed the Priestess's arm with it instead. She pulled her toward her and slammed the fist of her other hand into the Priestess's side. The Priestess pulled back, losing a dagger in the process and emerged to face Kala, each of them brandishing a single dagger.

Kala rushed forward, blade held in front of her. She thrust, and the Priestess parried, slashing upward to cut Kala's forearm. Kala ignored it and grabbed the Priestess's dagger arm. The Priestess did the same, locking them in a stalemate that Kala broke with a vicious headbutt to her nose, followed by a kick to her leg that off-balanced her enough

301

that she released her grip on Kala's arm. Kala yanked on the Priestess's arm, spinning her to the ground and slashing her back.

The Priestess rose to her feet stiffly, while Kala staunched the bleeding of her forearm. The Priestess lunged suddenly, and Kala rotated to let her stab through where she'd been, grabbing her arm and slashing her across her ribs as she moved past. The Priestess collapsed to her knees and rose unsteadily to face Kala.

"It's over," Kala told her coolly.

The Priestess stabbed wildly. Kala caught her wrist, twisted it cruelly, and drove her fist into her shoulder, then again and again until she dropped her dagger.

"Yield," Kala demanded

"Never," the Priestess spat.

Kala spun behind her and held her blade to the woman's throat. "Yield," she repeated.

"Kill me," the Priestess replied. "I would."

Kala drew back her dagger hand and punched the Priestess hard in the side of the head, knocking her sprawling to the ground.

"I'm not you," she informed her, standing astride her, looking down.

The Priestess struggled to get up, and Kala punched her back to the ground.

Grey rushed into the room, bloody, but whole.

"Deal with her, please," Kala told him, stepping away from the Priestess.

Grey nodded and took Kala's place, tearing a strip of cloth and binding the Priestess's hands behind her back with it.

"You've doomed us all," the Priestess declared. "Maybe not today, but someday our race will tear itself apart because you would not go quietly, you selfish little girl."

Kala sighed. "That may be, but it's our choice, not yours. And I believe that it's in us to be better than those that have come before."

Jarom called from the throne room, "We have a problem."

Kala hurried back, with Grey pulling the petulant Priestess behind him. They emerged to a room filled with monks with weapons drawn standing tensely before Brinn, Jarom, and Dhara, with Seline backed up to the wall behind them. Kala walked calmly to the throne and sat down. Grey guided the Priestess onto the dais, her pride keeping her silent.

Kala looked into the faces of the monks before speaking. "I am the Goddess's servant in this world," she proclaimed, her voice firm and commanding. "You serve Her through me."

The monks stood, unwavering.

A raven cawed from the balcony, and, as one person, the monks knelt before Kala.

"We enter a new age," she announced, rose, and stepped forward to place a hand on Brinn's shoulder. "This is the right hand of my Church. She has instructions for you. Now, if you'll excuse me, I have matters to attend to," she added and stepped off the dais to collect Amber's body.

EPILOGUE

38

Kala

Two airships landed at Bayre near dusk. Forest stepped out of the first, gingerly cradling the arm that was still in a sling and looking around the empty port. Lily and Cera followed her out, weary from the long trip. Dhara and Calix exited last and joined the other three in waiting for the second ship to finish mooring itself. When it did, Grey stepped out, followed by Seline and Jarom, then Skye. Kala exited last, carrying Amber's body. Her friends knew how deeply she felt the weight of Amber's death, so they let her shoulder the physical burden alone.

The returning party wound its way through the city to the temple at its center. Celeste had been woken by one of her charges who had taken upon herself to keep watch for the airships. She met them at the gates and directed them to bedrooms she had prepared for them. Kala carried Amber's body down to the catacombs. Skye followed her to make sure she would be all right and grabbed a torch to light the way. They descended the stairs to a large room where Kala laid Amber's body on a stone altar. She knelt on the floor beside it, held Amber's hand, and wept quietly. Skye placed the torch on the wall and slipped out to leave her alone with her grief.

Kala woke the next morning in bed, having fallen asleep in the night and been carried out of the catacombs by Skye. He was sitting in a chair facing her and got up when he noticed her eyes open.

"Good morning," he said tentatively.

"Is it really over?" she asked, emotionally shattered.

"Yes, it is," he replied and got up to slowly pull back the heavy curtains and let in the sunlight."

"It doesn't feel like the happy ending I was promised," she replied sorrowfully.

Skye moved to sit beside her and held her hand. "I'm sorry for that," he said tenderly and sat with her.

"What time is it?" she asked, noting the brightness of the day.

"Past midday," he replied. "You slept like a rock." After a while, he told her, "Councilor Fayre is outside and hoping to see you."

"She's *Councilor* Fayre again?" Kala asked.

"Yes. She was appointed to Bayre's Council while we were gone."

"I'm glad for her – for us all, really."

"So, you'll see her?"

"Of course, but I'll need a moment to finish waking up and wash."

"Celeste has a bath ready for you in the adjoining room. She's been a tyrant in having the children keep it hot all morning."

Kala almost cried at the thought of a warm bath.

"I'll fetch you some kai," Skye offered.

"No, thank you – just stay with me."

He squeezed her hand and helped her up and to her bath. She slid into it and gazed out the window at the brilliant blue sky while she soaked. The water warmed her, and she felt her heart begin the slow process of healing.

Skye picked up a pitcher and began washing her hair.

Kala banished her sorrow and allowed the pleasure of Skye massaging her scalp to wash over her. "You know how to treat a girl right," she purred.

"Just *my* girl," he replied.

Once she felt sufficiently herself, she rose from the bath, dried off, and dressed in a simple white dress that Celeste had thoughtfully laid out for her. She looked herself over in the mirror, wondering if she'd ever worn white before. Her bare arms were covered in cuts and scars, but the cuts were already beginning to heal, and the scars fade. She let Skye know that she was ready to see Fayre, returned to her room, and took a seat by the fireplace while she waited. A few moments later, there was a gentle knock on the door.

"Come in," she called and rose to greet Councilor Fayre.

Fayre poked her head in, saw Kala, and stepped in. "Don't get up," she said, but Kala walked over and hugged her warmly.

"Please, sit," Kala offered, gesturing to the chair opposite from the one she'd just risen from, and sat back down herself. "What can I do for you?" she asked.

Fayre leaned forward in her chair. "There are two things I'd like to discuss with you, if you don't mind."

"Of course, I don't mind. What are they?"

"First, do you remember Lennox?"

"Soren's man?"

"Yes. He's an eel, but he knows things. He's been trying to leverage that knowledge for a reduced sentence, and even though he deserves every day of his incarceration, I'm inclined to be accommodating if it can save lives."

"I agree, but I don't see why it matters what I think."

"I'll come back to that," Fayre replied. "He tells us that Soren divided his forces as he moved south, and a second army moves west, ignorant of the fact that the war has ended in the east. Lennox will tell us where they are if we half his sentence."

"Do it," Kala replied without hesitation. "Find out where the army is, and I'll take care of it."

Fayre nodded but didn't ask how Kala planned on dealing with the army.

"The second point?" Kala asked.

Fayre shifted in her seat, clasped her hands, looked directly at Kala, and replied, "The Council would like to crown you Queen."

Kala stared at her, blinking, thinking that such a ridiculous statement made a terrible joke, and puzzling over Fayre's beseeching stare. "You're serious?" she concluded.

"Yes, quite."

"It's not a wise precedent to vest power in a single person."

"We understand that. It's largely symbolic. The Council will still govern."

"Then why do we need a queen?"

"We're transitioning to a new world, and you are a symbol of the ideals we'd like to base it on."

Kala couldn't help but laugh. "I'm hardly a symbol."

Fayre got up and held out a hand. "Let me show you something," she said.

Kala took her hand tentatively and allowed herself to be guided to the balcony. Fayre opened the doors and motioned Kala outside.

She stepped out and looked out over the railing. Thousands upon thousands of people lined the streets below. A thunderous cheer went up when they saw her.

Fayre stepped out behind her. "They beg to differ."

Kala reluctantly agreed to be crowned, but only if it could be put off while she tended to what she felt to be the more pressing matter of Amber's funeral. Fayre was happy to oblige, saying that there was much that she needed to organize before there could be a proper coronation.

Kala's first order of business as queen-in-waiting was to request that Amber be given a state funeral, to which the Council agreed, not fully understanding why, but sensing its importance to Kala.

Amber's body was dressed in white and laid in an open casket, which was placed on a horse-drawn carriage. Kala lead the funeral procession through Bayre, and people lined the streets to watch them pass.

Kala overheard a young girl ask her mother, "Who was she?" to which the woman replied, "Her name was Amber, and she was beloved by the Queen."

Yes, she very much was, Kala thought, holding back tears.

310

The procession wound its way to the gates of the temple so that Amber could be interred beneath it. The carriage stopped, and Kala, Forest, and Dhara lined up on one side of the casket, with Skye, Grey, and Calix on the other side. They each grabbed a handle and carried Amber's body inside the chapel. They laid the casket on a low dais beneath a painting that Twill had created of Amber. Kala had cried when he showed it to her, saying that it captured the beauty of her spirit perfectly.

Celeste sang a dirge as people filed in to pay their respects. Kala stood by the casket and greeted each person who approached. The girl at the front of the line had dark hair and a scar across her cheek. Kala recognized her from Baron's. "You got out," she said as she hugged her.

"Thanks to you, and Amber," she replied and deposited a white rose before the casket.

Kala's peeked out the carriage window as it pulled up to the temple on her coronation day.

"I don't think I can do this," she said to Skye, who held her hand.

"Dire wolves, armies, and monsters you can face... but not an adoring crowd?" he asked, incredulously.

"Everyone has to be afraid of something," Kala replied sheepishly.

"I'll be with you every step of the way, he reassured her and placed his free hand on the handle of the carriage door. She breathed in deeply, nodded, and he opened it. It rained rose petals, and she smiled shyly and waved as she stepped out. She wore a flowing silver dress, with black binding, and delicate chains looped around her waist. Her dark hair was tied up and threaded through with silver thread. She looked as regal as she did beautiful.

Skye escorted her inside. She held her composure, and only he could tell that she was petrified. Kala stepped up onto the dais, and Skye wheeled off to the side and winked at her.

She looked out over the crowd. Her grandfather sat in the front row, smiling proudly at her. A lump formed in her throat, and she smiled back. Forest and Addis sat beside him, holding hands, and Lily and Cera sat beside them, looking radiant. Dhara and Calix sat across the aisle with Nina between them, who looked none too happy to be there. Kala suppressed a laugh. Brinn sat beside Grey, both looking uncharacteristically relaxed. At the end of the row, Eden sat beside the Pirate Lord Eryl, causing Kala to raise an eyebrow. Eden blushed and smiled shyly.

Councilor Fayre opened the ceremony with an address, but Kala heard nothing she said. Finally, a young girl brought forward a finely-wrought silver crown on a satin pillow and stood before Fayre, who lifted it high as everyone held their breath in anticipation. Kala knelt as she'd been coached, and Fayre placed the crown on her head. Fayre turned and announced, "Your Queen." The crowd surged to its feet, applauding.

When the crowd quieted, Kala addressed them, "Gone are the days when we sat behind our walls, ignorant of the world," she began. "We have awakened to the fact that we are one people spread wide. It is our duty to care for one another and this precious world. It is a duty that I, as your servant, embrace." People cheered wildly as she looked out into the crowd.

Skye escorted her out after the ceremony. "Do you know they're planting a tree in your honor in the city square?" he told her. "We totally have to build a tree fort," he joked.

"This is too much," she told him, exasperated, but was content to lean into him as they walked.

He walked her back to her room and stood with her outside her door.

"You have that glint in your eyes," he remarked. "Should I be scared?"

She grabbed his shirt in her fist, placed her crown on the doorknob, and pulled him into her bedroom.

"Terrified," she replied.

Kala, Dhara, Forest, and Brinn traveled in the lead airship, guided by the information that Lennox had provided. He had forecast that the army would be nearing the city on the west coast where Forest had found Soren's mother. Forest informed them that the city had no defenses and would likely fall quickly to the five-thousand-strong army that marched on it. Kala stared out the window and hoped that they were not too late.

It was a long trip, but eventually, the airship began to drift lower. Descending through the clouds, Kala could see two armies assembling on the fields outside the city. Just as Lennox had predicted, Soren's western army looked to number about five thousand. They were arrayed against a force of perhaps one thousand, few of whom were trained fighters, and none of whom had seen battle. Kala breathed a silent prayer that they might still arrive in time to sway the outcome.

The ship sailed over the armies, and everyone on the field watched it land outside the city. Kala pushed the door open and emerged, resplendent in her black leather, with the emblem of a wolf's head newly stitched in silver across her breast. Her silver crown rested on her mane of jet-black hair, as she strode forward, every bit the Queen of Bayre. She strode to the head of the army of defenders, where an older woman in a helm stood surrounded by her generals.

Kala saluted her and proclaimed, "The East stands with the West." She did not wait for a reply from the confused woman and marched past her to the front lines.

Forest followed her, wearing the leather dress of the plains horsemen, and carrying her bow in her hand. "The Northern Plains stands with the West," she said and continued after Kala.

Dhara approached next, spear in hand, wearing little beyond that which was strictly necessary to ensure modesty, war paint across her body. "The South stands with the West," she declared and marched after Kala.

Brinn came last, wearing an outfit of mottled green and brown, a hood obscuring her face, cloak trailing, and sword in hand. "The People of the Shadows stand with the West," she stated and continued after Kala.

Kala and her party walked through the front line of defenders, who made way, unsure what to make of them. Kala marched half-way to the opposing army and stopped. She pulled her swords from the scabbards at her back and drove them into the ground in front of her. Dhara, Forest, and Brinn fanned out behind her.

"This city," she declared loudly to the army before her, "is under my protection." She paused. "Soren is dead, but his dream of a world in which all people are free lives on. The forces that have held us enslaved have been overthrown. There is no need for further bloodshed." She placed her hands on her hips and awaited their response.

The army before her stood silent. Its leader strode out of their midst. She was a formidable woman, even without the armor she wore and the weaponry strapped to her. She walked toward Kala and, once close, slowly unsheathed an enormous sword.

Kala stood her ground.

"I've heard of you," the woman said. She lifted her sword and dropped it at Kala's feet. "It is an honor to surrender to you," she added and knelt before Kala. The army at her back hesitated, then knelt as one.

Kala held out a hand to the woman kneeling before her. "The honor is mine."

The woman took her hand and rose. A shadow passed over them, prompting them to look up at a sky dark with airships.

"The cavalry," Kala told her, smiling, and placed a hand on her shoulder.

39

Seline

Seline took time off from teaching at Bayre's newly founded university to rebuild the Fortress in the Wastes, as Kala requested her to do. She pulled her furs tighter against her as she mulled over the problem of how to move the giant ice blocks that were being quarried nearby. She looked forward to returning to the level on which the geothermal heat had been harnessed.

Grey was off retrieving another crystal so that it could be relocated to the Fortress. Seline liked to stare at them and wonder about the technologies that lay before them, just begging to be rediscovered. Grey simply looked forward to completing his mission and returning to Brinn's village and Winter.

40

Celeste

Kala came to see Celeste and Petr off at the airfield. They were the first to use Seline's redesigned passenger compartments.

"It isn't safe out there," Kala tried a final time to dissuade them.

"When has that ever stopped me before?" Celeste replied for the hundredth time. "But there's always room for my favorite assassin," she said, gesturing to the airship.

"Tempting," Kala sighed. "For now, you'll just have to travel with my love – but if anyone gives you a hard time, you tell them that the weight of an empire will fall on them."

"That might put a damper on our world tour," she laughed. "Relax – we've been received warmly so far. Besides, we're traveling with several young people eager to be reunited with their families. You should see the look on people's faces when we bring someone back. It changes you."

"*You* change people," Kala said ardently.

Celeste blushed. "I hope you don't mind my making notes in your journal."

"I told you – it's yours. Eden is making me another. She's working on it right now on her pirate beau's island, or I guess I should say, ex-pirate beau, given that he's establishing trade up and down the coast and generally becoming a respectable businessman. Eden says she's happy to stay busy when she isn't joining him."

Celeste gave her a final hug and boarded the ship.

Kala watched it rise until it disappeared.

41

Forest

Forest sat beside the fire in the camp of the plains horsemen that still stood outside Bayre, listening to songs celebrating the lives of the lost.

Addis walked their horses over to her. "Ride with me?" he asked.

"Love to," she replied, getting up. "Are we going far?" she asked, walking up to stroke the neck of her steed.

"No, just far enough to have some privacy."

"I'm ready now, then," she said and climbed onto her horse.

Addis stepped into the stirrup and swung himself up and into the saddle. He pulled the reins and steered their horses away from the city.

Forest got a sense of the direction they were headed and spurred her horse to a full gallop. The wind blew her hair back from her face and filled her with joy.

Addis caught up to her quickly and rode beside her until she felt that her horse needed to rest, and slowed to a trot.

Addis turned to her after a moment. "My father has passed away."

"I'm sorry," she replied and reached to take his hand.

"I have to leave immediately to attend his funeral."

"Of course."

He stopped his horse, prompting Forest to stop hers. He leaned toward her. "I'd like you to come with me."

"Oh," she replied.

"Please say, 'yes.'"

"Seeing how you asked so nicely — yes, I will."

"Don't joke with me. I'm serious."

"So am I," she said earnestly. "I'd love to see your lands again."

He cleared his throat. "Our stay there won't be quite as rugged as it was when we first met," he said guardedly.

"Why's that?" she asked, suspiciously.

"My father's crown has passed to me."

"Aren't you the youngest?"

"I am, but my brothers and sisters support our late father's decision. Apparently, my raising a host to ride against Soren pleased him and impressed them. I didn't have the heart to tell anyone I did it for you."

Forest didn't know what to say. "You're telling me."

"Because you already have my heart," he replied earnestly.

Forest squeezed his hands. "Addis, I'm flattered, but we're young."

"I don't know how this will end, but I'd like to see where it goes."

"So would I."

"Hold out your hand," he requested, pulling his away.

She complied, uncertainly, and he tied a beaded bracelet around her wrist.

"What's this?" she asked.

"It's your story, according to the customs of my people. I'll teach you how to read the beads." He handed her a bracelet to tie around his wrist.

She noted the bright blue bead on both their bracelets. "What's this one?" she asked.

"That's us," he replied, smiling.

They rode back to Bayre chatting until Forest excused herself to go tell Nara that she was leaving.

Nara saw her coming and could tell right away that something was different.

"What's that?" she asked, pointed at Forest's bracelet.

"Nothing gets past you, does it?" Forest replied.

"That's not an answer," Nara said impatiently.

"Addis gave it to me," Forest admitted.

Nara squealed. "That's *so* romantic. What does it mean?"

"I'm not sure, but I think we're an item."

Nara hugged her, but Forest detached herself and held Nara by the shoulders. "Addis needs to return home, and I'm going with him."

Nara looked crushed.

"Come with me," Forest urged her. "Thorvyn is from the north. He probably wants to return home too."

"I'm not going to follow a boy on merely the hope that it leads somewhere."

Thorvyn emerged from the tent behind them. "I was getting to that," he said, surprising them.

"How's that?" asked Nara, recovering.

He dropped to one knee and took her hand. "Marry me."

"Maybe," she replied but swept him into a hug so tight that she nearly suffocated him. She peeked over his shoulder at Forest and told her, "We're going to have such beautiful babies!"

"My gods, Nara!" Forest exclaimed.

Nara winked at her and looked down at Thorvyn. "Of course I'll marry you," she said, holding his face in her hands and kissing him deeply. "We're going to have a wedding," she squealed and pulled Forest into their hug.

"Awkward," Forest protested, but Nara would have none of it, and only released her when Thorvyn suggested that they go ask for her father's blessing.

Thorvyn glanced at Forest's bracelet and inclined his head before excusing himself. "Raina," he said deferentially.

I am going to kill Addis, Forest thought as she watched them walk away and turned to go tell Lily.

42

Lily

Lily and Cera walked down the seaside path to the village. The wind off the water never seemed to let up, but it was warm, so they didn't mind it. They arrived at a fork in the path and kissed goodbye for the day. Lily continued on to the bakery that she'd taken over from its former owner. She'd renamed it "Raven's" over Kala's objections, who only relented when presented with Cera's alternative – "An Unkillable, Killer Scone." Lily propped open the door and fired up the ovens. She tied an apron around her waist, sprinkled some flour on the table, and began singing.

Cera headed to the school, which was bursting at the seams with a diaspora of refugee children. Despite the early hour, several were already waiting for her. She picked up a small girl and carried her into the classroom. "Want to help me set up the paints?" she asked. The girl nodded, and the two of them got busy.

Kala's grandfather had also chosen the village as his home, preferring its quiet to the bustle of Bayre. Besides, he'd said, Evelyn had returned to her home there too, which gave Skye and Kala twice the reason to visit, which they did often.

43

Dhara

Dhara knocked on the door to Calix's room, Nina on her hip.

He smiled broadly as soon as he saw it was her. "Come in," he invited, opening the door wide.

Dhara stayed in the doorway. "We're leaving," she told him.

"Fine. Let me gather my things," he replied and turned to stare at his dresser.

"I meant Nina and me. We're going home."

"Then I'm coming with you," he replied matter-of-factly and began to assemble piles of clothes on his bed.

"Calix, it's not *your* home," she said.

Calix stopped what he was doing and turned to her. "*My* home is wherever *you* are," he told her, and locked eyes with her.

Dhara wavered. "I can be difficult."

"You can say that again," he chuckled and reached out his hand.

"Nina is my daughter now."

Calix placed his hand on her arm. "She can be ours."

Dhara's resolve evaporated, and she melted into him. "I'm in charge, though," she reminded him.

"As though you know any other way," he laughed and kissed her.

44

Kala

Skye bent down to give Kala a kiss, then handed her a steaming cup of kai. She slid an arm out from under the sleeping cat to take it, took a sip, and placed it on the arm of her chair. He sat down beside her, and she rearranged the blanket to cover them both. She leaned her head against his chest and resumed gazing out to sea. The wind blew up, he put his arm around her, and she snuggled closer. She was just a girl, he was her boy, and she was happy.

Read on for a preview of

Unlucky Sevens

First book in

The Innocents Series

Unlucky Sevens

FIRST BOOK OF THE INNOCENTS

COLIN LINDSAY

PROLOGUE

Jenna grabbed Grace by the wrist, glanced about to confirm there were no witnesses, and pulled her into the barn.

"We have chores, Jenna!" Grace protested.

"I'm going to tell your fortune," Jenna announced, ignoring her cousin's protests and pulling a deck of cards from the folds of her skirt. She sat down on the blanket that she had spread out before going to find Grace.

"That's easy," Grace teased. "Ten more years of school, then I marry Gabriel and live next door to you forever."

"The future is murky," Jenna intoned in her spookiest voice and pulled a reluctant Grace down beside her. "Draw a card," she commanded.

Grace did as she was told and held up the seven of diamonds.

"That's you," Jenna informed her, and laid the card down in front of them. "Not an exciting card, sorry."

"Then it fits," Grace sighed and smoothed out the blanket.

"Draw seven more cards," Jenna instructed her. "Those are your sevens."

"I know who my sevens are. I was assigned them at birth," Grace reminded her.

"But do you know if they'll rise to the occasion if needed?" Jenna asked.

"I guess not."

"Then draw the cards!"

Grace relented and turned over a queen, three jacks, a king, an ace, and another queen.

"Your cheating!" Jenna accused her.

"How can I cheat when you haven't told me the rules?"

"I guess," Jenna replied, only slightly convinced. "Your sevens really have your back."

"Isn't that the whole point?"

"Sure, but not everyone gets the A-team. My sevens are boring."

"They come to your birthday. Mine don't," Grace countered.

"My six gave me socks as a present. Your six is the ace of hearts."

"I've never met my sixth."

"Well, she's a lion," Jenna assured her, then leaned in excitedly. "Now for the best part… draw another card."

Grace sighed but reached for the deck.

"Not with that attitude!" Jenna declared, pulling back the deck. "This card is your love," she informed her.

"I should have known this was coming," Grace replied, rolling her eyes and snatching the top card before Jenna could stop her. "Ha! The seven of hearts. What does that mean?"

"Matching sevens," Jenna observed reverently. "She's your soulmate," she added wistfully.

"She?" Grace asked. "Gabriel is *not* going to be happy about that."

"I want *your* life," Jenna lamented.

"You can have it," Grace assured her. "Does that mean I get your socks?"

Jenna unfolded her legs and wiggled her toes. "Nope."

"What about her sevens?" Grace asked.

"Who's?"

"My supposed love."

"That's not part of the game."

"I want to know," Grace demanded.

"Okay," Jenna accepted. "Draw seven more cards."

Grace drew two twos, a three, another two, two more threes, and the last two.

"Oh, no," Jenna declared. "She has no one. Poor girl."

Acknowledgements

I would like to thank my daughter, Katherine, for being the impetus for this project. It would also not have seen daylight were it not for the forbearance of my wonderful family, who tolerated my frequent disappearance to write and the addition of the characters of this series into the family. I am indebted to Dolores, whose reverence for proper comma use kept me on the straight-and-narrow, and Kim, whose insightful feedback helped me see the book through fresh eyes. I am also grateful to Andra Moisescu, whose illustrations brought the main character to life.

COLIN
LINDSAY

is the author of Queen's Sacrifice, the third and final book in The Goddess's Scythe series that he began writing for his daughter. He was born in the year in which a person first set foot on the moon, a year in which anything seemed possible. It is.

Manufactured by Amazon.ca
Bolton, ON